# Cat Cross Their Graves

Also by Shirley Rousseau Murphy

*Cat Fear No Evil*
*Cat Seeing Double*
*Cat Laughing Last*
*Cat Spitting Mad*
*Cat to the Dogs*
*Cat in the Dark*
*Cat Raise the Dead*
*Cat Under Fire*
*Cat on the Edge*
*The Catsworld Portal*

# CAT CROSS THEIR GRAVES

A JOE GREY MYSTERY



Shirley Rousseau Murphy

HarperCollins*Publishers*

This book is a work of fiction. The characters, incidents, and dialogues are drawn from the author's imagination and are not to be construed as real. Any resemblance to actual events or persons, living or dead, is entirely coincidental.



HarperCollins books may be purchased for educational, business, or sales promotional use. For information, please write: Special Markets Department, HarperCollins Publishers Inc., 10 East 53rd Street, New York, NY 10022.

FIRST EDITION

*Designed by Nancy B. Field*

*Illustration by Beppe Giacobbe*

Printed on acid-free paper

Library of Congress Cataloging-in-Publication Data

Murphy, Shirley Rousseau.
Cat cross their graves : a Joe Grey mystery / Shirley Rousseau Murphy.—1st ed.
p. cm.
ISBN 0-06-057808-4
1. Grey, Joe (fictitious character)—Fiction. 2. Women cat owners—Fiction. 3. California—Fiction. 4. Cats—Fiction. I. Title

PS3563.U355C26 2005
813'.54—dc22

2004054246

05 06 07 08 09 ❖/RRD 10 9 8 7 6 5 4 3 2 1

*To the memory of Phyllis Wright.*

*To the memory of J.,*
*and to what might have been.*

*And with thanks to Peter S. Beagle**
*for allowing Lori to read aloud passages from*
*his delightful* A Fine and Private Place,
*a book and a voice that I treasure.*

* www.peterbeagle.com

I do not know that I ever saw anything more terrible than the struggle of that . . . Ghost against joy. For he had almost been overcome. Somewhere, incalculable ages ago, there must have been gleams of humour and reason in him . . . But [now] the light that reached him, reached him against his will . . . he would not accept it.

—C. S. Lewis, *The Great Divorce*

# Cat Cross Their Graves

# 1

UP THE MOLENA POINT HILLS WHERE THE village cottages stood crowded together, and their back gardens ended abruptly at the lip of the wild canyon, a row of graves lay hidden. Concealed beneath tangled weeds and sprawling overgrown geraniums, there was no stone to mark the bodies. No one to remember they were there save one villager, who kept an uneasy silence. Who nursed a vigil of dread against the day the earth would again be disturbed and the truth revealed. On winter evenings the shadow of the tall, old house struck down across the graves like a long black arrow, and from the canyon below, errant winds sang to the small, dead children.

There had been no reports for a dozen years of unexplained disappearances along the central California coast, not even of some little kid straying off to turn up at suppertime hungry and dirty and unharmed. Nor did the three cats who hunted these gardens know what lay beneath their hurrying paws. Though as they trotted down into the canyon to slaughter wood rats, leaping across the tangled flower beds, sometimes tabby Dulcie would pause to look around her, puzzled, her skin rippling with an icy chill. And once the tortoiseshell kit stopped stone still as she crossed the neglected flower bed, her yellow eyes growing huge. She muttered about a shadow swiftly vanishing, a child with flaxen hair. But this kit was given to fancies. Joe Grey had glanced at her, annoyed. The gray tom was quite aware that female cats were full of wild notions, particularly the tattercoat kit and her flights of fancy.

For many years the graves had remained hidden, the bodies abandoned and alone, and thus they waited undiscovered on this chill February night. The village of Molena Point was awash with icy, sloughing rain and shaken by winds that whipped off the surging sea to rattle the oak trees and scour the village rooftops. But beneath the heavy oaks and the solid shingles and thick clay tiles, within scattered cottages, sitting rooms were warm, lamps glowed and hearth fires burned, and all was safe and right. But many cottages stood dark. For despite the storm, it seemed half the village had ventured out, to crowd into Molena Point Little Theater for the week-long Patty Rose Film Festival. There, though the stage was empty, the darkened theater was filled to capacity. Though no footlights shone and there was no painted backdrop to describe some enchanted world and no live actors to beguile the audience, not a seat was vacant.

Before the silent crowd, the silver screen had been lowered into place from the high, dark ceiling, and on it a classic film rolled, a black-and-white musical romance from a simpler, kinder era. Old love songs filled the hall, and old memories for those who had endured the painful years of World War II, when Patty's films had offered welcome escape from the disruptions of young lives, from the wrenching partings of lovers.

For six nights, Molena Point Little Theater audiences had been transported, by Hollywood's magic, back to that gentler time before X-ratings were necessary and audiences had to sit through too much carnage, too much hate, and the obligatory bedroom scene. The Patty Rose Film Festival had drawn all the village back into that bright world when their own Patty was young and vibrant and beautiful, riding the crest of her stardom.

Every showing was sold out and many seats had been sold again at scalpers' prices. On opening night Patty herself, now eighty-some, had appeared to welcome her friends; it was a small village, close and in many ways an extended family. Patty Rose was family; the blond actress was still as slim and charming as when her photographs graced every marquee and magazine in the country. She still wore her golden hair bobbed, in the style famous during those years, even if the color was added; her tilted nose and delighted smile still enthralled her fans. To her friends, she was still as beautiful.

When Patty retired from the screen at age fifty and moved to Molena Point, she could have secluded herself as many stars do, perhaps on a large acreage up in Molena Valley where a celebrity could retain her privacy. She had, instead, bought Otter Pine Inn, in the heart of the village, and moved into one of its third-floor penthouses, had gone quietly about her everyday business until people quit gawking and sensibly refrained from asking for autographs. She loved the village; she walked the beach, she mingled at the coffee shop, she played with the village dogs. She soon headed up charity causes, ran benefits, gave generously of her time and her money.

Two years ago she had bought an old historic mansion in need of repair, had fixed it up and turned it into a home for orphaned children. "Orphans' home" was an outdated term but Patty liked it and used it. The children were happy, they were clean and healthy, they were well fed and well educated. Eighty-two percent of the children went on to graduate from college. Patty's friends understood that the home helped, a little bit, to fill the dark irreparable void left by the death of Patty's daughter and grandson. Between her civic projects and the children's home, and running the inn, Patty left herself little time for grieving.

She took deep pleasure in making the inn hospitable. Otter Pine Inn was famous for its cuisine, for its handsome and comfortable accommodations, and for the friendly pampering of its guests. It was famous indeed for the care that Patty extended to travelers' pets. There are not so many hotels across the nation where one's cats and dogs are welcome. Otter Pine Inn offered each animal velvet cushions by a window, a special menu of meaty treats, and free access to the inn's dining patio when accompanied by a human. Sculptures of cats and dogs graced the patio gardens, and Charlie Harper's animal drawings hung in the inn's tearoom and restaurant. Police captain Max Harper had been Patty's friend from the time she arrived in Molena Point, long before he met and married Charlie.

When Patty first saw Charlie's animal drawings, she swore that Charlie made some of her cats seem almost human, made them look as if they could speak. Patty Rose was perceptive in her observations, but in the matter of the three cats who lived with three of her good friends, Patty had no idea of the real truth. As for the cats, Joe Grey and Kit and Dulcie kept their own counsel.

Now in the darkened theater, as the last teary scenes drew to a close, Charlie leaned against Max's shoulder, blowing her nose. On her other side, Ryan Flannery reached for a tissue from the box the two women had tucked between them. Patty's films might be musicals, but the love interest provided enough cliff-hanging anxiety to bring every woman in the audience to tears. Over Charlie's bright-red hair and Ryan's dark, short bob, Max Harper glanced across at Clyde with that amused, tolerant look that only two males can share. Women—they always cried at a romantic movie, squeezed out the tears like water from a sponge. Charlie cut Max a look and wiped her tears; but as she wept at the final scenes, she looked up suddenly and paused, and her tears were forgotten. A chill touched Charlie, a tremor of fear. She stared up at the screen, at Patty, and a fascination of horror slid through her, an icy tremor that held her still and afraid, a rush of fear that came out of nowhere, so powerfully that she trembled and squeezed Max's hand. He looked down at her, frowning, and drew her close. "What?"

"I don't know." She shook her head. "Nothing. It . . . it's gone." She looked up again at Patty, at the twenty-year-old Patty Rose deep into the love scene, and tried to lose herself again in the movie.

But the sense of dread remained, a feeling of regret so vivid that she was jolted completely out of the story. A sense of wrongness and danger that made her grip Max's hand more tightly. He drew her closer, uneasy himself now, and puzzled.

Patty really hadn't been herself these last weeks, and that had concerned Charlie. Patty was usually either all business or cutting loose, laughing with her friends, singing her old songs and making fun of herself, hamming it up. Whatever Patty did, she was completely in the moment, giving of herself fully. But these last weeks she had seemed distracted, drawn away and quiet, her attention wandering so, that sometimes you had to repeat what you said to her. Charlie had glimpsed her several times looking off across the inn's gardens or out through its wrought-iron gates to the street as if her thoughts were indeed very far away, and her gamin face much too serious.

NOW, AS CHARLIE FROWNED over Patty's distraction, and the crowd in the theater was caught in the last tearful moments of Patty's love story, Patty Rose was out in the storm crossing the inn's softly lit patio.

Pulling her wrap close around her against the cold wind, she headed through the blowing garden for the closed tearoom.

The shifting shadows were familiar enough, the tile roofs, the dark, shivering bushes no different than on any windy night. The black tearoom windows rippling with wind reflected only blowing bushes and tossing trees and the long wing of the inn itself, and the guests' lighted windows. Then the dark, uneasy glass caught her own reflection as she moved quickly down the brick walk through the shifting montage of garden and dark panes, heading for the tearoom's small auxiliary kitchen. She meant to make herself a cup of cocoa, to sit for a while in the empty tearoom and get herself centered. Put down the silly sense of invasion that had followed her the past week.

**When Charlie shivered again,** Max squeezed her shoulder. She looked up at him and tried to smile. His lean, leathery good looks eased her, his steadiness reassured her. The deep lines down his cheeks were smile lines, the tightness of his jaw reserved for less pleasant citizens than his redheaded bride. She leaned into his hard shoulder, rubbing her cheek against his sport coat; he had worn the cashmere jacket she liked, over a dark turtleneck and faded jeans. He had bought their tickets for all six showings mostly to please her, but she knew he was enjoying Patty's films. She snuggled close, trying to pay attention as the last scene played out. Wadding up her tissues and stuffing them in her purse, she pushed away whatever foolish imagining had gripped her; but she was so engrossed in her own thoughts that when Max reached into his pocket to answer his vibrating cell phone, she was startled. The dispatcher knew not to buzz him here. Not unless the matter was truly urgent.

As he lifted the phone from his belt, the chill touched her again. As he punched in the single digit for the station, sirens began to scream across the village, patrol cars and then the more hysterical wailing of a rescue unit. Max rose at once and quietly left the theater, was gone so fast she had no time to speak to him.

Watching his retreating back, she felt Ryan's hand on her arm—and the chill returned, making her tremble, cold and uncertain. She could not remember ever having had that sudden lost, frightened sensation minutes before the sirens screamed. When Ryan took her hand, she rose helplessly and followed him and Clyde out the side exit, ahead of the departing crowd.

TEN MINUTES BEFORE the sirens blasted, the tortoiseshell kit awoke just as startled as Charlie, just as eerily scared. When the sirens jerked her up from her tangle of cushions on her third-floor window seat, she immediately pressed her nose against the cold, dark glass.

The time was near midnight. Above the village roofs and chimneys, above the black pools of wind-tossed trees, the distant stars burned icy and remote. Impossible worlds, it seemed to Kit, spinning in a vastness that no one could comprehend. Beyond the inn's enclosing walls, a haze of light from the village shops shifted in the wind as indistinct as blowing gauze; against that pale smear, the black pools of trees rattled and shook. She stared down past the lower balconies to the inn's blowing gardens and patio, softly lit but deserted. What had waked her?

Nothing moved on the patio but the puppets of the wind. She heard no faintest sound.

She and Lucinda and Pedric had been at Otter Pine Inn since before Christmas, enjoying the most luxurious holiday the kit had ever imagined. Over the hush of the wind, from deeper within the darkened suite, through the open bedroom door, she could hear Lucinda's and Pedric's soft breathing. The old couple slept so deeply. Lucinda had told her, laughing, that that was the result of a good conscience. The kit, staring down through the bay window to the courtyard and sprawling gardens, studied the windows of the bar and the dining room and the tearoom.

The tearoom was closed and dark at this hour, and the faintly lit dining room looked deserted; she thought it was about to close. No one came out of the bar, and its soft lights and black-smoked windows were too dark to see much. No one was returning through the wrought-iron gate from the street, ready to settle in for the night. As she pressed her nose harder to the glass, her whiskers and ears sharply pricked, her every sense was alert.

Otter Pine Inn occupied nearly a full block near the center of the village, just a short stroll from Ocean Avenue. Its wrought-iron gates, its three wings that formed a U, and its creamy stucco walls surrounded winding brick walks and bright winter blooms. The roofs of the inn were red tile, mossy in the shady places, slick and precarious under the paws, slick all over when they were wet.

There were four third-floor penthouses. Patty Rose's suite was at the back. Kit and Lucinda and Pedric had a front suite overlooking the patio and the front gate. In one of the other two penthouses this weekend were a young couple with three cocker spaniels, in the other a family with two children and a Great Dane, a dog the kit avoided, but only because she didn't know him. The cockers were more her size; she could easily bloody them if the need arose. Or she could terrorize them for amusement, if she liked. If Lucinda didn't catch her at it. Since before Christmas, Kit had enjoyed such a lovely time with her adopted family. The three of them had indulged in all manner of holiday and post-holiday pleasures—concerts, plays, long walks, and amazing gourmet delights.

Though for the concerts, she had to endure one of those abominable soft-sided doggie carriers with its little screened window. Of course, she could open the stupid thing from inside with a flick of her paw, but the embarrassment of being in it was almost too much. She was, after all, not a toy poodle! Lucinda laughed at her and made sure she had little snacks in there, but Lucinda really did understand. And their reunion was so amazing, after Kit had painfully mourned her dear old couple's death. When the TV newscasts had reported the terrible wreck that destroyed the Greenlaws' RV while the elderly couple was traveling down the coast, all their friends had believed them dead. The kit never really believed that. Then when no bodies were found in the burned wreckage, hope began to touch them all. And when Lucinda herself called to say they were alive, Kit had nearly flown out of her skin with joy. Now, to have her beloved adopted family back from the grave, as it were, was a never-ending wonder to the small tortoiseshell.

Settling into Otter Pine Inn for the holiday, visiting with their friend Patty Rose, the kit had every possible luxury—her own cushioned window seat, her own hand-painted Dalton china dinner service, and anything at all that she cared to order from the inn's gourmet kitchen or from attentive waiters on the dining patio. Now, twitching an ear, she listened harder. Had she heard, on the instant of waking, angry human voices?

Below, the bar's lights went brighter, and three yawning couples emerged, maybe the last customers, heading for their rooms. Molena Point was not a late-hour town; even the tourists turned in early, many to rise at dawn for a walk with their dogs or a run along the white-sand beach. The shore in the morning was overrun with wet, sandy dogs running insanely and barking at nothing.

Now in the bar, the lights blazed and she could see the waiters starting to clean up, wiping the tables; the cleaning staff would arrive soon to sweep and scrub. The smell of rain came sharply through a thin crack around the side of her window. She could hear voices now, hushed and angry, an argument from somewhere beyond the dining room. Maybe from the stairs that led down to the parking garage? She hated that garage; the vast concrete basement made her shiver with unease; she didn't like to go there. When she was little she had thought that caves and caverns were wonderful places, peopled with amazing and mythical beings. Now those grim, echoing hollows frightened her. Angrier and louder the voices came, though maybe too faint for a human to hear. Burning with curiosity and a strange sense of dread, she pressed at the glass of the side window with an impatient paw until it opened.

Yes, a man and a woman arguing. She didn't recognize the man, but the woman was Patty Rose; she had never heard Patty so angry. Impatiently Kit pushed against the screen. The way the echoes bounced and fell, she thought they were on the stairwell down to the garage, their words deflected by the inn's plastered walls. Patty's tone was hot and accusing, but the way the man was snapping back, Kit could make no sense of their words. She was pawing at the screen's latch when three sharp reports barked between the walls, echoing and reverberating across the patio. Slashing hard down the screen, she ripped a jagged hole.

Behind her she heard Lucinda thump out of bed. Before the agile old lady could stop her, Kit forced through the screen tearing out hanks of her fur and dropped to the second-floor balcony. Below her, doors banged open, people were running and shouting. She heard a tiny click as Lucinda snatched up the bedside phone, heard Lucinda alert the dispatcher as, likely, a dozen people were trying to do.

"Three shots, that's all I know," Lucinda said as Kit slipped beneath the rail. "Yes, shots, my dear," the old woman said testily. "That was not a backfire. I know gunshots when I hear them. And there was no smallest sound of a car engine."

Kit dropped onto the back of a bench and into a bed of cyclamens. Racing across the brick walk and through the taller flowers, she listened for the shooter running, but all she heard was her own fur brushing through the foliage. As she skirted a bed of geraniums, her nose tingled at the flowers' smell where she crushed them.

Strange, the stairwell that led down to the parking garage was dark, the little lights along the steps had been turned off. As she reached the top of the stairs, she heard running below, the faintest footsteps fast descending: soft shoes heading for the parking basement. She caught a whiff of geranium mixed with the sharp iron smell of blood, heard the squeak of rubber soles on concrete.

On the dark stairs, a body lay sprawled head down. Staring at the mutilated woman, Kit glimpsed, far below, a running shadow disappear through blackness into the garage. But Kit's attention, her whole being, was centered on the dead woman.

Patty Rose lay tumbled, unnaturally twisted down the concrete steps, her white silk dressing gown slick with blood. Her face was turned away but was reflected in the steel hood of the recessed light: bloody, distorted. The smell of blood filled Kit's nose; she could taste the heavy smell. Sirens screamed closer, muffled by the wind and by the walls of the buildings. Heart pounding, she crept down the steps to Patty. The sirens grew louder, coming fast. Trying not to look at Patty's poor torn face, Kit reached out her nose searching for breath. And knowing there would be none. Police cars careened around the building, slamming on their brakes. Then silence. Car doors slammed and the night was filled with the static of police radios, with the dispatcher's voice, with footsteps pounding across the patio above her, cops running down the stairs; and Kit ran, pelting down into darkness.

Crouched far down the steps in blackness, she smelled Patty's blood as strong as if it was on her own whiskers. Her tail was between her legs, her whole being felt shrunken.

Patty Rose had held Kit on her lap and loved and petted her, Patty had shared tea with her and fed her bits of shortbread all buttery warm, Patty had talked so softly to her. This kind woman had talked and talked to her and had never known that Kit could have answered her.

That seemed terrible now, that Patty had never known. Patty Rose would have been thrilled. Kit wished she could talk to her now, that she could tell Patty she loved her.

Below her she heard another scuffle of footsteps near the door to the parking garage, a faint squeak as of rubber soles on concrete, and then, from the far side of the garage, the cops surging down the two ramps and inside. Kit stood on the dark steps alone, heartbroken and shivering.

Oh, she longed for Joe Grey and Dulcie to be there with her, for the strength of the big gray tomcat and for tabby Dulcie's mothering. She knew she was nearly a full-grown cat, but right now all she wanted was to push close between the two bigger cats, like a lost kitten.

Joe Grey and Dulcie, and their human friends, had cared for Kit ever since she left the wild bunch she had run with. Always picked on, she hadn't had the courage to leave until she met Joe and Dulcie, and Lucinda and Pedric. Oh, then her life had so changed. To find two speaking cats like herself, and to find humans who understood—that had been an amazing time.

But right now this minute, she ached just to feel Dulcie's nose against her ear, to hear Dulcie and Joe Grey tell her that everything would be all right—she longed, most of all, for this terrible thing to have never happened, for Patty Rose to be alive and unharmed.

Above her, two medics knelt over Patty's poor bloody body. Kit's nose was sour with the smell of death. Far below, she could hear the faint scuffs and voices as the officers searched. Strange, she'd heard no car screeching out to escape. Was the killer hidden among the parked cars or under them? Or ducked down in a car, thinking the cops would miss him? She imagined him creeping out later through the confusion of police cars and rescue vehicles and somehow eluding them. Was that possible? Oh, the officers would find him, they *must* find him!

But if they didn't catch him, Kit thought . . . she knew something about that man that the law didn't know.

Racing down, she hit the bottom step and fled into the garage dodging a confusion of swinging spotlights, the officers' torches burning leaping paths through the blackness. Crouching in shadow under a small black car, she listened, paws slick with sweat.

At last she began to creep along between the cars, scenting the concrete, seeking the smell of crushed geranium—and listening for the sound of softer shoes slipping away accompanied by that telltale little squeak, that chirp of rubber against concrete.

# 2

WHEN SIRENS CAREENING THROUGH THE night woke the village, the most curious or adventuresome residents threw on whatever clothes were handy and followed, running through the streets to form an unwanted crowd, so many unruly onlookers that they had to be forcibly kept in check by half a dozen busy officers; the more considerate folk sat by their open windows tuning their radios to the local station, or stood in their miniscule front gardens asking their neighbors what was happening.

In the village library, which should have been empty at two in the morning, the racket jerked a little girl sharply from her troubled sleep. She sat up flinging herself off her thin mattress and against the cement wall, scrambling like a terrified animal. The sirens screamed overhead nearly above her, heavy vehicles thundering down the street as if they were right on top the basement. Sounded like the rumbling engines were coming down at her. In the tiny, hidden basement, she wondered if she would die crushed by trucks and by fallen concrete.

She didn't flick on her little flashlight, she was afraid to.

There was no window into her hiding place, no one could see her, but still she was afraid. Was there a fire somewhere near? She pulled the thin blanket tighter around her. The basement was always cold. A damp cold, Mama would say. She missed Mama terrible bad.

She hadn't run away until Pa boarded up the kitchen window, long after he'd nailed plywood over the other windows and locked the doors with key bolts that she couldn't open. When he covered the kitchen window, too, she knew she couldn't stay there anymore. He'd nailed that plywood on after the neighbor saw her looking out, a big, bony, nosy woman, saw her at the window and came over to ask him if she was sick and why wasn't she in school. That's when Pa found her footprint on the tile counter where she'd climbed up to see if she could unlock the window, where she forgot to wipe away the waffle mark of her jogging shoes. He told the neighbor she was home with the flu but afterward when the neighbor was gone, he was white and silent, and he locked her in the bathroom all night. She didn't know what was wrong with Pa except he didn't love her anymore and wasn't like that when she was little.

She was six when he'd started yelling at her and locking her in the house and wouldn't listen to Mama, and that was when Mama packed a suitcase and the two of them slipped away after he went to work and drove clear across the country to North Carolina to live. Where Pa wouldn't never think to look. They'd lived in Greenville for five years.

After Mama died and the social workers put her in foster homes one after another and she kept running away, that was when she told them she had a father in California, and they sent her back.

She'd thought he'd be different, anyway better than foster homes. But then she was sorry. Pa didn't hurt her like some of the kids had told her about, but he kept her like an animal in a cage, and the cage seemed smaller every day. She was afraid to call the social worker, though, call the number they gave her, she didn't like social workers.

The rumbling had stopped, the sirens were fainter. Lying in the dark listening to them move away, she hugged herself. She wished she had another blanket. She imagined growing old in this basement, living her whole life here and no one knowing. She thought that over the years everyone must have forgotten this small space behind the library's basement workroom, the way it had been walled off to itself. It was just a cubbyhole with rough concrete calls, not smooth walls like the workroom, and it wasn't as big as their little bathroom at home. She'd known about it since she was six, though. She'd found it when Mama worked in the library; she'd used to come in here to play, slip in behind the bookcase and no one knew.

Now it wasn't play anymore.

She only had enough food for another week. The welfare woman took her money, that Mama gave her. The welfare woman in Greenville, with the big nose, said she'd keep it for her but she never gave it back. Twenty dollars Mama gave her, and Pa never gave her even a nickel.

Now when she ran out of cans to open she'd have to go out in the dark and steal food from the back of restaurants like the homeless did.

Well, she guessed she was homeless now, too.

Or in a kind of prison.

Except, Mama would say, *This isn't a prison, you're here by your own choosing, Lori. You can leave when you want, no one is making you stay here.*

But where would she go?

Mama wouldn't tell her to go back to Pa; Mama hadn't stayed, had she? But Mama wasn't here to tell her where to go, where to hide.

Well, she was done with the welfare people and the foster homes. The other kids said the homes were out for blood, took in kids just to make money. The more kids the foster homes got, the more money they made. Didn't matter to them if you had to sleep on the floor, ten to a room, what did they care? She'd heard plenty from the older kids. She wondered where those sirens were going, wondered what those cops were like, out in the night with their sticks and guns, wondered what they'd do with a runaway child.

Call child welfare? Call Pa? No, she wasn't going to the cops. She curled up shivering on the thin mat, pulled the blanket tighter, and snuggled into the old, stained pillow. As hard as she hugged herself she couldn't get warm and she couldn't go back to sleep.

**Joe Grey and Dulcie crouched** out of the way among a tangle of ferns as officers' feet raced past them, the cops' hard black shoes thundering on the brick walk. Within the lacy foliage, Dulcie's dark tabby stripes rendered her nearly invisible. Joe Grey's pewter coat was the color of the shadows; his white markings among the lacy fronds might be mistaken for bits of blown paper. Both cats' eyes burned with interest—though there was an unusual unease between them. They were not snuggled close. They sat apart, and they had not, as was usual, raced onto the patio together. Joe had been hunting. Dulcie had been home in bed with Wilma as her housemate read aloud. Neither cat was in the best mood. As the officers crowded around the stairs to the garage, Joe glanced at Dulcie, stiff and wary.

For nearly two weeks, they had hardly spoken. Joe didn't know what was wrong with Dulcie, and he certainly wasn't asking. If she didn't want to talk, that was her problem. When, among the village rooftops or gardens, he happened on her by accident, he remained as aloof as she. Tonight, racing onto the inn's patio from different directions, they had eyed each other like strangers, Dulcie's stance defensive, Joe swallowing back a hiss.

Yet now as officers moved down the stairwell toward an objective the cats couldn't see, both slipped quickly through the garden to look, glancing shyly at each other. Beyond them across the patio two uniforms guarded the inn's front gate, and two more strung the traditional yellow tape against the gawking crowd that had gathered even on this rainy night. Dulcie glanced at Joe. Padding closer, she gently touched her nose to his. "Where's Kit?" she said softly. "Is she down here in the middle already?"

Joe glanced, scowling, up at Kit's third-floor window. The lights were on but Kit was not in sight. The side window was open and he could see a rip in the screen. He turned to study the shadows around the stairwell, but he saw no gleam of yellow eyes. Dulcie, rearing up, scanned the windows, too. "The screen's torn. Maybe Lucinda tried to keep her in."

*Fat chance,* Joe thought.

When Dulcie nuzzled him, he didn't respond. She gave him a sideways look. She could imagine Kit leaping down the roof to the balcony, down again—at the sirens' call, she thought, amused. She slipped closer to Joe, who had shifted away, and this time he didn't move. He was watching Ryan and Clyde, who had come in before the tape was strung, and watching Lucinda and Pedric hurrying down the stairs from their penthouse, the tall elderly couple pulling on their jackets. Softly, Lucinda was calling the kit. Both she and Pedric looked worried.

The stairwell was mobbed now with uniforms, the flash of police torches reflecting up from below projecting gigantic shadows up along the stucco walls. The lights beside the descending steps, which marched down to the garage, and the garage lights below, had been extinguished. Joe wondered if the killer had disconnected them, or if perhaps a gunshot had shorted them out.

Was Kit down there in the stairwell, below the crowd of officers? Or maybe above them, peering over from the deep shadows of the balcony that ran above the stairs? Looking along the balcony, Joe searched for her but saw no gleam of yellow eyes. He glanced at Dulcie, and his look softened. For a moment the two cats were close again, of one mind, their noses filled with the smell of death. Sliding into the bushes at the top of the steps, staring down among the flashing torch lights, both cats froze.

Patty Rose lay below them, her white satin robe bloodstained, her face brutally torn. Dulcie was so shocked she felt her supper come up, her mouth fill with bile. Joe's ears were back flat to his head, his whiskers laid flat, his eyes burning like yellow fire.

Detective Garza knelt beside Patty, feeling for a pulse. The cats knew there could be no pulse. When at last Garza rose and backed off, the medics knelt over her trying for a pulse, too, trying to stop the bleeding, trying to start her heart beating again. They worked for a long time before they rose and turned away. Beside Dulcie, Joe's face seemed suddenly thinner, his whole body smaller and limp. Shivering, the tomcat nosed at her. She looked at him helplessly, read in his eyes exactly what he felt—as if all that was good in life had vanished, as if the negative forces of the world had suddenly won. Never had either cat imagined Patty Rose murdered. Such wanton violence to someone so good, so innocent of malice, filled them with defeat. Crouching with Joe above the stairs, Dulcie watched Detective Garza unpack his cameras.

Peering from behind several uniforms' dark trouser legs, shuttering their eyes against the bright strobe lights, the two cats watched Dallas Garza begin to shoot the scene. The big, square-faced Latino was dressed in soft jeans and a wrinkled blue T-shirt, as if he had grabbed the first clothes at hand. He wore scuffed tennis shoes but no socks. His short, dark hair was uncombed. His tanned jaw was darkened by a day's growth of shadowy whiskers, and set with a cop's controlled anger at this death of a good friend. As he stood above the body, Garza's dark, solemn eyes searched every inch of the stairwell as he decided where to shoot, making sure he missed nothing. Some of his close-ups were made more difficult by the steep flight of steps, some were assisted by the dropping angles. When he had shot a roll of film, he began to set up additional lights to eliminate shadows, to do it all again. The two cats fled to the concrete walkway above the stairwell.

Crouching there on the cold cement, tasting the smell of death, they tried not to look down directly at Patty, but the lights brutally illuminated her. Sickened, Dulcie couldn't help but imagine a grisly film shoot, macabre and shocking. A horrifying farewell for a great star, a surreal and disgusting final drama too much like the sickest of human culture.

She watched Captain Harper and the coroner approach the stairs through the crowd of officers. At the top of the steps, the two men paused, waiting for Garza to finish so Dr. Bern could examine the body before taking it to the morgue. There, the final bits of fiber and debris would be removed from Patty's clothes and body. She would be examined for all manner of trauma and of course for bullets. Samples would be taken before her body was tagged and locked away in a cold metal drawer. The cats knew the drill. They had attended more murder scenes than some of the rookies present. But that didn't make this death easier.

Certainly Captain Harper looked sick, so stricken that Joe wanted to put out a paw to him. The tall, thin chief watched the procedures in silence, his lined face pale and grim. Watched Garza finish photographing the body and surroundings and wind back the film of the old, reliable Rolleiflex camera, then shoot a few minutes of video, moving up and down the stairs. When he started toward the walkway above, the cats melted into the deepest shadows, Joe hiding his face and chest and paws by curling into a furry ball.

When Garza seemed sure he'd missed no shot, he tucked

the cameras into his black leather bag, then knelt and began lifting samples, picking up small bits of debris with tweezers, and using a small soft brush to sweep the tiniest flecks into evidence bags. Garza had been with Molena Point for just a year, since Max Harper hired him away from San Francisco PD, a change that Garza had been more than happy to make. Leaving behind him too many years of big-city crime, he had moved into his family's vacation cottage at the north side of the village, a small old hillside cottage they jokingly called the Garza/Flannery estate. At about the same time Dallas left San Francisco, his niece, Ryan, after a painful divorce had also relocated from the city, to start her new construction company in Molena Point.

As the cats crouched among the flowers watching Garza, they heard a woman start across the patio behind them, coming from the front gate, her hard-soled walk quick and decisive. They didn't need to look, they knew Detective Davis's step. Juana Davis crossed and stood at the top of the stairs beside Dr. Bern, studying the body, watching Detective Garza collect evidence on the steps below. The case seemed to be Garza's call, but maybe both detectives would work this one, as they sometimes did. The cats could imagine the hours of interrogation as Harper and his two detectives questioned all the many hotel employees and guests. At last a stretcher was carried down the steps, Dr. Bern supervising the lifting and securing of the body, and Patty Rose was taken away.

Garza studied the crime scene and photographed the area beneath where she had lain, then lifted some samples. When at long last he turned off the strobe lights, when the stairwell was once more in darkness, the cats dropped down onto the concrete steps, well below where the two detectives stood talking.

"Was she alone?" Davis asked, puzzled. "Alone on the back stairs in the middle of the night? In her nightie?"

Garza shrugged. "You know she was famous for that, getting a snack in the middle of the night, raiding the tearoom pantry."

Davis nodded. "Never could understand how she kept her figure. Patty's . . . she's slim as a girl." Davis had a problem with weight; she was squarely built and, despite lengthy workout routines, the burgers and fries all went to fat.

"Harper's photographing and printing the pantry. The door was open, the light on."

Davis glanced toward the tearoom. "He need help?"

"He took a rookie to lift prints. Cameron, she's good with that." Jane Cameron had been on the force just a month, having come straight from San Jose PD, where she'd served her apprenticeship after graduating from San Jose State.

"Where's Dorothy?" Davis said, looking back to where a small group of employees had gathered, kept in check by Officer Brennan. Dorothy Street was Patty's personal secretary. Davis glanced up to the narrow balcony that ran above the stairs. The dim, chill walkway, even in the daytime, gave no hint of the sunny apartments to which it led. At intervals beneath the concrete roof, the five doors were closed. No one had come out or gone in while the cats were there. Yellow crime-scene tape closed the doors now. Each door opened to a large and comfortable room reserved for members of the hotel staff. The cats, when they prowled the garden behind that wing, always peered in through the wide glass doors at the spacious residences. Dorothy Street had a two-room apartment down at the end. "She should have heard the shots," Davis said, studying the closed doors.

Garza shook his head. "She's in L.A. Flew down last week; her daughter's having her first baby. Max called the number she gave the staff." He handed Davis a slip of paper. "First one is the daughter's home number. No answer. You want to try the hospital?"

Davis nodded. "You've gone over Patty's suite?"

"Not yet. We've secured both doors."

Again the cats heard Lucinda calling the kit, her voice harsh with worry. "How long has she been gone?" Dulcie whispered.

Joe shrugged, and Dulcie began to fidget. "She can't have followed the killer?"

Joe's yellow eyes burned. "She can't?" Both cats rose and began to sniff along the concrete, seeking the kit's scent. The two detectives were discussing the witnesses. ". . . get their preliminary statements tonight," Garza was saying. "Bartender and two barmaids, ten customers, four kitchen staff. Dining room closes at ten. No other guest so far has come forward. I'll take the bar group. You want the kitchen staff?"

Davis nodded. The officers would, the cats knew, question each witness individually, keep them from talking among themselves. When witnesses started comparing what they remembered—thought they remembered—everything got garbled. With a little imagination, the pop of a beer can opening could turn into the sound of a gunshot.

"Maybe Max will take a few," Garza said. "We might get a couple hours' sleep before breakfast."

"Right now I'd settle for breakfast," Davis said wistfully.

"Finish questioning your bunch, maybe they'll fry you an egg."

Listening to Garza and Davis, the cats grew increasingly uneasy about Kit. It wasn't like her not to be on the scene. Prowling the balcony, they picked up no scent of the tortoiseshell. Lucinda was still calling her. They looked at each other and forgot their differences.

"You want to catch the interviews?" Joe said, knowing she would not. They could read the interview reports on the dispatcher's desk at the station or in one of the detectives' offices. A cat lolling on a cop's desk was not unusual at Molena Point PD, Joe and Dulcie had long ago seen to that.

The urgency of the moment was to find the kit, and neither cat could pick up her scent. Joe was so concerned that he'd almost forgotten his anger with Dulcie; he glanced at her now with speculation.

Well, he wasn't asking questions. And he wasn't sneaking around following her, he wasn't lowering himself to that. If she wanted privacy, that was her affair—but she couldn't keep a secret forever.

It was the possibility of another tomcat that worried him. He *had* checked for the scent of a strange tom around the village, and had found none, nor had he detected the scent of another cat on Dulcie. But what was so sacrosanct that she couldn't share it?

UNCOMFORTABLE BENEATH JOE'S STARE, Dulcie put her nose to the concrete again. She hated keeping secrets from him, she considered that the same as lying, and she wanted to share every aspect of life with Joe. But she couldn't tell him this. Leaping down from the concrete walk to the steps below, she landed on a spot far beyond the chalk marks where Patty's body had lain. Moving on down, scenting for the kit, she couldn't smell much over the sharp stink of death. She was shaky with shock and grief. Now that the harsh strobe lights had been removed, the shadows leading down to the parking garage were thick and black, even to her eyes. She sensed Joe behind her, felt him brush against her, and in darkness they moved down together toward the bottom of the stairs.

Had Kit come down here before the police arrived? All alone, trying to sort through the smells of blood, shoe polish, and scorched dust from the harsh spotlights, through the smell of camera equipment and gunpowder. There was black fingerprinting powder on every surface. They didn't want that stuff on them. Not only did it taste bad, but their respective housemates would pitch a royal fit. Joe could just hear Clyde. "Stuff's hell to get off, Joe. Can't you think about these things? And do you have to have your nose into every damn crime scene?"

As the cats slipped into the black garage, they would have

been nearly invisible except for the snowy gleam of Joe's white nose and his white chest and paws. His disembodied white markings moved beside Dulcie like tiny white ghosts. The garage stank of cigar smoke, of hair cream, of various scents that could belong to anyone. They could find no trail of the kit. Padding between the cold wheels of cars that had been parked there all night, they kept their noses to the concrete like a pair of tracking hounds.

Back and forth they quartered the garage, under and around the cars. They caught whiffs of cops they knew, little air trails of human scent—shoe polish, aftershave, tobacco—swirled with the automotive stinks until, mixed by the sucking wind that swept through the garage, all became mucked together like an overdone stew, and nothing of value remained. When, after an hour they had found no trace of the kit, they left the garage feeling decidedly cranky. Trotting up the short drive, they slowly circled the block-long building, then padded in beneath the yellow crime-scene tape, where the wrought-iron gate stood open. The gate did not smell of the kit, nothing smelled of the kit, all was a mishmash of too many human scents. Stopping among the patio flowers, they stared up at the Greenlaws' windows.

The kit was not looking out; they saw no figure, no movement within. The one light was burning, as before. The patio was silent except for the faintest murmer of voices from the tearoom and dining room, and the soft crackle of a police radio turned low. And then, from across the gardens, they heard Lucinda calling again. Softly calling and calling the kit. Calling for a cat who might, by this time, be very far away and deep into trouble.

# 3

THE HARSH LIGHTS THAT HAD ILLUMINATED the patio had been extinguished; only the fainter garden lights remained, sending their soft glow low among the flowers. The tearoom lights were turned up brighter, and the cats could see Dallas Garza inside, beyond the flowered curtains, seated at a little table, talking with one of the waiters. The windows of the dining room, too, were bright where other employees or guests waited their turn. In the garden, two police guards moved back and forth along the walks, one of them yawning, their radios hoarse in the silence. Beneath the maple tree, Lucinda stood beside a wooden bench calling the kit. The thin old woman sounded more angry than pleading. When she saw Joe and Dulcie, she sat down on the bench and put out a hand to them.

Leaping to the bench beside her, Joe Grey crowded close. Dulcie climbed into Lucinda's lap, staring up into the old woman's long, thin face. Dulcie's voice was only a whisper, not audible to the guards above the mumble of their radios. "You've been out searching, out on the streets." It was not a question.

"Where is she?" Lucinda said. "You've been looking, too?"

Dulcie twitched an ear.

Lucinda frowned. "She slashed through the screen. I woke hearing gunshots, very close, three shots. By the time I threw on a robe and went to find Kit, she was gone, the screen torn, her fur caught in the wire." Lucinda went silent, cuddling Dulcie close as an officer wandered past them. Then she looked down at Dulcie and Joe. "We've tramped the village for over an hour, looking for her. Clyde is out there somewhere. Pedric's still looking. I'm worried for him, he's been gone a long time. Did you know that Kit's been watching a stranger? Some tourist, I thought."

The cats' eyes widened.

"She's so secretive. All week, she's been peering out the window at him, watching, and sometimes she would slip out and follow him—though she's never gone long. As if maybe he takes off in a car. A thin man, small. Maybe five feet tall. I don't—"

At Joe's expression, Lucinda stopped. "What, Joe?"

"Black hair," Joe said. "Small hands like a child?"

Lucinda nodded. "No taller than a twelve-year-old." The old woman stared at him, just as Dulcie was staring. "Do you know him? Who is he? I'm terrified of what might have happened to her."

Joe kneaded his claws nervously on the redwood bench. "I only saw him once, don't know who he is. Guy made me edgy as hell." Just thinking about that little man made Joe's fur stiffen with apprehension.

Three nights ago when he saw the small, strange man, he had backed away for no reason and hidden from him, not even ashamed of his cowardice. Maybe it was some subliminal scent, or maybe something in the guy's movements. Whatever, he'd kept his distance.

That was Monday night; it had been raining all night but had finally eased off. Entering Jolly's alley, he had enjoyed a leisurely and solitary midnight feast, finishing up the fresh leftovers George Jolly had set out. Crouching beneath the little roof of the feeding station that Mr. Jolly put out in bad weather, a little decorative structure like a hand-decorated doghouse, Joe had taken his time enjoying his meal, hoping wherever Dulcie was, with her stupid secrets, she was hungry and cold. Jolly's alley was one of Dulcie's favorite places, and Joe had taken perverse delight in going there alone and pigging out on the fine deli offerings, including one of Dulcie's favorites, creamy salmon salad.

He had been sitting beneath the jasmine vine washing salmon off his whiskers when a strange little man passed by, out on the sidewalk. He watched the guy pause and turn back to stand at the mouth of the alley, looking in. Being that the man was silhouetted against the streetlights, Joe could see only that he was short and frail, couldn't see his face. But even his silhouette made Joe's fur stand up, gave him a jolt that he didn't understand but that sent him backing deeper among the shadows.

The stranger had peered in at the potted flowers and shrubs, idly studying the inky recesses beneath the benches and around Joe's concealing vine. Joe, already crouched down, ducked his head to hide the white stripe down his nose, concealing as well his other white markings. Hunched there like a rolled-up porcupine, he had felt icy fear course through him, puzzling but quite real.

Maybe the guy had stirred an ugly memory. Triggered an unpleasant association. Maybe jarred in him some emotion from that other incident in Jolly's alley, three years earlier, when those two men entered and Joe witnessed one kill the other with a crescent wrench. Maybe this little man's appearance reminded him of that singular and shocking moment.

And maybe not. A cat couldn't always account for his fear-driven reactions. But a cat had the sense to pay attention.

Watching the small man, Joe had licked his shoulder, which was wet from the recent rain, and had wondered why this tourist was out in wet weather. A little rain was no big deal to a cat; there were countless niches where one could shelter out of the downpour and lick one's fur dry. But not many tourists walked for pleasure on a rainy night. The man had seemed so interested in the stained-glass doorways of the little out-of-the-way shops that lined the alley that Joe had wondered if he was planning to break in.

Yet his body language had seemed wrong for a break-in, relaxed but not stealthy. Not watchful enough of the street behind him, not attentive enough to the two open ends of the alley.

The stranger was such a small guy. His bones looked as thin as bird bones. His skin was very white, his hair as sooty black as the crows that bedeviled Joe from their clumsy perches among the oak trees. The guy's cheeks were thin and narrow, his pointed chin darkened by black stubble. His pale, child-size hands looked frail and weak. Moving suddenly, he had entered the alley.

Wandering along the narrow brick walk, he glanced without interest at the empty paper plate in its wooden shelter; he looked into the jasmine vine but didn't seem to see Joe, who was still rolled up like a frightened caterpillar. Joe thought the guy was maybe fifty or sixty, he could never be sure about human age. To interpret a person's age from a set of facial features was for Joe a far more difficult science than reading their body language.

The guy's high forehead was feathered by wispy black hairs that lay thinly across his pearly scalp. Thicker hair grew on his thin arms and the backs of his small hands, as if the maker of all living creatures had somehow gotten his wires crossed and put most of the hair in the wrong places. Joe imagined that if this man were to shake hands with a normal-size person, one would hear his bones cracking. The man seemed *unfinished.* Moving on through the alley, he paused beside a wrought-iron bench. What did he find of such interest in Jolly's alley that he remained standing there, looking? What was he looking *at*? But then when a car came down the street, its tires swishing on the wet pavement, he headed out of the alley fast, as if he didn't want to be seen there.

Joe looked up at Lucinda, feeling cold. This had to be the same man the kit had been watching. How many child-size men were there? The population of Molena Point wasn't all that big. If Kit had seen him tonight, what *had* she seen? Joe imagined too clearly the kit's yellow eyes, round and huge with curiosity, with shock at Patty's death—and perhaps with secret knowledge. If Kit had seen the killer, there was no telling where her rage and determination would lead her.

**EARLIER THAT NIGHT** as the detectives and coroner worked over Patty's body, photographing and videotaping, collecting fingerprints and lab samples, and then as Joe and Dulcie and their human friends searched for the kit, Kit moved alone through the windy night tracking Patty's killer. Or, she started out to track him.

Frightened and cold, filled with hatred of the man, she had followed the geranium scent as far as she could, hurrying along the icy concrete, her small body shivering with chill and grief, hurting so for Patty that all her senses seemed numbed. Besides geranium, she had picked up the stink of dirty socks and dog doo, all three mingling in the same gusts of air. As nasty as that was, it made her tracking faster; she galloped along following that wafting sourness, scanning the airy drafts like a small bird dog. His trail led her straight to Molena Point Little Theater.

The movie crowd that had enjoyed Patty's films was just dispersing. Had there been no announcement, then, of Patty's terrible murder? Maybe not. The cops had had enough trouble keeping people out of the inn's patio and away from the crime scene. Maybe they'd encouraged the theater personnel to say nothing, to simply continue with the filmed interviews that followed the movie. The programs were sometimes quite long. That was why Lucinda and Pedric had skipped this one after four nights' running. Drawing back among the bushes at the edge of the sidewalk, Kit watched people hurrying to their cars, or starting to walk home bundled up against the stormy cold. Rearing up on her hind paws trying to see through a forest of human legs, she looked and looked for the man—she could smell him close to her, he'd come here, all right, to mix with the crowd, as if this would this be his alibi, that he was at Patty's movie.

There, she saw him—the small man who had watched Patty, and who carried the scent of the killer. Kit wanted to leap on him and claw him, hurt him as he had hurt Patty. Dulcie said, and even Joe said sometimes, that in the case of human crime it was better for human law to punish the killer. But right now it would be more satisfying to tear at the evil creature as she would at a rat, dismembering it. Racing between hard oxfords and women's high-heeled boots, she slid into the bushes behind him.

Phew. The scent of dog doo laid over geraniums and dirty socks. When the man turned and nearly stepped on her, she spun away. If she were a cop, she could stick a gun in his ribs. So frustrating sometimes, being only a cat. When he moved away through the crowd, she followed, dodging people's feet and drawing surprised and interested looks. She followed him up the sidewalk, swerving and running, falling back behind people then hurrying ahead. After five blocks he got into a car, an old gray Honda parked at the curb a block from the library. Got in and took off, the smell of exhaust choking Kit. She followed the car, running down the middle of the street, until she had to streak for the curb or be crushed, landed pell-mell on the sidewalk, tumbling and scared out of her little cat wits.

The car had vanished, its stink lost among other cars, among the smell of tires and asphalt and diesel. She crouched on the concrete, shivering at having been so close to being hurt, so foolishly close to moving cars, telling herself she must not do that again.

But at last she shook herself and licked her cold paws, then started on in the direction the car had gone, looking ahead for any gray car, hunting stubbornly.

As she searched hopelessly along the endless dark streets, rearing up, scanning the side streets, twice she heard, far behind her, Lucinda calling her. She did not turn back, she kept on even when her friend's voice grew louder, closer. Lucinda would pick her up and hold her and make a fuss over her—and force her to go home. Later as she raced up to the roofs to better see the streets below, she heard Clyde, and then Pedric's low, gruff voice calling and calling her. Obstinately she turned away and kept on searching.

She had watched this man for nearly two weeks as he hung around the inn. She knew he was watching Patty but he'd never seemed threatening, such a small, frail man. Lucinda had seen him once, and they'd thought he might be a fan of Patty's. Now he had turned suddenly into the most terrible of monsters. Kit felt guilty, deeply guilty that neither she nor Lucinda had told anyone about him, and that Lucinda had never asked Patty about him.

Was this man the *reason* Patty had been distracted? Had she known he was watching her? And all the time, had he been waiting to kill Patty? And Patty herself had told no one. Had she not thought he would attack her? Never dreamed he would shoot her? A deep, terrible remorse filled the kit.

She tried to remember if she had ever seen his car, before tonight. Tried to bring that car clear again, that gray Honda. It was old and battered. A two-door, she thought. She had been so focused on the man and on dodging people's feet that she had not, as Joe or Dulcie would have done, set to memory its license number. Now that omission, too, was a matter of shame.

But she knew that car. And once, coming from along the seashore where she'd been hunting alone in the weedy shoulder above the sand, she'd seen it, she was sure she had. That time, her mind had been so intent on breakfast because she'd caught nothing in the tall grass, not even a mouse, that she'd hardly paid attention.

But now she paid attention. Where? Where had she seen it? Squinching her eyes closed, she made that picture come back to her, that old gray car. Parked. It had been parked way back down a weedy driveway beside a dark-sided, neglected cottage with tall grass in the yard, a cottage half hidden behind a bigger house, not a typical Molena Point cottage, well kept and pretty.

As the first fingers of dawn crept above the eastern hills, that was where Kit headed, to find that house. To that part of the village where, on one of the side streets off Ocean, she'd seen his car.

Padding along trying to remember which street, which block, she doubled back and forth. Where the collie barked? Where the yard seemed always to smell of laundry soap? Around her, dawn lightened the street between the shadowing oak trees, leaving pools of blackness beneath. She was tired, so tired that when at last she saw the gray Honda, she didn't believe it.

But there it stood way at the back behind the bigger house just as she remembered. Why hadn't the man skipped, why wasn't he out on the highway heading for L.A. or San Francisco? He had his nerve, coming back where he must have been staying. She caught his scent, she sniffed again, she swished her tail. She approached warily down the cracked, overgrown walk, staying within the tall grass, past the main house and through the scruffy yard like an overgrown jungle. Both houses were brown-shingled boxes with small, dirty windows. At the side of the cottage on a patch of gravel beside a black Ford sedan and a blue Plymouth stood the gray Honda, its fenders pushing into the rough bushes.

Approaching the steps on silent paws, looking up at the grimy windows, she stalked the cottage. These dark-shingled old buildings didn't look so much like Molena Point as like a pair of deserted houses she'd seen on her travels while running with that wild band of feral cats. He must be renting. Surely he was a visitor; she'd never seen him before he began to hang around Patty. Above her against the brightening dawn sky the roof shakes curled up, warped and black with rot. The boards on the steps warped up at the ends, too, and the narrow wooden porch sagged to the left. The path beneath her paws had run out of paving stones, was now rough dirt and gravel. She padded over to investigate his car.

Its tires were nearly cold, but she could feel the faintest heat lingering around its engine. When she glanced up at the house and saw movement beyond the glass, she crouched down as if hunting mice, sneaked into the bushes lashing her tail as if hot on the track of escaping game. There, deep within the shrubs, she looked out, again studying the window. Now the figure had disappeared inside beyond the murky glass, but then in a minute the door opened.

The little man stood in the doorway looking out, his thin face caught in a shaft of weak light. She wondered again why he hadn't run. He had to know the cops were after him. Did he think he was that clever, mixing with the theater crowd? Did he think the law wouldn't track him? He had very black hair and very white skin, and little, fierce black eyes. His forearms sported as much matted black hair as a mangy dog, a white-skinned sickly dog.

Dropping two bulging garbage bags on the rickety porch, he swung back inside, perhaps for another load. She could smell from the garbage bags the stale odor of old food; an empty can rolled out, crusted with something unpleasant. Crouched and tense, the kit waited. Was this the behavior of a killer, taking out the garbage?

He came out carrying a cardboard box, came down the steps, and headed for the Honda; behind him, he had left the door ajar. The minute he turned to open the trunk of the car, she fled up the steps and across the porch and into the cottage.

But once inside, she saw that there was only the one room, only one door. One path of escape. The other door, which stood open, led to a tiny bathroom. Watching the door behind her, she slipped beneath the bed, her heart thudding. She hadn't been smart to come in here. Should she scorch out before he returned? This man wasn't right; no sane person, no one with any gentleness, would have killed Patty.

Outside, he slammed the trunk and his soft soles crunched across the gravel. *Run, Kit. Run*. But she didn't run; stubbornly, she backed deeper beneath the bed.

# 4

**THE ROOM WAS MUSTY AND DIM. SHE PEERED** out from under the far end of the bed, watching him. He picked up the box and returned to the car; she heard him making noises as if loading it into the seat. In the dim room, dirty curtains were closed across three small windows, one window on each of three walls. On the fourth wall, through the open door to a bathroom, she could smell the stink of black mold. The window curtains must once have been bright plaid but were now a faded grid of colors as sickly as scrub rags. What kind of landlord would rent a place like this? There was no accounting for humans. Above her the dirty, dark ceiling absorbed what little light came in. Thin cobwebs clung to the dark old rafters, and the boards above them were crude and rough, as she'd see in some old garage.

Overlaying the other sour odors was the smell of stale food. The worn linoleum beneath her paws was so dirty that, when she crossed the room, grit and sticky stuff had pressed into her pads. She hated licking that gunk away. Where the linoleum had worn through, the fibers were filled with goo, like old ketchup.

A small, rusted cookstove stood in one corner between a dirty little refrigerator and a sink that was fixed to the wall with no cabinet or counter, its rusty plumbing hanging out underneath. A wooden table next to the sink was piled with cardboard boxes.

There was no closet. Next to the bed, five big nails had been driven into the wall. Some limp shirts and a tan windbreaker hung from these. She wondered if the bigger house, in front, was any cleaner. What a strange, forlorn place to find in this village, where most of the cottages were pampered and painted and their gardens lovingly tended. Maybe Lucinda was right, maybe some folks didn't want to do a thing to their property—just wait, and sell at inflated prices. Make a killing and move on. Strange, Kit thought, how some humans loved beauty and tried to make things nice, while others clung to ugliness.

She'd learned a lot since she left the band of ferals. When she was a little kitten, all she'd seen of humans were people's abandoned cars left to rust along the back roads, dirty streets, and garbage-strewn alleys. She hadn't understood until later that her band of strays had kept warily to the ugliest places, where humans expected them to be, where they were less likely to be chased or captured.

Hearing him outside at the car, clattering and walking around on the gravel, she slipped out from under the bed and leaped up on the table, peering into the boxes. One contained crookedly folded underclothes, and packs of letters and papers shoved in beside them. Another box held his dirty laundry. Phew. And two smaller boxes overflowed with empty beer cans. He was coming back, the grinding of gravel, the scuffing of his shoes up the steps. She flew under the bed.

Coming in, he slammed the door behind him and moved directly to the table, his rubber soles squeaking—something about the way he twisted his foot, she thought. She crept out as far as she dared, watched him set down a brown paper bag. He opened the refrigerator, pulled out a can of beer, and popped the lid. He picked up the box of laundry, tucked it under his arm, and left again, swilling beer, slamming and locking the door; she heard the bolt slide home. She listened, as nervous as a cornered mouse, as he started the Honda. Listened to it back out the gravel drive. As it turned onto the street, bits of gravel crunched under its wheels against the blacktop. What a strange man. He kills a woman, apparently follows her for weeks and then murders her, and now he's, what? Going to the laundromat? Taking out the garbage and doing his laundry? As Lucinda once said of someone, his mind was wired wrong. Drug dealers, thieves, killers. Not wired up right, Lucinda said. She listened to the car head away to the south but she remained still and shivering, more and more frightened by his strangeness.

When at last she came out from under the bed again and leaped onto the table, she looked into the bag. Yes, groceries. Peanut butter, bread, soup. As if he planned to stay awhile? Did he think no one would look for him? Or did he want them to look, did he want to be caught? Or was this food to take with him when he left, when he belatedly ran? She pawed into the cartons of clothes and papers hoping to find something that the law would want, something that could give the cops a handle, the way Joe said.

Nosing through the jumble of papers and jockey shorts and paperback books, she found, at the bottom of the second box, two big brown envelopes like magazines came in. Because he had sealed them closed, she wanted to see inside. Gripping them in her teeth, she pulled them off the table, dropping down with them, dragging them under the bed through a haze of dust to the back wall.

Crouching, she clawed the flaps open as neatly as she could, which wasn't very neat at all. When she shoved her nose in, her nostrils tickled with the smell of old newspapers. Slipping her paw inside, she was more careful now as she pulled out the contents and spread it in the dust.

There were three yellowed newspaper photographs, fuzzy and unclear, and a tangle of newspaper clippings. The photos were dull pictures of four men standing before a building. In all three pictures, the small man stood at the end, like some wizened-up child who had been made to stand next to his elders. The names in the short captions were Harold Timmons, Kendall Border, Craig Vernon, Irving Fenner. If they were in order, left to right, then the man she had followed was Irving Fenner. The columns below the pictures told about a series of murders in Los Angeles. There were no dates but the clippings were old, dry and brittle. Scanning the text as Lucinda or Wilma would have done, she went cold and still; she crouched unmoving, her paw half lifted, her eyes black and huge. Patty's name was there. In the article. And something about Patty's dead daughter, Marlie Rose Vernon.

This was about the murder of Marlie and her little boy. About Marlie's husband, Craig Vernon, who had been convicted of killing their child. Kit knew the story from Lucinda. The article said that Irving Fenner was an accessory to the murder.

Kit stared at the clippings and stared. After a long time she pawed them back into the envelope, her paw unsteady and damp with fear.

The second, fatter envelope was filled with glossy photographs, real professional portraits that made Kit catch her breath. Glossy magazine stories, too, with big colored pictures. Every photograph and every magazine picture was of Patty Rose when the famous actress was young and very beautiful indeed, her blue eyes huge, her short blond hair curling around her face. Pictures of Patty in elegant clothes, Patty in all kinds of scenes from her movies, all with other famous actors. Pictures of Patty singing with Stan Kenton, with Artie Shaw,

Glenn Miller, with all the famous bands that Wilma liked to listen to; Wilma and Lucinda had wonderful collections of Patty's old music.

In each picture, Patty's smile was the same that Kit knew, a smile filled with joy, as if nothing bad could happen in the world. In each picture, someone had punched a small, round hole in the paper—through Patty's forehead. A hole like a bullet hole.

Kit sat for a long time, shaking all over. Thinking about Patty, hurting bad inside, like huge hands crushing her. As she huddled there miserable and terrified and lost, she heard, outside and far away, a faint voice calling, calling her. A voice garbled in the wind but one she loved so dearly. She longed to cry out. Oh, she needed Lucinda. She longed to run out—if she could *get* out. Run to Lucinda where she would be loved and safe.

But she didn't cry out, and she didn't try to get out—not yet.

Pawing the pictures back into their envelope, she left a mark on one from her dirty pad. Trying to lick the page clean, she only smeared it. She didn't like to contaminate the evidence; that's what Joe would call it. Max Harper would need these, they might help very much to convict Irving Fenner.

Closing both envelopes as best she could after clawing them open so raggedly, she heard Lucinda calling her again, and this time Lucinda was closer, so close that it was all Kit could do not to leap to the window and claw at it, claw at the door and yowl.

And why not? She had the evidence, amazing and valuable evidence. If Lucinda came now, if Lucinda could let her out now . . .

But how could she, if the door was locked, if the windows were locked?

Snatching the two envelopes in her teeth, she dragged them just to the concealing edge of the crooked bedspread. Heavy to drag, they would be cumbersome indeed to carry. Once, she had helped Joe Grey carry a similar brown envelope for blocks across the village. Such a big, bulging package that it had taken the two of them together to pull it all the way to Joe's house and inside, and get it up the stairs.

Joe wasn't here to help her now, no one was. *You are alone, my dear,* she thought primly, as Lucinda or Wilma might say. *You are on your own.*

Leaving the envelopes out of sight beneath the edge of the bedspread, she leaped up at the knob of the front door knowing very well the door was locked; she could see the thrown dead bolt. She didn't hear Lucinda now. Had she gone on, searching in another direction? Moving farther away, along the dark street? Leaping up the door again and again, she fought the bolt until her paws were bleeding; at last she turned away and tried the windows.

All three windows were locked and were probably stuck, too. They were filled with ancient paint in the cracks, paint chipped off in layers of gray, cream, white, each layer thick between the sill and window. What did people do for fresh air? Even if she could have turned the round brass locks, she doubted these windows would open for anything less than a crowbar in human hands.

Was Lucinda carrying her cell phone? Inspired, Kit searched the room for a phone. She had long ago learned, from Joe Grey, how to paw in a number; and she had learned from the wild band she ran with how to remember stories, numbers, whatever she chose. When she was running with the wild ferals, the only joy she knew was their tales of the ancient speaking cats, the Celtic cats, and she had absorbed those delights word for fascinating word.

Finding no phone, circling frantically, she stared up at the ceiling. There was no way out, and no phone, and she could feel a yowl starting deep inside. She heard the car again, he was back, skidding to a gravelly stop. The car door creaked open, then slammed; he scrunched across the drive. As he squeaked up the steps she snatched the envelopes in her teeth and, hauling them, made for the bathroom. She didn't panic until she was inside. There, trapped in that tiny space, she went shaky.

The front door banged open. She stared helplessly around her, then pawed frantically at the two little doors under the sink, pawed and pulled until she fought one open. He was coming, his footsteps crossing the hard, gritty floor. Dragging the envelopes into the dank, moldy space, she pulled the door closed with her claws, her heart pounding so hard she thought it would burst.

The oilcloth beneath her paws was sticky but it was encouragingly loose, curling up at one corner. She'd barely pulled it back when he barged into the bathroom flinging the door wide. She crouched, shivering. If he opened the cupboard door, she'd go for his face. His feet scuffled on the other side of the cabinet, inches from her. Carefully pawing the oilcloth farther up, she slipped the envelopes under. Above her, he used the toilet and flushed, then turned on the water of the basin.

Working fast beneath the sound of running water, she smoothed the oilcloth over the envelopes. The wood beneath was black with rot, so soft that shards of wood came loose in her claws. Crouching atop the lumpy oilcloth, she watched the cabinet door.

But there was nothing under there for him to reach in for, not even scouring powder—not that he seemed to feel a need for cleaning products. She crouched there for what seemed hours, listening to the pipes groan. When she put her nose to the hot water pipe, it burned her. He must be shaving. She heard him brush his teeth. The water went on and off several times. She longed to hear Lucinda calling her again, even from far away, longed just to hear her friend's voice. He was rummaging around in the medicine cabinet. She felt so tired, so very hungry and thirsty. Her paws were beginning to sweat, and the cabinet walls seemed closer, the space growing smaller. She listened to him rummaging around. What was he doing? Why didn't he leave, what was taking him so long? She began to tremble with the panic of being shut in, trapped in that dark closed place. *She wanted out! Wanted out now!*

Panting, she told herself that she lay atop something so valuable, atop the very evidence that might fry Patty's killer. Told herself she had what the cops needed, that she would get out, that she would get the envelopes out of there. But all she could really think of was that she was locked in, caged, trapped in this dark, close cupboard in this horrible old house and that maybe, for her, there was no way out. Huddled atop the envelopes panting and shivering, she was scared out of her little cat mind.

# 5

No one knew the kit was trapped in the old cottage. Lucinda and Pedric, Wilma and Clyde searched half the night for the little tortoiseshell. They looked everywhere they could think to look—underneath porches, through any open windows, into the back gardens of shops and cottages, and in all the little alleys. Clyde had climbed fences and Wilma had hurried up exterior stairways onto private balconies. Several times she'd stepped out from the balconies to wander the rooftops like a cat herself. She heard Lucinda and Pedric calling, too, calling and calling the kit. But at last they had given up, had all turned toward home, silent and worried and angry.

Charlie would have been out searching, but she was unaware of the small cat's absence; she and Ryan had left the murder scene early, before anyone had begun to search for Kit. Now, this morning as Ryan turned her red pickup into the long lane, Charlie was just coming out of the barn leading Max's big buckskin, turning the horses out for the day. Charlie looked up and waved.

Ryan waved back, but her mind was on the weather that so

stubbornly dictated the work on this job. California winters could be windy and nasty, but this bout of storms seemed to have gone on forever. She had been able, between heavy rains, to pour the foundation for the Harpers' new living room and frame and dry-in the new mudroom; and now, this morning, the weatherman promised their first clear day, so maybe they could get on with framing the living room.

Of all those who complained about the extended wet weather, the building contractors had grown perhaps the most irritable, cursing the succession of storms that decisively halted construction schedules. All through the Christmas season, construction jobs had waited while cold storms battered the California coast, wind and rain lashing Molena Point until the village seemed ready to wash out to sea. The Molena River rose so high that many lowland houses flooded, their carpets and furniture soaked with mud, driveways washed out, streets closed. South of Molena Point, on Highway 1, rock slides shut down both lanes for over a week, just before New Year's Eve. The wet weather had caused Ryan to put off not only the larger portion of the Harper job, but the start of a new house in the north hills, and had forced her to give three carpenters unwanted vacations. This, coupled with the obdurate reluctance of the county building department to issue any permit on a timely basis, had left her highly ticked. Not until after New Year's had she been able to sweet-talk the county inspectors into issuing the Harper permit, employing what charm she could muster. Ask any Molena Point contractor, working with their county building department was like working with bureaucrats from hell.

But now, in the wake of the murder, her irritation seemed only petty and without substance. The death of someone who had done wonderful things in her life, things that made a difference in the lives of others, that death seemed to Ryan an enormous loss.

She and Charlie had left Otter Pine Inn around one last

night, leaving Max and Ryan's uncle Dallas and a handful of officers interviewing witnesses. She'd lost track of Clyde—her date, she thought, amused, had gone off on some serious errand with Wilma and the Greenlaws. Now, as she swung out of the truck, Charlie came out of the barn again and hurried toward the house, having apparently finished with the horses. Ryan let Rock out the passenger side, gave him a command, and the big weimaraner raced for the house.

Charlie moved ahead of Ryan into the kitchen to pour fresh coffee, letting Rock in. She stood warming her hands around the coffeepot, then knelt down to give Rock a hug. He was so sleek and healthy, and so much the gentleman, it was hard not to hug him. Rock had been good for Ryan, and the big dog had had his own part in spotting Ryan's husband's killer and thus clearing Ryan of the suspicion that had surrounded her.

Of course no one except Charlie herself, and Clyde and Wilma, knew that the gray tomcat and his two ladies had, as well, pointed the department toward evidence that convicted the real killer. Charlie hoped the cats would stay out of this murder—though she wouldn't lay money on it.

Leaving Otter Pine Inn last night with Ryan, Charlie had wanted only to be quiet, to grieve for Patty alone until Max got home and could hold her and they could comfort each other. Setting the alarm, she had fallen into bed wondering if Max would get home at all, if he'd get any sleep. The next days would demand a lot of everyone; this was not just a remote police investigation. They were all grieving; certainly Max was. Patience would be required of them all. This was not like the murder of a stranger, and not like a natural death, where after a few days there would be a funeral and some kind of closure.

Arriving home alone to the few lights she and Max had left on, she had brought the two big dogs inside from where they roamed the fenced-in yard around the house. She'd wanted them inside with her as she crawled gratefully into bed. She had soon slept, the dogs sprawled on the rug snoring. But she did not sleep well; she kept waking, seeing Patty's torn face in the harsh, glaring lights, the officers and coroner moving around her, busy at their work. Seeing the awful pain in Max's eyes.

She had dozed and waked until Max came in about four. He had crawled into bed ice cold. She had clung to him, warming him, had held him close, not talking, until he slept.

This morning, letting him sleep, she had risen with some renewed strength and resolve. She had quickly showered, then gone out to feed the horses and clean their stalls. Returning, pouring a cup of coffee, she heard Max get up. She had stood at the kitchen window looking out at the morning, letting the long, unbroken view down the hills strengthen her. The first early light, when the broad expanse of sea and hills was dressed in rich, dawn colors, seemed always new to her. Leaning against the counter sipping coffee, she'd heard Max get out of the shower, the silence as the water stopped pounding in the pipes. Putting bacon in the skillet, she'd mixed the pancake batter listening to the dogs' impatient barking. Going to the door, she had made them be still. Max's buckskin gelding, not to be outdone, began banging his stall, wanting to be in the pasture, making her laugh. She tested the griddle that was heating, flicked water on the hot metal, and watched the drops bounce and dance. As she poured pancake batter, the sea wind blew harder, rattling the tarp that covered their stacked lumber. If they got any dry weather, she wondered how long it would hold.

Setting the bacon and pancakes in the barely warm oven, she went to turn the horses out. They had finished eating and were eager for the sunshine that the clearing sky promised. Looping a rope around Bucky's neck, she led the big buckskin out, letting the two mares follow him. As she was shutting the gate, Ryan's red truck had pulled off the road and into their long lane, Rock with his head out the window. Above Ryan's truck, the sky over the sea was truly brightening.

• • •

"WE CAN START FRAMING the living room this morning," Ryan said. "Don't know how far we'll get. Don't know whether Scotty will want Dillon to help us or work with you—you can rip out the Sheetrock between the two bedrooms this morning, take out that wall." It amused her to be giving the owner of the house orders. Charlie was, with some experience behind her, turning into a fair carpenter. The tear out would be an exercise in violence that might help Charlie work off some of her anger at Patty's death. And they were both eager to finish Charlie's new studio. Charlie couldn't wait to bring her desk and easel over from the barn, her drafting and work tables and boxes of art supplies that were stacked in the grain room inviting the mice to sample her inks and paints and her expensive drawing paper.

The kitchen was warm, its bright colors always welcoming. Red and blue pillows were scattered on the window seat, and the breakfast table was set with red place mats. Charlie was dressed this morning in a pale blue sweatshirt and jeans; blue always helped to cheer her.

"You sleep?" Ryan said.

"A little. You have breakfast?"

Ryan nodded. "Rock and I had leftover steak. I had an orange and some kiwis, but he likes his kibble." She sipped her coffee. Standing in the kitchen, the two women looked out at the increasing brightness as the clouds blew south, and watched Ryan's uncle Scotty pull in, his old white truck muddy halfway up the sides. Dillon Thurwell was with him, the girl's red hair catching the light as he turned in the yard to park. Someone usually picked her up in the village; she couldn't drive yet and it was a long bike ride. Dillon worked with them on weekends and when she wasn't in school. With their fiery red hair, Scotty and Dillon might have been related, though they were not. The big, burly Irishman and the slim young girl got along like a pair of redheads, too. The two waved, pulled on their work gloves, and headed for the covered lumber pile, where they began pulling out two-by-fours, stacking them along the foundation for the new living room. When they had maybe two dozen placed, Scotty stood explaining something to Dillon, talking with his hands as he always did, making Ryan laugh. In a minute they headed around the far side of the house where their tools were stored underneath.

Dillon, having worked with Scotty through Christmas vacation, seemed to like this new twist in her life. The fourteen-year-old had learned quickly once she had knocked the chip off her shoulder. She'd settled in well to help with cleaning up the debris, filling the tarp-covered Dumpster that had been hauled up to the site; and in the old living room, which would become the new master bedroom, she was learning to mud and tape drywall. With the constant rain, all work seemed twice as hard—taking out the demolished drywall and wood scraps, hauling new building materials into the mudroom, trying to keep the house halfway clean. And then draining the foundation for the twenty-by-thirty-foot living room so they could at least frame the walls. The earth within was still a pool of mud, but the concrete foundation was firm and deep.

"I always wanted a swimming pool," Charlie said, looking out at the mud where the living room would rise.

"Don't knock it. Bring in a masseuse, add a steam room, you can make a bundle. Harpers' spa, restorative soaks in Molena Point's rare and rejuvenating beauty clay." But Ryan looked at Charlie shyly, a bit embarrassed by making jokes this morning. "You promised to help the senior ladies with their garden today, if it didn't rain. Will they go on with that, after last night? And even if they feel up to gardening, will the ground be dry enough?"

"Should be nice and soft to get the weeds out. They've never had a problem with slides on that hill; there are railroad ties to retain it. Somewhere underneath there's supposed to be a shoulder of granite running along above the canyon." Charlie pushed back her unruly red hair. "The ladies will be up to it. Work is better than sitting around grieving. While they weed, I'm going to take out whatever geraniums they don't want; I can pot them until we finish building. Those overgrown pelargoniums are magnificent."

"You have so much time to garden. Five commissions pending for animal portraits, the picture book you're working on, your own repair and cleaning business to oversee, to say nothing of the fact that you're working for me on the house."

"You can't spare me this afternoon? Call it my lunch break."

Ryan laughed. "I can spare you. It comes out more even, for framing, with just Scotty and me, and Dillon doing the odd jobs."

Finishing her coffee, Charlie rinsed her cup and headed for her soon-to-be studio. Ryan and Charlie and Max had planned the renovation together, the three of them taking their time, paying attention to how the sun would slant into the new great room with its high rafters and stone fireplace, how much more view down the falling hills the raised floor would allow. Standing in the front yard on ladders, they had made sure how much of the sea and the village rooftops would be visible.

While the old living room became a large new master suite, their present bedroom would be Max's study. The two smaller bedrooms would become Charlie's spacious studio, and she could hardly wait. The renovation might seem wild to some, but to Charlie and Max and Ryan, it made perfect sense. By the time the phone rang at eleven-thirty, Charlie had finished the tear out and, with help from Scotty, had finished putting up the new drywall. She was drunk with the big new space; she wanted to whirl around shouting and swinging her arms, she could hardly wait to cut through the wall for the large new windows with their north light; but that would have to wait until the weather settled. Hurrying into the kitchen, she picked up the call.

"It's Wilma. We haven't found Kit, no one's seen her. I just . . ."

Wilma didn't sound at all like herself. "She disappeared before . . . right after the murder. I didn't tell you last night, I thought . . ." Charlie's aunt, a tall, capable, no-nonsense former parole officer, was not given to a shaky voice and tears. "We're headed out to look again, Lucinda and I. Pedric is already out, after just a few hours' sleep."

"I can join you. I—"

"No. I just . . . wanted you to watch for her as you head down to the seniors'. Dulcie and Joe aren't nearly as concerned as we are. They say she's been gone before."

"The last time, she turned up in the middle of a double murder," Charlie said. "I'll look out for her, and leave my cell phone on. Call me if I can join you." Charlie didn't like to see her aunt so upset. Those three cats were so dear, so very special. And Kit was so damned headstrong. How could Joe and Dulcie not worry? And how did you look for one small cat, if she didn't want to be found?

In the mudroom she pulled on a pair of rubber boots, then hurried out to her van. Her cleaning crews didn't need it today; when they did, she had to use Max's old wreck that he'd kept for emergencies and which, they agreed, laughing, was an emergency in itself. Heading down toward the village, she drove slowly, watching the roadside and the hills, searching for that dark little hurrying tattercoat. Praying the kit was on her way home, praying she was all right. Several times she stopped to scan the trees, looking for a dark lump perched among the branches. Below her, the hills glowed brilliant green against the indigo sea. The grass, fed by the heavy rains, had sprung up tall and lush, as vibrant as living emerald. The horses could think of nothing but that tender new growth, all they wanted to do was race out and gorge on it.

Between the hills and sea, the white shore stretched away scattered with black boulders, and down to her right, the village rooftops shone with shafts of sunlight striking between dark smears of cypress and pine. Could Patty Rose, wherever she was now, still glimpse this lovely land? Might Patty from her ethereal realm crave a last look at the dimension she had left behind?

Or did she no longer care, now that she moved in a far more fascinating realm?

Or was Patty simply gone? Was there nothing more?

Charlie didn't believe that.

Coming into the village, slowing among the cottages, she watched the streets and rooftops for Kit, trying not to let Wilma's distress eat at her. Maybe Joe and Dulcie were right, that Kit would show up in her own time, sassy and wondering what all the fuss was about.

But it wasn't only the missing kit that made her edgy about the cats. She was puzzled by Joe and Dulcie, too. For nearly two weeks, they had been acting so strangely. Wilma said Dulcie had hardly been home, that when she was home, she was silent and remote. Or nervous and completely distracted. And Clyde said Joe was cross as a tiger, that the tomcat was so bad tempered he sometimes wouldn't talk at all, would just hiss at Clyde and stalk away.

Clyde thought Joe's anger was because of Dulcie's preoccupation; and Clyde, with Joe's grouchy silence, had become just as bad tempered himself. A pair of surly housemates snarling at each other and at their friends—until last night. Then all minor concerns, it seemed to Charlie, had been put into proper perspective.

And as she'd descended the winter hills, Charlie had had the feeling that it all was connected: the kit's disappearance, Dulcie's secrecy, and Joe's distress somehow all linked together—and that those puzzling situations had a bearing on Patty's murder. She had no idea how that could be, but she couldn't shake the thought.

# 6

Crouched in the dark cabinet beneath the bathroom sink, Kit listened. Irving Fenner, having brushed his teeth and presumably shaved, seemed to have crouched down himself, just outside the cabinet door. She heard the faint hush of fabric against the sink cabinet as he knelt, imagined him reaching for the door. Two unlike creatures facing each other on either side of the thin wood barrier. He was totally still. Her heart pounded so hard it shook her whole body.

She heard his hand brush the door. The door creaked, and the left-hand side swung out as she slid, silent and fast, behind the other door. He had to hear her heart pounding, had to smell her fear as she pressed into the corner, into the deepest dark.

He reached in as she watched through slitted eyes. His hand passed just inches from her face. He reached back, thrust his hand straight back to the drainpipe that hung down in a rusty gooseneck curve. His face was so close to her she could have shredded it. She was deeply tempted. He was half turned away, a perfect target, his forehead and shoulder pressed against the edge of the cabinet, so close that she had to draw back to keep from touching him. His arm smelled sour, of old sweat, of soap caught in the swarthy hairs, of sleep. Reaching down, he slipped his hand into the hole where the pipe went through, where the black wood had rotted. Forced his hand down inside, his hairy wrist knocking off additional flecks of soft wood, some falling away beneath the house.

Leaning in, feeling around inside the hole, he drew out a package. It was about the size of a shoe, a strangely shaped package wrapped in brown paper. Its smell nearly made her cry out. Gun oil. The package smelled of gun oil, the same smell as Captain Harper's regulation automatic and as the guns the detectives carried. The same smell as the .38 that Wilma kept in her night table against a possible but unpleasant contact with some bitter ex-parolee; the gun that Wilma took up to the range once a month so she wouldn't be out of practice, then cleaned with gun oil at her little workbench in the garage, a tawny, nose-twitching scent. Kit remained stone still as he backed out with the package and shoved the cabinet door closed.

She listened to his footsteps cross the room. Listened as the front door opened and then closed. Listened to his footsteps on the gravel, then the car door open and slam, and the car start and pull away. What was all the coming and going? Her paws were slick with sweat. Her heart pounded like trapped birds flapping in her chest; she felt too weak to run away and too terrified to remain where she was. She was trapped in this house and there might be no way out.

Except, there was the underhouse, the crawl space, if she could get down there. Tasting the stink of mold and rotting wood, she nosed at the hole where the pipe went through. There was always a way, always. Kit did not take well to defeat; she did not believe in defeat.

She wondered if the gun had been used to kill Patty, and if it held his fingerprints. Wondered, if ballistics had that gun, would they find the proof the law needed to convict that man?

The little hole beneath the sink would take her a long time to dig out and get through. Backing out from under the sink, leaving the envelopes hidden, she stood in the middle of the dark little room looking around her. Leaping to the sink, she tried the bathroom window, but it was as thick with paint as the others. She tried the front door again, leaping up, snatching at the knob that would move the bolt, that was too small to get her claws around. Her paws started bleeding again. If she had more leverage, if she could get up higher . . .

Stalking a wooden chair, she set her shoulder against it and pushed, heading toward the front door.

The chair didn't slide along the floor, but fell over onto its back. She shoved again, throwing all her weight against its side, edging it slowly across the floor. Its journey was much too loud, a sliding scrunching that made her skin twitch with fear. But at last she had it across. Pushing it against the door, she stood on its side and worked at the knob with both paws. Desperate now, ever more frantic at being closed in, she grew angry enough to try to claw through the wood itself.

When the knob wouldn't move, she gave up at last and returned, defeated, to the bathroom, leaving the overturned chair behind her and her faint, bloody paw prints on the dirty floor. Maybe Fenner wouldn't notice the paw prints.

But he sure would notice the chair. Going back, she tried her best to right it. She pawed and fought until she'd slipped her front paw under, and then her shoulder. It was a light chair; she guessed that was why it had fallen. A small ladderback. Maybe if she . . .

Crouched with her shoulder beneath it, slowly she reared up, pressing it with her shoulder. When it was as high as she could reach, she grabbed it between the slats and lifted higher. Lifted, rearing up as high as she could. And when she gave it a little push, up it went, rocking back and forth, threatening to fall again.

Catching it in her paws, she steadied it until it stopped rocking and stood as it had before. She gave it a lovely loud purr, and returned to the bathroom, her tail lashing.

She didn't like to think what would happen if the cops were to search this place, after they had the evidence, and found her blood and paw prints. There would be hell to pay—she had no idea how she would explain such a thing to Joe Grey. She licked her paws trying to stop the bleeding, but the damage was already done. Pushing into the tiny bathroom, she immediately felt so caged that she wanted to race out again. It was very hard indeed to press into the dark cupboard beneath the sink.

Clawing at the hole beneath the drain, pawing and tearing the rotted wood away, she could feel the niche where he had tucked the gun. A little space, back on top of a floor joist. She dug and dug, dug at the rotting sides of the hole until her paws were nearly raw. Until, at last, she had a hole big enough to slip through.

Bellying in, she hung halfway through the crumbling wood, peering around into the blackness below her. The underhouse space stretched away to the front of the cottage, and was maybe three times as tall as a cat, tall enough for a large dog to walk around in without crouching—though he would scrape his back on the floor joists and pipes and wires running through. Away in the far walls, three small louvered vents let in faint light through their grids. The space smelled of wet mold and rat droppings.

Hanging farther down inside, her round, furry butt planted on the cabinet floor above, her hind paws braced against the edges of the rotting floor, she stared through the black, cobwebby crawl space to those far bits of dust-filtered sunlight and let loose with her hind paws and dropped down, landing on the sour earth and the scattered bits of rotted wood.

Ears and whiskers back, and carrying her tail low, she padded beneath the cobwebs, brushing over rusty nails and pieces of ragged screening or wire. According to human myth, cats loved dark, hidden places. Well, certainly in her younger days, before she knew better, she'd been drawn to mysterious caves, but not like this place. The caves in her wild dreams led to wonderful underneath realms to be discovered—not to a dark, stinking underhouse strewn with rusty nails. Easing through the black, cobwebby labyrinth of cement supports and cast-iron pipes and hanging electrical wires, she approached the vent that would face the front yard, and stood sniffing in the good, fresh air. She could smell green grass and pine trees, and from somewhere the lingering aroma of someone's breakfast of bacon and hot maple syrup. Rearing up, she hooked her claws in the vent grid and pulled.

She pulled harder. Bracing with her hind paws, she jerked and jerked, backing and fighting until she feared she'd tear a claw out. Giving up at last, and muttering softly, she went to try the vent nearer the drive.

She had no better luck with that vent. Crossing through the darkness and the spider curtains, she tried the last one; she fought until not only her paws but both forelegs hurt, then gave up, backing away, her tail limp and her head hanging. A little whimper of defeat escaped her. She was trapped in this prison of a house. Greedily she sniffed the small wisp of fresh air that filtered in through the dirty grid, the scent of pine trees and green bushes. And, she couldn't help it, staring out at the open, free world that she could no longer reach, the kit howled.

But at last she quieted and turned resolutely away, and headed back to the crawl hole and the bathroom to retrieve the envelopes, to get them out before he returned. What if he came back and reached in again, and happened to flip the oilcloth back? What if he found them?

*So?* she thought. *So? What was he going to think?*

She didn't know what he'd think; she couldn't imagine. But he'd tear the place apart looking for whoever had been there.

And, searching, what if he found her paw prints? What would he think then?

Dulcie would say she was losing her grip, would tell her to get hold of herself. What was he supposed to think? That a talking cat had taken his envelopes? She tried very hard to calm her shivering nerves as she hooked her claws in the rotting wood of the hole and crouched to leap up, prepared to retrieve the clippings and pictures. Prepared to get out of there somehow, and tip the cops about Kendall Border and Craig Vernon and Harold Timmons, whoever those men were. Tip the cops that Irving Fenner had indeed been connected to Patty Rose. Irving Fenner, who had watched Patty, and who had shot a bullet hole into each of Patty's pictures—Irving Fenner, who had killed her dear Patty Rose?

**ENTERING THE VILLAGE,** Charlie called Wilma on her cell phone, touching the button for her aunt's number. Wilma didn't answer. Turning down Ocean, Charlie watched the streets, among the feet of the locals and tourists, looking for the kit. She saw no one searching for Kit. But then, as she approached the library, she saw a dark little shape in the garden of the shop next door. With a surge of excitement she touched the brakes and pulled over.

But it was Dulcie, there by the building next to the library, not the tortoiseshell kit. Dulcie, prowling along through the front garden as if she was searching for Kit. When the dark tabby turned away, moving down the little lane between the buildings, Charlie didn't call out to her.

Dulcie had been hanging around that building a lot lately. It and the library stood close together; they were of the same Mediterranean style, same white walls and faded red-tile roofs, and had been built at the same time. They had once been part of an estate that included servants' quarters, carriage houses, stables, and outbuildings. This building now housed an exclusive men's clothing shop, with an apartment behind it and a larger apartment above. Its basement, if she recalled correctly, had once run beneath both buildings, and the narrow walk between the two buildings had been a passageway for delivery carts. Dulcie, as Molena Point's library cat, considered all adjacent gardens her personal territory, off-limits to the other village cats whether she chose to hunt there or not.

The three rentals in the smaller, two-story structure had produced a comfortable income for Genelle Yardley since she'd retired. Genelle's family had, years ago, given the larger building to the library foundation. Just recently, Charlie understood, Genelle had put her rental building in trust for the library as well, for when she died—and Genelle was dying. The party that Patty had been planning for Genelle was, in fact, a final goodbye. A gesture that could only be understood in light of the two women's long and sympathetic friendship.

*So much death*, Charlie thought. *Not a happy way to start the new year.*

Though Genelle's approach to death showed an amazingly matter-of-fact attitude. Quite methodically, Genelle had updated her trust to her satisfaction and had put all her personal and financial affairs in good order. She had left a nice sum of money to Patty's children's home, and Genelle's gift of her building to the library would, indeed, be well used. The library was so cramped for space that the librarians, including Charlie's aunt Wilma, had to discard far more out-of-date books than they cared to, to make room for the new books that were needed or were in demand.

Genelle was only in her sixties, young to leave this world; Charlie realized that fact ever more sharply with each of her own approaching birthdays, though she was only half Genelle's age. She supposed Genelle's matter-of-fact approach to death was in character with Genelle's practical turn of mind and organized thoughts, which had made her a very efficient business manager for Vincent and Reed Electrical before her retirement, and certainly she had managed her own inherited money judiciously.

Charlie watched Dulcie vanish, down at the end of the alley, and wondered again what this little tabby, of such special intelligence, was hiding. Wondered if it had to do with the lane itself or with the garden of the rental building, where Wilma had often seen her prowling lately. When Wilma had asked Dulcie what was so fascinating there, Dulcie's green eyes had widened with innocence.

"Mice," Dulcie had said, staring up at her housemate as if Wilma shouldn't have to ask. "I can smell mice inside that building and I can hear them." Charlie and Wilma had been sitting in Wilma's blue-and-white kitchen, at the kitchen table, Charlie and Wilma having coffee, Dulcie in her own chair enjoying a bowl of milk, and all three of them eating Wilma's homemade sticky buns. Dulcie said, "Maybe mice that were driven inside by the rain. Succulent little mice, Wilma. They smell lovely. But there's no way to get inside, no way to get at them."

Wilma had just looked at Dulcie. "You and Joe seldom hunt mice; you much prefer to go up the hills and kill jackrabbits—a catch, as Joe puts it, that you can get your teeth into. And," Wilma had said pointedly, "I notice that you're not hunting with Joe much these days."

Dulcie had lashed her tail with such annoyance that Charlie almost choked hiding her laughter.

"And," Wilma had said further, "prowling around that building, you didn't look as if your mind was on anything remotely connected to mice."

"What else would I be doing?" Dulcie had laid her ears flat, leaped down from her chair, and stalked out her cat door, her tail lashing with an angry hurt that had shamed them both—just as she'd meant to shame them.

Charlie moved on past the library without stopping, and

before heading up the hills to the senior ladies' house, she tried Wilma's cell phone again. Nothing. Then she swung by Clyde's to see if he might be at home, if he had any news of the kit. At one time in Charlie's life, she would have found it ludicrous to spend all night and day searching for a cat. But she hadn't known then what she knew now.

Clyde's car wasn't in the drive; he was either looking for Kit or had gone on to work. As she pulled up in front, Joe Grey was just leaping up the steps toward his cat door. When he heard her van he turned, scowling at her, his ears back, then ducked to slip through the plastic flap. She opened her door. "Wait, Joe!" she hissed. "Wait for me!" She swung out, glancing around to see if any neighbors were watching, if anyone had heard her. Joe had paused beside his cat door looking back at her, scowling with annoyance, the white strip down his nose drawn into a thin line, his yellow eyes narrowed.

"You didn't find her," she said softly, coming up the walk.

"We didn't find her," he snarled, hardly a whisper. She sat down on the steps.

The tomcat stopped scowling and sat down close to her. He looked tired, his ears and whiskers drooping; he looked resigned. "Lucinda and Pedric and Wilma are out looking, calling and calling her. Dulcie and I can't call her in broad daylight. And we couldn't pick up her scent. Not anywhere." He lay down, his paw touching her leg. "Lucinda and Pedric are worn out. Eighty years old, and only a couple hours' sleep."

"You don't look so great yourself."

"Village full of tourists, all you can smell is perfume and dog doo, gum wrappers and stale tobacco." Joe yawned. "Clyde went on to work. I need food and sleep, I'm bummed out. Nothing as exhausting as looking for that damned kitten."

Charlie didn't point out that the tattercoat wasn't a kitten anymore, only young and headstrong. "And you and Dulcie searched for her together?"

He just looked at her.

"You haven't been seeing much of each other these days."

"Dulcie doesn't share her appointment calendar with me," Joe snapped. He yawned again, rose, and headed for his cat door. Charlie reached out to stop him.

"What is this, Joe? What is this with Dulcie? What's *wrong* between you two?"

Joe laid back his ears and hissed at her.

"What? This is scaring me," Charlie said. "You're mad enough at Dulcie to eat rocks!"

His yellow eyes were fierce and unforgiving. He looked, with his angled head narrowed by anger, as formidable as a stalking cougar.

"Not another tomcat?" Charlie said softly. "I don't believe Dulcie would do that."

"What else would she be up to that she won't tell me? Even tonight, searching for the kit, she was closemouthed. Remote as all hell." He nosed at the plastic flap intending to terminate the conversation. She pressed on his chest and shoulder, making him pause, and imagining a bloodied hand. Joe had never slashed her, but now he looked like he might.

"Maybe she promised someone," Charlie said softly. "Maybe she's keeping someone else's secret, maybe she can't—"

"Promised *who*? Keeping *what* secret? There's no other cat she can talk to except the kit." His yellow eyes widened. "There's no human but the Greenlaws, and Clyde and Wilma and you."

She didn't want to mention the black tomcat that had once come on to Dulcie. They all thought, hoped, that cat was gone. Preferably, to a place where he *couldn't* come back. Charlie thought if Azrael ever did show up, Joe might kill him. "Couldn't there be some innocent reason for Dulcie keeping a secret? Someone else—some kind of promise that isn't meant to hurt you? Dulcie would never hurt you, Joe."

"You're saying she's spoken with someone new? That she's talked to some new human? That she's given away our secret?" His eyes burned into hers. "*I* don't believe *that*."

"I'm not saying she *told* anyone. I'm not suggesting she *talked* with anyone. I'm saying maybe someone's in trouble, and they made it clear that others mustn't know. That maybe Dulcie—"

"*What* trouble? What secret?"

Charlie just looked at Joe. He was such a big, dignified cat, all hard muscle and gleaming silver coat, and his white markings were polished like new snow. But now his yellow eyes burned with such deep hurt and wounded pride and anger that Charlie wanted to pick him up and hug and cuddle him.

But she didn't dare. Joe had always been too dignified to tolerate hugging.

And how could Joe's beautiful tabby lady keep secrets from her tomcat? How could his lovely and talented coconspirator in matters of criminal investigation, his skilled hunting partner, whether it be human felons or four-legged rats, how could his true love intentionally hurt him?

Wanting so to stroke Joe Grey and comfort him, Charlie shyly drew her hand away. She could no more cuddle this tomcat than she could pick up and cuddle Detective Dallas Garza. Than she would, at one time, have cuddled Chief of Police Max Harper—before she knew Max better. Instead, she rose. "Get some sleep, Joe. Get something to eat. Shall I come in and make you an omelet?"

"There's stuff in the fridge. Half a chicken," he said ungratefully. "Damn kitten. No more sense than to go off by herself after an armed—"

She reached to block his cat door. "Why would the guy shoot her? Why would he even guess what she is? Get a grip, Joe."

He stared back belligerently. "She's so nosy. Irresponsible. No telling what she might—"

"Give Kit some credit, Joe. She found that meth lab up in the hills, and she didn't give herself away. She . . ." She stopped talking and reached diffidently to scratch his ear. "She'll likely be back when you wake up. Call me on my cell, I'll come help you look; at least I can offer wheels. I'm just headed up to the seniors' to dig up some flowers."

Joe stared at her and yawned, and slid in through his cat door. Charlie remained crouched on the porch looking around at the houses across the street, praying that some neighbor hadn't seen them talking. Well, she could talk to a cat all right without causing raised eyebrows. As long as they didn't see the cat talking back.

But the neighbors' windows all looked empty, curtained and serene; she saw no one looking out. Rising, pushing back a loose strand of hair, she headed for her van and the senior ladies' house, armed with her shovel and empty pots and plastic bags. Maybe Wilma would be there, maybe Wilma would tell her the kit was home with Lucinda and Pedric—then maybe this queasy nervousness in her stomach would go away.

# 7

**D**ULCIE HAD THAT SAME SICK FEELING ABOUT the missing tortoiseshell that Wilma or Clyde must feel when she and Joe were gone for several days; surely it was the same uneasy worry that filled her now. They had looked everywhere for the kit; no one *knew* where else to look.

And she felt edgy about Joe, too. A dozen times last night as they searched for the kit, she'd wanted to tell him the secret that lay between them, tell him where she'd been going for the past two weeks. But every time she started to mention Lori, she reminded herself that she *had*, in her own heart, promised the child. That when Lori whispered, "You won't tell anyone, Dulcie," she had, by her purring and cuddling, really promised Lori, just as much as if she had whispered, "I'll never say a word."

Now, agonizing, all she did was get her mind in a muddle. She went into the library at last, not through Lori's secretly unlocked basement window, but through the open front door. As library cat, she had as much business padding in through the main entrance as had the head librarian—and there had been times in the past, with another head librarian, when Dulcie had been more welcome. Her appearance in the library always generated smiles and greetings and pets, and today was no different. Except that she made quick work of the petting and cuddling, only pretending to linger. Purring and winding around the patrons' reaching hands, she sidled toward the stairs in an oblique dance until she was able to disappear among the stacks. And in an instant she was down the steps and into the basement workroom.

She had been visiting the runaway child for nearly two weeks, but she still hadn't learned much about her. Lori's casual, disjointed remarks were only frustrating. And how maddening were their one-sided conversations, when Dulcie had to remain mute, when she couldn't ask questions.

She'd fared no better listening to conversations around the library and watching the daily paper. She heard nothing about a runaway child, and no missing child was reported anywhere near Molena Point. No mention on the local radio station or TV. And surely the *Molena Point Gazette* would jump on that kind of story.

Certainly there was no recent police report; she would have heard about that from Wilma or Charlie or Clyde—from Max Harper's own wife and his two closest friends. Max had grown up with Clyde; they were like brothers, brothers who had indulged in a good deal of beer drinking and bar fights during their young days on the rodeo circuit, Dulcie thought, smiling. It always amused her, and amazed her, to imagine either of the two men crouched atop the chute, settling down onto the back of a bull as the gate was opened; to imagine them riding the lunging, twisting, hard-landing bulls. Though she didn't like to think of the end of the ride, of the terrible, lunging horned danger, when they were on the ground once more.

In the basement, two librarians were working on a book order, sitting at the big, scarred worktable. The room was cool, its concrete walls emitting a perpetual chill that on a hot day was delightful, but was not so pleasant in the winter. Both ladies were wearing heavy sweaters. Dulcie, leaping onto an empty table, lay down between the stacks of new books where a slant of watery sunlight seeped in through a basement window. Five basement windows opened into deep wells that were cut into the sidewalk. All but one was securely locked, although all of them appeared to be locked. Settling down for a light nap, waiting for a chance to get in to Lori, Dulcie sleepily watched the librarian at the computer preparing orders. She was worn out, what with keeping Lori's secret from Joe and with worry over the kit.

Well, she could do nothing about Joe at the moment; he would just have to sulk. And they'd have to trust the kit. Just as she herself wanted Wilma to trust *her* and not always to be calling her and hovering. Kit was a big cat now; she would have to take care of herself.

But the worst of her tiredness came from her pain over Patty's death. Patty Rose, who would have hurt no one. No one . . . She was nearly asleep when the two librarians rose from their desks, picked up their purses, and headed for the stairs to go to lunch. She waited for some time, to be sure they didn't come back, hadn't forgotten anything. When neither hurried back down the stairs, she squeezed behind the small bookcase; there was barely room between it and the wall.

She didn't try to shove the bricks aside to reveal Lori's hidden entryway. Instead, pawing at the loose heat vent, she reared up, pushing the swinging grid aside. Crawling up and in, scrambling through where the big plastic pipe had fallen away from its connection, she entered the hidden part of the basement.

She had always known that grid was loose, hanging by one rusty screw, the other three screws not secure in the soft, old plaster. Long ago she had sniffed around there for mice but had never found fresh scent. She was more likely to find the occasional unwary mouse in the workroom itself, drawn by a candy bar left in a desk drawer, or upstairs among the books and the reading-room couches, both of which offered delightful nesting material for a mouse family. While she had long ago eradicated the main populations of library mice, an occasional optimistic newcomer would venture in, only to find itself summarily dispatched and on its way to mouse heaven.

Slipping in, pausing in the darkness, sniffing child scent and the sharp aroma of peanut butter, she dropped to the cold concrete floor. The cement-walled room was so dark that even a cat had to squeeze her eyes closed for a moment before she could see anything at all. But she could hear the child's slow, even breathing.

It still dismayed her that, all these years, she hadn't a clue that this room was here. She had assumed that behind the vent was just crawl space, dirt and foundation and spiders. Apparently the library's drainage system was well constructed, because the little basement room had remained dry even during this winter's heavy rains. The floor beneath her paws was dry as dust, though icy cold. And there was no faintest scent of mildew. Moving by the thin light that seeped through the vent behind her, she approached the sleeping child.

Lori lay curled up on her old sun pad, which maybe Lori's mother had once used. She had pulled her thin blanket tight around her as if to shut out the tiniest finger of cold, and had spread her windbreaker over that. For a long while, Dulcie stood watching Lori nap, her little hand under her cheek, her brown hair tangled across the stained old pillow.

Lori had moved into the hidden room surprisingly well equipped: the thin little pad, the old blanket, the backpack on the floor beside her with its canned provisions—though the pack was thinner now. Dulcie thought the child had brought as much food as she had been able to carry, but it wouldn't last much longer. Whatever the reason for her running away, and wherever she had come from, this little girl wasn't playing games. The puzzle was, if no one had reported a child missing, and if no one was looking for her, did she not have a family? That hardly seemed possible. Where, then, had she come from?

Or was someone searching secretly for her, someone who did not want to go to the police, who wanted to remain unknown? And why? Because they had hurt her, or meant to harm her? The child woke suddenly and sat up, startled, knowing someone was in the room. But then, staring into the darkness, she saw Dulcie. Catching her breath with pleasure, she put out her arms. Her voice was a whisper.

"Dulcie? You mustn't let them see you come in here." She glanced warily toward the workroom. "You mustn't let them know. Maybe they're at lunch? Oh," she said, shivering, "I wish you could understand. No one must find me! I wish I could make you understand."

*But I do understand,* Dulcie thought. *I wish I could speak, I wish we could talk. Who would find you? Where do you come from and what are you afraid of?* Leaping onto the blanket, Dulcie curled up close to Lori, basking in Lori's warmth, breathing in her little-girl scent—and wishing not only that she dared speak, but that she could share this child with Joe Grey. She longed to tell Joe about Lori, to discuss the child with him. Longed for Joe to help her come up with some answers. But she didn't dare, not until she knew who or what Lori was hiding from.

Because what if Joe, thinking only to help, placed one of his anonymous phone calls to Captain Harper about a lost child, a runaway child? And Harper came and scooped Lori up? What if, in the eyes of the law, Lori must be returned to the person she had run from? Sometimes the police could do little but what the legal statutes told them to do.

The Molena Point police were Joe's friends, Joe believed those officers could do no harm. In relying on the men he admired, the tomcat could be as hardheaded as any street cop. If he decided that Captain Harper should find Lori, no matter what Dulcie said, the tomcat would take the matter to the chief.

When Joe Grey got stubborn, got his claws into a matter, no one could turn him aside—and once Lori had been returned to whoever was her legal guardian, the law might not be able to protect her.

Dulcie stayed with the child for a long time, curled up close to her on the thin mat with the blanket wrapped around the two of them. With her thick tabby fur, Dulcie was really too warm, but the child clung to her as if she were starved for warmth. When at last Lori dozed, Dulcie slept, too, for a little while, then woke and lay wondering.

She knew that Lori slept during part of the day and then prowled the library late at night feasting on the books, as Dulcie herself often did. She had to smile at the way the child lugged books through the hole in the wall. Lori reminded Dulcie of herself when, slipping through her cat door late at night into the closed library, she would paw a book down from the shelves onto a reading table, paw open the pages, and read into the small hours, lose herself to the world around her as she wandered through even more fascinating worlds.

When Lori ran away, she had brought with her, besides her bedding and food and her little flashlight, a battery-operated lamp of the kind sensible humans kept for power outages. Each time before turning it on, Lori would check the loose bricks in the wall, which she kept to block her makeshift door. Making sure she could see no light between them, she would carefully hang her jacket over the roughly closed opening, anchoring it on the rough bricks. And all the while she would listen for any sound from the other side. Even at night she did this, to make sure no one was out there working late, who could catch a glimpse of light in the wall where there should be none.

Now, sighing, Lori snuggled even closer. It must be hard for a child to hide in this cold place all alone. For a kid of maybe twelve, Lori was amazingly disciplined.

But Lori was a reader; her world and experience had

expanded her thinking far beyond the here-and-now everyday world she occupied. There was no question that she was a bright child. Dulcie had seen adult nonfiction books on every subject from model trains and miniature dollhouses to a history of Molena Point and one on the various breeds of dogs. All were books that, if any patron asked for them, would be recorded by the librarians as missing, but then would be found a few days later. Dulcie liked best that three Narnia books were stacked neatly against the wall, that Lori loved C. S. Lewis and his magical world—that not everything in Lori's life centered around fear, but still could embrace wonder.

Lori woke, whispering into Dulcie's fur, "He was there when I went out this morning, Dulcie. It wasn't hardly light yet. I don't think he saw me; I slipped back through the window real quick and slid it closed."

Who *was there?* Who *are you hiding from?*

In the dark, the child looked intently at Dulcie. "*Was* he looking for me?" She shivered. "If he'd seen me, he'd of followed me.

"But he couldn't of seen me, he was looking straight ahead, driving." She squeezed Dulcie tight. "How long can I stay here, though? My food is nearly gone." She stared hard at Dulcie. "And then what? I try to ration it, but I sure get hungry."

Dulcie reached a soft paw to touch Lori's cheek. There were no marks on the child as if she'd been beaten, as if whoever she was talking about had hurt her. No scars or bruises. But certainly Lori was scared.

"Mama would say, 'Go to a grown-up,' someone I can trust. A grown-up to help me." In the darkness, she shivered. "Who? There aren't no grown-ups I trust. Not those child-welfare people." Dulcie found it interesting that, though Lori was a voracious reader, her English sometimes faltered. She had lived way out in the country, in the south, since she was six. Maybe in that rural area, such usage was natural. Dulcie nuzzled Lori's cheek, purring. But she looked up when she heard voices beyond the wall, heard the two librarians on the stairs, coming down, and she leaped away, toward the heat vent.

"Dulcie?" Lori whispered.

But Dulcie was into the air duct and through it and slipping out from behind the bookcase as the two women entered, taking off their coats. Yawning and stretching, she looked up at them blearily and wandered away under the tables, where she lay down to roll and wash her paw.

And the moment they settled to work she trotted away again, up the stairs, and raced across the reading room before someone wanted to pet her. She was out the front door and around the corner, up a bougainvillea vine, moving eagerly to the rooftops. There she investigated every cranny between the peaks and chimneys, every high balcony and little penthouse window, searching for the kit's scent, hoping maybe Kit was headed home or had come to look for *her*, in the library. Or maybe, worn out from her unknown journey, had stopped in some unlikely place for a nap.

Padding through stark noon shadows and shafts of sunlight, Dulcie had searched the roofs for maybe ten blocks, slipping along the gutters looking down at the busy streets and into the trees and little yards. She was just above her favorite fish café, sniffing the good smells, when a police car turned down the street below her, moving as fast as it dared on the busy street, but without a siren. A second unit sped by, and a third. Something was happening; the officers' sleek white cars moved together as purposefully as three hunting sharks. Quickly she followed, running across the roofs, over and around peaks, keeping the cars in sight as they slid through traffic. They were heading up into the hills; she was going to lose them. Curiosity drove her faster. As she crossed the roof of the police department, below her another car left the station and instead of following farther, she scorched up the courthouse tower, where she could watch from its open parapet, from the highest lookout in the village.

Crouched on the high, open rail of the parapet, she watched the five cars turn onto a street that led high up into the hills. The senior ladies' street? Yes, the street of her four retired friends, of the house the ladies had bought together for their retirement, the tall old house that they were slowly renovating.

But that didn't mean anything, there were lots of houses on that street, including their friend Genelle Yardley's home. Stretching as tall as she could on the wall of the parapet, balancing on the narrow bricks, she counted the streets and the blocks, counted the rooftops. And she caught her breath, dropped down to the brick paving, and leaped down the tower's winding stairs hitting every fourth step, then took off across the roofs. As she raced across oak limbs and more rooftops, icy fingers crawled up her spine. That *was* the seniors' house, where the police units had turned in, the home of Cora Lee and Mavity and their two housemates. What was happening? What was wrong?

# 8

**HALF AN HOUR BEFORE DULCIE FLED ACROSS** the rooftops following Max Harper's police units, Charlie parked her van on the wide, cracked drive in front of the senior ladies' tall old house. The dark, peak-roofed structure rose above her, shabby and neglected, but it would not remain so for long; these ladies, given time, would have it looking as fresh as new. They planned for repairs and softer paint, new landscaping, and a granite-block parking apron to replace the cracked drive. In the meantime, the five bedrooms plus the two small downstairs apartments offered ample room for the four ladies and their future plans.

Swinging out, glancing at her aunt Wilma's car, which was parked at the edge of the drive, she looked in through the driver's-side window. Yes, Wilma had left her cell phone on the seat. Had she given up searching for the kit then? If Kit had been found—had come home—Wilma would surely have called her.

Moving around the side of the house between tall weeds, toward the backyard, she tried to imagine how the landscaping would look when the ladies were finished with it. The fifty-year-old house had seen many tenants, the more recent of whom had done little to care for it; the ladies *had* pruned the neglected old apple tree and the pear trees and had dug the choking growth away from them, leaving wide circles of dark, turned earth. The four senior ladies liked to say that their house marked the last boundary between civilization and the wild, unspoiled land that had once graced all of these coastal hills. While the front of their new home stood snug between its neighbors on a tame and civilized village street, the back of the house overlooked the wild, dropping canyon where black-tailed deer browsed, and raccoons and possums slipped through the grass. One might, on occasion, while sitting quietly on one of the two decks, see a bobcat or even a cougar or black bear. Certainly there were coyotes, the ladies heard them at night just as Charlie and Max heard them up in the hills, their primitive song engendering a strange mix of wonder and ancient fear. Their yipping stirred a restless unease in those who loved their cats. It gave rise to added fear in those who knew Joe Grey and Kit and Dulcie, who knew their secret, who imagined those three cats out in the night venturing too near the hungry beasts.

But the cats were wise, Charlie told herself, they were clever. And she could not change their ways. She glanced up at the windows where new white interior shutters caught the light. So far, the ladies had concentrated their limited funds and time on the inside of the house; the day they moved in they began to renovate the living area and kitchen, patching and painting, then each had designed her own bedroom to please her individual taste. Susan Brittain liked lush potted plants around her and hand-thrown ceramics, lots of sunlight and bright watercolors. Blond Gabrielle Row preferred more formal and expensive furnishings, which, even when purchased used, spelled money. Little, wrinkled Mavity Flowers went in for solid comfort if she could get it cheaply, and lots of bookshelves fitted out with her beloved paperback romance novels.

Tall, elegant Cora Lee French had done her top-floor bedroom and studio with an eye to maximum work space, plenty of white walls where she could hang her bright landscapes, and room to paint and to work on other projects. Now, with the rooms sparkling, the four ladies were impatient to get at the outside. The hired painter would have to wait for dry weather, but the ladies could sure dig out the weeds and tame the overgrown perennials that crowded the back flower beds. Charlie could imagine the masses of colorful blooms they would plant down there, overlooking the canyon.

As she passed the wide back deck she could smell coffee and see empty cups and a thermos on the picnic table. Down below at the lip of the canyon, the ladies were hard at work. She didn't see Wilma. Wherever her aunt was at the moment, she would soon be down there digging enthusiastically; among her other talents, Wilma was an eager and expert gardener.

Now she saw only Mavity and Cora Lee kneeling in the dirt of the long, raised flower beds, both of them up to their elbows in weeds, attacking the tangle with such vengeance you'd think the plants had attacked them. Stacks of wilting weeds lay behind them. They had freed the geraniums, which now stood leggy and rank, reaching in every direction for the sun. The other two members of the foursome were off in San Francisco for the week visiting Susan's daughter. Maybe Wilma was walking Susan's two big dogs. The standard poodle and the dalmatian were a handful, but Wilma loved them; she'd jump at any chance to walk them. And today, she was likely looking again for the kit. Charlie watched Mavity and Cora Lee fondly.

Both women were in their sixties, and were very different from each other but they got on famously. Mavity's short gray hair was always wildly frowsy, and this morning as usual she was dressed in a white maid's uniform, one of a dozen similar garments, all limp from uncounted launderings, that she bought in the secondhand shops. Her white pants and tunic were streaked with dirt, as were her wrinkled, sun-browned hands. By contrast, Cora Lee was as neat and immaculate as if she'd just stepped out of the house. Not a speck of dirt, not a wrinkle, her cream cotton shirt and beige jeans fresh and clean. Not a hair of her short, salt-and-pepper bob was out of place. Her flawless café au lait skin was like velvet, her subtle makeup as carefully applied as if for a party—but when Cora Lee looked up at Charlie, her eyes were red from crying.

She searched Charlie's face and put out a hand to her.

"I'm so very sorry," Charlie said. Cora Lee and Patty Rose had been close; they had done three musicals together for Molena Point Little Theater after Patty retired.

"She was a fine lady," Cora Lee said softly. "Such a joy to work with. Who would do this? Do the police know anything yet?"

Charlie shook her head and patted Cora Lee's gloved hand. "There were no direct witnesses, or none they've found so far. Not a clue yet to a motive. Patty's secretary has been out of town; she's flying back this morning." Charlie never knew what to say to someone grieving; there was so little one could say that would help. Digging a cap from her pocket, she pulled it on and tucked her red hair under, trying to capture the escaping wisps of curl.

Cora Lee tossed another weed on the pile. "Is Lucinda all right?"

Charlie nodded. "She's all right, she's tough. We're all devastated, Cora Lee. But how's Genelle Yardley taking it? She and Patty were such dear friends."

"I dreaded telling her this morning. But when I went to fix her breakfast, she already knew. She was up, as usual, sitting on her terrace reading the paper, the tears just running down. I . . ." Cora Lee shook her head. "I wouldn't have told her, so early. Though I suppose Patty's secretary would have called her, if she'd been here. The paper arrived before I did. But she . . . She believes so strongly that death is not the end. She . . . she'll be all right. I'll go over again later."

The four ladies had been seeing to Genelle Yardley since Genelle had gone on oxygen, helping their neighbor through what they all knew was a terminal illness. Helping her get around with the cumbersome oxygen cart, fixing her meals and cleaning her house, taking her out in a wheelchair. Genelle had no one, no family. A home-care nurse came in to help with her medications and to bathe her. Genelle, despite her increasing difficulty in getting a full breath, was in surprisingly good spirits—or she had been until this happened. Belief in an afterlife or not, this had to be devastating for her. Patty had been close to Genelle's family since before Genelle was born. Coming home to the village even during her busy Hollywood years, Patty had always spent some time with the Yardleys. Patty said your real friends were the old friends, before you got famous.

Now, Charlie thought, Patty's death might set Genelle back severely. She could only hope this wouldn't make Genelle turn away from her stubborn battle to enjoy the last of her life as best she could. Wouldn't change her so she let herself go into a deep depression. And Charlie thought, *I will enjoy life while I'm young. I will love and enjoy Max every moment I'm given; I will enjoy my friends while we're all young and strong, can ride and shoot and work and dance. And I will enjoy them when we can no longer do those things.*

Kneeling farther along in the flower bed, she began to dig around the roots of a tall old pelargonium. She didn't know what color its blooms would be, but she remembered seeing masses of bright-pink blooms in these flower beds, as vivid as peppermint ice cream.

She knew she wouldn't be at work five minutes before her jacket and jeans would be muddy and she'd have smears of dirt over her freckles and in her escaping hair. And she could never work in gloves, could never do anything in a garden without wallowing. It was a wonder her cleaning and repair customers, who included gardening in their varied lists of jobs to be done, didn't drop her services for someone who looked more professional. *Like Cora Lee,* Charlie thought, watching the older woman with speculation.

Cora Lee French's smooth presence was a talent Charlie knew she'd never master. If she felt rocky, she looked rocky. If she was mad, she knew she looked like a vixen. Max said she was always beautiful—but Max loved her. Charlie thought, not for the first time, that Cora Lee would make a perfect manager for Charlie's Fix It, Clean It. She was getting to the point where she desperately needed a manager, yet even to ask Cora Lee seemed an imposition. Cora Lee had cut back on her waitress and hostess jobs, for which she was always in demand at the best village hotels and restaurants, to pursue her other interests. She had been painting a lot, these past months, not theater stage sets but exciting canvases. And now she had this new venture, at which she was making such good money that she didn't need to wait tables or manage Charlie's business. Cora Lee's hand-painted chests, cabinets, and armoires were selling for very nice sums through the local interior designers. Ryan's sister Hanni had put Cora Lee's pieces in some very exclusive homes.

No, Cora Lee was not a prospect as manager, she was far too busy. Charlie wondered for a moment if Mavity would want a stab at the job. Wizened and leathery little Mavity Flowers could still outwork many men; Charlie couldn't run the business without her. She was fast and efficient at cleaning, at painting and plumbing repairs, and at most gardening chores. But planning and directing the crews' work made Mavity nervous. Watching Mavity put all her weight on her trowel to send it deep beside a doomed weed, Charlie shook her head. It wouldn't work; Mavity would balk at the responsibilities of interviewing, hiring, firing, and keeping the records.

Still, she had to find some kind of manager. Her own interests, like Cora Lee's, were moving her powerfully in other directions. She didn't want to abandon the business; she was proud of what she had created and the income was good. Charlie's Fix It, Clean It was the only service in Molena Point where a client could have all manner of small chores taken care of with one phone call, from a broken garden gate to planting spring flowers, from everyday housekeeping to ironing, shopping, helping with parties, or painting a room or two. She would feel like a traitor to her regular customers if she didn't keep the service alive.

Though the rain had ceased early this morning and the sun had tried to shine, moving in and out of cloud, now the cloud cover was lowering heavily, laying a muted silver haze across the garden. *Lucky that the ground was so wet,* Charlie thought. The root structure of the pelargonium she was digging went deep. Even with the softened earth, she was making quite a pit getting the plant out without hurting it. And the weeds the two ladies were pulling had roots as big as turnips. Suddenly, as she dug deeper to free the last of the root, a chill slid down her spine, a coldness that left her shivering for no reason.

Where had that come from? Frowning, she slipped a pair of clippers from her jacket pocket. Pruning the giant geranium before she replanted it in a big plastic pot, she looked around her, puzzled.

Behind the two kneeling women, the old house rose up tall and awkward, its peeling exterior darker still where rain had soaked the siding. Its blackened roof shingles curled up as if surely rain would leak inside. What a dour old relic it was, hunched in the center of its ragged yard like some unkempt old man in worn-out, smelly garments. But the price had been right. This would be the ladies' last home, a comfortable retirement residence for Mavity and Cora Lee, Gabrielle and Susan, and, perhaps later, Charlie's aunt Wilma. Single, aging women banding together for comfort and security in their last years rather than seeking institutionalized living. Their buying a house together had seemed to be asking for trouble, but so far it had worked very well. Soon they would rent out the two basement apartments, though these, in the future, could accommodate caregivers. Potting the pelargonium, firming soil around its roots, she had set it aside and moved on to the next rangy plant when, again, icy fingers touched her.

And in the next flower bed, Cora Lee knelt among the weeds, suddenly very still. Frozen, her trowel in midair, her hands shaking. Her dark eyes were huge, staring at the earth before her.

# 9

Cora Lee didn't move. She might have been molded into a frieze. The color of her face was no longer warm café au lait, but that of gray cardboard. Had she dug out a snake? Disturbed a rattlesnake? Or uncovered one of those huge potato bugs with the vicious pincers?

Slowly Cora Lee reached down, her hesitant, wary hand hovering above something hidden from Charlie's view in the turned earth.

"Cora Lee?"

Cora Lee glanced up, then down again, staring at the earth before her.

"*Cora Lee?*"

Cora Lee looked up, focusing on Charlie, her face twisted, her dark eyes frightened and helpless. Her mouth moved in a soft, begging way, but no sound came. Down the row, Mavity was equally still, watching them. After what seemed hours, Cora Lee whispered, "In the storm, all the bodies floated up."

Charlie rose and stepped closer.

Where Cora Lee had dug the soil away, she could see dark bones. Bare bones, stained by earth. The bones of a hand. A small human hand. A child's hand.

Charlie had spent countless hours in art school drawing human bones, human hands. This was not an animal paw that might be mistaken for human, not a raccoon or a possum. She knew a child's hand when she saw it.

A child's hand, the fingers all in place as if the hand had been securely embedded in older, harder soil, allowing the loose, wet dirt above to come away. The stained bones were woven through with the little pale roots of the weeds. She could see the wrist bones, but the arm was still hidden by earth—if there was an arm. Cora Lee's trowel lay abandoned atop the turned soil. Charlie wanted to pick it up and pull the dirt away, free the poor creature if indeed a body was buried there. *Call Max. Don't touch anything. Call him now.*

Cora Lee's thin, lovely face was crumpled with such distress that Charlie rose and gripped her arms, gently helping her up. She stood with her arms around Cora Lee, the frightened woman shivering against her. Charlie didn't know what Cora Lee meant by bodies floating up, but Cora Lee was far more terrified than seemed reasonable. Charlie reached into her pocket for her cell phone, then drew her hand back and looked at Mavity.

"Go in the house, Mavity. Call nine-one-one. Tell them we need a detective up here; tell them what we found." Mavity, too, was pale. She needed to do something, to take some action.

As the little wrinkled woman hurried away, the back of her white uniform stained with earth, Charlie held Cora Lee close. Cora Lee was not a weak person; last summer when she'd been attacked in the alley behind the charity shop and so badly hurt, when she'd spent that long time in the hospital, she had been as stoic and strong as rock.

This little hand had brought back something that touched

Cora Lee in a way Charlie did not understand. Leading Cora Lee up to the picnic table, Charlie got her to sit down, and poured her the last of the lukewarm coffee from the thermos. They waited, not speaking, until Mavity came out again. She was scowling, her wrinkles multiplied, her fists clenched with annoyance. "Dispatcher had to go through the whole routine of what to do. I *told* her *you* were here, Charlie. That you already know what to do." Turning, saying nothing more, she picked up the thermos and went back in the house.

She returned in only a few moments with a fresh thermos of coffee and clean mugs on a tray. Mavity's response to any calamity was to keep busy. And even as Mavity poured coffee, they heard the police radio, heard the unit patrol pull into the drive. To Charlie, that harsh static cutting through the still morning was as reassuring as a hug. Eagerly she watched the corner of the house as hard shoes clicked on the concrete, coming around the side.

But it wasn't Max; she knew his step. Officer Brennan swung into view coming down the overgrown walk, his high forehead catching the light, his generous stomach bulging over his uniform trousers. Brennan nodded to her. Charlie rose and led him down the yard to the lower flower beds.

She was standing with Brennan, describing how Cora Lee had found the hand, when she saw Dulcie leap from the neighbor's roof to a tree, and back down, dropping into the tall grass. At the little cat's questioning look, Charlie glanced down at the excavation. At Charlie's questioning look, Dulcie twitched her whiskers and flicked her ears. Dulcie had not found the kit. Quietly Dulcie approached the flower bed.

When she saw the hand, her ears went back and her eyes grew huge and black, the way a cat's eyes get when it is afraid or feels threatened, and Dulcie's rumbling growl shocked Charlie. Officer Brennan spun around, waving a threatening hand at her.

"Get out of here, cat! What the hell do *you* want? Cat's worse than a dog! Dig the bones right up! Get out, get away!"

"She didn't do anything," Charlie snapped. "She's just curious. She won't hurt anything!"

"More than curious," Brennan growled. "Cat'll dig up the bones and carry them off!" He stared at Charlie strangely. "How do you think the captain would like that?" When he raised his hand, Charlie snatched Dulcie up in her arms. Dulcie didn't resist, but she was still growling, her enraged glare turned on Brennan. Charlie moved away from him quickly. What had gotten into Brennan? She'd never seen him so grouchy.

For that matter, what was with Dulcie? This wasn't the little cat's usual crime-scene behavior. Dulcie and Joe Grey always stayed out of sight, they had no desire to stir questions among the law. Surely the little tabby would not be so bold around Max or the detectives. Neither cat wanted to be seen near a crime scene, nor did they want paw prints or cat hairs fouling the evidence.

In Charlie's arms, Dulcie seemed to shake herself. More cars were pulling in, the slam of car doors, the multiplied cacophony of police radios. Brennan was still looking surly as Detective Davis came down the drive, her hard shoes clicking on the concrete, three officers behind her. Exchanging a comfortable look with Charlie, Juana Davis moved carefully along the weedy path where Brennan indicated that he had already walked.

Juana Davis was in her fifties, a stocky Latina with a usually bland expression and a keen mind. She had been on the force since long before Max became captain. She was pushing retirement but not looking forward to it. Though few detectives wore a uniform, Davis preferred to do so. Maybe she felt that the uniform gave her more status, more clout—not that she needed it. Davis was a skilled and capable officer. Or maybe she thought black made her look thinner. Dressed in regulation jacket, skirt, and black oxfords, she stood a few minutes looking around the yard, seeing every detail. She studied the hand, the heaps of earth around it. She looked up at Charlie to ask the usual questions. Who had found the hand? Who was present? Would Charlie ask them to remain until they could be questioned? Then she readied her camera and got to work. First the immediate scene from a standing position, before she knelt to take close-ups. She looked up briefly when the chief arrived.

Max moved down the yard, giving Charlie a glance and a solemn wink. Staying to the broken, weedy walk, he didn't speak or stop. Standing at the edge of the flower bed, above Juana, he studied Cora Lee's excavation, the small, frail bones, the piles of earth and weeds. And Charlie studied Max, taking comfort in his tall, lean frame, his sun-weathered face, his thin, capable hands, and the hard breadth of his shoulders. Max Harper, particularly in uniform, made her feel so safe—and always made her heart skip.

Max stood studying the little hand, then stepped back out of Juana's way. Behind them, Brennan and two other officers moved around the edge of the yard stringing yellow crime-scene tape. Everyone present would be asking the same questions. How long had the hand been buried? Was there a full body lying beneath the earth, or only the lone hand? Who was the victim? How old? Boy or girl? If a child was buried here, where had that child come from? How long dead? How many years alone beneath the cold earth? How many years had a report on this lost child been filed away, inactive? Where were the grieving parents, presumably suffering their loss without knowledge of the death, or closure?

Shivering, Charlie returned to the picnic table to sit beside Cora Lee. She looked up as Mavity returned balancing a tray with cocoa and fresh coffee cake and another pot of coffee, enough for an army. Not only was keeping busy a comfort to Mavity, she considered warm beverages and rich food a comfort for everyone in times of need. Charlie guessed she was no different, though, as she reached greedily when Mavity passed the tray, taking enough for herself and for Dulcie. Cora Lee took nothing, she simply squeezed Charlie's hand in her cold one. Charlie poured hot cocoa for her and put the piece of coffee cake before her, hoping the sugar would help strengthen Cora Lee's shaky, chilled spirit.

# 10

"THE BODIES FLOATING AWAY . . . ," CORA Lee said, "the sight of that little hand brought it all back, from when we were children."

"You needn't talk about something painful," Charlie said, putting her arm around Cora Lee where they sat at the picnic table.

Dulcie, crouching low on the bench, peered around Charlie, watching Cora Lee. She had never seen her friend so distressed. What had happened in her childhood? *Let her talk, Charlie, I want to hear this.* She knew that Cora Lee had grown up in New Orleans, on the Mississippi delta. She remembered Cora Lee telling about the vast city cemetery where, as a child, she would sneak inside the gate with her friends and race, terrified and screaming, among the rows of concrete boxes that all stood aboveground. Because of the shallow water table, no grave could be dug, no corpse could be buried; there they all stood, rows of granite and marble boxes with the dead inside.

"One year, we had a terrible flood," Cora Lee said now. "The water rose so high, the caskets were washed out from under their raised tombs. Some coffins broke open and released the corpses, to float away down the streets of the city." She looked up at Charlie. "That's what I saw when I uncovered that little hand. I saw again those helpless, gruesome bodies floating, floating away, that had so terrified me."

Charlie didn't take her eyes from Cora Lee's. She squeezed Cora Lee's hand in her own freckled hand.

"And then," Cora Lee said, "a year after the flood, Kathy's bones . . ." She looked devastated. "My best friend . . . We were nine, we played together, were constantly together. Like sisters. She disappeared one night, three days before her tenth birthday.

"Her bedroom window was broken, the jagged pieces of glass scattered on the ground, and there was blood on her blanket. No note, no phone call. She was simply gone. It wasn't as if her family had much money, to pay a fancy ransom. There was never a request for ransom. It took two years for the police to find her. They found . . ."

Cora Lee swallowed, and put her other hand on Charlie's, in a hard grip. "They found Kathy's bones washed up from a shallow grave in someone's garden. That," Cora Lee said, "that came back to me, too, this morning, seeing those newspaper pictures again. Pictures of her little bones. My mother hid the paper, but you can't hide something like that, it was everywhere, Kathy's bones strewn across a tiny yard in the French Quarter." Cora Lee turned away, but Charlie drew her close again. After a moment, Cora Lee leaned her face against Charlie's shoulder.

"I thought that life in the French Quarter had toughened me." She looked down the garden, and was quiet. "I guess it didn't." She said nothing more. Beside them, Dulcie felt cold and sick, distressed not only for Cora Lee, but also for that long-ago dead child. And for the child who might be buried here, in the garden. And she was suddenly frightened for Lori, for the living child. *Can that be why Lori's hiding? Because she knows something about that grave down there? Because someone wants to keep her quiet? Oh, but this is only coincidence . . .*

Sitting rigid on the picnic bench close to Charlie, Dulcie didn't know what to think or what to do about Lori, but now, suddenly she was afraid to do nothing. Should she take Lori's story to Captain Harper? An anonymous message such as she and Joe often managed, to tip the cops? She knew she could trust Harper—but trust him to do what? To follow the law, as he was sworn and committed to do? If there was something badly wrong in Lori's home, and if Lori had no other family, Harper might have no choice but to petition the court to send Lori to child welfare—where Lori seemed afraid to go.

Watching the three officers drive their metal stakes into the lawn and string the last line of tape, she wondered how many miles of yellow tape she and Joe had seen strung in such a way, around some grisly scene. No crime scene they had yet encountered had been like this, with the shocking impact of that one small hand, a hand that seemed to reach out so beseechingly, like the victim in a nightmare come alive.

When another car arrived and Detective Garza came around the corner of the house, Dulcie felt an added sense of security and strength, much the way a cat feels when all her family is at home. They were here now, the chief and both detectives, and they would make things right.

Garza looked tired, his square, smooth face drawn into deep, serious planes, his dark eyes studying the cluster of officers as he moved down the garden. He walked slowly, looking everywhere, taking in every detail. He was still dressed in the sport coat and slacks he'd worn to the theater the night before, the slacks wrinkled; and his jaw was dark with stubble. Had he not been home at all, had he not slept? He moved to where Max Harper stood at the end of the garden watching Juana photograph the scene.

Garza studied the hand and looked up at Harper. "I finished up with the last witnesses. Not much more of value. Nine people heard the shots, no one saw a damn thing. Except one of the inn's guests we had waiting. Said she saw a man running out through the side entrance to the patio, but she was vague about whether it was before or after the shots. Couldn't describe him. I'll talk with her again.

"Besides Lucinda Greenlaw, two more witnesses say they've seen a man hanging around the inn. Small man, much like Lucinda described. Lucinda thought he might be watching Patty, but said he was casual, laid-back, so meek and harmless looking she thought maybe he was a fan. She knew Patty had seen him, that Patty didn't seem concerned. She never asked Patty, and Patty never mentioned him." He looked at Max. "I'd like to use the newspaper, let the *Gazette* run a clip. See if anyone coming out of the theater last night saw him. Four blocks from the inn; he could've doubled over there, strolled out with the crowd. Someone might remember a car, or where he was headed."

As the two officers stood talking, watching Detective Davis at work, Dulcie wondered if Davis would take this case, and leave Garza with Patty's murder. She'd observed the department long enough to know that the two detectives meshed like clockwork, that Harper seldom told them what to do. When Captain Harper motioned to Charlie, Charlie went down to join him. Dulcie was tensed to leap down and follow quietly through the weeds, when she saw Wilma coming around the side of the house leading Susan Brittain's standard poodle and dalmatian.

Rearing up on the bench, her paws on the table, Dulcie looked questioningly at Wilma. Wilma shook her head. *No Kit. Nothing.* Dulcie's tall, silver-haired housemate studied the yard full of uniforms only briefly, then she hurried the big dogs inside the house, getting them out of the way. Lamb, the chocolate standard poodle, looked around with dignity at the action, but the young dalmatian pranced and huffed and pulled, wanting to join the fun. Dulcie imagined Wilma inside wiping paws and offering doggie treats; but Wilma was soon out again, having settled the dogs, probably where they could watch the action. Wilma sat down at the picnic table, between Mavity and Cora Lee. Apparently, she already knew what had happened.

Stepping into Wilma's lap, Dulcie stood looking over the top of the table, watching the officers at work. Wilma's faded jeans and sweatshirt smelled of dog and of the juniper she'd brushed in passing the overgrown neighborhood bushes. Dulcie could hear the dogs inside the nearest empty apartment, probably jockeying for position at the sliding door, with both noses pressed against the glass. She heard a car door slam out in front, but this time no police radio. In a moment the coroner, John Bern, come around the house.

Bern was a slight, bald man, his head as shiny as a clean supper bowl. His face was thin, fine boned. He wore rimless glasses that reflected glancing light. He was dressed in tan chinos, Dockers, and a pristine white lab coat buttoned over a bright-red polo shirt. He paused to speak with Captain Harper, then approached the dirt excavation to study the small, skeletal hand and to ask Juana the usual obligatory questions: had anything been removed or touched, that sort of thing, expecting Juana to answer in the negative. He made a few notes in a spiral binder, then adjusted his camera and began to take his own set of pictures. He took maybe two dozen shots very close up, then stepped away for longer angles, then turned to speak with Harper.

"We'll want a forensic pathologist on this, Max. I'd prefer a forensic anthropologist. I'd like to get Hyden down here. Meantime, I can do some preliminary digging."

Harper moved around so the noon sun was not directly in his face. "I have a call in for Hyden. We sure don't want to ship the bones to Sacramento if we can help it. If Hyden's not available, we'll try for Anderson—maybe luck out and get them both." Alan Hyden and James Anderson worked out of Sacramento. Dulcie supposed that, even if they left the state capital at once, the drive would take maybe four hours.

"I have a tent on the way," Max said. "We could be getting more rain, and there are coyotes in the canyon. We'll put guards on the site, of course." It was at this moment—as if additional assistance might be needed—that Joe Grey strolled on the scene.

Dulcie considered with interest the gray tomcat's bold entrance as, in plain sight, he sauntered across the cop-filled yard exhibiting all the casual authority of a high-ranking police detective. The tomcat made no effort to hide himself, and this was not Joe's usual mode of operation. In fact, why were neither of them taking their usual secretive approach? Her own attitude puzzled her nearly as much as Joe's brazen entrance.

Was it because there was such a crowd in the yard—cops, the senior ladies, Charlie and Wilma? But last night, even in that crowd, they had made some effort to keep out of sight. Or was it because this was a much more bucolic scene, the weedy yard, the open, wild canyon, where a cat would not seem out of place? A slower scene, too, and less frenetic. And because there was no hurried urgency, because a murder hadn't *just* happened.

But even so, she thought, watching Joe, half annoyed and half amused, even if *she* had let herself be seen, *she* hadn't swaggered. His in-your-face behavior around the cops was not in anyone's best interest.

Yet there he was, tramping across the weedy grass, as bold as the detectives and taking in every detail—the crime-scene tape, the little hand, the coroner at his work. Strolling across the yard, Joe turned and looked up toward the picnic table, looked right at her, then moved on down the garden ignoring her. Well, he hadn't found the kit, then. If he had, he'd be up there letting her know about it, no matter how miffed he was. Strolling on down across the trampled grass, he looked as if she didn't exist.

Padding boldly beneath the yellow barrier, he picked his way with disdainful paws along the length of the retaining wall. Every movement, every line of his sleek gray body challenged the officers to chase him away, though he knew very well that if he took one step off that retaining wall, Dr. Bern and every cop within sight was going to shout and throw things, and that someone would snatch him up in swift eviction. Dallas Garza and Juana Davis stared at Joe. Dr. Bern waved his arms and rattled a paper bag at him. Coolly Joe looked back at them, and sat down to study the little hand in its earthy excavation.

Dulcie watched him until he rose at last and moved on down the wall of railroad ties and stretched out along the top. Joe's questions would be the same as hers, as everyone's, questions that couldn't be answered until forensics had done its work. Questions that couldn't be answered completely until Harper and the detectives had obtained countless old, dead files, until they had examined whatever unresolved cases of missing children lay half forgotten among California's law-enforcement records.

When the answers did surface, Dulcie thought, she'd like to be lying on the dispatcher's counter beside Joe, reading the computer printouts or fax dispatches. She wanted to share with Joe, she didn't like this cold treatment.

He'd been fine last night as they searched for Kit, fine when she left him saying she'd just prowl the library, make sure the kit wasn't in there, that she'd be out again within the hour and would keep searching—a bold lie she wasn't proud of as she'd headed down to see Lori. She wanted so badly to tell Joe about Lori. She longed for Joe to gallop up the yard right now, leap on the picnic bench beside her, and give her a whisker kiss, let her know he was sorry for being angry.

But the tabby cat had to laugh at herself. *She* wanted *Joe* to say he was sorry! *She* wanted Joe to say he was sorry because *she* had lied to him? Because she was keeping secrets from him? She knew she was being totally unreasonable.

If she wanted Joe to forgive her, she would have to grovel.

And groveling was not in her nature.

What human said the road to hell was paved with good intentions? She guessed, if humans could make a mess with their good intentions, so could a cat.

But now, knowing that Joe hadn't found the kit, she grew edgy again worrying about the missing tattercoat. This, and her unease about Lori after the discovery of what could be a child's grave, made her want to claw the plank table. She began to fidget and scratch nonexistent fleas, drawing a surprised frown from Wilma.

CONTRARY TO POPULAR HUMAN BELIEF, all cats do not love, or gravitate to, dark, enclosed places. Not when that confining crawl space smells like an old sewer and is strewn with jagged rubble. Having scrambled back among the pipes and floor joists that formed the underside of the rental cottage, Kit was clawing to get back up through the rotted hole in the bathroom floor when she remembered about search warrants. Remembered Joe Grey's admonishment regarding the laws surrounding police work.

"The cops can't remove anything from a house without a search warrant, Kit. And they can't get a warrant without seeing a judge, the judge has to sign the warrant. But we can, Kit. We can take anything we can carry, anything we can haul out."

Leaping again at the hole, she dug her claws into the rotted wood, scrabbling and breaking off disintegrating splinters. Praying that Fenner hadn't returned, to hear her, she hoisted herself up into the bathroom. She was making so much noise, she must sound like a battalion of giant rats clawing at the bathroom floor. But she *couldn't* leave the envelopes under the sink. If the cops couldn't come into this house without a warrant, she had to move the evidence.

Surely an officer could casually slip into the yard when the house was empty, and happen to see the envelopes lying inside a floor vent—with the envelopes at the right angle, they would be visible; the department could say he'd just been walking by and seen that pale, smooth paper beyond the grid, and had wondered. And surely a cop could get those vent grids off. The use of tools, of screwdrivers and pliers, was a wonderful skill.

Such a story, for the law to use, sounded implausible even to Kit, but it was the best she could think of. They could do it, they could slip up to the vent and reach in for the envelopes. Slipping a paw under the linoleum, she clawed the two big brown envelopes out, her heart racing like a freight train, listening for Fenner to come back, listening for him in the next room.

Clawing the envelopes free, she had to bend each one double to force it down the hole. Silent and alone, she fought the evidence through the little hole, heard it drop onto the rubble below. She was so hungry and so very thirsty. But she wasn't going to drink out of that toilet, no way. She wished the other cats were there with her, wished longingly for Joe Grey and Dulcie, someone to help her, someone to lean on. Someone to lovingly wash her face and lick her ears.

She wished, most of all, that she had some breakfast. Her stomach was so hollow it ached. Squirming, wriggling, she dropped down beside the envelopes. Between her clawing at them and dragging them over the dirt and rusty nails, they were going to look pretty strange.

Well, she couldn't help that. Pulling them across to the far vent, one at a time, she listened and listened for his car. She still didn't know how she was going to get out.

If she didn't get out, if she didn't let Captain Harper know where to find the evidence, it would rot under there. And so would she. But she daren't dwell on that. Maybe when Fenner came back, if she went back up into his room and waited until he came in, maybe she could scorch out behind his heels, slide out through the door before he closed it. It was worth a try. She didn't have much choice.

# 11

DULCIE COULDN'T STAND, ANY LONGER, THE painful chill that separated her from Joe. Dropping from the picnic bench to the ragged grass, she started down the garden. She had never meant to hurt him; she was only keeping a secret she felt bound to keep. Trotting down through the rough grass, she crouched beside the low retaining wall just below where Joe stood brazenly watching the coroner photograph the little hand. Dr. Bern and every cop there was aware of Joe; they were all poised to chase him away.

Was it something about Joe's bold attitude that kept them from shouting at him again or carrying him, clawing, out of the yard? If someone tried that, she thought, smiling, all hell would break loose. She couldn't believe Joe was doing this. What was wrong with him? Slipping up onto the wall beside him, she crouched close. Was his nervy defiance the result of his anger with her?

But as much as she loved Joe, she wasn't going to lay his problems on her own back. She was doing what she had to do about Lori, what she felt was right. When Joe turned to look at her, his yellow eyes fiery with challenge, she gave him a long, steady look in return. His stupid tomcat rage wasn't going to cow *her*.

Joe stared, then returned his attention to the coroner. Had she seen a twitch of amusement, a willingness to make up? But she'd have to make the first gesture, Dulcie knew. Below them, John Bern worked with a teaspoon and a tiny, soft paintbrush, removing fragments of earth from the little bones. And then, working with tweezers, he pulled away thin, evasive roots and lifted any tiny fragments of unidentified debris.

Carefully Bern removed a bit of rotting cloth from the soil, then picked out what looked like a dirt-encrusted button. At intervals he stopped to take pictures, shooting close-ups from every angle. Both Dulcie and Joe, held by the scene, nearly forgot their differences. Bern, while waiting for the forensics people, was doing more than Dulcie had expected. Twice as he worked, the cats listened as he spoke on his cell phone with Drs. Hyden and Anderson, eager to follow their wishes. Apparently the two were on the road already, heading down from Sacramento. Had this discovery sparked an unusual eagerness in the two forensic anthropologists, to send them so quickly on their way? With the seeming age of the little hand, this grave might, for many investigators, mark the possible end to a long and discouraging search.

Within half an hour, Bern had freed the child's lower arm, digging so slowly that Dulcie wanted to yowl with impatience. The arm was so frail and so entangled with roots that it had to be a touchy job. It was so darkly stained by the earth in which it had lain that it seemed almost fused with the ground. Bern tried once, carefully, to remove it, but then he left it in place. He continued slowly removing the softer soil around it, fragment by tiny fragment, until he reached the little shoulder.

Despite the heavy rains that had wet the garden, the deeper earth was not sodden but only damp. As if the rainwater had drained quickly through the topsoil and, perhaps forming rivulets through the lower clay, had run off between the timbers of the retaining wall to the canyon below. Joe lay with his front paws tucked over the edge of the wall, so fascinated with Bern's work he seemed to have forgotten that the doctor might look up any minute. When he did remember, he jerked up quickly, turning to lick his shoulder. He looked straight at Dulcie, too, but now his look was gentler. She softened her own gaze, and lifted a paw to him.

Below them, Dr. Bern had uncovered the child's shoulder bone, working so slowly, Dulcie thought she'd explode from impatience. Both cats waited, unmoving, as inch by excruciating inch Bern's excavation revealed the child's head and, much later, the little upper torso. Bern's face and high forehead were slick with sweat, not from heavy digging but from tension. Twice more he talked with Dr. Hyden, following the anthropologist's instructions. The cats stared down at the child's rib cage, at the delicate bones, at the little thin neck bone and the child's fragile skull, and the friction between them, the foolish misunderstanding, seemed pointless. Except, when Dulcie thought of Lori's unnamed fears, she saw too sharply the shadow of Lori superimposed over those little bones.

She started when she heard Wilma's voice, and turned to look back up the garden. Wilma was leaving, telling Cora Lee and Mavity, loud enough for Dulcie to hear, that she was going to look again for "that runaway cat, help Lucinda and Pedric look. That kit will be the undoing of us all." Glancing down the garden, Wilma gave Dulcie a reassuring look, then was gone. Dulcie heard her car door slam, heard her pulling away.

It was perhaps four hours later, when the little body was fully revealed, that Hyden and Anderson arrived. The cats heard their car pull in, heard two doors slam and a trunk open, then close. The first softer light of evening was falling, not dark yet but softening, and though the wind had died to a whisper, it had turned colder. The two men came around the house, pausing to speak with Dallas Garza.

Hyden was tall, very thin, with brown receding hair. His long, smooth face seemed filled with quiet patience. He wore loose, faded jeans, a limp khaki shirt, and high-top tennis shoes. He carried a black leather camera bag. James Anderson was shorter, very square, with coal-black hair, and with his deep, vivid coloring and high cheekbones, looked like he might have American Indian blood. He was dressed in a faded blue jumpsuit that had seen many launderings, and he wore leather sandals over white crew socks. He carried a small canvas bag that he set carefully on top the wooden retaining wall. At their arrival, Dulcie and Joe had moved away from the dig—these two didn't look like they would tolerate cats in the way. They had a good enough view from the bushes without incurring any more wrath.

The men stood studying the body. Hyden talked with John Bern for some time, asking questions and making notes, while Anderson took pictures. Kneeling close to the bones, he shot just a few inches away, apparently aiming at the surrounding as much as the body, working so close Dulcie thought he must have a special lens. It was some time later that the coroner took his leave and the two anthropologists began, with painstaking care, to remove the frail bones from their grave. Fascinated, the cats didn't think of leaving, of missing the smallest detail. The day was nearly gone, and officers were bringing lights and drop cords from the squad cars, and two large canvas bundles.

The cats watched Hyden and Anderson place the bones, one by one, in a long wooden box like a coffin, carefully packing each in folds of clean, soft paper. As horrifying as was this child's grave, Dulcie was heartened by the care with which the doctors handled the little skeleton, exhibiting not only skill and precision but respect for this little human who had so violently lost its life. She looked with distaste at the head wound that had possibly killed the child, though there could have been any number of soft flesh wounds that the doctors would never find. They watched as four officers erected two long tents over the site, and two more officers set up the spotlights on tall poles, running a hundred-foot drop cord into the lower apartment of the seniors' house. Dulcie looked at Joe and laid her paw on his.

"I *have* to talk to you. I couldn't tell you before. But now . . . with that little grave . . . Now I have to tell you." Her mutter was so low that no human could hear. Joe looked at her and twitched an ear, and for nearly the first time in two weeks, the two cats were easy with each other. Moving close together, they left the bushes and made their way up the garden, through the falling dark. And as they padded away from the seniors' house, they watched every shadow, listened to every tiniest sound, searching for the kit. They glanced back only once, down at the lower garden where the spotlights shone bright within the tents.

"Will they work all night?" Dulcie asked.

"Maybe. There could be more bodies, those guys are feverish to find out."

"What kind of person would murder a little child?"

"Maybe there *is* just the one child, maybe it wasn't a murder, maybe an accident, and whoever caused it panicked. Buried the child and ran."

"Maybe," Dulcie said doubtfully. And she took off through the tangled neighborhood gardens, then scrambled up a vine to the rooftops, Joe racing close beside her. And they headed, without discussing the matter, for the courthouse tower, where, from its high platform, they could see nearly all of the village.

# 12

**GALLOPING ACROSS THE PEAKS AND SHINGLES,** swerving to the edges of the roofs, the cats peered over, searching the darkening streets for the kit. Dodging between stone chimneys and roof gardens, they scanned the alleys and the courtyards below them. They saw no cats at all, not one. Skirting third-floor penthouses with their tiled stairways and jutting dormers, they peered into windows blinded by drawn curtains or revealing empty rooms. They gained the narrow steps that spiraled up the courthouse tower, raced up thinking that they might, from the tower's high parapet, see Kit, a small speck on the streets or roofs below.

In this California village where occasional earthquakes were a given, only a few buildings rose over two stories. The taller clock tower was a singular exception; it provided for the cats, and for space-loving villagers and bold tourists, a dramatic view of the small village. Who knew how safe the tower was, how well it could withstand a really hard temblor? Such matters did not bother a feline; a cat could usually detect a shake some minutes before it hit, long enough to race down to solid earth again.

Now, circling ever higher through the deepening evening, Joe glanced back at Dulcie and looked down longingly at the red tile roof of Molena Point PD, almost directly below them. In the brightening light of the early half-moon, the department beckoned to Joe, distracted him from Dulcie's problem and even from searching for the kit. Fixed on Max Harper's domain, he wondered if the fax machine was already spitting out electronic information, or if the dispatcher's computer was feeding her data from long-dead files, buried intelligence that would provide Max Harper and Dallas Garza, and Joe himself, access to the lives of missing children—and perhaps of that one dead child.

Gaining the parapet, the two cats leaped from its open piazza to the top of the brick rail, five stories above the streets. Crouched on the rail, they watched the moon-washed clouds above them, and the car lights below flicking in and out beneath the pine and cypress trees. Scanning the ever-changing shadows of the rooftops, their gazes sought any small, dark shape racing or lurking, but half Joe's attention remained on Molena Point PD. On the files from across the western states and from archived FBI records that, combined with information the forensics team would develop, was all they would have to identify the small victim. Though Dulcie didn't see how, in this very old case, she and Joe could be of help. Even if the department was able to identify the child, this wasn't the kind of murder where a cat could track a suspect or toss his house. This killer was years gone, could be dead himself.

But, she thought, Lori was not an old, unsolved case. And she looked with speculation at Joe. She felt so strongly that Lori needed them now, needed their help now—if they *knew* how to help her, without stirring up trouble for the child.

Stretching along the top of the brick rail, in the slanting moonlight, she studied Joe, then studied the stark shadows below among the peaks and chimneys, the pale rivers of the streets, the dark pools of the crowding trees. The world below seemed totally empty of cats. From the other side of the parapet, Joe looked across at her, his gray coat gleaming silver in the moonlight, the white strip down his nose squeezed into a frown, his yellow eyes narrowed with impatience. "So, spill it, Dulcie. You've been as closemouthed as a crooked cop."

Dulcie looked at him, her tail twitching with nerves. "If I tell you, this is our secret. You won't tell anyone? Not Clyde, not Wilma or Charlie?" She wished with all her heart that the kit was there, so she could tell her, too.

"This can't be about the grave," Joe said, "about the dead child. So is it about Patty Rose? But why . . . ?"

Dropping down to the parapet, Dulcie stared up at him as he began to pace the rail, spinning back and forth on the thin barrier five stories above the roofs, his white paws seeming at every step to slide away into the night. He knew she hated that, hated when he indulged in fancy footwork on the edge of space.

"Come down and I'll tell you. Come down now."

Smiling, Joe paused on the edge, moonlight catching along his muscled shoulder.

"Come down, please. I promise I'll tell you if you won't grandstand."

He glared at her, but then he dropped to the bricks, a whiskery leer on his face.

"But you have to promise not—"

"I don't *have* to promise *anything*. Don't play games, Dulcie!" He crouched to leap up again.

She moved in front of him, stood nose to nose with him, her body drawn up tall, her paw lifted and her claws out, as sharp as razors. "If you want to hear, you'll promise not to bring Harper or the detectives into this, or any human. Not until we know the whole story."

Joe waited, his ears back, his whiskers tight to his tomcat cheeks, his yellow eyes wide with challenge.

"Promise?"

"Tentatively," he snarled, more a predatory growl than consent.

"I found a child, Joe. A little girl hiding in the library basement, in a walled-off part like a cave. She's around twelve, and so determined to keep herself hidden. She has food, a blanket, everything. But so alone."

"So why couldn't you tell me that? Where did she come from? How long has she been there? If she's run away, we'll have to—"

"*That's* why I didn't tell you. Because you'd say we have to tell Harper, that we have to drag in the law. Harper will only call county welfare to take care of her. That's what the law has to do. And I think that's part of the problem, I think she's afraid of someone in child welfare."

"Then tell Wilma. If you tell her the kid's afraid of someone in the juvenile system—"

"Joe, Wilma is service oriented. Family services, alcohol rehab, drug rehab, job placement. She depended on them all when she was a probation and parole officer." Dulcie lashed her tail with frustration; Joe looked back at her, his yellow eyes slowly softening. "Tell me about her, Dulcie. Tell me why she's locked herself in there; it has to be like a prison. Tell me why she's afraid."

**But while Dulcie and Joe** talked about Lori in her self-imposed confinement, the child was turning handsprings in the moonlight. Giddy with a few minutes of stolen freedom, she didn't guess that she might soon take fate into her own hands, might set in motion her own salvation.

Tonight she had waited, as she did every night in her black concrete hole, until the front door thudded closed for the last time and she heard its heavy bolt lock slide home. Until the last muffled sound faded, of library patrons and staff moving away down the walk and across the garden. She never felt safe until the library closed and everyone had gone, until nothing larger than the library cat could get in. Then, she had two choices. Some nights she just lit her little lamp and curled up under her blanket to read. Some nights she ran through the empty rooms and did cartwheels and laughed out loud, celebrating her freedom.

Tonight she went up into the children's room because she had finished the fourth book of Narnia and wanted the next one. She always hated finishing, no matter how many times she read them.

Moving the bricks and slipping out through the hole, she had pushed aside the little bookcase, leaving the space open for a quick return. Clutching her flashlight, she had hurried up the stairs. The library was hers, the big, empty, moonlit rooms were hers, all the thousands of books were hers. Lori had not the wildest idea that the library cat often had exactly the same thought. No notion that tabby Dulcie coveted the books as she did. That, like Lori, the library cat reveled in the fact that she could read whatever she chose, that she could read all night if she wanted.

Though if Lori ever discovered Dulcie's true nature, she would have no trouble believing. She was only twelve, and she was a reader. Despite her ugly brushes with the adult world, Lori's capacity for wonder had not yet been crippled; she was too strong for that. The powerful life-giving acknowledgment of wonder, that life force that should carry a child on through adulthood had not been twisted by the adults of the world. In Lori's case, maybe it never would be; she was a stubborn child.

In the main reading room she turned off her little flashlight and shoved it in her jeans pocket. Moving across the carpet, she stretched up in the moonlight and danced; she turned handsprings swimming through wavering fingers of light thrown by the wind through the tall windows. She was filled with wild, giddy freedom; she ran, she shouted softly in a breathy mock of a shout. She attempted backflips and collapsed giggling, fell over giggling, rolling on the carpet as wild with release as any caged young creature, celebrating the only freedom she was able to gain. Handspringing between the stacks and whirling across the reading room between the long tables, surrounded by thousands of books, Lori thought of Mama saying, "Be happy, Lori." Oh, Mama would laugh at her, Mama would love that she had hidden here, taking charge of her own life. Mama said you had to be a problem solver if you wanted to survive.

When Pa turned so strange, Mama did what she could for him, she talked to doctors and she got help from the county. But when nothing helped, when Pa started to lock Lori in the house, Mama waited until he left for work, then packed them up and they were out of there, heading for Greenville. She wished Mama was here to read with her. The first time she'd stepped into Narnia she was really little and Mama read to her, *The Lion, the Witch and the Wardrobe*, and she wished Mama was here now, to share it. To love her and hold her, the two of them wrapped in Mama's quilt, wished they could talk and talk like they used to do. Moving across to the big, soft chairs by the fireplace, she took the *Molena Point Gazette* from its shelf because Mama always read the paper and Lori didn't like to miss Snoopy or Mutts. The everyday funnies in this paper were in color just like on Sunday. Kneeling on the chair, she hunkered over the table. She liked "For Better or Worse," too, but sometimes that one made her feel lonely. How would it be to have brothers and sisters, to be a big family all together with so much going on all the time and a father who loved you? The page opposite the comics always had a boring list of notices like charity events and dance recitals, but Lori read everything—pill bottles, cereal boxes. Now, in last week's paper, she was reading about a boy at a beach barbecue who thought he could walk on coals when another article caught her eye. She grew very still. The name "Vincent and Reed Electrical Contractors" held her; the name was twice mentioned and that made her feel both proud and lost.

**Tea to Be Held for Genelle Yardley**

A tea will be held on Wednesday at Otter Pine Inn to honor Genelle Yardley on her sixty-sixth birthday. The tea will be hosted by Friends of the Library and by actress Patty Rose, in the inn's charming tearoom. Ms. Yardley has recently placed into trust for Molena Point Library her commercial building next door to the library. On her death, this will provide for a new children's wing and an enlarged reference collection. For many years, Ms. Yardley was known for her storytelling, for charming and original children's fantasies set on the central coast. A small edition was published locally. The book has long been out of print and is a collectors' item.

For the last twenty years of her career, Ms. Yardley was office manager for Vincent and Reed Electrical Contractors. She left the firm four years ago. She has continued to write folk tales that she has never sought to publish. She has spent much of her time working with Friends of the Library.

This Genelle Yardley had worked for Vincent and Reed, for Pa's company. She'd worked for them for ever so long, since before Lori herself was born. Lori had heard the librarians talk about a Genelle something, and about a tea party, when she was up in the children's room. One of the librarians said Genelle had something terminal, that meant you were going to die, like Mama. In Greenville, the doctor told the social worker that Mama was terminal; he thought she, Lori, wouldn't know what that meant.

The librarian said Genelle's neighbors would take her to the party, put her folding wheelchair in the car along with her oxygen tank. Mama had had an oxygen tank. Lori guessed that tea party must be something this Genelle wanted very much before she died. Where do you go when you die? *Mama, if you're somewhere, can't you tell me? Can't you just give me a sign, like a seagull flying around my head three times when I go out in the dark morning? Or like a seal rising up out of the ocean to look at me in a special way? Something so I'll* know *there's another place and you're in it?*

*Or are you too far away to do that?*

*Or is there nothing? Are you just cold dead, rotting in the ground?* But Lori wouldn't let herself think that, she couldn't think that Mama had just stopped being, disappeared into nothing. She had to be somewhere.

And this Genelle Yardley who was going to die like Mama. Was she scared? Had Mama been scared, underneath, and never told her? Or did Mama really know for sure where she was going? But how could anyone know?

And more important right now was the fact that Genelle Yardley knew Pa. She'd worked for Pa, had worked for him a long time. Maybe Genelle Yardley knew what happened to Pa to make him so different all of a sudden. Maybe she knew things that even Mama didn't know?

Did Mama ever go to Genelle Yardley to ask questions? No matter how Mama tried to understand what made Pa change, he would never talk to her, he only shouted at her.

As far as Lori knew, Mama had never gone to any of their friends for help. Mama would have been ashamed to do that.

Sliding down from the chair, Lori headed across the reading room with a whole new plan flaring in her mind. Genelle Yardley knew about Pa. Genelle Yardley knew secrets that she, Lori, needed to find out.

Up the little half flight of seven steps, two at a time, she slipped behind the checkout desk. Shining her flashlight into the shelves beneath the counter, she hauled out the phone book and laid it on the floor. She found a pencil on the desk and a scrap of paper, and knelt on the carpet. Licking the end of the pencil, she found and wrote down Genelle Yardley's address, then turned to the front of the phone book to find the village map. She tried to imagine what Genelle Yardley looked like. She was old. Lori didn't know that people worked until they were over sixty. She wondered if Genelle Yardley had ever been to their house when she, Lori, was little, wondered if she'd ever seen her. She kept wondering if Mama *had* ever gone to ask that old lady what was wrong with Pa.

Maybe Genelle Yardley didn't know, either. Maybe she couldn't help her, but Lori had to try.

This would be the farthest she'd ever gone from the library since she came to live here like a hobbit in a hole. Like Mr. Baggins, she thought, smiling. Only his hobbit hole was a lot bigger, with all kinds of rooms, and was full of hams and bread and cider that she wished her hideout had, too.

She'd have to go before it got light. Even so, she likely wouldn't get back from Genelle Yardley's house until it was bright morning. She'd have to wait all day, until nine that night, before she could be safe in her cave again.

And she couldn't hang around the library for too long, and draw attention from the librarians. Some of those women might remember her, from when she was little and Mama worked here. And she didn't dare be seen during school hours.

She wrote down the streets that climbed the hills to Genelle Yardley's, wrote where to turn and when to start looking for the number. The house was so high up the hills that it *had* a number. Those in the village didn't. If someone told another person where they lived, it was like, "Third house on Lincoln north of Fourth." People who lived in the village went to the post office to get their mail.

Going up the hills, she'd have to watch for Pa's truck, out early going to some job. Hide if she saw him. But what worried her was the other man, the man she'd seen standing in the shadows one morning when she went out. She'd seen him later, too, when she slipped out before it was hardly light to walk on the beach. Probably she imagined he was watching her. Probably some homeless man with nowhere to go. Anyway, he was very thin and small, not much taller than she was, and Mama said she was strong for her age. Mama showed her things she could do to get away from someone, things that could hurt a person, so she wasn't very scared of him.

Folding her slip of paper with the streets and address, she flicked off her flashlight and crossed the library to the stairs. As she headed down to the basement, the courthouse clock struck ten—two hours until midnight. She thought to set her alarm for really early, maybe four A.M. No one would see her on the streets then, it would be deep dark. Windy and cold, too. Pa sure wouldn't be out at that hour.

But that man, he'd been out there early, before dawn. She looked out at the moonlight, bright now with the moon right overhead. She could go even earlier; he wouldn't be out in the middle of the night, would he? Maybe no one would. She could hurry up the hills to Genelle Yardley's house and hide in the bushes until the old lady woke up. Until Ms. Yardley turned on a light in the morning or came out to get the paper. If anyone bothered her she'd kick them in the groin, the way Mama taught her.

As Lori bricked herself back into the basement room again and set her little alarm for one in the morning, five blocks away the kit pressed the two brown envelopes up between a floor joist and a plumbing pipe. Secure just inside the vent grid where a cop could reach in, they would not be seen by the casual passerby. Now, with the envelopes safe, the kit circled the underhouse again, frantic to get out. She circled, pawing uselessly at the other two vents, but both were fixed tight to the wall. With screws, she thought. She hooked her claws in but couldn't pull them out.

Studying the concrete foundation, wondering how deep it went, she found a soft place in the dirt where she could smell the old, dry scent of squirrels, where their digging had made the ground soft.

Thanking the little rodents that normally she would eat, she began to excavate the churned earth, kicking dirt behind her like a terrier. Her panic at being trapped was worst of all when she did nothing; she needed to move, it eased her to dig even if she had to dig to China. Listening for his car, she clawed down and down, wondering if he was coming back or if he was gone for good. She thought the time was past midnight. She dug straight down for nearly a foot, fighting the dirt away from the concrete wall, trying to find its bottom, scraping the skin from her paws until they bled again. And still the concrete went deeper.

After a long, long time of digging she found a straight edge to the concrete, where it turned under. Her paws hurt bad. She was very thirsty. And hungry. But the discovery of the bottom of that concrete filled her with terrible joy. Pausing, she thought she would just rest for a little while before she dug on through and up the other side. Soon enough she'd be free, be out of there and free.

# 13

**A**BOVE THE COURTHOUSE TOWER THE CLOUDS moved away; the full force of moonlight washed down across the parapet, caressing the two cats, etching Dulcie's black and brown stripes like a black ink drawing. She lay licking her paw, watching Joe, her ears back in a thoughtful frown but trying to remain silent, letting Joe come to his own conclusion.

"Maybe you're right about Harper," he said at last. "If we tell the cops about the child, they'll have little choice, they're bound by law to call child welfare—if the kid's really all alone, if there's no family." He studied Dulcie, his yellow eyes narrowed and appraising. "But Wilma's retired, she's a free agent, she's not beholden to the law. She can do as she pleases."

"But what would she do? You know how she feels about help from the proper officials, she's all for it."

"Maybe. But she isn't stupid. She knows how twisted some of those agencies can be. You get one bad apple . . ."

Dulcie shrugged. "I suppose. So frustrating that I can't ask

Lori questions. That I can only hope she tells me more. I don't know why she doesn't want anything to do with child welfare. And the man she talks about, she just says *he*. I don't know if someone's stalking her, or if the man is family. I tried to find her last name in the library database for library cardholders, for children's cards with the first name Lori. Took me all night, those computers are so temperamental. Why don't they make a steadier machine, one that doesn't go off in a hundred directions?"

"A cat-friendly computer."

"Exactly. Someone ought to write to Bill Gates. Well, there's no library card for Lori, not one Molena Point child named Lori in the system." She told him how she had discovered Lori in the first place, when the scent of peanut butter and jelly drew her across the library basement to the bricked-up wall behind a little bookcase.

"It was late, after the library closed, ten days ago. That's where I've been. She gets so lonely, especially at night. And it's dark in there all day. It took a lot of resolve for the kid to hide there, and I think it takes a lot more to stay."

Her green eyes were big with concern. "She's not playing, Joe. She's made a safe little home for herself; she's thought it all out. She keeps her toothbrush and extra clothes and a bedroll in her backpack, and hides it in a rough niche in the wall—I think she must have dug the loose bricks out herself, maybe with a pair of scissors from the workroom. There are bits of concrete scattered on the floor, which she's pushed into a heap. And the hole where she enters her little basement, she fits loose bricks back into that really carefully."

Dulcie smiled, her pale whiskers gleaming in the moonlight. "She does her laundry in the ladies' room after the library closes at night, hangs it in her basement from the rough, sticking-out bricks. Folds and hides the dried clothes when she wakes up in the morning, before the library opens, her little socks and panties, or a blouse, afraid someone might move the bricks and look in.

"It's hard," Dulcie said, "with librarians working just on the other side of the wall. Hard to stay there in the dark and cold, alone. To only come out at night and early in the morning to use the bathroom and get books. She has everything she needs, though. And she never lets herself look seedy, never misses brushing her teeth, combing her hair, keeping her clothes fresh. She took a little lamp from the library storeroom, and she has a big tin can she empties at night to use as a makeshift bathroom in the daytime. Most children wouldn't do all that. There's an electric plug in there, but her lamp is the battery kind. Maybe the room was part of the library basement once or of the basement across the alley."

Joe frowned but said nothing.

"That room is underneath the alley, it has to be. I think it must have once joined the basement of the other building."

"Why would someone build—"

"It was originally all one house, in the 1800s. Gardens, stables, a carriage house. A little estate that filled the whole block. I found pictures in a history of Molena Point. The alley was a carriageway between the big house and the servants' quarters, where those apartments and the men's shop are now. Genelle Yardley's parents deeded the main house to the village for a library, but kept the servants' building for rentals. Genelle has lived partly on that income since her husband died and she retired.

"Somewhere along the way, the lane became a paved service alley. Maybe it was then that the basement beneath was walled off. Maybe something to do with ownership or property rights. Or the weight of the garbage trucks on top of the basement, who knows."

"You did a lot of research."

"I wanted to know where that room came from. And where it

might once have led." She looked up past the little parapet roof at the slowly dropping moon. "I wanted to know if there might be another way in or out of there, but there doesn't seem to be." Talking about Lori made her sad. Lori, with her little heart-shaped face and the way her mouth tilted up at the corners, and her dark, huge eyes. Dulcie always wanted to touch her with a soft paw, rub her face against Lori and purr. When Lori's tears came, Dulcie had to snuggle close; and when the child pressed her face into Dulcie's fur, Dulcie licked her shining brown hair. "Somehow," Dulcie said, "she got hold of someone's library card, maybe stole it. With that she can open the card lock to the women's bathroom. She brought a flashlight with her, and even extra batteries, and she has a little battery-operated clock. And she *knows* that library, Joe. Knows her way around.

"Why has no one missed her?" Dulcie asked. "We'd have heard, if someone was looking for a lost child. When she slips outside, in the early morning before it's light, sneaks out through the basement window, she makes sure no one is on the street or sitting in a car. Makes sure no police car's parked around the corner.

"She's really skittery; she startles if anything moves, stays in the shadows against the buildings. She must crave getting out. Every couple of days, she goes to walk the shore and drop her little bag of trash and wet paper towels in the public garbage cans."

"And you follow her."

Dulcie twitched her ear. "The child's as clever as a cat herself."

"The streets are lonely that time of morning, Dulcie. Have you thought about someone grabbing her? Even in Molena Point—"

"I'd rake and bite so hard he'd never grab another child." Dulcie cut him a fierce green-eyed look. "The real problem is, Lori's little stash of canned food won't last much longer. Maybe another three or four days. I don't know if she has any money to slip out and buy more, or if she'd dare go in the market in broad daylight. It's so frustrating not to know who she's hiding from, not to know what happened to her."

"Maybe she has no one, maybe her parents are dead. A homeless child?"

"She doesn't look homeless. There've been no reports of a homeless person found dead. And why suddenly move into the library? To get out of the cold and rain? But . . . I don't know. It doesn't add up. And if someone died recently in the village, a neighbor or school official would report that the child was alone. Everyone would be looking for her."

"Maybe she ran away from home, and her parents think she'll get over it and come back?"

"After nearly two weeks? What kind of parents wouldn't report her missing?"

Joe shrugged. "The kind you know are out there. The no-good ones." He looked hard at her. "So why didn't you trust me enough to tell me?"

"I didn't trust you not to go to the law."

"That's not saying much."

"It's saying a lot. It's saying you think like a cop, Joe. That you'd start checking Captain Harper's desk for fliers on a lost child, watching the computers, listening to every conversation."

Joe shrugged. "The whole department will be looking now, with a body to identify. Checking the files for lost children."

"They'll be checking old cases, not recent ones."

"And the kit? Why didn't you tell the kit?"

She widened her eyes, and Joe grinned. Of course she wouldn't tell the kit—Kit would be right down there in the basement making up to Lori, so fascinated that she would find it hard not to speak to the child. Or to blurt out Lori's business to some trusted human.

"Anyway," Dulcie said, "before Patty's murder, Kit was too busy playing grand lady, living like a queen in her penthouse, letting Lucinda and Pedric spoil her. And now . . . ," she said, "now . . ."

"She'll turn up, Dulcie. Kit always turns up." But he leaped restlessly to the brick rail again, pacing, peering down at the moonlit streets for a small, dark feline shape hurrying along, and studying the darkly pooled treetops and shadows. Dulcie, leaping up to join him, wished with all her heart that Kit was at that moment safe in the penthouse, still being spoiled rotten, listening to Lucinda's favorite Dixieland jazz records and ordering outrageous delicacies from room service.

"So what happens," Joe said, "when Lori runs out of food? You plan to deliver takeout through the basement window?"

She looked at him bleakly.

"I'll keep my mouth shut, Dulcie," the tomcat said with unusual constraint. "I do promise. It's your call. But where do we go from here?"

She smiled and nuzzled him, purring and loving him. "I don't know where. Don't know where to go from here."

Joe licked his shoulder, then turned his yellow gaze on her. "You wouldn't consider asking for help? Someone who won't go to the law or to Harper."

Dulcie drew away, alarmed. "Who? Not Charlie, she's Harper's wife, we can't burden her. And Kate Osborne's out of the picture, moving up to Seattle. And Clyde, besides being Harper's best friend, really does think too much like a cop. And right now, Lucinda and Pedric are way too worried about the kit; I don't feel like putting anything more on them. So who . . . ?"

"But you've always trusted Wilma."

She licked her paw. "I know. I'm ashamed not to trust her this time."

"And it would be natural for her to discover Lori's hiding place," Joe said, "working in the library. Dulcie, Wilma won't blow the whistle. Wilma raised you from a kitten, she's your best friend."

"You're my best friend. Wilma's second best." She sat thinking. "But maybe you're right. Maybe . . . she always does listen. Pays attention to me, to what I think."

Joe studied again the angles and planes that tumbled below them, the jumble of rooftops and trees and balconies, and he dropped down to the parapet beside her. "You do what you think best. Meanwhile, I'll just nose around the department, see if there are any recent fliers on runaway children." And before she could reply, he was racing away down the tower's spiraling stairs, heading for the PD.

She watched him from the rail. He was burning to get his teeth into the files on those old unsolved cases. He was a racing streak as he rounded each curve of the stairs, appearing, then vanishing until he burst out across the courthouse roof and into the oak tree above Molena Point PD. There she lost him as he scrabbled down the thick trunk; she glimpsed him for a second as he dropped to the sidewalk twisting in midair to crouch before the glass door. And even before the door was unlocked from within by the cat-friendly dispatcher, Dulcie herself was gone, racing down the brick steps to the icy sidewalk, heading out to search for Kit. As she watched the shadows and circled, peering into crevices, looking for the tattercoat, the courthouse clock struck midnight; she was glad they'd left the tower, the chimes were hellishly loud when you were right on top of them. In her search this time, she looked for silent little unmoving forms, and prayed she wouldn't find one.

Turning to retrace an elusive scent, stopping to explore the blackness beneath steps and porches, she didn't dare call the kit. Even in the middle of the night, who knew when some human might be out late, or standing sleepless at an open window? Or someone homeless asleep in a dark niche, who would wake to hear a cat shouting in his face. Her eyes burned into the night, searching silently, her ears rigid, the delicate antennae of her whiskers following every twist of air.

And as Dulcie fretted and worried, not four blocks away the kit lay curled up beneath the old rental house, sound asleep beside the hole she had dug. The hole to freedom that she had only half finished. Exhausted and thirsty, feeling weak from lack of supper, she slept deeply. She had no notion that both Joe and Dulcie were so near, Joe approaching Molena Point PD, and Dulcie just a few blocks away quietly looking for her.

# 14

**P**AWING AT THE HEAVY GLASS DOOR OF Molena Point PD, Joe pressed his nose against its cold surface, peering into the booking area. Except for the dispatcher, the small room was empty. To his left, the holding cell with its barred door was empty of prisoners, too. Behind the dispatcher's U-shaped counter Mabel Farthy sat among her radios and phones and computers, half turned away from the door and busy with a call. He meowed loudly. Very likely she didn't hear him through the thick bulletproof glass and over the noise of the phone and radio. Mabel was square, sturdy, blond, and in her mid-fifties. She must just have had her hair done because the color was brighter than usual, the short, layered cut neatly coiffed. She had a phone to her ear and was talking into the radio as well, apparently fielding a call and sending out a unit. Through the heavy glass, Joe couldn't hear her words, but Mabel seemed well in control, keeping the caller on the line as she relayed information to a responding unit. From somewhere north of the village, a siren started to whoop, moving away fast into the hills. Mabel didn't look up until the siren stopped, likely as the unit arrived.

As she hung up the phone and turned to the fax machine, Joe reared up, throwing all his weight against the glass. He was barely able to rattle the heavy lock in its metal frame; his violent effort elicited only a tiny thunk.

But that small sound was enough to bring Mabel straight up from her chair, reaching for the alarm button and touching her holstered automatic. Then she saw Joe peering in.

Hitting the remote instead of the alarm, she released the lock and came around the counter to pull the door open. She shook her head at him, grinning. "You are such a little freeloader."

Smiling up at her, Joe sauntered in taking his sweet time, slow and unhurried, in the best feline tradition.

"Hurry it up, Joe! You want to let in the whole village?" She glanced up and down the street. "I haven't got all night. What is it with cats!"

Mabel had cats at home and, apparently, a husband who was just about as indolent. As soon as Joe strolled through the door, she pressed it closed again and tested that it had locked. He looked up at her innocently and rubbed against her leg. Mabel gave him an impatient but amused sigh. Mabel was always good about letting them into the station; she had no idea how much he hated having to ask.

There had been a time when Joe and Dulcie could paw the unlocked station door open whenever they pleased, to wander in and out of the big squad room. That was before Max Harper remodeled the interior of the building, increasing department security. Before the more dangerous elements in the world had extended their influence quite so stubbornly into the small village . . .

Before Molena Point rocked with an explosion that blew up the village church; before a meth lab sprang up back in the woods and another north of the village, poisoning surrounding land and water; before the Medellin cartel increased its visits to these small coastal towns, cars full of thugs driving up from L.A. to break out plate-glass windows and steal millions in precious stones. Now Molena Point had joined the larger world. This village might be small, but it was a well-to-do tourist retreat. There were, among the upscale shops, twenty-three jewelry stores, and many times that in the surrounding towns of the county. Tourists meant money, and Molena Point lived on the largesse of happy shoppers.

The tomcat didn't much like the increases necessary in departmental security that came with intensified village crime. But it didn't matter what he liked, one cat can't change the world. Though Joe had some thoughts on how to do just that, if ever the opportunity arose. In his view, if humans took a more feline stance in these matters, the crime rate would drop like a stone.

Meantime, he could fight the bad guys on his own terms, as much as he was able. And so far he and Dulcie and Kit had done all right. Over a dozen killers and assorted thieves were living very well at the expense of California taxpayers, including a couple of folks awaiting the state's attention on death row.

Joe wondered if evil came in waves throughout history. If tides of evil grew powerful, as in the Dark Ages, and then eased off. Maybe good and evil were forever changing balance over the decades, each increasing, then waning.

But to what end? And why did he think about this stuff! These were matters for human deliberation, these abstractions didn't worry most cats. Your ordinary everyday tomcat lived for the moment, lived to kill and make love, sleep in the sun, take happiness where he found it. Not waste his time pondering philosophical ambiguities. Your everyday garden-variety tomcat didn't give a damn about the state of the world. He whiled away his nine lives manipulating humans when the occasion arose, and thoroughly enjoying himself.

*So why am I different? Why are Dulcie and Kit different, why do we care about these things? Why do we spend our talents and energy so freely to cure the ills of the world?*

Joe didn't have the answer. That was the way he was made. His curiosity, his fierce predatory skills, and his natural ability to outsmart humans had combined in a new way. His enraged, often amused drive to set straight the flawed rejects of the human world seemed to Joe himself insatiable. Feline undercover work was a huge and fascinating chess game, with the highest possible stakes.

Leaping onto Mabel's counter, Joe looked up into her round, motherly smile wondering what she'd brought for supper. Mabel Farthy was always pleased to see him. Mabel's brown, laughing eyes and happy expression inspired total confidence from beast or child—just as her acumen with a .38 police special, when needed, could inspire respect from an assortment of miscreants who might misjudge her motherly appearance. A matronly lady with a little extra fat on the hips did not necessarily add up to ineptitude in the arts of law enforcement.

"So, you little bum." Mabel scratched behind Joe's ears in just the way he liked. "You hungry? When were you ever not hungry?" Reaching under the counter of her busy electronic cubicle, she drew forth the paper bag containing her lunch, which she'd stashed on a lower shelf. Mabel, in packing her lunches, seemed always to allow generous portions for any visiting felines.

Joe purred extravagantly as she unwrapped a piece of fried chicken. Mabel made the best fried chicken; Joe didn't know what she did to it, but it smelled like the kind of chicken he imagined would be served in cat heaven. And Mabel Farthy well understood that a helpless little cat, wandering many blocks from home, would be hungry on these cold winter nights.

Removing the chicken from the bone, she tore it into small

pieces, which she laid on one of a supply of paper plates that she kept beneath the counter for just this purpose. Next to Mr. Jolly, who owned the deli, Mabel had turned into the second-finest provider in the village in matters feline.

The chicken didn't last long; Joe tore into Mabel's offering as if he hadn't eaten in months. When he'd finished, holding the plate down with his paw, he licked it as clean as would a ravenous dog. Mabel, tossing the empty plate in the wastebasket, wiped her hands on one of those damp paper squares that she pulled from a little cylinder, then stood stroking him for a few minutes.

When she returned to the fax machine, sorting through the pages it had spewed forth, Joe wandered along the counter to Harper's report box. Still purring, he studied the fresh copy, smelling the faint aroma of the laser-jet toner. Reading the top sheet, he smiled.

He must be on a roll. He'd lucked out not only with fried chicken, but apparently with a full printout of the witness interviews from the murder of Patty Rose. Pretending to wash his shoulder, he sat reading, wanting badly to lift a paw and flip the top sheet away, restraining himself with difficulty.

But the top summary sheet said all that was really necessary. Max Harper's and the two detectives' interviews of the witnesses was one big ho-hum. One gigantic blank. Not one of those present in the bar or restaurant or in their rooms saw anything out of the ordinary. Half a dozen people heard shots, or what sounded like shots, but no one *saw* anything. Garza's summary described interviews so negative that one had to wonder if these folks were hiding something.

But that was a paranoid thought. *Now* who was imagining things? Turning away with disgust, he pushed close to Mabel to have a look at the growing pile of faxes that she was sorting into neat stacks. Rubbing lovingly against her arm, Joe scanned the reports beneath her fast-moving hands.

Nice. Very nice. These were the missing-child cases; and more were coming in, in a steady production from the fax machine.

All were old cases, five years, ten, fifteen years. Unsolved cases that might have been brought out now and then, at infrequent intervals, when an officer had some new line on child abductions, some new hint at a solution. But cases that were filed away again, unsolved. One case in Portland was over twenty years old.

Picking up the stack, Mabel thumped it on the counter to align the edges, put the stack in the copier, and ran two more sets. So many children lost, no closure to their disappearance, no answers for their families. What was the background on these kids? Did they have something in common? Joe burned for a long look, undisturbed. What kind of kids were they, what kind of families? Did these kids come from stable households, or live with drunks or in broken homes? Where did they go to school? Were they problem students? Runaways who'd been picked up by some lowlife—disaster waiting to happen?

Which child was this, buried in the seniors' garden? Was his or her background included among these cases? And would the forensics team, tonight or tomorrow, find more bodies? There was only one word for the murder of innocent children. Evil. Complete evil.

Licking his paw, he watched Mabel set up a cross-referencing chart on her computer, listing the cases by date and location, and by age of child. None seemed to have occurred any closer to Molena Point than Seattle to the north, and Orange County to the south. Dr. Hyden had said it would take some time to determine the age of the corpse but that, given the Molena Point climate, and if the body had been buried soon after death, it might date from four to ten years ago. When Mabel finished sorting, and no more faxes had come through, Joe curled up in her out box to await further electronically generated intelligence.

Yawning, he felt his eyes droop. It had been a long night. A long day and previous night; he had not had his cat's share of sleep. Tucking his nose under his paw, shielding his eyes from the harsh overhead lights, he felt himself drop into a doze. Just a few minutes, he thought, to renew his energy, to prepare for future action. Yawning again, Joe slept.

# 15

**S**TRETCHED ACROSS THE DISPATCHER'S OUT box, his hind legs sticking out, Joe woke blearily. Beyond the glass doors, the big front parking lot was alive with headlights. Cars were pulling in, officers coming on for last watch. Private vehicles, and half a dozen police units, as well, returning from late watch. He yawned heavily. He could hear, out behind the building, several units leaving the smaller, fenced-in parking area that was reserved for official cars. Cold blasts of air ruffled his fur as officers trooped in by twos and threes. Retracting his hind paws and licking one pad, he sat up in the box yawning. But when Max Harper swung in, Joe leaped down to a shelf beneath Mabel's counter. Mabel glanced at him sharply. Looking up, he yawned in her face and curled up for another nap as if the commotion had disturbed him.

But, listening to officers joking with Harper as they moved down the hall, Joe dropped to the floor and followed, pausing outside the squad room. Harper was saying, ". . . Brown and Wrigley will be posted. You have a be-on-the-lookout for a man Lucinda Greenlaw saw hanging around the inn." Harper described the small man, the same description that would appear in the be-on-the-lookout notice. He gave them some particulars on the murder, and on the bullets that had killed Patty. "Likely a small caliber," he said. "Could be a twenty-two." He filled the officers in on the child's grave. "Hyden and Anderson are down from Sacramento, may still be working. About an hour ago, they uncovered a second body . . ." In the hall, Joe's ears pricked up sharply and he edged nearer the door. ". . . child about the same age," Harper said.

A young rookie asked about the gender of the children, and how they'd died.

"Hard to tell what sex," Harper said. "May never know. First child died, apparently, from a blow to the head. Second body, they've only uncovered a leg and part of the torso so far."

There were a couple more questions, the chief discussed half a dozen more situations, and the officers filed out, heading for their units. Joe imagined them settling into the cold, black leather seats of their squad cars, their holstered guns and handcuffs and all the equipment they must wear pressing into their butts and backs, imagined them moving about into just the right worn position to get comfortable, some of them balancing coffee mugs. Imagined the late watch revving their adrenaline along with their engines, heading out on patrol not knowing whether they might have to use their handguns, might get shot tonight or have to shoot—or spend the shift bored out of their skulls.

They would be watching for Patty's killer, though. Smiling, Joe trotted on down the hall and into Max Harper's dark office, just beating Harper and Garza there. When they came in, he was curled up in the bookcase between two volumes of the California civil code. He watched Garza dump water in Harper's coffeepot and drop in a prepacked filter. He liked the scent of coffee, it spoke to him of camaraderie, easy friendship—and of ready information.

Harper, tossing the three stacks of faxes and printouts on his desk, eased into his leather chair. The chief looked tired. Garza poured their coffee and picked up a set of the printouts. From the shelf, Joe had a fine view of Harper's desk. On top the stack was the chart that Mabel had prepared.

Garza didn't glance up into the bookshelves, but the detective knew he was there. A change in Garza's body language and movement connected him to Joe almost as if he had looked straight up at the tomcat. Setting his coffee mug on the low table, he settled into the leather easy chair. And Joe settled down more comfortably among the books, thinking about the second body.

The officers were not surprised by the second grave. Nor was Joe. Nothing surprised a cop, and Joe had acquired much the same view of the world. That first grave had never really seemed like the cover-up for, say, a single accidental death. His natural tomcat cynicism, honed by close association with law enforcement, had left him expecting more bodies.

Now, with so many old, unsolved cases concentrated all in one area of the Northwest, his imagination had already jumped ahead to what he imagined Hyden and Anderson might yet find, and he shivered.

Though that preconception was not always wise police work, it was the way the tomcat operated; so far, it had worked for him. He looked around the office, waiting for Harper to flip through a stack of unrelated papers that had been left on his desk, checking for anything urgent, before he got down to the subject at hand. Joe liked Harper's new office, he liked seeing the chief in a more comfortable environment. With the building's renovation, the old, open squad room with its tangle of desks and noise and constant hustle was no more. The chief had had only a scarred old desk at the back of the busy, forty-by-forty-foot space, a habitat as spartan as that of a prison guard's.

Now Harper and his two detectives had private offices, and

all the officers had much-improved facilities. A more efficient report-writing room, an updated firing range in the basement, a larger and better-appointed coffee room. And thanks to Charlie, Harper's own office was a welcome retreat, with its brown leather couch and matching chair and an oriental rug, all of which had been wedding presents from Charlie, items not considered essential by those city officials who spent the taxpayers' money—though some of them hadn't stinted on their own offices.

But the city had sprung for a new walnut desk for Max, and walnut bookcases, as well, unwittingly providing a convenient though unofficial satellite office, as it were, for certain feline operatives.

Charlie's framed drawings of Max's buckskin gelding hung on the pale walls, lending a handsome finishing touch to the room. Joe was sure that, if not for Charlie's influence, Max would have moved into his new digs with the old battered desk that looked like some World War II government reject, the government-issue, service-grade vinyl-tile floor, and his dented and mismatched file cabinets. Max would likely have brought in a couple of hard chairs for visitors, and been perfectly happy with bare walls to look at—if the chief ever had time to simply look at the walls.

Below him, Max studied the faxes. "This one in Half Moon Bay is the only one in California."

"Sure doesn't fall in with the rest," Garza said. "Newer, too. Two years."

Juana Davis came in, poured herself a cup of coffee, picked up the other stack of copies from Harper's desk, and sat down on the leather couch. Placing her coffee cup on the end table, she slipped off her shoes. "Hyden and Anderson all tucked in?" Juana yawned, looking as if she meant to head for home, too, very shortly.

"When I left," Harper said, "they were still at it. They've uncovered a second body."

Davis nodded, as if she was not surprised. She looked at the chart, remarked on the Santa Cruz case, then was quiet, studying the comparisons. Joe could see Max's copy clearly, over the chief's left shoulder. Mabel had laid it out in three time periods, giving not only date and place but the barest facts as well. For Joe, this was far more legible than the computer screen where, too often, the lights bounced and reflected. From the preliminary forensics information on the new grave, some of these cases were way too old.

In two instances, twenty years ago, the suspected abductor had been a father who did not have custody and was never apprehended. Fifteen years ago, a missing Oregon child was later found, washed up from the ocean. The time frame of the other cases, where children hadn't been found, ran in three batches. The oldest three cases were children who had disappeared nearly fifty years ago. That seemed monstrous to Joe, that those cases had not been solved after half a century and, most likely, never would be. Their parents were dead and gone, their siblings growing old.

Seven cases in the Pacific Northwest had occurred between six and eight years ago. That would fit Hyden's guess on this time of death. Those children had lived in an area that ran from Tacoma to Seattle. All had disappeared from schoolyards or from playgrounds near their own schools. None had been found. "Full cases on the way?" Davis asked. Harper nodded.

In the largest group of missing children, the bodies had been found; that was some thirty years ago, again not a match. But the officers knew this case, and read with deep interest, making Joe frown. Looking for some connection? Those deaths had occurred in the L.A. area, from 1971 to 1974. All twelve children were found in 1974. Harper looked up at Davis and Garza. "You knew that Patty Rose's grandson was one of them."

The officers nodded. From the report, the bodies had been buried in the walls of a condemned and boarded-up church that was waiting to be torn down. Four men were subsequently arrested. A Kendall Border and a Craig Vernon of Norwalk, a Harold Timmons of L.A., and an Irving Fenner of Glendale. The children were between the ages of four and seven, all from the greater L.A. area.

Harper said, "Patty's daughter, the little boy's mother, was killed soon afterward in what appeared to be a one-car wreck. Car went over a cliff, up in Canada. No one could ever prove it was other than an accident." Harper had that intense, bird-dog look on his face that rang all kinds of alarms for Joe.

"Craig Vernon, the child's father, got murder one, as did Border. Both were put to death. There was not enough evidence to convict Timmons or Fenner for murder. Timmons got fifteen on circumstantial evidence, Fenner twenty-five, same charge.

"They were members of a small, pseudo-religious cult led by Fenner. They met three or four times a week, without city permission, in the condemned church. Over the years, Patty told me quite a bit.

"Marlie and Craig Vernon had been married about seven years. They both worked in the film industry, Marlie as a secretary, Craig in the script department of MGM. He started staying out late, not telling Marlie where he'd been. She had the usual suspicions, that it was another woman. But then he began to look at and treat their little boy strangely. Asking him a lot of questions. Acting, Patty said, more like the child's psychiatrist than his father. That's the way she put it.

"When children in the L.A. area began to disappear, Marlie grew uneasy. Started putting things together—Craig's actions, the newspaper stories. By the time she grew sufficiently alarmed to do anything, to report Craig, it was too late." Harper shuffled the papers on his desk. "The sitter usually left at five and Craig would be there with the boy until Marlie got home around six-thirty.

"She got home from work on a Friday night, both Craig and the boy were gone. When Craig got home around midnight, she'd already called the police. He said he'd left around four, had to run some errands. Said he left the boy with the sitter, paid her extra to stay late.

"Sitter testified that she'd left at the usual time, that Craig was there, no discussion of her staying later, that nothing had seemed any different than usual." When Harper moved his chair, Joe slipped along the bookcase so he could still see the reports.

"There were five additional cult members who were never tied directly to the murders. Timmons came out in 1990. The cult leader, Fenner, came out on parole in 1997. Two years later he was back inside on a molesting accusation, got out again just a few months ago."

"What *was* the cult?" Davis asked. "Another sick religion like Manson's?"

"Fenner started out as a schoolteacher," Harper said. "Misfit, apparently. Lost his position at several schools, never made tenure. After that he worked as a social worker in a dozen cities under different names, forged credentials. Sure as hell, if we looked at it, we'd find missing children in those areas. And find he was gathering disciples, even then. A pretty sick religion, from what Patty told me. Fenner believed that unusually bright children were put here by the devil. Sent by the devil to destroy the world."

Davis shook her head. "How were they supposed to do that?"

"Take over corporations, political groups. Slowly build up their own rule that would destroy mankind."

"Too many bad trips," Garza said. "Or maybe the bright kids in his classes got the best of him."

Harper shrugged. "He thought if he could rid the world of all the brighter-than-average children, he could bring about universal peace."

Davis looked sickened. She shuffled through the reports, scanning them, then looked up. "Patty Rose testified against Vernon."

Harper nodded. "She didn't like to talk about the trial. It was Marlie's testimony that really incriminated Craig, and, apparently, Fenner. Patty believed Marlie was killed because of her testimony—Patty said her own testimony didn't amount to anything, that she didn't have much to tell." Harper frowned. "Patty never described Fenner to me.

"I never asked her much about that time, just let her talk, vent when she wanted to." He bent to the reports again, as did Davis and Garza. Behind Harper, Joe lay down, drooping his paws over the edge of the shelf. The be-on-the-lookout message would have gone on the computer as soon as Lucinda told Harper about the small man, and would have been read over the radio to officers on patrol. The fact that Fenner hadn't been picked up likely meant he was long gone—if that man was Fenner. And if he did kill Patty, why would he hang around?

This line of thinking was a real long shot. That case was thirty years old. And yet . . .

After a few minutes, Davis rose. "I'll get on the computer, get a description from L.A. Run Timmons and Fenner through NCI, see if there's anything else. The little man Lucinda saw . . . We get a match, that'll give us enough for a warrant." Davis headed out the door, her midnight sleepiness gone, her dark eyes keen.

On the bookshelf, Joe lay thinking. Until ballistics was in, no one was going to know anything about the weapon. Only that Patty had been killed with soft-nosed bullets, probably small caliber, two lodged in the head, one in her throat. With this ammo, there really wasn't much likelihood of identifying the weapon; that lead would spread out like a mushroom. The officers had found no casings. Curling deeper among the books, the tomcat closed his eyes, as if set for a long nap. He could hear

Juana Davis down the hall in her office, talking. Maybe on the phone to NCI? Sometimes Davis liked to place a call rather than go through the computer. As Harper and Garza rose, moving toward the door, the chief's phone buzzed. He nodded to Garza to wait.

Half sitting on his desk, Harper picked up. He was just inches from where Joe lay. Joe could hear the deep timbre of the male dispatcher's voice—Mabel had gone home at shift change. "She is?" Harper said. "When did she get in? . . . Tell her . . . Yes, that should be fine. Hold on." He glanced at Garza. "Patty's secretary just landed, she's calling from the terminal. You want to talk with her first thing in the morning?" He handed the phone across to Garza.

Joe listened as Garza was put through to Patty's secretary; the detective made an appointment for seven the next morning. "No, not a bit too early. Yes, the tearoom's fine. At that hour, we'll have it to ourselves." The tearoom of Otter Pine Inn, which wouldn't be open until midafternoon, might offer, Joe thought, a less traumatic environment than Patty's suite or office, where Dorothy had spent so much time with her employer and friend.

"No," Garza said gently into the phone. "Apparently she didn't. She died in just a few seconds, she couldn't have felt pain for more than an instant." They talked for a few moments longer, Garza quiet and attentive, asking about Dorothy's new grandchild. Beside him, Harper waited.

"Tired," Garza said when he'd hung up. "And hurting. Sounded wrung out. She tried to talk about Patty, but she couldn't say much.

"Said her daughter had a long labor, fourteen hours. A little girl, seven pounds. They named her Patty. Patty Rose Street Anderson. Dorothy plans to go back down, help take care of the baby if she can get the preliminary work on Patty's affairs in order, put her assistant in charge."

Harper nodded. "She worked for Patty, what? Over twenty years. Patty was her daughter's godmother." He looked at Garza without expression. "You did check that Dorothy was in L.A.?"

"Talked with the daughter's doctor around dinnertime. Dorothy was there all yesterday, last night, and the night before. He heard her calling her travel agent after she was notified of the murder, making plane reservations. You plan to be there in the morning?"

Harper shook his head. "She'll be more comfortable one-on-one."

A quiet, private interview, Joe thought. Just Detective Garza and Dorothy Street—and one gray tomcat dozing among the shadows.

Garza moved down the hall toward his own office. Harper, turning off the light, headed up the hall for the front door. In the dark behind the two men, Joe Grey dropped from the bookshelves to Harper's desk.

He'd meant to trot on out, but now he paused.

He could hear Harper speak to the dispatcher on his way out, then heard the front door open and close. Lifting a silent paw, Joe knocked the headset off Harper's phone, selected Harper's private line, which didn't go through the switchboard, and with squinched-up paw punched in a number.

The phone rang and rang. Wilma didn't answer. He heard Harper's truck pull out. Cutting off the call, he tried Lucinda.

She answered muzzily, coming out of a deep sleep.

"It's me," he said carefully. "Has Kit come home?"

"Not home yet," Lucinda said after a moment, only slowly realizing it was Joe Grey. "We're worn out." She sounded sad, flat, both discouraged and angry. "The middle of the night, alone in places she shouldn't be. We've walked the streets everywhere, called and called her. Pedric's so hoarse he can hardly talk. We've been into every alley and yard. Where is she, Joe? Why is it that she's always, always into trouble!"

Joe's heart sank at her desolation. But he had to smile, too, at Lucinda's temper. Even if it was only anger to hide her fear and worry. And the old lady was right, Kit did gravitate toward trouble. A brand of trouble that made everyone despair—yet made them love her all the more.

"So headstrong," Lucinda said. "Look for her, Joe. We'll be out again as soon as it's light."

Pushing the headset back onto Harper's phone, Joe thought how simple life had been before the kit arrived in Molena Point with her insatiable curiosity and all four paws taking her where she shouldn't be.

He didn't remind himself that Kit had been a great help to the law in a number of cases. He only remembered that several times she'd nearly gotten herself hurt or killed. Now he told himself she was all right, that she was out there somewhere in the night having a ball while all her friends were sick with distress over her. *Damn cat,* Joe thought, just as on other occasions Clyde or Wilma had thought the same of him and Dulcie.

He left Harper's office and the department stubbornly determined to hit the sidewalks and roofs again to search for Kit—yet certain that if he didn't get another hour's sleep, he'd drop on the spot like a limp cat skin. That short nap on the dispatcher's desk had only left him yawning. Heavy with worry and exhaustion, Joe headed home, dragging his poor, tired paws.

# 16

By one in the morning the wind had scoured the village streets clean, scuttling odd bits of paper and debris against cottage steps and bushes; wind battered the gardens, sucking away dead leaves and bright flowers indiscriminately to pile them against fences and shops and in recessed doorways. Lori, in her concrete lair, listened to the wind slapping against the building and didn't much want to go out, wanted to stay huddled in her cold bed. Even through the thick concrete walls, the wind moaned and cried. She thought about the times she had gone to the shore in the predawn dark, when the wind had swept the sand clean of foot-prints, the prints of humans and dogs, and the little forked prints of birds. All swept away, leaving the sand as smooth as if no living creature had ever passed there. As if she were the only one remaining in an empty world.

When she reached out beneath the blanket to silence her alarm, the damp cold pushed right into her, its icy fingers reaching to her bones. During the night she had thought about going up into the dark library to see if someone might have left a sweater or coat, but it was too cold even to do that. Mama used to say she could feel the cold right to her bones. That was after she got the cancer. She would huddle under the blankets shivering with cold that, she said, was not like any cold she'd ever known.

Lori thought about before Mama got sick, Mama tucking her in under their warm, thick quilts and snuggling close when it was snowing outside. She thought about Mama so hard that she thought she could smell Mama's lavender soap and the scent of her tomato plants on Mama's hands, and the sleepy scent of her nightie. She would never smell those smells again.

But she would *never* go back to Pa. So angry and silent and then shouting and swearing at her and smelling of whiskey. And if he didn't smell of whiskey, he was just real quiet. She never knew if he was mad at her or so mad at someone else that he just had to shout. Maybe mad at the whole world. That's what Mama said, that Pa hated the whole world and Mama didn't know why. After Mama died, when child welfare brought her back to Pa, she thought it had to be better than those foster homes in Greenville but it wasn't. When he got up in the mornings he didn't talk to her; he drank coffee and locked her in the house and told her to eat peanut butter for lunch and not dare to go outside. She'd started school, but Pa made her stop. And their house was hot all the time. No way to open a window, he'd nailed them all shut.

He thought she couldn't open the heavy bolts on the doors but she found a hammer and hid it under her mattress. She could open the back door bolt with that but she was scared he'd catch her, scared to run away. She only went in the backyard in the sunshine. When he got home after work he just sat in his chair, didn't talk to her, and he never read books or the newspaper like when she was little. If he turned on the TV she didn't think he saw or heard it, he just sat there and never moved except to drink whiskey. Except if she did anything he didn't like. Then he yelled at her. He always heated a can of soup for their supper and made her sit at the table with him but he never said a word. If she went near the front or back door, he'd shout. And then one day he came home from work and she was in the backyard playing jacks. She'd forgot how late it was. He was real mad, and that night he found her hammer and he took it and nailed the back door shut. But he didn't find the pliers she'd taken from the garage. The next day he put padlocks on both doors and that night she lay in her bed thinking about what Mama would do.

She had that social worker's phone number. That lady that met her at the airport. Had it in her school notebook but she didn't want to call that woman, she didn't want to go to another foster home. When she knew he was asleep, when she could hear him snoring, she stuffed her clothes and toothbrush in her backpack, crammed in some cans of beans and plums from the kitchen, and a jar of jam and one of peanut butter. She used the pliers to open the kitchen door to the garage, where there were boxes of old, musty clothes from when she and Mama lived there.

She'd dug around real careful because there were spiders. She found the old plaid blanket and a rolled-up sun pad with a cord around it from when Mama used to lie in the sun. Both of them smelled like the boxes of clothes did. And when she was rooting around in the boxes, that was when she found the billfold—that was when everything changed.

That was when she really, really knew she couldn't stay with Pa any longer.

She didn't remember Uncle Hal very well except she didn't like him much. He was always too nice to her. Always asking so many questions about school. "You're finishing the first grade? Most girls your age are just going into kindergarten. Are you doing numbers yet? Do you like that? Do some sums for me, Lori. Or why don't you read to me? Your mama says you can already read real well. Read to me from your little book." She *hated* that. Pa scolded her for being rude to Uncle Hal but she couldn't help it. She was glad when he went away to British Columbia. To spend his days fishing, that's what Pa said.

The morning she found the billfold, she was surprised Uncle Hal would go away without his driver's license and credit cards. British Columbia was in Canada, but was that place so different that he didn't need a license or credit cards? Not likely. His snakeskin belt, that Uncle Hal wore all the time, was with the billfold, and his gold ring shaped like a dragon; she'd never seen him without that ring on his middle finger. She didn't know what made her take them when she found them, but she stuffed them in her backpack. She broke the garage window to get out. Hit it with a shovel then climbed on Pa's work bench and jumped out.

It was after she ran away that she thought about the terrible argument Pa and Uncle Hal had the night before Uncle Hal left. The two of them shouting and swearing so bad that Mama took her out for a walk to get away from the house and they ended up at a late movie. When they got home real late Uncle Hal was gone fishing. And after that, he didn't come over anymore. That was when Pa started being so cross all the time.

Had Pa been looking for her the day she saw him outside the library? She'd never seen him in the library, even if Mama used to work there; he didn't like libraries. Anyway he didn't know about the hidden room. She'd found it when Mama worked upstairs at the checkout desk. She was only six. She came down to the workroom to watch the library assistant, who was in high school, paste pockets for cards in the books. When the assistant went home for lunch and she, Lori, stayed there reading, that was when she found the loose bricks in the wall. She'd taken some of the bricks out and looked in. The hole was big and like a dark cave and smelled of old, dry concrete and mice.

Now, scowling at the silenced alarm clock, she sat up at last in the icy room and reached for her flashlight. In its thin glow she pulled on two sweatshirts and her jacket and then her jeans and jogging shoes, all the time keeping her blanket around her as much as she could, and listening to the wind howl around the library windows.

She didn't eat anything. She was really tired of plums and cold beans. She could choose among plain red beans or navy beans or baked beans. That got old. And the peanut butter and jam were gone; she'd dropped the empty jars in a trash bin at the beach. Now, moving the bricks, stacking them where she could reach them from the other side, she crawled through, then put them back, arranging them carefully. She was getting tired of this, and her hands were scratched raw.

Mama would say she was lucky to have such a cozy place. But Mama would hug her and kiss her and rub on thick hand cream and bring her a nice, thick quilt to make her warm again.

Well, she was acting like a baby. Mama said you did what you had to do. And tonight, right now, she had to do this, had to talk with Genelle Yardley. Find out about Pa so she'd understand. Find out why Pa was so angry.

Pushing the bookcase in front of the bricks, careful to get it exactly where it had stood before, she hurried to the dark basement window that opened to the sidewalk.

Sliding open the glass, she looked up and down the dark street. Molena Point had no streetlights. Only the shop lights, to light the sidewalks real soft. The sky above her was lighter than the village streets. From the stars, she guessed, and from the crooked moon that was smeared by clouds. She couldn't *see* anyone on the street. Climbing out into the concrete well that was lower than the sidewalk, she slid the glass back in place. The lock, the way she had broken it with tools she'd found in the janitor's closet, still looked like it was locked tight. She was proud of the way she'd done that. When she stood up out of the window well, the wind hit her hard, slapping her against the building. Climbing out, she stared up the street toward the hills to the north. She was scared to go way up there alone, she wished Mama could reach down and take her hand.

One morning when she'd slipped out of the library she'd stayed out too long. When she came back someone was already in the workroom. She hid in the bushes all day and was really hungry by nine that night when the library closed. She'd thought of going home and, if Pa's truck was gone, trying to get more food, but she was afraid to try. And that night when she got back the cat was there, the library cat, waiting in the basement workroom for her, and real glad to see her. Dulcie stayed with her all that night, snuggled close. You could talk to a cat and it couldn't repeat a thing. A cat couldn't tell Pa where she was. Dulcie was someone to talk to while she ate her beans and then rolled out her bed and got under the blanket and pulled the lamp close. The cat had curled up on the blanket close to her while she read, then came right up to snuggle in her hair. And Dulcie had lain there beside her cheek looking at the pages, almost like she was reading, too.

Then when she woke up in the morning, the cat was gone. Likely went out its cat door in that librarian's office, Ms. Getz. Strange that a cat would live in the library part of the time. Wouldn't find nothing like that back in Greenville; if Mama saw a sight like that, she'd laugh. Lori could just hear her. *A cat in the library? A library cat? What does it do, honey, read the books to the children?* But everyone loved Dulcie, all the kids wanted to hold Dulcie at story hour.

Mama couldn't make jokes anymore.

Mama couldn't laugh anymore.

Or, Lori thought, hurrying through the dark, midnight village among the little shops with their softly lit windows, *or could* Mama still laugh? Wherever Mama was, could she still laugh and be happy? And if she could, then could Mama see and hear her? Where did you go when you died? She missed Mama so bad, and she missed their home place in Greenville with just the two of them, the little cabin all among the trees; she missed being there with Mama.

She was leaving the shops now and it was darker still. Leaving behind the glow of their windows was like stepping into her basement cave in the middle of the night with no light at all. Hurrying uphill shivering with the wind blowing at her back, she startled at every shadow. There was only a thin moon. She didn't know whether to walk in the middle of the dark street away from the black pools of yards and gardens, or to slip along there where it was darkest and she might not be noticed. Pushing up into the village hills, she prayed hard that she was alone. She kept listening, but she heard no sound behind her except the scurrying sound of trees shaking in the wind. Glancing back every few steps, she saw nothing moving behind her but the faint, whipping shadows of blowing branches—until, over the sound of the wind, a soft and rhythmic hush, hush began.

The steady scuff of soft shoes? Tennis shoes or jogging shoes? She looked around, but saw no one.

But someone was following. Every few steps she could hear a little squeak, as of rubber soles on the concrete.

Glancing back into the shaking, shifting shadows, she stopped a minute, staring.

Then she ran.

He chased her, soft clump clump, squeak. Clump clump, squeak. He drew closer, louder. She dodged and twisted but couldn't get away; he grabbed her, his hands as hard as steel. Jerked her around hard and held her. So small a man, but so strong. She fought and twisted but couldn't move, couldn't move at all, it was like being held by an iron robot. She didn't know anyone was that strong, not to give at all. She tried to knee him where it hurt the most, but he threw her around off balance and tripped her, his foot pulling her leg out so she fell; she couldn't break his grip, tried to twist and kick and couldn't get loose from him. He dragged her down the street, his hand over her mouth, dragged her for blocks, then shoved her into a car, shoved her over, past the steering wheel, and got in. She was going to die. He was going to kill her. But why? What had she done? Or was he just a crazy, what adults called a predator? And that thought turned her truly sick with fear.

# 17

**HURRYING HOME ACROSS THE ROOFTOPS, JOE** Grey peered down past the gutters to the streets below, then studied the rising, falling roofscape once more. Scanning the shingled valleys and peaks around him for the kit, he felt heavy with fear for her—and silently he cursed her. Nearly dead on his paws, his poor cat body wanted more than anything a deep restorative slumber among the warm blankets. A healing snooze until morning and then a nice rich omelet thick with cheese and sardines and kippers. Comfort food as only Clyde could create, heavy with life-giving fat and cholesterol.

Dulcie would say, "How can you think of your belly, with the kit missing?" But he couldn't even search for a flea on his own back without sufficient fuel. Hunting for the kit was stressful at the best of times, and tonight, yawning and worn out, his belly as empty as a deflated balloon, he just wished the damn cat was at home, in bed, safe with Lucinda and Pedric.

But around him the night remained empty. The windswept rooftops were all deserted, no small shadow flicking through the cold blowing dark, not even a bat or a roof rat, the world as deserted as the mountains of the moon. Galloping across the last oak limb above the last narrow street, Joe headed for his own safe roof. Home looked mighty welcome, the new second story with its big windows and solid stone chimney, and Joe's private tower sticking up atop the peak—as fine a sight as a tropical island to a lost sailor. Galloping across the new cedar shakes, loving the feel of them under his paws and their new-wood smell, he slipped through his plastic cat door into his private retreat. Into his window-walled, hexagonal, cushioned aerie—and collapsed exhausted among the pillows.

With the wind rattling outside, he was thankful for the heavy, double-glass windows. Ryan, when she designed his tower, had installed them so Clyde could open them from inside the study simply by climbing the sliding book ladder and reaching up through the cat door. She had no idea that Joe could slide those windows to suit himself, from inside or outside, as his mood dictated.

But all the same, she had created a perfect design for the tomcat. Joe's retreat commanded a superior view of the village rooftops and of the sea beyond. It welcomed the ocean breezes on hot days and the low south sun in winter. And as the mean midsummer sun arced overhead, the generous overhang blocked its hottest rays.

Now, though, the winter rains had lashed wet leaves across his closed windows, dark red and brown leaves sticking as stubbornly as bugs stuck to a car's windshield. Windows sure needed washing, he'd have to speak to Clyde.

After a short restorative rest he rose, padded across the cushions, and had a long drink from his water bowl. Clyde did keep that washed and filled with fresh water every day. Then he pushed through the cat door. Slipping down through the ceiling of the master suite, he paused on the rafter, looking down and around him.

Nothing stirred beneath him. Desk and easy chair and bookshelves stood dark and tranquil. From the master bedroom, he heard only Clyde's snoring. Dropping onto Clyde's desk, barely missing an empty coffee cup, he sniffed it. Colombian with a touch of brandy. The desk was littered with catalogs for automotive parts, and a neat stack of orders stood beside the cup, all filled out and weighted down with the stapler. Since Joe was a kitten, given to tobogganing across desktops on a stack of loose papers, Clyde always left his papers weighted. During Joe's youth, Clyde's orders and correspondence were usually wrinkled or ripped and always embossed with tooth and claw marks that, he had told Clyde recently, turned each into an original and endearing memento. Pity Clyde hadn't saved them. Like those copper-encased baby shoes that little old ladies kept to remind them of when their aging children were babies. Imagine the joy of those trashed automotive orders, pasted in a scrapbook, to recall for Clyde Joe's kittenhood.

Leaping from the desk to the carpet, he crossed the study, past the file cabinets and bookcases, past the squat legs of the leather chair and love seat, and through the open sliding doors into the master bedroom. There he paused before the hearth, soaking up the last warmth from the dying logs. When, yawning, he leaped onto the bed, Clyde groaned, and his snores grew ragged as a buzz saw. Joe pawed at Clyde's cheek, politely keeping his claws in. Clyde jerked from sleep and sat straight up, swearing.

"Can't you go *around* the bed? To your own side? Why did you wake me?" Clyde stared at the clock. "It's one in the morning, Joe! Do you *have* to wake *me* before *you* can sleep? Do you have to ruin my night before you're happy? You want to make sure I see every stain of blood and mud smear you're leaving on the clean sheets?" Clyde's dark hair went every which way. His cheeks and chin were rough with stubble, and there were shadows under his eyes.

"My paws are scrupulously clean. I am not smearing blood or mud on the sheets. I woke you to ask if you'd found the kit. Wilma doesn't answer her phone. Lucinda and Pedric didn't find her. I thought—"

"You think if I'd found her I'd be asleep? You think I wouldn't have called Lucinda? I just got to sleep, Joe. I've *been* looking. Wilma's fine. We're all worn out looking for that damn cat. I just left Wilma. *I just got to sleep after looking all night for the damned cat!*"

"You can't dance the light fantastic until all hours the way you did when you were twenty?"

"You woke me up to assess my physical condition?"

"I woke you to ask if you'd found the kit."

"You woke me because you were hungry!" Clyde stared at him sharply. "Hungry! You can open the refrigerator. You know how to do that. So why wake me! Did it occur to you that I have to get up in the morning? Do you ever once think—"

"Spare me. I've heard it all. You have to get up and go to work. Someone in this family has to make a living. Someone has to pay for the kippers and smoked salmon with which certain cats insist on being provided." Turning his back, Joe pawed his own pillow into the required configuration, kneading it energetically. He was too tired even to go downstairs and eat. Behind him, Clyde turned over. Joe looked around, regarding Clyde's naked back. "You heard about the bodies, the buried bodies?"

Clyde rolled over, glaring. "I know about the graves. I know about the two buried children. I know that Hyden and Anderson are down from Sacramento. I know that they haven't finished digging, that there are tents over the back garden and uniforms guarding the scene. I know that you and Dulcie were tramping all over the crime scene, right in plain sight, which was patently stupid. Have I missed anything? That's not like you, Joe. It's not like Dulcie. What got into you today? You cats have always been—"

"We were *not* tramping all over the crime scene. We were most diligent about staying out of the way, about not contaminating evidence. What do you think we—"

"And I know that earlier tonight you were on the dispatcher's desk pawing through department faxes that are none of your business, and that Mabel Farthy fed you fried chicken that she took carefully off the bones before she gave it to you."

Joe looked at Clyde for a long time before he turned away again and began to wash his paws. He felt Clyde roll over. He debated whether to go downstairs for a snack. That fried chicken seemed days ago. Already Clyde was snoring. Joe sat on his pillow, frowning.

Clyde would know about the graves from Max or one of the detectives or Wilma or Charlie. But Joe hadn't thought Mabel Farthy would have occasion to blab. Why would she tell Clyde about something as casual as a little tête-à-tête that included fried chicken? You couldn't do anything in this village; a cat had no privacy.

The fact that Clyde cared enough about him to *want* to know what he was doing did not excuse Clyde from snooping. Stretching out across his pillow, Joe yawned and, like Clyde, was gone at once into deep, untroubled sleep.

# 18

THE TORTOISESHELL KIT WOKE TO A HARSH beam of light in her face; it brought her straight up, stiff and rigid, hissing and ready to fight, a light swinging in through a grate in the darkness above her, and the sound of a car, too, very close. Backing away, she didn't know where to run, didn't know where she was.

But then she smelled sour dirt, saw the loose dirt piled up, and remembered she'd been digging. Her paws hurt bad and were caked with damp soil and blood. She'd slept in the hole she'd dug; her fur was filled with dirt and smelled of sour dirt. Quickly she scrambled out, listening to the car outside scrunching on gravel, then heard the engine die. Fenner had come back. Now she might get out. Rearing up against the vent, she peered out into the yard, listening.

She couldn't see the car for bushes. She heard the car door open, then slam closed. His footsteps crossed the gravel and started up the steps above her. The front door creaked open. He pounded across the room toward the bed and makeshift kitchen. Abandoning the hole, she scorched through blackness beneath the house, hurting her lacerated paws on the rubble.

Pausing beneath the hole in the bathroom floor, she listened, licking the grit from her hurt pads and washing the caked blood away. Her ears cocked to catch every sound above her, she listened to Irving Fenner move about near the makeshift kitchen. When he paused there, and did not enter the bathroom, she crouched to leap up through the hole. But first she looked for the gun, just to make sure. The space had been empty when she fetched the envelopes. She would not want to tangle with that gun.

But the dank space was still empty. Swinging herself up, she dug all her claws into the rough timber and hung there, then scrambled up beneath the sink.

She heard him in the bedroom dragging something heavy across the room. He was muttering and laughing. Was someone with him? He laughed once, very loud, a crazy cackle, and moved across toward the chair in the corner, that old upholstered chair.

He must have left whatever it was in the chair, because when he moved back across the room he wasn't dragging it. She heard the bed creak, as if he'd sat down. Heard one shoe drop, then the other. She thought he'd lain down, but then he rose again, walking softly now, without his shoes.

He moved to the table; she heard glass clink against glass, then he set something down. In a minute she could smell liquor, its nose-tingling scent drifting in to her. Then softly he moved back to the bed.

His sudden voice came so clearly it shocked her. "You better sleep while you can. Lessons start early. If you do well, I might let you go home." Kit heard a little creak, as if he'd lain down, a thunk as if he'd set something on the floor. Maybe his glass, or a bottle. Who was there with him? If he was drunk, maybe he'd sleep.

She waited a long time. All was silent above her. She heard no sound from the corner, no sound from the bed. Shivering, and so very thirsty and hungry, she thought about water in the sink. Maybe she could turn on a tap—if he slept deeply, and if it was the kind of handle she could move.

At long last, she heard his soft snoring. Pushing out through the cupboard door, she hopped noiselessly to the sink counter and peered into the basin.

Talk about filthy! Stains she didn't want to identify, and grease. Long, black hairs, and short bits of black hair mixed with smears of shaving cream. Enough to make any cat lose her thirst.

But the handle was the lever kind. Pawing at it, she managed a small stream of water. Tilting her head, she drank the running water as best she could, wetting her whiskers and fur, unwilling to drink where the water settled in that mess. When she felt satisfied, she dropped down on silent paws, made sure he was still snoring, then nosed open the bathroom door.

She peered past the table legs to the bed. A faint haze of light from a pale night sky seeped in through the dirty windows. He lay sprawled on top the covers with the bottom part of the spread pulled up over his legs. And there *was* someone else in the room, a warmth, a presence, someone in the chair. A darkness curled up in the dark chair, in the darkest corner.

Encouraged by his steady snoring, she moved warily under the table and past the bed toward the lump in the chair. Sneaking across the room, belly to floor, she thought about the envelopes. If something happened to her, if she never got out, if he woke and caught her, the evidence she'd so carefully hidden would never be found. Who would think to look under the house, inside the vent, to feel around the joists for two brown envelopes jammed up under the floor among the spiderwebs and soggy insulation?

Oh, how sad. Captain Harper and Detective Garza might never have the pictures, and maybe Irving Fenner would go free, would never pay for Patty's death. She had to tell the captain—but if Fenner killed her here, or this unknown person in the chair killed her, the law would never find those pictures and clippings.

The gun was another matter. She didn't know where it was. And likely the law would need a warrant for that. She turned to look back at the bed, wondering if the gun was on him, maybe in his pocket. Then she crept closer to the silent presence in the dim chair—and now she could smell fear, sharp and quick. She could smell the person, too: A child! A little girl! The kit reared up tall, looking. He'd brought a child here? Had kidnapped a child? She could see the child now all huddled up, and as she dropped down and moved toward the chair, she heard a muffled gulp. Then silence. Rising up again on her hind paws, she wanted to whisper, *Don't be afraid.* And she could say nothing.

**Lori hoped it was a cat** creeping across the floor and not some other creature; the way this place smelled it could be a rat or anything. She drew her feet up as best she could, being tied like they were. Outside the dirty windows the sky was milky with clouds but not much light came in around the drawn drapes. The animal drew closer. Had some wild animal got in? Unable to move much, she could only watch, she couldn't kick or fight back. The idea of rats scared her bad. The kids in one of the foster homes said there were rats, and she'd seen big rat droppings. They said if a rat bit you, you died. They'd threatened to catch one and put it in her bed but she'd run away before they did.

It was coming. A silent shadow slipping toward her. She *wouldn't* scream. It reared up, looking at her—and she saw it clearly. A cat. It was only a cat. Letting out her breath, chewing at the tight, dirty handkerchief that bound her mouth, she thought at first it was Dulcie.

But it had a fluffy tail, not smooth like Dulcie's striped tail. Long, dark fur. It leaped to the chair arm, looked right into her face, then dropped into her lap, heavy and bold. And purring.

She couldn't pet it or touch it. It stared at the ropes that bound her arms, and it bent its head over her arm.

It began to chew. To chew the rope. Lori couldn't believe what she was watching, she felt her heart lift in wonderment. The cat had the rope right in its teeth, its teeth pressing against her skin but not hurting her. It chewed ever so carefully. Chewed and gnawed the rope, and all the time its purr rippling and singing really bold. And its furry warmth pressing against her. The cat smelled of sour earth but she didn't care. Watching it gnaw on the rope, she thought of magical animals. In Narnia, in the fairy tales, in "Cinderella." She thought of the mice nibbling the lion's bonds and she wanted to laugh out loud.

But those were stories. That didn't happen in real life.

Except, it was happening.

She wondered if she'd wanted someone to help her so much, she'd made up a dream. She'd been so scared all night since he grabbed her on the hill and tied her up and hoisted her in his car and made her have a lesson. An algebra lesson in the middle of the night in that cold, stinking car, and that was what scared her most. A school lesson, with her tied up. A flashlight and a workbook and he said they were in school and that he was a teacher and his eyes were crazy, all black and strange. A grown man playing school. What did he want? Why did he force her to answer questions? Said that if she answered all of them right, he'd let her go, but she knew he wouldn't—yet she hoped he might. And then he'd brought her here, drunk in the car swigging on that bottle. From the time he'd first caught her, he'd stunk of booze. Well, maybe it was the booze that made him sleep.

And then the cat came.

She still thought maybe she was imagining the cat, that there was no cat, that maybe he'd drugged her, given her a shot when he tied her up and she didn't feel it and she really was imagining the cat.

Except, the cat had chewed nearly through the rope. When she twisted her arm back, the rope gave and flew apart. Swallowing, she jerked her arm free.

Quickly she got the ropes off, around her body, her legs. She was free. She jerked the handkerchief down from her face. Free! She could breathe! The cat stared up at her once and leaped from her lap and went straight to the door.

Lori didn't tell herself she was imagining anything. She slipped to the door shaking so much she could hardly grab the knob. So scared she thought she'd throw up. She turned the dead bolt real careful, turned the doorknob ever so slow, not to make a sound, and eased the door open.

The cat flew out between her feet, and Lori flew out after it. They were free. Free, together. Out in the cold black night free. She was certain, then, that the cat had been trapped in there, too.

Turning, silently she closed the door before the cold breath of night woke him. And they ran, away through the night, Lori on tiptoe on the gravelly rough walk, then faster when she hit the sidewalk. She ran straight back to the hills, but the cat swerved away in the other direction, seemed to know exactly where it wanted to go. How did you thank a cat, when it maybe saved your life? But, oh, she was free. Racing through the empty village and uphill in the cold night, running so hard she was warm, then sweating, she fled as fast as she could toward Genelle Yardley's house. She knew no other living person to go to. She couldn't go back to the library, he knew where she'd been, she was sure of it. She needed to be with someone, she needed a grown-up, bad. Running and running, she knew that what had happened was impossible. But that it *had* happened, that a cat had saved her, that a little cat had chewed her ropes and freed her.

# 19

**In the black predawn that enfolded the** village, Lori slowed her running at last. Her heart was pounding hard, but pounding, now, more from her wild flight than from fear. Down in the village behind her, the courthouse clock struck five-thirty, its chimes wavering like underwater in the gusting wind. She ached with hunger. Mama wouldn't have let her go out in the night without eating and without another sweater. Well, Mama wouldn't have *let* her go out at one o'clock in the morning. No way. Mama would say, "You went out alone in the middle of the night, and look what happened!" But all the same Mama would hold her tight and be thankful she was home.

Except, she wasn't home. She didn't have a home.

She tried not to think about what that man might have done to her, what he meant to do. She'd never heard, not from Mama, not from the kids in foster care, of someone asking school questions before they did bad things to you. Those foster-care people in Greenville, after Mama died, they hadn't told her nothing like that—but then, they hadn't told her anything straight. And then that one welfare woman, she took the money from Mama's purse, Lori saw her take it.

She'd still had almost ten dollars of her own, in her book bag, money that Mama gave her for an allowance. But then in that first home that was like a big jail, they took her book bag, too, and when they gave it back, her money was gone.

She'd pitched a fit, just like Mama would've done. And that made 'em mad, they said she had some kind of mental disorder and shut her in a room by herself for a week. Of course they didn't give her money back. It was five foster homes later that she told welfare she had a pa, and they put her on the plane and sent her home, had a welfare person meet her and take her home to Pa.

She'd been so excited that she'd be with Pa again; and it'd been nice at first, just her and Pa, but then he saw her talking to that man on the street, old Mr. Lummins from the shoe shop. Pa got real mad, told her not to talk to no one. Then he found out she had a man teacher that she liked and he kept asking her questions about him. She didn't know what was wrong with Pa, he started getting real strange again, like before she and Mama left.

When she was little, before she and Mama moved away, Mama was so pale and didn't talk much, and then they moved. Packed up Mama's car and drove for five days to North Carolina where Mama had a friend, Bonnie, they could stay with and Mama went to work in the library in Greenville. After that, Mama was happy, she started to smile again and have fun; they were happy there, just the two of them.

Dawn was coming, the sky getting lighter. She kept looking behind her and listening for his footsteps or the car. She hoped he was dead drunk, out like a light—or better, that he was dead. There was no one on the street. The wind hit hard against her back, pushing her so hard uphill she could almost lean against it. Lights were coming on in a few houses. She wondered how long she'd have to wait until Ms. Yardley woke up. Wondered if she could be rude and ask for something to eat. Maybe old women slept really late and she'd have to hide in the bushes forever.

Was she crazy to come up here and try to ask that old lady questions?

In the yard of a tan frame house, she could see a faucet beside the steps. Crossing to it, she drank from it, getting her shoes wet, then ran because maybe they'd hear water banging in the pipes and come out. She thought she'd never reach Genelle Yardley's number, but then at last there it was. She stood looking up at Ms. Yardley's tall old house. It was the color of pale butter, its walls covered with round shingles like fish scales.

Above the windows were fancy decorations like a fussy old lady wearing lace. Victorian, Mama would say. The house stood close to the street and close to the house on its left. Its yard seemed to be all on the right behind a high wall that was shingled like the house, with fancy stuff on top. Gingerbread. A Victorian house with fish-scale shingles and gingerbread, but not a storybook house. Just strange, and different. Stepping close to the wrought-iron gate, she peered in—and caught her breath.

A faint glow washed across the garden from little lights down low among the flowers, mushroom-shaped lights like houses for tiny people, maybe for *The Borrowers.* Maybe it was, after all, an enchanted place. She wanted to be in there. Safe, all safe like in *The Secret Garden*, behind its locked wall. Far at the back, she could make out pale round boulders lining a little dry streambed. Suddenly, looking in, she felt a ripple down her back, and she spun around.

But there was no one on the street or in the other yards. Well, she'd heard nothing; just a feeling. She could make out no one standing in shadow, no movement, but she was not comfortable there.

Moving quickly, she lifted the wrought-iron latch. She felt a surge of excitement that it wasn't locked. She slid inside, closing the gate behind her. Wishing she *could* lock it, she hurried down the stone walk between flowers and little trees. There were surprises everywhere, flowers among big boulders, benches tucked under the trees. A roofed stone terrace ran along the side of the house, and glass doors looked out on the garden. In one, a light shone. Did Ms. Yardley keep the light on all night? Maybe because she wasn't well? When Mama was so sick, she didn't sleep much except if she took pain pills, then she slept a lot.

The glass door was open, she could see the thin white curtain at the side blowing in and out. Maybe a nurse had come real early. When they took Mama to the hospital and Lori had to go to juvenile, she didn't see Mama anymore. They wouldn't take her to see Mama. Mama died alone. That hurt so bad. Approaching the glass, she paused.

Maybe the old lady was undressed in there, with nurses doing things to her that she didn't want to see.

Maybe she should go away now. Go back to the library before it got light, hide in her cave again. She didn't know what to say to Genelle Yardley, she didn't know how to explain why she'd come.

Except, that old woman had worked for Pa for a long time before he got mean and silent. She would know things about Pa that she, Lori, didn't know, that she needed to know. If she wasn't too sick, maybe Genelle Yardley could help her understand why Pa had turned so mean. She wished her stomach would quit growling. She hoped Ms. Yardley wasn't so sick that *she* was cross and wouldn't talk, like Pa.

Drawing close enough to the glass to just peek in, she saw that the room was empty. The bedclothes thrown back, a wheelchair standing in the corner. She could smell bacon, and syrup warming. That made her stomach really rumble. Was Ms. Yardley in the kitchen eating breakfast? She stood looking in, wondering if she should knock.

"Good morning," a voice said behind her. She spun around.

Down at the end of the terrace, in the shadows, there was a bench, and someone sitting there.

"Good morning," the woman said again. "Have you come for breakfast, child?"

"I . . . I'm looking for Ms. Genelle Yardley."

"I'm Genelle. Come sit down. Cora Lee's cooking pancakes. She'll make more than I can ever eat, she always does."

The thought of pancakes was like a warm light in a dark cold room. Lori approached the woman. Drawing near, she saw the shiny metal tubing of a walker standing beside the bench where she sat, and a cart with an oxygen tank on it, like when Mama was sick. Was this Cora Lee a visiting nurse come to cook Ms. Yardley's breakfast? Mama had had a visiting nurse, arranged for by the welfare people, but that nurse didn't make breakfast, she'd been sour and unpleasant; Lori hadn't liked her any better than that first welfare woman.

"Come, child. Come sit down."

Lori went to sit beside the old lady. She was tall, you could tell that even when she was sitting, tall and very thin. She had dark hair with gray in it, cropped close to her head. Her eyes were so dark they looked black. Her face was lined and sagging and her eyes were red, as if she'd been crying. She was dressed in a pink satin robe and pink slippers. She had a wadded-up tissue in her hand.

Lori remembered her now, from the shop office. But she'd looked stronger then, not so frail. The old woman's mention of pancakes and the smell of bacon cooking made her lick her lips. Ms. Yardley must have been weeping for a long time because there was a really big wad of tissues in the wastebasket beside the bench. Lori sat sideways on the bench, not quite facing her; she didn't like to look at someone who was crying.

"I like to eat early," Ms. Yardley said, tossing the tissue in the wastebasket. "I like to see the dawn come." She looked hard at Lori. "Even this morning, I love the dawn. Especially this morning. You can call me Genelle."

Lori looked at her with interest.

"You must like the morning, too, child, or you wouldn't be out so early. Are you all right? Is something the matter?"

Lori nodded that she was all right, then shook her head. No, nothing was the matter. She thought it funny that Ms. Yardley didn't ask *why* a child was out alone, so early, almost still the middle of the night.

"What is your name?"

"My . . . my name . . ." Lori could see, behind the old lady, a little table set for two, with a white cloth and wicker garden chairs. She listened to the comforting kitchen sounds from inside the house, the clink of plates and the scraping of a spoon on a pan.

The old woman squinted, leaning closer. "Could you be Lori? Lori Reed? Jack Reed's child?"

Lori was so surprised she wanted to leap up and run away. "I . . . I'm Lori." How did she know? Did Ms. Yardley remember her? She'd only been six, a baby. Now Genelle would start asking questions.

But she didn't, she only smiled, and blew her nose, which was already red from blowing. "I'm sorry about the tears. A dear friend has died. But surely that isn't why you have come?"

"Oh," Lori said, embarrassed. "No, it isn't. I'm sorry."

"I'm not weeping for her, she was in her eighties. Though it was an ugly, terrible death. I'm weeping for me because I'll miss her."

Lori didn't know what to say. She didn't really know how to think about people dying. It was hard enough to think about Mama. She didn't know *what* to think about dying. Grown-up talk about death made an emptiness come in her. "It's a nice garden," she said. "It's like *The Secret Garden.*" Probably this old woman had never heard of *The Secret Garden.*

But Genelle's face lit right up. Her wrinkles deepened into a smile and her eyes brightened. "That's exactly what it's like! That's what I meant it to be when I planned this garden, when I had the wall built. A secret garden. You're a reader, child."

"I love *The Secret Garden*, I almost know it by heart. And have you read the Narnia books?"

"Oh, many times. I still read them every few years. I almost know *them* by heart! Sometimes Aslan comforts me as no formal religion could ever do." The old woman laughed. "I decided long ago that when I die, that's the first place I'll go. To sail with Reepicheep into Aslan's country and on, 'beyond the end of the world.'"

"Through the water lilies," Lori whispered, enchanted. "In a little coracle among the water lilies."

"Exactly. 'Where the waves grow sweet, there is the utter east.'" Reaching, Genelle took Lori's hand. "Why *are* you out so early? I'll tell Cora Lee to set another place." She seemed not to expect an answer. Or maybe she'd forgotten her question. Lori remained quiet.

"There's a little cat farther up in the garden," Genelle said. "Do you see her? How intently she's watching us. Up by the wall, among those white flowers." Genelle pointed up among the round boulders.

Lori looked up the garden. In the first faint gleam of dawn, she could see a cat crouched among the shadowed rocks, a dark silhouette that at first had seemed only another shadow. It was definitely a cat, looking down at them. It made her think of the library cat. But Dulcie wouldn't be way up here. There were cats all over the village, lots of cats.

"I used to have cats," Genelle said, "I'd always had cats until my Melody died. When Melody went, I grieved so. I never let another cat into my life, not ever." She reached for another tissue, but she wasn't crying now. "I remember that you used to go to the library with your mother when you were little; you learned to read long before kindergarten. I used to tell stories to the children on Saturdays; do you remember? You used to come to listen, you were always there for Saturday-morning stories, curled up in a corner of the window seat."

Lori remembered those story hours, sitting snug with the other children all among the cushions. How could she have forgotten that Genelle Yardley was the storyteller? Ms. Yardley *mustn't* tell Pa that she was here.

But better she tell Pa than that horrible little man with his rope and scary questions. The memory of his hands snatching her and hurting her, the feel of the rope tight around her; being unable to move or get out of that place filled her again. Afraid she would die there; a drowning, falling emptiness, with no one to cling to.

Genelle squeezed Lori's hand. "I'm sorry about your mama; I read it in the paper. I supposed you'd come back after she died, come to live with Jack."

Shaken, Lori nodded.

"It's hard to talk about death. My friend Patty wasn't young, and she'd made a good life. But your mama was so young. She went before her time, and that was very hard for you." Genelle touched Lori's chin, lifting her face so their eyes met. "Death is not the end, child."

Lori just looked at her. She didn't know what to say. She squeezed Genelle's hand. "The stories you used to read to us in the library, they were good stories. I liked Bran and the Celtic kings."

Genelle smiled. "You remember the correct way to say Celtic. I hear Cora Lee coming with breakfast; she'll be happy that we have company." Reaching for her walker and pulling it to her, the old woman rose unsteadily, leaning into the metal cage. Lori wanted to steady it as she had for Mama, but the old woman seemed so self-sufficient that she was shy about offering help. And the old woman moved slowly to the table.

"Cora Lee lives down the street," Genelle said as she swung herself from the walker into the wicker chair, shoving the walker aside. "She's my neighbor, one of the four ladies who come to help me out. They've been very kind." She hadn't touched her oxygen cart. Mama, when she was so sick, if she got the least bit excited she had to put on the oxygen mask. "Cora Lee's a singer, she's with our Little Theater. She's quite wonderful."

Cora Lee appeared on the terrace carrying a tray. The smell of breakfast, of bacon and pancakes and syrup, wrapped around Lori like warm arms. Made her long for Mama and for their little pine kitchen in Greenville where they'd been so cozy. Lori knew Cora Lee, too, knew this tall woman, knew her from the library when she, Lori, was little. She was the first lady with darker skin that Lori had ever seen; she used to come in the reference room and talk with Mama. She was so beautiful with her close-cropped curly black hair and her dusky complexion, with her creamy silk dresses and long legs. Lori hoped Cora Lee wouldn't remember her. She kept very quiet, and she breathed easier again when Cora Lee went back to the kitchen for another plate and silverware and a glass of milk.

"When I die," Genelle said, "I'm leaving the household things to Cora Lee and her three friends to help pay for their new home. Oh, they know about it, it's no secret."

Lori squirmed and stared at her hands.

"Child, one can talk about death. Death is a natural thing. At my age, I have a special license to talk about anything I choose—I can say what I wish!"

That made Lori smile.

"I figure if the four ladies have an estate sale of my things, they can clean up. There are some fine old antiques and paintings, and my jewelry. The house and some other property I own go to the library. I have no one else." Genelle looked at her, gently amused. "I'm quite matter-of-fact about death, it doesn't scare me anymore. Now I'm more curious than afraid. Like Reepicheep, I keep wondering what exactly does come next. What that world will be like."

"*Does* something come next?" Lori whispered. "How can you know that? How could anyone be sure?"

Cora Lee sat down at the table where she could see the garden, and served Genelle and Lori's plates from a huge stack of pancakes. She took two small cakes for herself, passed the bacon around, and poured two cups of coffee.

"You can't doubt that there's more after this life?" Genelle said softly to Lori. "Sometimes, don't you sense your mother nearby?"

"Maybe," Lori whispered, glancing uneasily at Cora Lee. "I want to."

Genelle put sugar and cream in her coffee, looking over at Lori as casually as if they were talking about the weather. "Someone once said that this world is a nursery for souls."

"Like school lessons?" Lori said with dismay.

Genelle laughed, and slathered butter on her pancakes. "No, I don't think of it like that." Lori had already buttered her pancakes and poured on syrup; she tried to eat slowly, but they were so good. She couldn't get them and the hot crisp bacon down fast enough. "I think we just dive into this world," Genelle said, "and start swimming—among all its splendor and its pain. That we make the best strokes we can, swim the best we can. That we make a little glory around us, or we don't. Does that make any sense to you?"

Lori nodded, chewing. She wasn't sure. A picture came in her head of Mama diving down through green water to be with her, but then turning and flying away again too soon. Genelle looked up at Cora Lee. "You look tired, my dear."

Cora Lee nodded. "I guess we're both tired, grieving for Patty. Did you sleep at all?"

"Yes, my dear. I slept. My grieving is partly a celebration of

Patty's life and what she did. It . . . it's the shock of how she died that's so hard."

Cora Lee nodded.

"But you did not sleep well," Genelle said.

"There . . . there was . . . some excitement at our place. We were up late." Cora Lee's voice was soft as velvet. Instead of saying more, she opened the morning paper that she had brought on the breakfast tray and handed it to Genelle.

Large on the front page was the picture of a skull and part of a skeleton. A man in a white coat knelt over the small bones half buried in the dirt with weeds growing around them. The bones of a child. Shivering, Lori rose and stood behind Genelle where she could read over her shoulder.

> The grave of a child was discovered yesterday at 2792 Willow Lane, when Cora Lee French, one of the four owners, was digging weeds in the back garden. Another resident, Mavity Flowers, was also present, along with the police chief's wife, Charlie Harper. When Ms. French uncovered the child's small hand . . .

The picture of the child's skeleton shocked Lori so that she backed away. Cora Lee reached to take her hand. "It scared me," Cora Lee said. "Reminded me of something that happened when I was a little girl. The police came—Captain Harper and both detectives and then the coroner. And later a forensic anthropologist. But the paper says that." Cora Lee did not talk down to Lori, like in juvenile hall where some of the case workers had talked down to her because she was twelve. Like if you weren't grown up, you couldn't understand anything.

> The identity of the child is not known, nor has the cause or date of death yet been determined. The child has a wound in the skull. Police have cordoned off the area and guards are

> posted. They request that residents stay away. Forensic anthropologist Dr. Alan Hyden has . . .

Lori read with more interest, her fear subsiding. No one knew how old the body was, or if it was a boy or a girl. Couldn't they tell? The child was about nine, *Younger than me*, Lori thought. The police and anthropologists were still digging, as if there might be more bodies, when the paper went to press. As she read, Lori glanced up the garden at the cat among the boulders. It was still watching them, staring so hard that it almost seemed to be listening. And it *did* look like Dulcie. Same black, curving stripes, same tilt of its head. Beside Lori, Genelle watched the cat, too. When Lori thought about dead children, she thought about throwaway children in the foster homes. That was what the cook in juvenile called them, throwaway children that no one wanted. She watched Genelle pull her oxygen mask to her, and breathe deeply. She didn't realize she was pressing against the old lady until she felt Genelle's arm around her. She hoped she wouldn't be afraid to walk back down the hill to the library now, after seeing that picture.

She'd be safe once she was inside, though. He wouldn't dare come in there after her, would he? Had *he* killed that child, years ago? How long had that body been there? When she went into the library, if she put the screws back in the window lock, maybe he couldn't get in. The rest of the library was locked tight. When she looked up, Cora Lee was watching her almost as if she knew what Lori was thinking—and as if she really cared.

# 20

INSISTENT FINGERS OF ICY DAWN WIND CREPT through the thinnest crack beneath the closed tearoom door, and across the pine floor, and rattled the windows; but bright flames snapped on the stone hearth, pressing back the dark, reflecting across the little table that was set before the fireplace. The welcome blaze warmed the faces of Detective Garza and dark-haired Dorothy Street, and warmed the gray tomcat, too, where he crouched above them, unseen, atop the tallest china cabinet. Firelight danced across the brightly flowered curtains and braided rugs, across the hand-rubbed blue walls and the flowery-papered walls, turning the small room into a retreat as cozy as a quilted cat basket. The brown wicker tables and wicker chairs gave the tearoom a homey charm that, Joe knew, Dulcie had always loved, an ambience that, until the tomcat had known Dulcie, he would never have thought about. Before both cats' perceptions warped so inexplicably into a vastly wider view of the world, he'd had no eye for beauty, homey or otherwise.

Peering down at the two lone occupants of the quiet tearoom, he commanded, as well, a clear view through the leaded windows to the lighted patio and gardens and across them to the far wing of the inn. To the third-floor windows of the Greenlaws' penthouse. But the kit's bay window remained empty, nothing but cushions leaning against the glass, no dark little shadow to tell him the kit had come home.

Below him, Dallas Garza poured sugar in his coffee, his muscled bulk and square shoulders dwarfing the slight woman. Dorothy Street was maybe in her early forties. As far as Joe could tell, she wore no makeup. She had short, dark hair curling casually around her face as if she had given it a swipe or two with the brush, then let it find its own way. She was delicately built, fine boned. A pretty, athletic-looking woman whose jeans and sweatshirt gave off the cool aroma of salty sea and pine boughs, scents that must have clung to her clothes even during her absence. She looked up when a waiter came through the door of the little kitchen, a thin, gray-haired man bearing a tray of fresh coffee and cinnamon rolls. As he set down the tray, Dorothy laid her hand on his for a moment in a gesture of mutual grieving for Patty. Patty's employees had been more than friends, they had been like family. After a moment, the waiter left, quietly shutting the door, proffering the needed privacy.

Dorothy's eyes were red, and she clutched a damp tissue. A packet of tissues lay in her lap. Garza, beneath his relaxed demeanor, was tense and watchful. The smell of sugar and cinnamon made Joe lick his whiskers. Dorothy took a cinnamon roll and split and buttered it. They had been talking about Dorothy's long friendship with Patty, since Dorothy was a little girl.

"Her daughter, Marlie, used to baby-sit me," Dorothy said, "when she was in college. West L.A. was nicer then." She looked at Dallas intently. "There was a man hanging around the inn, Detective Garza, for a few days before I left. I feel terrible about him, now. That I didn't call you, call the station. Something about him bothered me. Patty was aware of him, and I asked her about him. She said she'd keep an eye on him.

She said nothing more. Left something unsaid, I thought. That wasn't like her, to be less than open with me.

"She said at first that she hadn't seen him. When I pressed her, she said she guessed maybe she had seen him, that she hadn't paid much attention. She wanted to let it drop, didn't want to talk about him. I said nothing more.

"Now I wish I'd checked on him myself. Do you know who he was? Did anyone see him that night? A really small man, like a boy." She cupped her hands around her warm coffee cup. "I guess that's why he didn't really frighten me, because he was so small. I could—if that's the man who shot her, I might have prevented what happened." She looked up at Garza. "She might be alive if I hadn't let that pass."

Garza sat waiting for her to collect herself. At last she leaned forward, still cradling her cup. "After I saw him, I kept wondering about that terrible time in L.A. It was the only time in Patty's life that there was any ugliness. Until now."

Garza was quiet. Not, Joe knew, simply from courtesy, from wanting to give Dorothy time and space. If the interviewer was silent, didn't respond, the interviewee experienced a powerful need to keep talking, a natural compulsion to fill the empty spaces.

"How much do you know about that time in L.A., Detective Garza? About what happened to Patty's grandchild, and then to her daughter?"

"The child's father was convicted for the murder?"

Dorothy nodded. "Yes, and for some of the other Sepulveda church killings." She pushed back her short hair. Despite her healthy good looks, there were smudges under her eyes, and stress lines creased her forehead. "The murders filled the L.A. papers. Patty always found it hard to talk about it. But then sometimes she needed to talk."

Listening to Dorothy's version, Joe glanced out through the window, watching for the kit. Nothing in the third-floor window had changed, except that the sky was growing lighter so that it reflected a silver sheen across the glass. Not only had Patty helped Marlie get out of L.A. after the trial, after Craig Vernon was convicted, but she continued to have Vernon's friends watched. She thought that Craig might send someone to hurt Marlie. She didn't want him to know where Marlie had gone, didn't want anyone snooping around.

"Patty was headed for France, on a short film shoot. When Marlie was safely out of the country, Patty flew on to Paris. She . . . It was all she could do to finish that film, the hardest thing she ever did. Marlie had insisted she go, had convinced her it would look better, might draw off anyone who meant to follow Marlie. They tried to make it look as if Marlie had gone with her mother, a plane reservation in Marlie's name, a double for Marlie, a film stand-in.

"Marlie's little boy had been just six, and so very bright. He . . . I loved that little boy. Those last weeks before . . . before he died, he'd started avoiding his father. Didn't want to be alone with Craig, was nervous and cross with him. That was what first puzzled, then alerted, Marlie."

Dallas poured fresh coffee for them from the carafe the waiter had left.

"That was what had prompted Patty to first hire a private investigator, have Craig followed. That was how they found out about the boarded-up church, the meetings there. The other people who slipped inside, same faces every night. The investigator never did see a child, only adults, but in the preceding weeks, several children had gone missing.

"Patty always felt that if she hadn't had Craig followed, he might not have taken Conner there, that Conner and Marlie might both still be alive, that it all might have turned out differently." Dorothy folded her hands together as if trying to keep them still. She was quiet for a moment, looking at Garza. "Think how that made Patty feel, that she had failed them."

Crouched atop the china cabinet, Joe Grey thought about those murders, and about the small graves in the seniors' backyard. The L.A. children were apparently all exceptionally bright. As were all the missing children in the reports from the Seattle area. But, cases thirty years apart, more than a generation apart, what did that mean? That was stretching for it, to assume that those thirty-year-old L.A. murders could have any connection with the two bodies in the seniors' garden. And yet . . .

"Silly," Dorothy said, "but I had the feeling, even when I was so young, that Fenner wanted those children dead out of some kind of, oh, jealous resentment. Some sick rage that, when I watched him during the trial, I really thought I felt. I went to part of the trial, against my mother's wishes; she thought that was terrible. Well, my feeling was just a child's reaction. He *had* killed Conner, and I loved Conner. The whole thing affected me terribly. I was only about ten, but I had such a sense of evil about those events. I thought, not just from what happened but from watching Fenner, that I was seeing pure, dark evil." She lifted her cup in both hands, looking up at Garza.

Caught in Dorothy Street's description, Joe stared almost unaware across the patio at the empty windows where still no small shadow looked out, no lamp was lit against the dim morning. Above the penthouse the dawn sky was as gray as the stormy sea. When he heard scrabbling on the roof above the tearoom, he thought at first it was leaves or twigs blowing.

This wing of the inn, tearoom, dining room, and kitchens, was just one story, its sloping red tile roof a handy route that the cats often took when crossing the village. When the sound came again, a hard thud, then sharp scrabbling on the tiles, Joe stared hard up at the ceiling. The next moment, he saw through the window a dark small shape race across the garden and up a bougainvillea trellis and in through the Greenlaws' third-floor window. Her fluffy tail lashing, she disappeared inside. Joe's heart was thudding so hard with relief, it felt like kettledrums. She was home. The damn cat was home. He stared around the tearoom searching for a phone, looked off toward the little kitchen pantry trying to remember if he'd ever seen a phone in there. He wanted to call Dulcie, to tell Dulcie.

# 21

**D**ULCIE WAS NOT NEAR ANYONE'S PHONE, SHE was crouched in Genelle Yardley's garden, the wind carrying the smell of bacon to her so powerfully that her pink tongue stuck out, tasting that lovely scent. Peering down from among the boulders, enduring her hunger with what she considered incredible fortitude, she studied the little group on the terrace. The child and the two women had taken forever to finish that lovely feast; and still they lingered, pushing back their empty plates. The morning was brightening, dawn chasing back the shadows, bringing up the bright yellows of the acacia trees and broom bushes so that, in spite of the gray and stormy sky, the garden appeared to be washed with the magic warmth of sunshine. How intently Cora Lee was watching Lori.

Surely Cora Lee was curious about this child who had made such an early visit to Genelle, but her interest seemed far more than that. Cora Lee seemed quite enchanted with the frail, brown-haired child whose dark eyes burned so very big and intense in that pale little face.

Did Cora Lee see herself in Lori? A gangling little girl

adventuring out in the night all alone, as Cora Lee might have done when she was a child? Did Cora Lee see a child filled with her own bold spirit? But a child very frightened now.

Dulcie worried sometimes about Cora Lee. Since her friend had been attacked last year, and hurt so badly that her spleen had to be removed, she had seemed frail indeed. Cora Lee no longer had the stamina and strength that had sustained her when she could work most of the day at waitress jobs, paint stage sets in the evenings and on weekends, found time to rehearse, and at night had belted out wonderful songs in the productions of Molena Point Little Theater.

Watching Cora Lee rise at last to leave, Dulcie supposed that someone else from the seniors' group would come later to clean up the dishes and help Genelle dress for the day. Without the assistance of those four ladies, and of Charlie's cleaning service, Genelle would long ago have moved to a nursing home, an idea she detested. Dulcie wondered if Friends of the Library, and Charlie and Wilma and the older ladies, still meant to have the special tea for Genelle—and if Genelle would feel well enough to attend her own party.

Wilma said it seemed barbaric to enjoy a lovely party in the face of Patty's death. But, she said, it was after all Patty Rose's party; Patty and the volunteer group had planned it and, even from her grave, Patty would pitch a fit if the party was canceled; Wilma was quite certain of that.

As Cora Lee left the terrace and garden, slipping out through the front gate, Genelle glanced up to the back of the garden, not for the first time, and far too intently for Dulcie's comfort. Genelle was watching her.

But why? To Genelle she was only an ordinary cat; the old lady could have no notion that she had followed Lori's scent here to the garden and was listening to every word. She had, heading up through the night for the seniors' house while searching for the kit, stumbled suddenly across Lori's scent. A trail as clear as, to a human, would have been a path of stones. Leaping through the wrought-iron gate into Genelle's garden, she'd had no idea why the child was out in the night. What could the child possibly want badly enough to disturb an old woman in the middle of the night, an old woman dying of lung cancer? Genelle's fatigue was plain to see in her pale color, in her labored breathing and the slow clumsiness of her movements. Several times during breakfast she had turned on her oxygen and held the mask up to her face for a few moments, her body rigid with her distress.

But now down at the gate, Cora Lee was coming back, letting herself in again, hurrying across to the terrace. "Lori?"

Lori watched her apprehensively.

"You don't really want to walk down that hill alone." Cora Lee took Lori's hand. "Have you run away, Lori?"

Lori didn't answer.

"Okay. If we don't ask questions," Cora Lee said, "if we don't pry, will you stay with us? You could come home with me; we have lots of room, and two nice dogs for company."

Lori's cheeks flushed; she looked and looked at Cora Lee, and lifted her hand as if to touch Cora Lee's hand, but she didn't reach out. "I have to go back. All my things are there, I have to go back. I . . . I'll be fine."

Dulcie wanted to race down the garden and shake the child, tell her to go with Cora Lee, tell her this might be her one opportunity to keep herself safe. Why was she so reluctant? What was she afraid of? At times, this morning, fear had seemed to spill out of the child so powerfully . . . and yet she did not want Cora Lee and Genelle to help her.

Surely coming here in the dark seeking out Genelle had not been, in any way, asking for grown-up protection. There was something else involved, Dulcie was sure of it.

"Lori?" Cora Lee said softly. "You can get your things, I'll come with you. You can stay with Genelle or with me."

"I . . . I have to go back. I can't . . . I have a nice place."

Cora Lee looked steadily at Lori. "Then I'll get my car, and take you there when you're ready."

"No, I . . ."

Genelle put her hand on Lori's. "Cora Lee can keep a secret. And so can I. Child, it would be so nice having someone here with me. Someone who cares, to stay with me, read with me. And for you . . . Even if you were to go back, wouldn't it be nice to have someone who knows you're safe, someone who cares about you? Where is it, child? Where are you . . . hiding?"

Lori looked at Genelle for a long time. "The library basement," she whispered at last, so faintly that Dulcie could barely hear her. "A hole in the basement."

But Genelle laughed out loud, a shout of laughter that startled them all. She choked and coughed, and had to have oxygen again, and was still laughing.

When finally she was better, she looked at Lori. "I used to play there, that was my hiding place, that basement. When I was your age and younger. The hiding hole under the alley."

Lori's eyes had widened; she was very still.

"I grew up in that house, Lori. Before it was the library. I used to play in the basement. That little part under the alley was open then, with a door. It was a walkway long ago, even before my time. A walkway for the servants to go back and forth. But how are you getting in? It was all bricked up. Bricked up from both sides. How . . . ?"

"I take the bricks out," Lori said. "In the wall of the library workroom. They were loose, they were just fitted in."

"And you just walk into the library through the front door? And go down and . . . ?"

Lori shook her head. "I go in one of the sidewalk windows." She looked up at the sky, which was now bright silver. "Before it gets light, though. Before the library opens." She shifted nervously.

"I will take you down the hill when you want to go back," Cora Lee said. She looked at her watch. "But it *is* getting light, Lori."

"Sometimes I go in when it's open, then I hang around the children's room."

"If I'm with you, it will be different. We'll get you safe inside. I'll just get my car," Cora Lee said, touching the child's shoulder. "I'll be a few minutes, time to shower and dress properly."

But Cora Lee's answer made Dulcie smile. Cora Lee hadn't said she'd allow Lori to say there, and she hadn't said she wouldn't. Dulcie watched the little scene, wondering. Strange, Lori seemed far more frightened this morning. But maybe it was being so far away from the library, up here in the hills in the dark that had scared her. A journey into a strange neighborhood in the middle of the night would be far more stressful than slipping out to run the shore at dawn.

Down at the table, the child looked very nervous, as if she'd like to disappear before Cora Lee got back. Was she afraid Cora Lee wouldn't let her stay there after all, wouldn't let her return to her cave? Dulcie was fidgeting, herself, shifting from paw to paw with curiosity and with worry.

Lori settled down into her chair as if she had decided to cooperate. She looked as if she burned to ask Genelle something. Something that now, when Cora Lee would so soon return, filled her with anxiety. Genelle remained very still, watching Lori. Dulcie, fascinated, slipped closer.

After a little silence, Lori said, "You worked for my pa."

"Yes, until I retired four years ago. You and your mama had already moved to North Carolina. I imagine you missed him, while you lived there."

Lori didn't answer.

"He was a quiet man." Genelle studied the child. "Or he turned quiet."

Lori looked at her with interest. Then, disconcerted, she

speared the last two pancakes in a frenzy of movement, slathered on butter, and poured on a deep pool of syrup.

"Was he quiet when you were little, when you were together?"

Lori spoke with her mouth full. "He used to laugh and we went to the park and the beach and he played ball with me, helped me build sand castles. He and Mama laughed a lot."

"When did he change?" Genelle said softly.

Watching them, Dulcie slipped closer still, down the garden through the bushes, to pause just above the terrace. Listening, she grew so intent that a beetle crawled across her paw in absolute safety, the tiny morsel totally ignored. When Lori didn't answer her, Genelle said, "I worked for Vincent and Reed for thirty years. At the reception desk, just in front of Jack's office. You used to come in, you and your mama. The three of you would go out to lunch."

Lori nodded. "There was a tall plant in the room, like a tree, next to your desk, and that room had yellow walls, like butter. We always had our lunch at that little cabin place; I liked their spaghetti."

Genelle nodded. "I took Jack's dictation, typed his letters, did the billing. Learned to use the computer when we changed over." The old lady seemed, in her own way, as hesitant as the child. Something unseen was sparking between them, some unspoken truth that made Dulcie's heart pound.

Dulcie knew Vincent and Reed Electrical from seeing their trucks around the village, and because they had done some work for Wilma when she'd enclosed the carport; Jack Reed had put in their electric garage-door opener. He was a tall man, well over six feet, she thought, very thin, and he walked with a twisting limp. He always looked shy, and he was very quiet. He did work for Ryan Flannery Construction sometimes; she'd heard Ryan say he was reliable. Interesting, Dulcie thought, how much a cat could pick up hanging out with humans.

"I was sorry to see your dad's brother leave so suddenly," Genelle said. "I liked Hal, none of us had any idea he'd take off like that. I always wondered if they'd had a falling-out, he and Jack. But it would have to be a very serious matter for two brothers to remain parted for so long."

When Lori didn't answer, Genelle put her arm around the child. "I liked to think of the company as Reed, Reed, and Vincent, that was my private name for it. Your father is a good man, Lori. A gentle, good man. I haven't seen much of Jack since I retired."

"When did he . . . Why did he . . . He wasn't always . . ."

"Angry?" Genelle asked.

"Yes, angry!" Lori said fiercely, her voice bursting out. "Like he hates me."

"He doesn't hate you, how could he hate you? You are his joy. He had pictures of you all over his office; he used to tell little stories about you, how you loved to chase the seagulls, how well you could read before you ever started kindergarten so they put you in first grade, how good you were at arithmetic, years ahead of the other kids."

"It was after Uncle Hal left," Lori said. "After that, Pa was always angry. Like he hated the world."

"After your Uncle Hal left?"

Lori nodded. Genelle took Lori's hand in both of hers. Lori looked up at her as if she wanted to say more, to tell her something she couldn't bring herself to say.

"Do you remember their arguing, Lori? Do you remember anything about why Hal left?"

Lori shook her head quickly. "I was little. After he left, Pa didn't talk much. He didn't want me to go to school either, or go outdoors. That made Mama yell at him that I couldn't be a captive. And then after a long time, we went away."

"Did Hal ever phone your pa, or come back for a visit?"

Lori shook her head. "He was just gone. Before he went

away, he used to always bring me candy. Once when no one else was in the room he wanted me to read to him but Pa came in and was real mad. I never did know why. I didn't do anything wrong. When Uncle Hal went fishing, he brought home tons of fish; we had to eat fish for weeks. Sometimes Mama let me eat in my room with my dolls, made me a jelly sandwich."

"He went fishing in the San Juan Islands," Genelle said. "He used to bring *me* smoked salmon, and I loved that. Jack said that's where he went when he left, back where he went every year.

"He left in September," Genelle said, "the year you were six. Seattle, Tacoma, or Canada, Jack said. He wasn't sure." And still there was something unspoken between Genelle and the child, something Lori was burning to tell the old woman, something she seemed afraid to tell.

Genelle breathed into her oxygen mask for a few moments, then pushed it away. "Now that Cora Lee has gone home, and before Mavity comes, do you want to tell me the rest of it? Tell me what you're holding back?"

Startled, Lori looked at her, very still.

"Why did you run away, Lori? Did Jack hurt you?"

Lori let out a breath, as if letting something hard and hurting escape. "He didn't hurt me, not *that* way. But he didn't talk to me, hardly. And he locked me in. Padlocked the doors and nailed plywood over the windows. And he was so angry all the time. I couldn't stand being shut in; I took some food and got out through the garage window, I broke it with a shovel."

Genelle nodded, as if this was not unusual behavior, as if she would have done the same. "Were you warm enough in the basement? It's cold as sin down there."

Lori nodded.

"How long have you been gone?"

"Ten days."

"You must have planned very well. What did you take to eat?"

"Canned plums, and canned beans," Lori said, making a face. "And peanut butter and jam." She glanced down at her empty plate. "Nothing like this, nothing hot and good."

Genelle looked harder at Lori. "And you came to me to learn why he locked you in?"

She nodded. "He took out the phone, too."

"But he didn't hurt you. Did he touch you in a bad way?"

"No. He never did *that.* I know about that from kids in the homes, they told all that at night when the lights were out."

"What does he do when he comes home from work? Does he go out again?"

"No, he stays in, locks the door, turns on the TV, but I don't think he sees it or hears it. Makes dinner from a can, then lies on his bed in his clothes and stares at the ceiling. He locked me in my room at eight." Her eyes grew huge, and very dark. "Why did he stop loving me? That's what I came to find out."

**FARTHER UP THE GARDEN,** Dulcie licked at a tear. She could observe adult humans who had been maimed or killed and she might not turn a whisker. But to see this child, like a soft little kitten, hurt so in her spirit, that was a terrible thing. What did a child have if her spirit was shattered, if someone destroyed her true and living self?

And yet, Dulcie thought, Lori's spirit seemed in pretty good shape, considering. Look at how the child had taken action on her own, to protect herself. She was taking care of herself very well. Lori was, Dulcie decided, fighting back just fine.

"And what else?" Genelle said, taking Lori's hand in both of hers. "What else is it that so frightens you? That you can't bring yourself to tell me?"

Again Lori was silent, watching Genelle. At last, "The bill-fold," she whispered so softly that Dulcie wasn't sure what she had heard. "Uncle Hal's billfold." The child touched Genelle's hand. “And his belt and ring. I found them in the garage. The ring and belt that he always wore, that he never took off. His billfold that was always in his pocket. That, if he went away to go fishing, he would never leave behind.

“That’s what scared me most,” she said. “That those things of Uncle Hal’s were there in our garage, Pa’s garage, after Uncle Hall disap— After Uncle Hal was gone away.”

# 22

**Leaping in through the third-floor** window that Lucinda had left ajar for her, Kit burrowed among the pillows trying to get warm. She was freezing. She was hungry. Thirsty. *Cold.* Behind her out the window the sky was cold, was the color of ice cubes. Her poor bloody paws were all ice from the rooftops, so cold that every cut burned and ached. She wanted hugs. She wanted soft creamy stuff rubbed on her paws the way Lucinda would do. She wanted to tell Lucinda and Pedric that she was home and what she'd found and what had happened to her; she wanted so many things at once she was ready to explode, but she needed most of all to call Captain Harper.

Call him now. At once. Tell him about the pictures. About the man she had followed and who had captured that child. Tell him everything that raced around in her head, like trapped mice.

But where were Pedric and Lucinda?

She stopped wanting everything and listened. Sniffed to catch fresh scent.

They weren't here? She did not smell coffee brewing in the

little kitchen, and no lights were on, and there was no good breakfast waiting on a little cart by the fireplace. It was usually brought there by dawn because they all three liked to eat early. The room was still cold, so no one had turned the thermostat up the way they always did, even though dawn was brightening. Were Lucinda and Pedric still out looking for her? Had they searched all night? How hard it had been when she heard Lucinda last night calling and calling her and she couldn't cry out.

But then the kit thought when she listened and sniffed again that the apartment didn't quite feel empty. Had her dear old couple come home very late and gone sadly to bed defeated by not having found her, and were now still asleep?

Leaping off the window seat, she fled to the bedroom and stood in the doorway looking. And her pounding heart slowed at sight of the double lump in the bed, at the scent of their sleep and the lovely rhythm of their breathing. She wanted to leap up and wake them, tell them she was all right, tell them she loved them—but maybe she should let them sleep.

With uncommon restraint the kit turned away remembering that Lucinda and Pedric were not young and that sometimes they tired easily and that she had likely worn them right out making them search for her. Reluctantly she returned to the window seat and nosed down among the velvet and brocade, making a little nest in the pillows to let the heat build around her. And she thought about the child and wondered where she had gone, and prayed again very hard that she was all right.

It took only a few minutes until she was warm again, then she leaped to the arm of the easy chair by the phone. Pushing the headset off its cradle, she punched in the number of Max Harper's cell phone. Lucinda was always amazed that she could remember so many numbers. But Kit had trained her wily memory on the ancient Celtic tales, and that delighted both Lucinda and Pedric. Kit had loved those stories when she was very small; they were the only wonder she knew in her miserable life. She had devoured every word the older cats told each other as she listened from the cold outer edges of that swift-clawed, bad-tempered crowd.

Settled down for the night among the garbage cans in some stinking alley, Kit had soaked up those stories as the only sustenance and the only warmth she knew. She had held the magic of those stories to her until they were a part of her and she knew every word, could repeat them all.

The phone rang four times before Captain Harper answered. Kit swallowed. She always found it hard to speak to him. "Captain Harper, the man who killed Patty Rose is staying in a cottage behind a house on Dolores. A brown-shingled house with a weedy yard, just south of Tenth. Peeling paint, his car and two other cars parked back at the end of the gravel drive. He is small, like a boy. His car is an old gray two-door Honda, 9FFL497," Kit said, seeing the license plate in her head like a little picture. She knew Harper would be writing it down.

Was he taping her call? He'd told Wilma once that taping the snitches' calls might be the only way he would ever learn who they were. Wilma had said, "Do you really want to know, Max? Seems to me you have a good thing going. You sure don't want to blow it."

Now, when Harper had been silent for too long, Kit said, "He had pictures of Patty Rose, Captain Harper. When she was young, a star. In every picture, there was a hole in her head like a bullet hole. And he had newspaper pictures of four men including him, so I think his name is Irving Fenner. After Patty was shot, someone ran away down into the parking garage. I think it was him, but I . . ." She couldn't say that the fresh scent of a man on the stairs near Patty went down into the parking garage.

"The pictures are in two brown envelopes, but they're not in the cottage anymore. They're under it. Under the foundation jammed up in the floor joists just inside the front vent."

So far, Harper had said nothing. But she could hear him

breathing. The kit didn't expect him to say anything, and she sure didn't want him to ask questions. But then Harper said, "The cottage behind a brown house on Dolores. South of Tenth. We can retrieve the envelopes by reaching through the vent."

"The vent's on tight, though. Take some tools."

"How did you . . . ?"

"He has a gun, Captain." She started to tell him to look under the bathroom sink, then she knew she couldn't tell him that. He was already wondering how the envelopes got under the house. How could they, when the vents were jammed tight? She had to hope, when they searched the house, that they'd find the murder weapon under the sink but wouldn't find cat hairs clinging to that ragged hole! Or paw prints and spatters of her blood—cat blood. She didn't dare think about a lab report that would show cat blood.

Pushing the phone back on its cradle and leaping to the window seat, she snuggled down, shivering again, trying to get warm again, and looked out at the slowly brightening morning that, despite the hint of coming sun, was all gray winter colors. Why was the light on in the tearoom? It had been burning when she got home.

Who was there this early? Against the dancing firelight, she could see the silhouettes of two figures sitting at a little table; the woman had short hair, but the man was more in shadow. Was that Detective Garza, the broad shoulders, the hint of a square jaw? She watched the firelight shift and leap, reflected across the glass china cupboards—and atop the cupboards, a small, dark shape crouched, intently listening. The kit smiled. She could see the gleam of his white markings, too. Whatever was going on in the tearoom, she would hear about it, hear it in detail from Joe Grey.

She imagined Captain Harper going to retrieve the envelopes, and that warmed her. She thought about the child and was thankful they'd found each other—without her, the child would still be tied up. Without the child, she would still be locked in there, too, with that insane little man. And the little girl—who knew what would have happened to her? She wondered where the child had gone, all alone in the night and so frightened. She prayed he wouldn't go looking for her, prayed she had a place to hide. She wondered, if Irving Fenner found the pictures missing, if he would think the little girl had taken them, and that could make everything worse for the child. From her window she watched an escaped newspaper twist and flap along the street like a live thing, then a flock of blowing leaves skitter; the hastening wind carried scraps of debris dancing and teasing and making her paws twitch—and the wild need to chase sent her leaping down again and racing for the bedroom.

She stopped at the doorway, looking in. The room was dim, the draperies still drawn. Lucinda hated closed draperies during daylight. The two lumps beneath the covers didn't move. Alarmed, Kit leaped up.

But the minute she hit the bed, Lucinda woke with a cry.

"Kit! Oh, Kit!" The old woman grabbed her, hugging her so hard that Kit couldn't breathe. Pedric woke and threw his arms around them both. "*Oh, my,*" Lucinda said. "Oh! So good to have you home. To hold you safe! Where were you? We were all *so worried*. Where have you *been*?"

"I found something," Kit told her. "And then I got trapped in the bathroom and I was afraid he'd come back and find me and I . . ."

Lucinda laughed. "Slow down. You're not making sense." The old lady set Kit down on the bed, and rose, pulling on her robe. "Come on, let's make some coffee, Kit, and warm milk, while Pedric gets dressed."

Sitting on a kitchen chair at the tiny table, in the little bar/kitchen, lapping up warm milk and devouring leftover steak, she told about the man. Listening to the shower running and knowing she would have to tell it all again, and not caring, she told Lucinda about the pictures, the gun, the tied-up child. With the smell of coffee filling the apartment, and Lucinda dressed in her quilted robe with yellow buttercups on it, Kit told her all about the man who had killed Patty and how she'd followed his trail and lost it and found it again, and about the pictures of Patty with the holes in them and how she'd called Captain Harper. When she'd finished, Lucinda hugged and hugged her.

"It was a courageous thing to do, Kit. To chase him like that, to keep on until you found him and then to slip into that cottage behind him. Oh, I do love you." She held Kit away. "And I do worry so about you. It was a courageous, dangerous, foolish thing to do. I'm so very glad you and the child are safe. Without that child . . ." Lucinda wiped at her eyes. "Without the two of you together, neither one alone might have left that place."

Kit felt very warm, deeply content. Tucking her face down in the crook of Lucinda's arm, she pressed against the old lady purring so hard that her reverberating body shook them both. But after a while, Lucinda got up and laid some logs in the fireplace and lit the starter, then carried her coffee to the window seat. Picking up the phone, she called Charlie. "I hope they're awake," she told Kit as the phone rang.

Kit crawled into her lap, listened to three rings, and then Charlie picked up.

"She's home," Lucinda said. "The kit's home."

"Oh, Lucinda. I'm so glad. Tell . . . Tell Pedric I worried all night about her." Lucinda grinned down at Kit. Max must be right there, listening, not guessing at the disguised message meant for Kit. Charlie sounded as if she'd just woken up. They talked for only a few minutes, then Lucinda went out to the veranda to fetch the morning paper.

She spread it out on the coffee table as Kit lay across her lap yawning, watching the fire blaze up. Very soon now, Captain Harper would have the evidence that she hoped would fry

Irving Fenner, fry him good. It was lovely here in their beautiful suite—so different from life when she was a kitten, before she knew that humans' houses were wonderful, when she'd thought that all of life, for a cat, was dirty alleys, mean dogs, broken glass, jagged, empty tin cans, and mean boys with rocks. When she was little, running with that wild clowder of feral cats, she had thought every cat in the world grew up on the street scared and hungry and cold. That was the way life was. The big cats took the only warm sleeping places, and snarled and slashed when you tried to eat. She'd stayed with that wild band because they were the only cats like her, the only speaking cats she knew of. She'd stayed because she was little and alone and they were better protection than nothing. She'd run with them until they found their way to Hellhag Hill. But there she'd discovered Lucinda and Pedric, and life was suddenly all different. Now, as Lucinda read the paper, Kit snuggled closer. "What?" she said, looking up at the thin old lady. "What's so fascinating?"

Lucinda turned the paper so Kit could see. The expression on her face was both sad and fascinated. "You'd better have a look, Kit. I knew this yesterday, but until now, I didn't . . . Not until you told me about the little girl did I think there might be . . . more to the story." Lucinda picked Kit up and held her on her knee so she could see the page better.

**Old Graves Found in Village Garden**

> The graves of two young children have been discovered in the village, the first yesterday morning by Cora Lee French as she dug in the backyard of the home she shares with three other Molena Point women . . .

Kit read the article, and read it again. Yesterday while she was trapped in that house, Captain Harper and the detectives were all looking at the graves of those poor children. Surely Joe

Grey and Dulcie were there, they would have been right in the middle. The article said that no one knew who the children were. It didn't say they'd been murdered, but why else would someone bury them in secret? She looked up at Lucinda. "You knew all about this, while you were out hunting for me, you knew all about the dead children. Could the same man have done it, that Irving Fenner?"

"The man who we think killed Patty? But these bodies aren't new, Kit, they've lain there a long time. Well," she said, "I guess anything's possible."

"How could humans murder little children? That man will burn in hell, Lucinda," Kit said, with no doubt in her mind.

Lucinda stroked Kit until Kit felt a little easier. "You don't think," Lucinda said, "that that killer should be forgiven?"

"No," the kit said, hissing. "I don't imagine that." She looked up intently at Lucinda, at the old woman's wrinkled face and lively blue eyes. "No, Lucinda, I don't think that. Nor do you and Pedric."

# 23

"WHEN PATTY'S DAUGHTER RAN," DALLAS said, "could you tell me more about that?" The tearoom fire had burned low, the pastry plate was empty save for one lone cinnamon roll, the coffee in its thermos getting cold.

"Because Marlie had testified against Craig and Irving Fenner," Dorothy said, "Patty was afraid for her. She got Marlie out of the country, had a driver take her to Vegas. Marlie flew out of there under an assumed name, headed for Canada, for Calgary, where Patty's secretary had arranged for a new car to be waiting, and an apartment and a job. Marlie went to work as a secretary.

"Craig was in prison and would likely be executed. And Irving Fenner was in custody, awaiting trial. But Fenner was so enraged by Patty and Marlie's testimonies, and so vindictive. Patty was convinced he would send someone to find Marlie and try to kill her. Patty didn't worry too much about herself, she always had people around her.

"Everything was fine for about a year. Marlie stayed in Canada, working. Fenner was convicted and serving time. Then one night, when Marlie had taken a weekend to drive to Alberta, her car went over a cliff in the rain. She died in the wreck.

"Some people said she'd committed suicide, that she hadn't been able to deal with life after Craig killed Conner. Patty knew different, she knew her daughter. She was certain that Irving Fenner had had Marlie killed.

"It could never be proved. No witnesses, no evidence that would hold up. When Fenner was released, Patty was more angry that he was free than afraid of him. Her friends convinced her to hire a bodyguard. She finally did; she kept him for about a year, then gave it up. Convinced herself that Fenner had left the state. Another of the group was already out, Harold Timmons. She heard rumors that he stayed in California, but she never found out where."

Dorothy finished her coffee. "I don't know, Detective Garza. I seem to be going on about this and I'm not sure I'm helping. I don't know if those cases are connected to Patty's murder. I just . . ." She snatched a tissue from the pack, a fit of weeping silencing her.

When Dorothy's crying had subsided, Garza rose. She stood up and was pulling on her jacket when Garza's cell phone rang.

He answered, and talked for a moment, growing very still. A slow smile touched his dark eyes. "Hold a minute, Max."

He shook hands with Dorothy and hastily thanked her for her time. "Will you let me know when you're leaving and how I can get in touch?"

"I will." She gave him a watery smile and left the tearoom.

"Okay, Max. I'm in the tearoom, Dorothy just left." Garza sat down at the table and, listening, poured the last of the coffee into his cup and picked up the last cinnamon roll. Above him atop the china cabinet, Joe Grey peered over, his silver ears sharp with interest, his claws silently flexing, every nerve in his tomcat body on alert. Harper had something, something was happening. He wished he could hear Harper's side of the conversation.

Garza smiled. "Yes, I know the cottage, I'll be right there. It takes two of us to collect evidence?" He listened again and shook his head. "Our woman snitch this time. Well, maybe she had a cold. How far in from the vent, did she say? Some of these old foundations—"

He was quiet, then, "I have tools in the car. I'll be there ASAP." Rising, he gulped the last of his coffee, wolfed the cinnamon roll, wiped some sticky sugar from his lips, and headed out. Joe didn't know where Harper was going, but he didn't intend to be far behind. There was no question, Harper's caller had to be either Dulcie or Kit. Very likely the kit, who had just rushed home in such a swivet. He stared across the patio to her third-floor window, but he didn't see her. As he leaped from the china cupboard to the table, he heard Garza's car start, out front. Hitting the cold tile floor, Joe was out of there, pushing open the tearoom door, heading across the patio for the bougainvillea vine that would take him, faster than any stairs, up to the Greenlaw penthouse. Where was Garza headed? Under what house? If Dallas Garza and Max Harper were about to crawl under someone's house, presumably without a search warrant, he sure didn't mean to miss the entertainment.

**DULCIE WATCHED LORI** leave the garden with Cora Lee, the child slipping through the gate as warily as if she expected that any minute someone would snatch her up. Dulcie looked after her, frowning. If Lori was in danger from more than a bad-tempered father, why hadn't she told Genelle and Cora Lee what more was wrong? Probably, Dulcie thought, because the stubborn little kid didn't want anything to do with the police. When they'd gone, Dulcie approached the terrace, watching Genelle Yardley with interest.

Genelle, pushing back the breakfast dishes, had spread out the front page and was reading about the little graves. Something drew Dulcie to the old woman, something about the way Genelle kept looking up the garden at her. Such a knowing look, so secretly amused. Shivering, Dulcie padded nearer, but she stayed beneath the bushes. This woman couldn't know what she was, that wasn't possible. But yet . . . Why that secret smile? Too many people knew already. Though those who shared the cats' secret in friendship would never tell, the more who knew, the more chance there was of some unintended slip.

Genelle looked up from the paper, her faded blue eyes widening. Dulcie remained very still as the old woman studied her where she crouched in the bushes, looking straight into her eyes.

"Good morning," Genelle said in much the same way she had greeted Lori.

Dulcie's heart dropped. Warily she trotted across the bricks and smiled up at Genelle, as friendly as any neighborhood cat, waving her tail as if longing for a nice gentle pet and a bit of breakfast.

"You are Wilma's cat, the library cat. I think your name is Dulcie?"

Dulcie purred and rolled over, waving her tail, pretending that she was used to people talking to her, carrying on one-sided conversations.

"You can speak to me, Dulcie. I know who you are." The old woman smiled gently. "And I know what you are. You live with Wilma Getz. Oh, Wilma doesn't know that I know the whole story. Wilma took you home from this garden, Dulcie, when you were very small."

Dulcie tried not to stare at her.

"She had no idea what she was getting when she took one of our litter of kittens. Nor did I, I wasn't sure. I only knew that my own dear Melody, your mother, was a very unusual cat, that she could speak," Genelle said softly.

"Melody and I had many talks here in this garden, many long and fascinating discussions in this house. She was with me until she died," Genelle said sadly.

Dulcie looked at the old woman as blankly as she could manage, dropping her ears as if she were shy or frightened. Genelle paid no attention; she kept talking.

"I didn't know how her one litter of kittens would turn out, nor did Melody herself. She said that none of her six brothers and sisters could speak." Genelle reached out to stroke Dulcie, but Dulcie backed away.

"This morning," Genelle said, "you came here following the child. I gather you've been watching her." She put out her hand, toward Dulcie. "I am terminal, my dear. In a few months, I'll be dead. Your secret will be dead with me. I will tell no one."

Dulcie could only watch her. Her heart skipped, as if it had lost all sense of timing.

"Melody had five kittens, three orange, one calico, and you, a dark, striped tabby. You were the tiniest. The others kept pushing you out. They didn't seem to like you, didn't want you to eat. I guess all young animals are that way with the runt, it's the way of nature. But something about you . . ." Genelle shook her head. "Melody would carry you up onto an easy chair and feed you alone, so you did indeed thrive. But she worried over you."

Genelle looked at Dulcie. "I kept the other four kittens. Neither I nor Melody knew—there was no way to guess—if you would be the most likely to speak. We thought you would, but we didn't know. And I . . . I thought even then that I wasn't well. We found the best home for you, where we could keep an eye on you. We chose Wilma with great care, but I told Wilma nothing.

"Your calico sister died when she was just six weeks old, a twisted intestine, the vet said. But you grew healthy, a wild, strong kitten. It was not until you began to steal your neighbors' lingerie, when you were little, that I felt sure you were more than you appeared to be. Melody did that when she was small; she so loved beautiful things."

Dulcie dared not speak. She couldn't stop shivering.

"Melody was not a young cat. She seemed determined to have that one litter. She died four months later." Genelle's voice shook. "It was . . . it was as if she knew. She wanted to produce at least one kitten like herself.

"And you were the only one." Genelle smiled and reached down to touch the peach-toned markings on Dulcie's nose and ears. "A bit of the Irish orange," she said with a fond, faraway look. "The other three cats are with me, orange tabbies, you've surely seen them around the village; they are dear, sweet cats, but they are normal, ordinary cats, not like you and Melody." Genelle rose, gripped her walker, and slowly crossed the terrace to the edge of the garden.

"It has taken a lot of self-control not to speak to you until now, my dear, nor to speak about you with Wilma. I thought that best. You have both guarded your secret as well as you are able, considering your busy life—you and your two friends," Genelle said softly.

Dulcie swallowed and backed away, slipping into the bushes again. That Genelle was aware of her ability was one thing. That Genelle knew about Joe Grey and Kit deeply alarmed her.

"Nor will I speak of them, to anyone," Genelle assured her, peering after her into the bushes. "I promise that. But I have enjoyed observing from afar the adventures I imagine for you three. From bits of news, my dear. From glimpsing you in the village, very busy and intent. From news clips about the crimes that have occurred in the village, and from the anonymous tips the police often receive. I know a couple of officers in the department, Dulcie. And I know a reporter or two. I hear things, things no one else would put together." The old woman laughed and winked. "And more power to you, my dear. The three of you are remarkable."

This was too much. Crouching deeper among the bushes, Dulcie was filled with feelings of chagrin, of betrayal.

She had no reason to feel that way. Indeed, she felt she could trust Genelle Yardley. But for a stranger to know about them, to have known all this time, to have been watching them . . . To Dulcie, the implications were immense and terrifying.

Stepping away from the walker but still holding on to it, Genelle knelt at the edge of the bushes, an exercise that took a great effort. "Please come out, please indulge an old woman. Mavity won't be here for another hour. Please come out so we can talk? And help me decide what to do about Lori?"

And Dulcie could do nothing else. She came out at last, her ears back, her tail switching.

"I don't mean to tell anyone about Lori," Genelle said. "It's very clear that she's afraid. But it seems to me that the child must go to the police on her own. Before her father knows she has the billfold." She looked hard at Dulcie. "Have you thought about what that billfold could mean?" Genelle rose, the effort so tiring that Dulcie longed to help balance her. Clutching at her walker, she turned away, making for her chair. Dulcie came out from the bushes then and leaped into the chair opposite, eyeing the last crumbs of bacon; crumbs were all that Lori had left.

Pushing the plate across to her, Genelle said, "It would be far safer for Lori if she'd go to the police now, of her own volition. Before Jack Reed knows what the child suspects, and that she has what could be damning evidence."

AS THE SUN LIFTED above the eastern hills, and Dallas Garza hurried away from Otter Pine Inn to meet Max Harper, Joe Grey leaped into the bougainvillea vine, heading up to the kit's window. He wanted some answers. He halted halfway up, as, below him, Lucinda and Pedric emerged from the stairs into the gardens. Looking down, he watched the kit race ahead of them, all fizz and ginger and switching tail. The old couple, in the first cold light of dawn, was headed for the dining patio. Quickly Joe dropped down again to the bricks and followed.

No one else was out there at the garden tables; it was too early and too cold. Bundled in fleece coats and sheepskin boots and caps as if they were at the north pole, the Greenlaws seemed fixed on indulging their young runaway with a welcome-home patio breakfast. Even beneath the patio heaters, and seated beside the fire pit where flames danced, they had to be freezing. The moment they were seated beside the warming blaze, Joe trotted over and, before Kit could leap into a chair, he pressed against her, nosing her toward the far end of the garden, away where nosy waiters wouldn't overhear.

She followed him, scowling, but wide eyed with questions, glancing back at Lucinda and Pedric with a be-back-in-a-minute look. Lucinda and Pedric, watching the little drama, could say nothing, observed by an approaching waiter.

Deep beneath a pyracantha bush whose branches hung heavy with red berries, Joe stood looking at the kit. "I see you got home."

She hung her head, ashamed that she had worried everyone, but then smiled with smug delight. "I found him, Joe, I found the man who killed Patty and I went in his old dirty cottage and watched him and saw his car, too, and all the garbage like he's been there awhile and I—"

"Will you slow down, Kit? Tell me where. Does Harper know? Did you . . . ?"

"I called Captain Harper just now from upstairs and told him it was an old gray Honda two-door all dented and the license number and told him where to find the newspaper clippings and the pictures of Patty and I put them where he can get them without a warrant like you told me and I told him about the gun but I don't know where that is except he might have it on him and I—"

"Kit!"

She tried to slow down, tried to be coherent. She told Joe what she had found and where, and the names of the four men in the clipping, and where she had hidden the envelopes. "Captain Harper said he was on his way."

Joe nodded. "So is Garza, he just left the tearoom." He was about to race away, when she raised a paw.

"The worst thing was the little girl . . ."

Joe stiffened.

"I chewed her ropes through like in that fairy tale and we got out all right and she ran and—"

"*What* little girl!"

"*I* don't know, Joe. I don't know her name, I couldn't *talk* to her. She got out with me, *she* opened the door, I couldn't, and we both ran in different directions."

"How old was she?"

Kit thought about this. "Maybe eleven or twelve, I guess. Brown hair."

"*Lori?*" Had this guy gone into the library and found Lori? Was this the guy she was hiding from? Patty Rose's killer, and not her own father? He didn't know what to think; this wasn't making sense. He nosed the kit's ear by way of thanks, and glanced toward the patio and the Greenlaws' table. "Your breakfast's getting cold," he said softly. And as Kit raced away to her eggs Benedict, Joe scorched out of the patio fast, his own stomach as empty as a drum. Taking to the rooftops, he headed across the village. His own breakfast seemed eons ago. Well before dawn, Clyde had fixed him a memorable omelet, tossing in some leftover salami and a slice of goat cheese, a delicacy to which Ryan had introduced their household—one of the benefits of a new woman in Clyde's life.

Joe was beyond suggesting that Clyde marry his current romantic interest. He'd done that with Charlie, and Charlie ended up with Max, though they were all three still the best of friends. But Joe was through with matchmaking, Clyde and Ryan would have to work out their own scenario. Which was at present more platonic than wildly romantic, but he guessed they had their moments. Just in case, Joe was careful about returning home late at night through his rooftop cat door.

He came down from the roofs just up the block from the brown-shingled cottage Kit had described. It stood back from the street behind the two-story house and some crowding pine and cypress trees. Joe had wondered about that house; who would let even a rental look so decrepit in this high-priced market? The place had a lurking, secretive air, as unappealing as the set for an old horror film. Max Harper's Chevy pickup was parked at the curb. Across the street, facing the other direction, was Dallas Garza's Ford. Joe paused beneath a tangle of overgrown oleander bushes, observing a scene that made him smile.

# 24

Joe approached the cottage behind the old house, concealed beneath overgrown bushes, padding through a morass of rotting leaves. The whole yard smelled of rot and mildew. Keeping out of sight, he watched Max Harper, standing on the cottage porch talking with a hefty woman in a red muumuu. Landlady. She was rattling off a list of complaints about her tenant. On the gravelly parking space before the cottage stood a black Ford sedan and a blue Plymouth. He could smell the faintest whiff of exhaust, as if a car had left within the past hour. The front door stood open. The landlady was so frowsy she matched the cottage exactly, and matched what Joe could see of the grim interior. He'd seen her around the village. Had Harper gotten a search warrant, just on Kit's phone tip? That would be unusual.

But if the landlady invited him inside, that was another matter; he could search then. And indeed, in a moment Dallas Garza emerged from within the cottage as if perhaps he had finished a search. Joe listened to Harper wrap up the conversation, to the effect that if her tenant returned she was to call him, and that he had just a little more checking to do; the old doll seemed fine with that. Waddling down the steps, she headed for the larger house and disappeared inside. Joe watched Harper and Garza walk along the foundation and kneel before the first of two ventilation grids.

Producing an electric drill that he'd shoved into his belt beside his black holstered radio, Garza removed four screws from the grill and pulled off the rusty grid, revealing a hole large enough for a small terrier. The detective looked up at Max. Max Harper smiled. "Be my guest."

Garza gave Harper a patient look, and pulled on a pair of worn work gloves. Lying down on his belly in the mud and wet leaves, he reached in through the hole. Pushing in and twisting, he felt around blindly, probably even with the gloves, praying he didn't disturb one of the more deadly varieties of poisonous spiders for which California was known. The bite of a brown recluse would dissolve the flesh from within like ice melting in a warm kitchen.

"Not a damn thing," he grumbled, adding a Spanish expletive. Groping farther into the darkness for whatever evidence the phantom snitch had found or deposited, he twisted onto his back to explore above him among the floor joists. Harper, standing over him, was highly entertained—as was Joe Grey. As Garza searched, he had to be wondering about protruding rusty nails as well as unfriendly spiders. After some moments, he withdrew from the underpinnings of the house and stood up. Scowling at Harper, he moved to the other vent and knelt again.

Removing the second grid from its frame, he lay down again reaching, groping and searching up among the floor joists until suddenly he shot out of the hole.

Swinging to a standing position, grinning, he clutched in his gloved hands a pair of large brown envelopes. Handing them to Harper, he was just replacing and screwing down the vent grids when Harper's radio squawked. Max picked up and listened.

Then, "No, just watch it. Put a man on it. With luck, maybe he'll come back for it." He glanced at Garza. "The Honda's parked up on Drake, behind a vacant house."

Garza looked pleased. Harper nodded toward his truck, perhaps not wanting to attract further attention from the neighbors and morning joggers. And as Garza followed the chief to his Chevy pickup, Joe, in a swift but maybe foolish move, sped behind them.

At the moment they opened their doors and thus were turned away, he slipped up like a flying gray shadow into the open truck bed. Onto the cold, hard metal floor. Sliding between an old saddle blanket and a fifty-pound bag of dog kibble, Joe braced himself as Harper started the engine. Likely the chief was heading back to the station, to his office where they could examine the contents with added privacy. Very good. In Harper's comfortable office, a cat wouldn't freeze his tail. The sea wind scudding into the truck bed felt like an arctic blizzard.

Getting soft, Joe thought as Harper eased the truck around the corner and down a block. But then the chief parked again, in a red zone beneath the branches of a Monterey pine. Joe, hearing him rattle one of the envelopes, wondered if he dared rear up for a look through the back window.

Sure he could. Right in line with the rearview mirror.

Glancing overhead at the spreading branches of the pine, he slipped up real quiet onto the metal roof of the cab, keeping away from the back window, out of sight behind the wide metal post, then up onto an overhanging branch. Its foliage was thick and concealing. But the branch was so limber that it rocked and swayed under his weight, dragging across the door frame and roof, alerting the two cops like a gunshot. Garza stuck his head out, glaring up into the tree and up and down the sidewalk. Cops never rode with their windows up, even in freezing weather. Their inferior human hearing, impeded by the thick glass, might block all manner of sounds they should hear, from a faint cry for help to a distant car crash to a muffled gunshot. Perched precariously above Garza, Joe was barely out of sight as the detective scanned the tree. Squeezing his eyes shut and tucking his white nose down, he was perched so unsteadily that he thought any minute he'd be forced to take a flying leap. He held his breath until Garza ducked back inside the cab.

"Probably a squirrel."

Harper grunted, opened the envelopes, and produced a third brown envelope from behind the seat. Removing from this a sheaf of clear plastic folders, he opened the first envelope and carefully shook out its contents. Using tweezers, he inserted each piece of paper into a plastic folder before they examined it.

From among the pine needles, the tomcat peered down at the old, yellowed newspaper clippings of strangers, and at the brighter magazine pictures and photographs of Patty Rose. Fidgeting, Joe edged this way and that on the branch, trying to see better. Were they going to go through the entire contents sitting out here in the cold? The officers were silent for some time, passing the plastic sleeves back and forth. The newspaper pages were creased where they'd been folded, and darkly discolored with age. Considering that feline eyesight was superior to that of humans, Joe wondered just how much facial detail the officers were able to discern in those old newspaper photographs. All were of the same four men, though. Three were in profile to the camera, one facing it. It was certainly not a posed shot. In fact, it was so casually candid that it might have been taken without their knowledge. The one man facing the camera full on was a head shorter than the others.

The chief glanced at Garza. "Fenner. Little creep should have burned long ago." Then he smiled. "Fenner turns out to be our man, you can chalk up one more for the snitch."

"Makes you feel pretty lame," Garza said. "Some civilian comes up with this stuff, we don't even know who she is."

"They," Harper said. "I'm pretty sure the guy and the gal

work together. And don't knock it." His thin, sun-lined face was thoughtful. "Weird as it is, so far they've been a hundred percent. So far," he said thoughtfully, "they've produced information that we had no authority to look for. No reason for a warrant. Stuff we might have found farther down the line, or might not. Might never have had cause to search for."

"Some of that stuff," Garza said, "who knows how they knew about it? That's what's weird. That's what gives me the willies."

Harper said nothing more. Above the officers' heads, Joe Grey peered hard at the old, yellowed newspaper. Even in the blurred clipping, Fenner's face looked sour and pinched; not an appealing fellow. After some minutes, Harper said, "Guy on the left, Kendall Border. I remember him from that San Diego case two years before L.A. And Craig Vernon, Patty's son-in-law, he was on death row for three years before he died."

Watching a mouse hole for hours was nothing compared to Joe's tension of the moment. He was so wired with questions that every muscle twitched. Edging closer along the frail branch, he watched Harper tilt the paper to the light.

"Those are the four," Harper said. "The great guru and his disciples." In the truck, the two men crowded shoulder to shoulder, reading, as Joe teetered on the thin branch above them.

"There were eight or nine women in the group," Harper said. "L.A. couldn't make any of them. Guess the men did the dirty work."

Dallas examined the last clipping, and looked up at Harper. "Mighty damned strange the snitch found these; I have way too many questions about this woman."

Max shrugged. "You can get used to anything if it works. "

"So what does she . . . what do they get out of it?"

Max shrugged again. "Ego trip. Moral satisfaction, the thrill of the hunt, who knows? Maybe they're a couple of frustrated cops?"

Garza grinned, shook his head, and let the subject drop. He

opened the truck door. "I'll get on the computer, get started on Fenner; hope L.A. kept good files."

As Garza swung out of the truck and headed up the street, Joe backed up the branch to a more solid perch, and sat thinking. Kit had tracked this guy, all alone. Had made his car, and had surely moved the evidence from inside that shack to where the cops could find it, in case the landlady wasn't home or didn't want to let them in. Fenner was as good as behind bars, Joe thought, thanks to the kit.

It remained to be seen if this might wrap up the other deaths as well, the little unmarked graves. Might. Might not. But plenty was falling into place, making Joe smile. Falling into place as neat as a mouse into waiting claws. Backing down the trunk to the sidewalk, into the stinking exhaust from Harper's pickup as the chief headed for the station, the tomcat took off to find Dulcie. To bring Dulcie up to speed, and then to find and praise the kit—if the little tattercoat wasn't already feeling too high to reach. Knowing Lucinda and Pedric, Kit was probably getting all the extravagant praise she could handle.

# 25

JUANA DAVIS SET THE DELI BAG ON HER DESK, filled her coffeepot, and switched it on. Glancing through a stack of fresh memos and reports, she signed three routine forms requesting information, returned four phone calls, which she kept as brief as possible, signed three requests to the DA. Shoving the rest of the stack aside, she carried the forms and requests up to the dispatcher. Returning to her office, she poured a mug of coffee, added creamer and sugar, and shut the door.

Placing the new stack of faxes on a tilted holder for easy reading, she opened the deli bag and unwrapped her breakfast sandwich. Eating Jolly's bacon, cheese, and egg on sourdough, she studied the more detailed background reports that had just come in on five of the missing children in the Seattle area.

Benjamin Alden was only seven. He had skipped the second grade. The two color pictures of Benjamin showed a freckled, redheaded little boy with a tooth missing in a wide grin. He was so advanced in arithmetic and English that he did not belong in third grade, either, but the school had been reluctant to let him skip another grade so soon, afraid this would create a social misfit. The kid didn't look to Juana like a misfit. Just full of high jinks, maybe. He had the same devilish twinkle as her own boys when they were small.

Benjamin's mother had transferred him to a private Catholic school in Seattle where he could advance at his own speed. She told the investigator that she had never pushed the child, that he ate up arithmetic and English grammar the way other kids did puzzles. Benjamin disappeared from the play yard of his new school around three P.M. during his third week in attendance. School had just let out. The other kids had waited for the bus or for their parents. No one saw Benjamin leave or saw him with anyone. His backpack and school books were on the steps when his mother arrived to pick him up. She searched the school and grounds for him, asked a few children. Drove home again watching the streets, checked the house and neighbors, then called the police. Police waived the requisite time of delay before the child was declared missing. Benjamin was not the first child to disappear that fall.

Officers found the fresh prints of a man's shoes in the woods that bordered the schoolyard, and signs of a struggle where the prints went deeper and were churned up. Police made casts of the prints, including the cast of a partial that turned out to match Benjamin's shoe size.

In the days preceding the disappearance, no one had seen anyone watching or following Benjamin. The child had not seemed disturbed about anything. After his disappearance, there were no phone calls or letters. No communication. Tracking dogs found a trail across the woods, which ended at the street. No one had seen a car parked there. Tire marks were photographed. Police had not turned up any suspects.

Juana finished her breakfast, which now tasted like cardboard, and swilled more coffee. Nancy Barker of Eugene was nine; she was in the fifth grade, two grades ahead of her peers. She excelled in gymnastics and world history. She was the youngest child on the elementary school's history debating team. She had disappeared from a sleep-over with five other girls at approximately two in the morning. Her friends, asleep all around her, heard nothing. No child woke. In the morning, the window was open and Nancy was gone. The girls were to go swimming that morning at a neighborhood pool. Nancy's overnight bag with a change of clothes and her bathing suit was missing. This was found later in an irrigation ditch north of Eugene. All the girls at the sleepover were neighborhood children, all from her school. Her absence was discovered about six A.M.

Police found traces of acepromazine, a tranquilizer used for animals, on her pillow, and on the carpet flecks of grass that matched the lawn. There were no fingerprints other than those of the girls and the sleep-over family. No one saw a car, no neighbors heard or saw anything. No one heard a dog bark. The family dog, who slept in the fenced yard, and three dogs on the same street had been tranquilized. There were no follow-up sightings of the child. There was no request for ransom.

Juana rose to refill her coffee mug. Unusually bright children and no request for ransom. A dangerous nutcase; dangerous, irreparably twisted. If these were the children found in the senior ladies' garden, they had to consider that the killer had lived in or near Molena Point. She sat looking at the reports, wondering. Could he have lived in the house that now belonged to the seniors? She had already been through the old tax records, she had the names of the two previous owners. That took her back twenty years. There was no record of the tenants; most of those rentals were illegal. All such small illegal apartments, termed granny flats, were presumably kept for family members. She planned to talk with the neighbors this morning. Rising, she was headed out, had stopped at the dispatcher's counter when Garza and Harper came in, the chief carrying a couple of full-size brown envelopes and both of them wearing smug grins.

"Come on," Harper told her, and moved down the hall to Garza's office. Davis followed. Garza sat down at his desk and booted up the computer. Davis and Harper stood in the doorway. Both the chief and Dallas were still grinning. Harper said, "Those old L.A. cases, when Patty's grandchild was murdered?"

Juana nodded.

Harper opened the two brown envelopes, shook the contents out on the desk. She looked down at the newspaper clippings, read them, picked up the photographs. Patty, young and smiling. Looked again at the small man in the clippings, then was grinning like the two of them. Like the cat that ate the canary.

"Sick," she said. "Those poor, bright children. All five, way ahead in school." She picked up one of the old newspaper photographs of Irving Fenner.

Harper said, "We have Fenner's car. He's staying in a rental cottage. Envelopes were under the foundation."

Juana looked at him. "The snitch?"

Harper nodded. "Landlady says Fenner was there last night, at least she heard him come in. Place reeks of booze. And there's more," he said, frowning. "You had breakfast?"

She nodded.

Harper picked up a single doughnut from beside Garza's empty coffeepot, stared at it, entombed in its plastic wrap, and tapped it on the desk. It sounded like a rock. Picking up Garza's phone, he asked Mabel to call Jolly's, see if they could send over some breakfast. He looked at Juana. "Anything from Hyden this morning?"

She shook her head.

He told Mabel, "If Hyden or Anderson calls, put them through."

Juana went down the hall, brought back her pot of fresh coffee. Pouring three mugs, she settled across from the chief in one of Dallas's two worn leather chairs. Reaching to Dallas's desk for the news clippings, she began to read them as Dallas set in motion retrieval of the files from L.A.

SEARCHING FOR DULCIE, Joe found not the smallest scent of his tabby lady, no hint of a trail until, giving up and heading for the seniors' backyard, he stopped suddenly, sniffing the black iron grill work of a wrought-iron gate.

Yes, Dulcie had gone in there, sometime early this morning; had leaped through the gate into Genelle Yardley's garden. And a child had gone in, too, a little girl. He caught Cora Lee's scent, and then he found Dulcie's second trail, very fresh, coming out again. He followed it up the street toward the seniors' house, and it vanished up a jasmine vine two doors away. When, staring up at the rooftops, he didn't see her, he trotted into the seniors' garden, down the cracked driveway, and around the house. Looking around for her, he approached the tent that had been erected over the dig; he preferred thinking of this crime scene as a dig. He'd never before felt this revulsion at a scene of human death. He didn't see Dulcie. Approaching the tent, he could hear the two scientists inside, softly digging. And a faint swishing sound that told him they were brushing earth from the buried bones.

The first child had been taken away, so he guessed they were still working on the second. Sticking his nose under the canvas, hunched low beneath its heavy folds, he peered at Dr. Anderson's thin, denim-clad posterior where the scientist knelt brushing away earth with a small paintbrush. Joe tried to see around him. Looked like they'd found a third grave. Slipping out and moving farther to the side, peering under again, he could see that two little skeletons lay there. The one that was still here from last night, after the first body was taken away, and now a new victim. Most of the child's side had been uncovered;

Anderson was brushing soil from the leg and the little foot. Hyden crouched just a few feet away also using a small paintbrush, removing loose soil from the child's shoulder. This body was smaller than the others. Compared to the heft of the two grown men, it seemed as frail as a baby mouse.

Joe had seldom seen a baby mouse clearly before he gulped it—until recently. The last nest of baby mice he'd encountered, he had turned away, leaving them. Leaving them to grow big, he told himself. Sensible game management, more for later. He did not acknowledge the more compassionate, human side of his nature, except to snarl at his own foolishness and tell himself he was getting soft. Now, when suddenly something pressed against his flank, he went rigid.

A breath tickled his ear.

He turned his head slowly, so not to attract the doctors' attention. Even though he was crouched behind them, he still felt as conspicuous as an elephant in a fishbowl; and these guys were not fond of cats. As he turned, Dulcie's green eyes met his so intently that he had a sharp memory flash of the first time he'd ever seen her. Her green gaze was just as wide then, and intent. That moment when they'd first met, the gleam in her eyes had turned him giddy; it was at that instant that he fell head over paws in love.

Now her little pink mouth curved up in the same secret smile, that smile that still turned him helpless. She nuzzled his shoulder, but then gave him a very businesslike stare, and backed out from under the tent.

He followed her toward the far bushes where they wouldn't be heard. Beneath a bottlebrush bush, they crouched together in the chill shadows. Her voice was faint, but tense with excitement. "Did you check at the PD? Are the reports in yet on those old cases? Any fix on when these children died?"

"You're in a hell of a swivet. What . . . ?"

She didn't answer him, but plunged on, her tail lashing, her paws shifting, her ears and whiskers rigid. "What about the old case files? Surely by this time they—"

"*What*, Dulcie?"

Her eyes blazed.

"The reports are coming in," Joe said patiently. "I don't think these forensics guys'll have any kind of fix on the dates until they do the lab work. *What, Dulcie?* What do you have?"

"Were there missing cases, say, around six to eight years ago?"

"Yes. Quite a few." He stared hard at her. "*What?*"

She was dancing from paw to paw, her green eyes like searchlights, nearly exploding with excitement. "Children from the Pacific Northwest? *Seattle? Tacoma?*" She was so wired that her tail lashed against the twiggy bushes like a high-powered weed eater.

"Yes, that area."

"Did *he* kill those children, and then run?"

"Did who kill them? Slow down." He glared at her until she calmed, slowed her lashing tail, and turned away to wash.

Sitting with her back to him, she had a thorough wash before she was cool again, before she turned to look at him once more. "Lori has been to visit Genelle Yardley," she said. "To the old lady's house."

"I know that. I caught your scent, coming up the hill. And a little girl's scent."

"Lori. She went up there to find out about her pa. Find out why he was so mean to her, why he locked her in."

"You're saying her pa killed those children?"

"No. Let me finish."

"And what could an old woman—"

"Genelle Yardley worked for him, Joe. For years and years. She was his office manager. She didn't know why he'd turned so strange. But she and Lori hit it off right away."

Impatiently, Joe chewed at his left-front claws, pulling off the loose sheaths, leaving the claws bright and knife-sharp.

"Joe, they were so . . . Genelle said Lori's pa turned peculiar after his brother went away." She looked at him smugly. "Hal Reed went away suddenly, six years ago. Never came back. Story was, Hal moved to Seattle, to spend his time fishing."

"You're saying Lori's uncle killed those children, then left? Come on, Dulcie. Why—"

She hissed at him, her ears back, her tail lashing. "Just listen, Joe. Lori found his billfold, Hal's billfold with his driver's license and credit cards. And with it, his favorite belt and a gold ring that Lori says he always wore. Found them in her pa's garage, in a box of old clothes. She has them," Dulcie said, "in the library basement, in her backpack. Why would he go away and leave his billfold and driver's license and credit cards?"

"Why, indeed," Joe said, licking her ear. "Very nice, Dulcie. You had an interesting morning. And what else might be found hidden in Jack Reed's house?"

"Exactly," she said softly, and gave him a sly smile. And the cats rose together and slipped out of the bushes. They were galloping up the cracked drive, their minds on tossing Jack Reed's house, when a startled "*Whoa!*" from down inside the tent stopped them as if they'd been snatched back by their tails. Alan Hyden's voice was so excited, the cats nearly fell over each other racing back to the tent.

"Hand me the camera," Hyden said. "Get Harper or Garza on the phone."

Dulcie, because she had no white on her face, slid under first to look. She was there for only an instant, just her striped haunches visible, her striped tail twitching. She backed out suddenly from under the canvas, whirled around wild eyed, and fled for the bushes. Alarmed, Joe raced close beside her.

Peering out, they didn't breathe. Joe wanted to scorch away, but Dulcie remained frozen, watching as Hyden stepped out the tent door and began to circle the big canvas shelter, studying the ground and the surrounding bushes. As Hyden approached their hiding place, his footsteps squished though the wet leaves, his trouser legs rattling the branches as he knelt to examine Joe's paw print in the mud. Leave it to a forensics detective. At his approach, they backed deeper in, pressing hard against the heavy branches. Crouched to run, both cats told themselves, *So what? What if he sees us? We're cats! Cats creep around under bushes all the time. What's the big deal? We're hunting. So we looked under the tent, so we're nosy. So cats* are *nosy!*

But Hyden did not like cats, did not want cats anywhere near to contaminate his work. Who knew what he would do? They kept their eyes squeezed shut, and their pale parts hidden, Joe knotted so tightly into a gray ball that he felt like a hedgehog. They listened for some time to Hyden poking around and under the bushes. At last he turned away, parting the shrubs farther on, making Dulcie smile. Had the great cat god once again given them a little help? Or was Alan Hyden, despite his superior professional reputation, beginning to need glasses?

Hyden stood for a moment in the garden looking down into the ravine before he returned to the tent. Watching him, Dulcie wondered if he was more concerned about paw prints among the evidence, or about some cat making off with the bones. Some feral cat, or a neighbor's cat leaving chew marks on the bones, marks the anthropologist would have to sort out and account for. In a few minutes, both men came out and began pounding additional stakes around the edges of the canvas. The cats listened to Hyden call the station, leaving a message for either Harper or Garza, an urgent message that gave no information, just said to be in touch ASAP; a message that made the cats glance at each other, wondering if they should risk another look under the flap.

"What did you see?" Joe asked.

"Nothing! He was in the way. But they sure were excited."

"Come on, let's try again for a look."

"It's too risky," Dulcie said. "These guys' minds are way too inquisitive. You can find out later, at the station." And, their own inquisitive minds totally frustrated, they slipped away at last to Jack Reed's house for a quiet break-and-enter.

# 26

**Looking out at the bright morning,** Charlie switched on the coffeepot. Standing beside her at the counter, Ryan cut a coffee cake she'd brought for their morning break, from Jolly's Deli, a confection of dates, pecans, and honey. "That'll put on the pounds," Charlie said.

"Not at all. Work it off by the end of the day."

"Maybe you will." Charlie took an experimental bite, and closed her eyes with pleasure. "That is purely sinful. I have to save some for Max, he didn't eat breakfast. He got a call before we were up; I guess we slept in, a little. He left right away, didn't say what it was." She glanced at Ryan uneasily. "Just—another message where the informer won't give a name." She reached to pour the coffee. "Guess I shouldn't knock it, that pair is good. It was the fe—the woman's voice this time."

Ryan took four plates from the cupboard, doling out generous slices of coffee cake. She looked Charlie over, laughing. "You used to be a redhead. There's so much Sheetrock dust in your hair, you've gone prematurely gray." Charlie's green T-shirt, too, was white with dust. Reaching up, she felt the grit on her face. "Are my freckles gone?"

"Almost. I like you better with."

Turning on the tap, Charlie ducked her face under and scrubbed. She was glad she'd covered the kitchen floor with a tarp to keep from tracking the white dust; it got into everything. She'd been sanding the taped and mudded Sheetrock intently for two hours, needing to keep working, to do something after Max left. She'd skipped her own breakfast and gotten right to work, her mind filled with the kit.

*Had* that been the kit who called this morning, after she was safely home? Or had it been Dulcie? Max said it was a woman, that was all. "Gotta go. Damned snitch—claims to have a lead. Some kind of evidence." Hanging up, he'd called Dallas on his cell, given him directions to some cottage in the heart of the village, then taken off. He'd been cross, the snitch always made him cross, Charlie thought, smiling. But he'd been wired, too, with a satisfied excitement.

She hated lying to Max, keeping secrets from him that, in her mind, amounted to the same thing as lying. Though it did amuse her that he hadn't a clue who his informants were. And it surely amused the cats. But now she stood seeing again Patty Rose lying dead, imagining the blaze of the firing gun as Patty must have seen it in the last seconds of her life. And then seeing the little graves, too, and wondering if there was any place in the world where ugliness no longer happened. Since yesterday when Cora Lee uncovered that little hand she kept imagining the faces of those children, and of their frantic parents.

Setting down her coffee cup so hard she nearly broke it, she watched Ryan carry coffee cake in to Scotty and Dillon. It was Saturday, and young Dillon Thurwell worked every weekend. Though the child had arrived for work this morning so silent and pale that Charlie had thought she was sick. Dillon had gotten right to work, though. No one said anything about the graves, but maybe Dillon had seen the morning paper, maybe the death of those children had upset her.

Charlie had wanted to speak to her about the tea party for Genelle Yardley, to make sure Dillon would join them. It seemed barbaric, to go ahead with such a celebration. But when Dorothy Street called last night, she'd assured them Patty would want them to, that the tea party was Patty's final gesture of friendship for Genelle. That if Patty was anything, she was hardheaded, that Dorothy wouldn't be surprised to see Patty's ghost striding across the inn's patio giving orders for the tea, telling the staff exactly what to serve and where everyone was to be seated. Charlie looked up at Ryan. "I've never been to a proper tea."

Ryan shook her head. "Nor I. Would you call this high tea?"

Charlie shrugged. "I haven't the vaguest. It can be what we want, now that it's smaller, just close friends."

"Whatever, we're going to make it lovely for Genelle. What are you wearing?"

"Something warm. Maybe that paisley cashmere sweater, and that smashing India necklace Max bought me. And a long wool skirt and boots. You think Dillon really will go? Patty so wanted her to."

Dillon had said several times that she wasn't going to any tea party. Ryan told her she *was* going. That, as Dillon's boss, she required it. Dillon said that was a lot of horse hockey. Of course Ryan hadn't wanted to go either; she viewed afternoon tea with as much disdain as did Dillon, but she hadn't expressed that opinion in front of the fourteen-year-old. "The experience will do you good. Maybe you'll learn some manners."

Dillon had looked hard at Ryan. "I have manners, when I care to use them." They had been working at the back of the house, tearing out a wall. "*You'll* have to put on a skirt for a *tea* party," Dillon had told Ryan. "*You'll* have to put on panty hose, *you'll* have to get all cleaned up."

"So? That won't kill either of us. That old woman is dying. This is something she's looked forward to, a lovely, cozy tea among her friends, at an elegant inn. The only element missing will be Patty, and she'll be there in spirit. *You* can at least be there in person, Dillon, and put on a happy face."

"You are so sentimental. How can Patty be there in spirit, after some guy blew her away! Besides, I don't even know Genelle. You hardly know her. Why should—"

"You knew Patty, and Patty liked you, though I don't know why. Patty wanted you there, Dillon."

"I don't see—"

Ryan's look had silenced Dillon, that fierce green-eyed stare that came from growing up around cops. Charlie, who had been sitting on a sawhorse among the torn-out walls, had watched the two, highly amused. But she'd kept her mouth shut. The thirty-something contractor and the quicksilver girl had been going at each other like this since before Christmas, when Dillon, who had fallen into shoplifting and running with a bad crowd, had made the mistake of sassing Ryan.

Ryan Flannery, cop's kid, excellent carpenter, crack shot, was not intimidated by a sassy fourteen-year-old. She had thrown Dillon's challenge back in her face, told Dillon to straighten up. And Ryan had offered her a job.

Dillon had sneered at the suggestion of working for Ryan, but a month later she was doing just that, as carpenter's apprentice. Working over Christmas vacation. She had dropped the truant, thieving girls she was running with and was getting her act together.

Dillon's sea change was, however, not entirely Ryan's doing. Dillon had straightened up quickly, too, when her mother began to put her own life back together after a more-than-foolish affair. Now, finishing her coffee cake and wishing for more but not taking it, Charlie rose. Rinsing her plate and cup, she headed back to work. Her mind was too full this morning, full of fear and death. She needed to drown her thoughts in the simple routine of sanding Sheetrock, put life to rest for an hour or two and get herself centered.

• • •

**LORI LEFT GENELLE YARDLEY'S** with Cora Lee, her stomach full of pancakes and bacon, and her mind in a turmoil of questions. Had she done right to tell Ms. Yardley about Uncle Hal's billfold? She was certain the old lady would keep her secret, but what if she didn't? What if Genelle Yardley went straight to the police after all and they arrested Pa because Uncle Hal was gone? Arrested Pa for *murder*? She didn't want to think that word, Pa wouldn't do that. There had to be another explanation. Uncle Hal was his brother.

Genelle Yardley said there might be any number of reasons that Pa had Uncle Hal's billfold and belt and ring. But Lori could tell that she really didn't believe that. And why, when Genelle first read the newspaper about the little graves, did she glance at Lori and go so quiet?

Sitting in the car beside Cora Lee, they were halfway down the hill, almost to the first shops, when she thought she saw the little man, but he was turned away, she couldn't be sure; he was standing in the doorway of the village grocery. She glanced at Cora Lee, but said nothing, just looked straight ahead watching the streets, praying she was wrong. Cora Lee turned toward the library looking for a parking place, and let out a little yip of pleasure.

"All right!" Cora Lee said, pulling into a twenty-minute green zone just in front of the library. "The parking gods are with us." Cora Lee laughed, and winked at her, and they got out. "I'm going to take you inside," Cora Lee said softly. "You can get your things."

Lori's anger flared. "You said—"

"I didn't say I'd bring you back to stay." Cora Lee took her hand. "I won't leave you here, Lori. It's dangerous. Do you understand that I can't leave you with no one to help you, that I'd be sick with fear, and so would Genelle?"

"But you—"

"I did not promise to leave you here. Think back to what I said—only that I'd bring you down."

Lori stared, scowling. But Cora Lee was right, she spoke truly. That was all she had said.

"Come on, then, let's get your things."

Lori didn't like standing out in the open, and she did feel safer with Cora Lee as they hurried up the stone walk through the library garden. Together they slipped in through the big double doors, and headed down the stairs to the lower floor. They had turned toward the basement workroom when Lori glanced behind her, up to the main floor, and saw him.

He stood just at the top of the half flight of stairs, near the circulation desk. Catching her breath, she drew back into the stacks pulling Cora Lee with her. Cora Lee looked at him, and her eyes widened. "You're afraid, Lori. Of that man."

Lori nodded.

"Go into the ladies' room. Quick. You have your card? Wait for me." Cora Lee's dark eyes were steady on hers. "Whatever this is, I'll get rid of him. Wait there for me, and don't unlock the door. Promise me!"

Lori nodded. "I promise."

Cora Lee gave her a gentle shove toward the door of the ladies' room, and watched while Lori fished her card from her pocket; she didn't start up the stairs until Lori had slipped into the ladies' room. Lori peered out as Cora Lee moved away, then locked the door and leaned against it, listening.

She could hear little through the thick door and walls. What would Cora Lee do? She waited for a long time. She washed her face, then brushed her hair with her fingers. She brushed her teeth with soap and her finger. There was no soft knock to say that Cora Lee was back. She put down the toilet lid and sat on it. She thought about Mama, and about Pa. Thought about Genelle all alone in that big house. Where was Cora Lee? She had to get her things, she didn't want to leave Uncle Hal's billfold in the basement, in her pack. She drank water from her cupped hands, and then at last she unlocked the door and cracked it open.

Peering out, she heard Cora Lee talking to someone, heard the end of Cora Lee's words, but couldn't see her, up beyond the steps. ". . . *must* be there, I *can't* stay. Oh, this is dreadful. Where is Wilma? Where is Ms. Getz?"

"She comes in late today. Noon. Sometimes she comes in earlier to do some things on her own time, but . . ." It was that Ms. Wahl, a dumpy, bossy little woman who was always hushing everyone and thought that children should be allowed to read only stupid baby books.

"Please, Nora. Please . . . There's a little girl in the ladies' room. Lori. Please, before you do anything else, go get her, keep her with you. Don't let her leave the library; I'll be back for her." Cora Lee sounded like she was holding the woman by the shoulders, trying to get her full attention. "Lori could be in danger, do you understand? Tell Wilma, the minute she comes in. See that Lori stays with her." They were moving away now; the woman said something Lori couldn't make out, her voice soft and faint; they were beyond the steps, among other voices. When Lori slipped farther out to look, she saw Cora Lee hurrying away out the door.

What was wrong? Something was very wrong. Was it Genelle? Was she worse? Oh, it mustn't be Genelle, and she hoped it was nothing bad for Cora Lee. She wondered what time it was. If it was coffee-break time, maybe the workroom would be empty, maybe she could slip in before that Ms. Wahl started looking for her. What had happened, to take Cora Lee away like that? She didn't like that Ms. Wahl, she didn't like being passed around, either, from one grown-up to another. She was headed along beside the stacks, for the workroom door, when she saw him again, up on the main floor. As if he had been waiting for Cora Lee to leave?

Ducking between the stacks, she saw Ms. Wahl turn away from the stairs and walk right past him. Trembling, Lori looked around her. Would he dare grab her in here? She could yell, or run to Ms. Wahl. But what could that rabbity little woman do? And now Ms. Wahl was gone again, and he was coming down. The soft sound of his shoes and a little squeak every few steps, rubber against the hard steps. Lori knew she could make a scene, bring everyone running.

Right. And someone would call the cops. And the cops would call Pa. She turned and fled, racing through the stacks and up the back stairs, her heart pounding hard. *Stay here in the library,* she thought, *don't go out!* But she was too afraid to stay. Racing past the circulation desk to the front door, she burst out across the garden and dodged across the street between cars. Slipping into a narrow walkway between two shops, she fled down the little lane and around the back into a courtyard. Then through a shop of model trains and out its front door to the next street. Across that, across another street, another courtyard, running, running until she was among the cottages on the south side of the village. Ducking through the bushes along the side of a tall stucco house, she fled into its backyard praying there wasn't a fence.

Finding only bushes, she scrambled through into the next yard, bloodying her legs and arms and tearing her shirt. Dodging into the shadows beside a little shed, she paused to stare in through its open door.

Clay pots, bags of fertilizer, garden tools, a bucket. She could hide in there, pull the door closed and maybe lock it.

Yes, and be trapped there.

Slipping out again, she pushed the door shut. Maybe he'd think she was in there, waste a few minutes looking.

Zigzagging through a tangle of trees and bushes, she raced for the next street and the next; and she heard him behind her, running. Making for the next block, she doubled back toward the shops where there were people. A snapping sound behind her, like a branch breaking. Dodging between houses, she crawled under a porch, squeezed back under the steps and out of sight. The street before her was busy with traffic, and lined with parked cars. He was coming, his feet squinching the wet leaves.

Slipping out from under the porch again, she fled between the parked cars and into the middle of the street. Running down the street between the two lanes of slow-moving cars, he didn't dare grab her. Horns honked. A woman yelled at her to get out of the street. She couldn't hear, in the traffic, if he was behind her. She was across Ocean again. What did he want? Dodging between the northbound line of cars, she ducked into the brick-paved alley behind the deli. Swerving around the little benches and potted trees, she startled a group of cats and they scattered everywhere, some into the street, some up a vine. He was still coming, running, his footsteps squeak, squeak, squeaking on the pavement. She considered the wooden trellis. Would it hold her? Racing past the closed back door where the cats had been gathered, she leaped at the frail trellis slats and climbed fast.

But he swerved into the alley, lunging for the trellis. Grabbed her foot, jerked so hard she fell. At the same instant the door was flung open and a fat man appeared. Round, shiny face, round, smooth head, and dressed all in white. He stood, startled, staring. The small man froze in place holding her, his face all sharp lines and dark stubble. "Keen." That was Mama's word. Keen with hate. Why? Through the open door, the shop smelled of spice and sugar, cinnamon, hot cheese browning in ovens. The small man stared past her at the round man. When the round man grabbed for Fenner, as if he'd squish him, Fenner twitched and backed away, dragging her; then he dropped her and ran, pelting through the alley and into the street. Her heart was pounding so hard she wanted to throw up. She stood with her head down until the feeling passed.

When she looked up, the man in white took her hand. "Come into the deli. I'll call the police."

"No! Oh, no!"

"The deli's safe enough."

"Please. Don't call anyone."

"I . . . All right." He looked surprised, but he didn't fuss like most grown-ups. He led her inside, into a big bright room filled with little tables and wire chairs, long windows all facing the street. A tall counter along the back with a glass front was crowded with cakes and pies and roast beef and sliced ham and salads.

He led her to a table in the corner, away from the windows. Sitting down, she stared out at the sidewalk but didn't see the small man. Only cars moving, and tourists, some with dogs on leashes, and locals going to work in jeans and sweatshirts. The round man disappeared into the back. There were people at three of the tables. Two women in jeans drinking coffee and eating something that smelled of bacon and onions and cheese, three men in sport coats and jeans, and a young pale woman drinking tea and reading a paperback book. They all glanced up at her and then turned politely away. The round man returned with a glass of milk and a slice of cake. She wasn't hungry but when she started to eat she devoured everything—the cake was carrot like Mama made, and the milk was cold and good. Maybe she was making up for lost meals. When she had finished, the fat man sat down across from her.

"I'm George Jolly, this is my shop," he said with pride. "You know that man?"

"No! I . . . He just . . . He just chased me."

"I thought maybe you didn't want to get him in trouble."

She shook her head. "I just . . . I don't want the police."

"Okay. But shall I call someone else? Your mother? To come and take you home, safe?"

*My mother's dead. Mama can't take me home.* "I'll be all right now." She knew she was being foolish. Mama would scold her for being so foolish. He could call Cora Lee. When she first got in the car, Cora Lee had slipped a piece of paper into Lori's pocket, with her house phone and cell phone numbers. Now, when Lori hesitated, he said, "Who should I call?'

She shook her head. "No one. He won't dare follow me again, not in the middle of the village, with so many tourists and cars."

He started to speak.

"I'll be fine. Some weirdo, that's all. When . . . when I've gone, you could call the police then, if you want. Tell them what he looked like."

"I can do that," George Jolly said, brightening.

"Just don't tell them what I look like."

Mr. Jolly grinned at her. "*He* looked like a little, hard beetle, all angles and as if he had a hard shell."

Lori grinned back at him. "That's exactly what he looked like! Hard, beady eyes, too, like a beetle." Like a beetle you'd find in the garden that the kids in Greenville liked to squish under their boots to hear it pop. She rose and took George Jolly's hand. "Thank you," she said softly. She left Jolly's Deli telling him she'd be fine, but the minute she was on the street she was scared again. That cold, falling feeling again, in the pit of her stomach.

She could go to Genelle's, but the library was closer. Hurrying along the street among window-shopping grown-ups, she wanted, now, only to get back into her cave.

And she knew something more about the beetle man. She knew, now, she'd seen this man when she was little. It was the same man, she was sure. He came in the schoolyard when she was six. In the second grade. In the schoolyard, standing inside the fence by the drinking fountain. They were playing kickball. Every time she ran near him, he watched her. He was there again the next day. She was eating lunch alone on a bench, reading. He sat down next to her and asked her what grade she was in and could he see her arithmetic and spelling papers that she had in her backpack. She stared at him and ran, back into the building. She'd called Mama, and Mama came for her. Mama didn't know who he was. That day had scared them both.

Uncle Hal always wanted to see her schoolwork, too. Or wanted her to play numbers games and do puzzles. At first she'd liked that. But Pa would make him stop, Pa didn't like those games. And *that* made Mama mad. Mama said, "What's wrong with her being smart? Why are you so set against a girl being smart? What if she were a boy?" Pa said it wouldn't make no difference, and then they'd fight and she, Lori, would go in her room and turn on her little radio loud and read a fairy tale that ended up happy.

Now, hurrying along the sidewalk staying in a crowd of people, she looked across at a shop window where a shadow moved, then jerked away suddenly behind the china and glassware. Fenner? She stopped for only an instant to look, but now there was nothing. Two women inside; she saw no one else. Hurrying across the library garden and in through the library's front door, she glanced back at the street. When she didn't see him, she slipped into the children's room.

The librarian was starting story hour. He didn't dare come here, among the children. She sat down on a floor cushion beside the crowded window seat, leaned against its cushioned edge beside the dangling feet of a four-year-old who was in turn snuggled up to an older child. She looked at the kind face of the librarian and listened to her quiet voice, and slowly she let the story take her away, saw the goats and the mountain and the grandfather and let the story become real, let the ugliness fade away until it was gone. Almost gone. He couldn't get her here, not in this safe place.

# 27

JACK REED'S HOUSE STOOD FIVE BLOCKS below the home of the senior ladies, and Genelle Yardley's, but seven blocks over the crest of the hill, closer to the sea. The two cats, leaving the seniors' garden and Drs. Hyden and Anderson to their dig, stopped only once, when a yapping terrier chased them. Spinning to face the frenetic animal, they smiled, and Joe Grey lifted an armored paw. The little dog stopped. Dulcie flattened her ears and crouched to spring. The dog backed up a step. Joe's burning yellow eyes and Dulcie's poison-green gaze made the terrier tremble right down to his hard little paws. Tucking his tail between cringing haunches, he moved back three steps more, let out a screeching challenge, then spun around and beat it out of there yipping for human protection.

Enjoying his retreat, the two cats smiled at each other and trotted on through the crowded backyard gardens, their path following the rocky ridge that began in Genelle's garden. An outcropping that ran for half a mile, cresting the hill in a ragged, stony spine. The yards through which it thrust were, for the most part, planted to enhance its sculpted curves. The ridge ended across the street from Jack Reed's bungalow, in an unbuildable jutting shoulder of stone. The cats paused among the boulders. They had seen this house many times, and they had never liked it.

None of these homes had much front yard, and little more backyard. A second row of roofs could be seen close behind them. The house was stark, forbidding, without any of the welcoming air of a beloved retreat, like most of the village cottages. Against the front of the one-story gray frame, with its dull-brown trim, was a line of dead or dying shrubs. The rest of the yard, where there might once have been flower beds, was covered with brick-colored gravel uglier than a parking lot.

The concrete driveway was empty, and Jack's white pickup with its neat side boxes and "Vincent and Reed" logo wasn't parked on the street. The two cats, padding up the concrete drive to avoid the gravel, stood for a moment assessing the windows and vents, looking for the easiest route of entry.

The foundation vents were so big that Lori could have gotten out through there, if ever she'd found a way down from the house above. The cats circled the house, but all seven vents were nailed shut. Slipping along between the bushes, they leaped up to the sill of the garage window and peered in.

No room in there for a vehicle; the place was stacked with cardboard boxes of clothes and other items spilling out, cast-offs that looked too old and tired even to give to charity. The window itself was new and clean but nailed shut, a dozen nails angled into the inside molding.

"What kind of man is this?" Joe Grey said irritably.

"Paranoid."

"All this to lock in one little girl?"

"Nutcase."

"You think he hurt her?"

"She's never said that, and she talks to me a lot. When

Genelle asked her if he'd done anything ugly, any kind of touching, Lori said no. That she'd heard all about those things from the other kids in the foster homes." She turned to look at him, the late-morning light catching across her green eyes and peach-tinted ears. "She's really afraid of going back to those foster places. I think, if she trusted the foster-care people, she would have called them, gotten some help."

"But help from what? What did he do to her?"

She turned on the branch. "He locked her in, Joe! Nailed the windows shut! How would you feel? You detest being locked in! Took her out of school, and she loved school. She was a prisoner!" Leaping from the narrow sill into the oak tree that towered above them, she trotted along a branch to examine an attic vent.

It was stuck tight. She examined the other vent on that side, then leaped to the roof and across it, into another oak. There appeared to be two vents on each side. All were stuck, but no new nails were visible. These vents were too small for a child to get through, and who would fear that a cat might enter or even want to. It was not until they were pawing at the last vent that they were able to rattle the wooden grid.

Pressing harder, then pulling with hooked claws, they loosened the hinges in the rotting frame where it had succumbed to dampness and maybe termites. Digging in harder, Dulcie flung herself backward on the branch, pulling with all her might—just as she would jerk a giant rat from its hole. The grid flew off, nearly taking her with it. In midair, she fought her paw loose, snatching at the branch. Teetering, grabbing for balance, she watched the grid spin away to the ground. She realized only then that Joe had his teeth in her shoulder, a mouthful of fur and skin to keep her steady. Turning, ignoring the pain from his teeth, she gave him a whisker kiss.

Joe released her and leaped to the edge of the hole, peering in. Dulcie edged up beside him. The attic was black and stunk of dead spiders and insects and mouse droppings, filling Dulcie with visions of black-widow spiders and the brown recluse arachnids and surly raccoons waiting in the dark to defend their lair. She wanted no truck with raccoons, better to face tigers. In Molena Point, raccoons were so well protected by the do-gooders of the village that they had grown unnaturally bold. Pet dogs had been attacked in their own yards, and just this winter, raccoons had badly bitten not only several family dogs but two different women, and a child, who tried to rescue their screaming pets. And only a few blocks from the Reed house, she and Joe and Kit had barely escaped a predatory band of raccoons in just such a black attic as this. That escapade had ended with gunshots. Dulcie still woke from nightmares in which she and Joe and Kit had been blown away instead of the raccoons.

"Dulcie?" Crouched on the branch beside her, Joe nosed at her impatiently.

She flicked an ear at him.

"You going to hang there all day? Is there a problem?"

Fixing her back claws in the molding, she gave a tail lash and bolted into the unknown dark, onto a soft surface that gave unpleasantly until she realized it was a matt of dust-embedded fiberglass insulation between two rafters. The faint echo as she scrambled in implied that the attic was empty, she didn't even hear mice, though her nose tickled with the smell of dry mouse droppings and the leavings of generations of squirrels. She was peering around her as Joe landed behind her. "Go on, Dulcie. *What* is *the matter?*" He pushed hard against her. She moved on hesitantly, picking her way along a rafter and watching through the blackness for the trapdoor that every house must have to give access to the attic—praying *that* wasn't nailed shut.

It would be just their luck if Lori's pa was at home after all, lying motionless on the bed below them, as Lori had described.

Morosely staring up at the ceiling just where she and Joe might emerge. This was, after all, the weekend, when most folks didn't work. Maybe he'd loaned his truck to someone.

But, she thought, it was only Saturday. Contractors did often work on Saturday, catching up on an ever more demanding building market. Maybe he was on some extensive job or some difficult old remodel, or maybe, hopefully, deep into a tangle of ancient, frustrating wiring that would take him the better part of the day. She watched Joe leap across the rafters searching for a way down, his white nose, chest, and paws in the blackness seeming disembodied.

"Here," he said softly. "Here it is. Come on, Dulcie, shake a paw."

Leaping after him, she crouched beside him at the edge of the trapdoor. His head was bent over the plywood square, his ears sharply forward, listening to the house below.

When they had listened for some time and had heard nothing, he clawed at the edge of the door. He was able, just barely, to wiggle it in its molding. "Come *on*, Dulcie." He turned to look at her, his patience wearing thin. "I've never seen you so reluctant."

She'd seldom felt so reluctant. All Lori's unhappiness in this house seemed to have collected like a chill around Dulcie's own heart, and she didn't want to go down there.

Well, the trapdoor was probably bolted, anyway. Padlocked maybe, from the inside. She set her claws in, and on his count of three, she jerked upward.

The door lifted an inch, then dropped back.

Again they listened, Joe as still as a snake about to strike, Dulcie's heart pounding.

When the house remained silent they tried again. With their back paws well under them, and their front claws deeply engaged over the lip of the door, Joe whispered, "One, two, three, heave."

The door flew up—but then dropped back again, forcing some swift paw work to leap clear.

On the next try, they were able to lift it far enough to get their shoulders under it. Cats were not built for this stuff, for using their bodies like wedges. But they heaved, heaved again, and finally with their backs under it, the rest was kitten play. A last heave and the door fell backward onto the rafters. They flew cringing away, out of the sight of anyone below.

But they saw then why the door had given.

"We pulled the hasp out," Joe said, amazed.

Dulcie stared at the softer wood where the hasp had pulled loose. Splinters had flicked off, scattering on the carpet below. When there was no sound, when the house remained as still as death itself, they crouched on the edge, looking down.

Below them down the dim hallway, they could see a living room at one end and next to it a kitchen. Along the hall were four narrow doors that probably led to a bath and three bedrooms. All the doors stood ajar. The rooms beyond were dark. The place reeked of stale air. They could see, inside the door to the farthest bedroom, stacks of newspapers and an unmade bed that even from this distance smelled of unwashed human. Glancing at Dulcie, Joe dropped the eight feet to the worn carpet, his heavy landing causing a muffled thunk. Dulcie, flehming at the smells, dropped down beside him, her legs and shoulders jolted by her landing. And, staring high above her at the attic crawl hole, which was now unreachable, she felt her courage drained away. Without a ladder or a tall piece of furniture, they were not going back out that way. And maybe, with the windows all boarded up, there was no other way out. Crouching on the stained carpet, breathing in the stale smells, Dulcie was filled with the terror of being trapped, unable to escape, a feeling so debilitating that it turned the little tabby cold and weak.

# 28

**In the children's reading room, Lori had** concealed herself as best she could, tucked up among the pillows at the end of the window seat. Story hour was over. She had fetched a book from the shelves and was pretending to read, holding the book in front of her face, glancing out the library window every few minutes watching for the beetle man. The children's librarian was right there at the desk, and another librarian at the circulation desk, two more in the reference room, so she felt safe enough. Ms. Wahl did not come looking for her, and no one said anything to her. She guessed Ms. Wahl didn't really care about what Cora Lee had said, or hadn't believed Cora Lee. Being a grown-up didn't automatically make you real smart, or turn you into a nice person.

Beyond the glass, the library's peaceful garden made a strange contrast with the turmoil in her mind, with the dark shadow of the beetle man, and with worry over what had taken Cora Lee away. Then, when she did read a few pages, the pictures in her head of Harry Potter were equally dark, all among the gloomy caverns.

And when she looked up suddenly, she saw him. The beetle man, standing across the street. Standing inside the door of the china shop, his back to her, standing in shadow and talking with someone inside.

Pressing deeper among the bright pillows, she was mostly hidden behind the wall where it met the window. She could see him gesturing, his hands making stiff movements. She didn't know whether to slip away again, out of the library, to run again, or to stay where she was. Stay here and watch him, see what he would do. It would be worse not to see him, not know where he was. He was waiting for her to come out; why else would he be there in a china shop?

Mama would always stop at a china shop window and stand dreaming, setting in her mind some lovely pattern of plates and silver, imagining them laid out on an embroidered cloth. She and Mama, they ate their meals on Melmac and flowered oilcloth—pretty oilcloth, though, and pale-yellow Melmac. But not china and linen like Mama loved. Their silverware was from the Greenville Woolworth's. He was coming out, turning to look straight across to the library window. Cringing deeper into the cushions, she was telling herself she was safer here, when she saw Pa. Saw his white truck coming around the corner. "Vincent and Reed" on the side. Pa driving real slow, looking out at the street. "Oh!" she said aloud, sucking in her breath.

The librarian looked up, startled. Lori smiled quickly and held up the thick copy of *Harry Potter*. "I'm sorry," she mouthed in silence. The librarian smiled at her and nodded—she was the children's librarian, she loved Harry Potter, too. She understood how you could get caught up in that world and forget your own. How you could get lost in a world so you just shouted out when you didn't mean to.

Out on the street, Pa had slammed on his brakes and swung out of the pickup, right in the middle of the street with all the cars stopped behind him. Pa ran across, Pa, tall and thin, reaching and grabbing the beetle man by the shoulders, swinging him around.

The beetle man fought him, trying to get away. Pa had on his dark uniform jacket with the red-and-white "Vincent and Reed" emblem on the pocket, his brown hair slicked down under his baseball cap. He shook the beetle man, shouting at him so violently that people crossed the street to get away. Any minute, someone would call the cops. Pa's anger scared her, and excited her, too. Pressing hard against the glass, she watched him shove the smaller man into the cab of his white truck, Pa still shouting in his face as if threatening him. Pa slammed the truck door. The man cowered, crouching down as Pa went around the front, watching him, and swung into the driver's seat. Pa pulled away in a chirp of tires. In a moment they were gone, turning away at the next corner.

Pulling the pillows closer around her, she felt hot, then ice cold. She wanted with all her heart to believe that Pa had come to find her and protect her.

But why would he care, after he'd kept her a prisoner? If Pa hated the beetle man, he hated her, too. He didn't care for no one. She longed to be down in her cave alone but she couldn't go there now in the middle of the day. When she looked back across the street, she saw a cat on the roof of the china shop. Dulcie?

But no, it wasn't Dulcie. A little dark cat, though. This cat had long fur and was darker than Dulcie, with a huge fluffy tail lashing, really comical. It stared down from the gutter, looking after Pa's truck.

It was the cat that had saved her, had chewed her ropes and freed her. Sliding off the window seat, she wanted to run out to it. She was safe now from the beetle man and from Pa, she felt suddenly so free she wanted to race into the street shouting and spinning cartwheels, she could run across to the little cat, she could race away up the street, free.

But first she had to get her backpack, in case she might not come back. She didn't think about what Pa might be doing to the beetle man, she didn't want to know. She waited until the children's librarian rose and headed for the reference room, then she crossed to the stairs. Hurrying down the half flight to the basement, she paused beside the workroom door, looking in, making up an excuse to go in there, feeling bolder than she ever had.

There was only one librarian, with her back to Lori. Lori watched her, puzzled, then alarmed.

The thin, blond woman had pulled the little bookcase aside and was sweeping up bits of broken brick scattered across the floor. Lori watched her edge the bookcase out farther and peer around it. Where Lori had always fit the bricks neatly into the hole, now they stuck out all ragged, with big gaps, bricks every which way. Someone had been there, someone . . .

Had the beetle man come here last night, before he found her? Come in through the basement window, through *her* window? He must have followed her, known she was hiding in the library. Then had come in at night in the dark after she left, thinking to find her alone in the middle of the night. To find her where, if she cried out, there would be no one to hear her? That thought filled her with a fear far deeper than when he tied her up and locked her in that house.

That time, he hadn't touched her in a bad way. And she'd thought there might be neighbors close, thought if she had to, she could yell. Had thought if she could escape she could come back here to the library, to her own hiding place, and be safe. But all the time, it wasn't safe? All the time, he'd known about the basement?

And there in the beetle man's room, tied up in that chair, she'd been more mad than scared. *Deep, cold angry*, Mama would say. But now she was only scared, now that he'd found her cave she was real scared. He knew her one last secret, her one secret place to hide.

As the blond woman finished sweeping and started to turn, Lori drew away into the shadows and fled, nipped silently up the stairs and out. Leaving her hideaway for the last time. Leaving her backpack, her blanket, Uncle Hal's billfold. Now she daren't come back. If the beetle man knew where she'd hidden, maybe Pa knew, too. And Pa would come looking. Even if Pa did mean to save her from the beetle man, she still couldn't go home with him, not and be locked up again. Sick with the pounding of her heart, she fled away through the village and into the hills knowing where she must go, the only place she had to go, the only place to put her trust.

PADDING DOWN JACK REED'S HALL, their noses filled with the sour, musty smell of the boarded-up house, their ears swiveling at every tiny creak that was probably only a house noise, the two cats pressed in through the first door. A small, dim bedroom hardly big enough to hold a little girl's delicately carved ivory-colored bed, neatly made up with a faded pink spread, a little matching desk and chair, and a narrow chest of drawers. The windows, covered on the outside with plywood and darkened with grime, were veiled within by dingy lace curtains hanging limp and tired. They had been lovely once. Lori's mother had taken great care to make a pretty room for the child, but now, with the thick dust, and the boarded-over windows, how grim it was. Windows were the eyes of a house; windows should be bright, should look out with joy on the world. But the eyes of this house, turned inward, were as sightless as if squeezed closed in shame. She watched Joe leap to the sill and put his nose to the glass, inspecting the nails in the plywood.

He dropped down again, disgusted, and headed for the hall and the next door. "We'll come back," Joe said, nervously moving on, looking intently for a way out, trotting into each room to check the windows. They had entered this house gambling that somewhere there would be a route of quick escape. Now they'd better find it.

The next room was just as tiny a cubicle. No lace curtains here. Faded plaid draperies and, again, plywood covering the dirty glass. A scarred oak desk nearly filled the room, one of those ancient government-surplus models from World War II that, Wilma said, were beginning to go for respectable prices. On the walls hung cheap landscape reproductions that Dulcie imagined a budget-conscious young homemaker might have picked up cheap from the discount table at Kmart. The pale rectangles between the pictures, where other frames had been removed, were more interesting than what had been left.

"Maybe he removed family pictures," Dulcie said. "Pictures of Lori and her mother? Because he didn't want to be reminded of them? Strange, though, to hang landscapes and family photographs all mixed up." Joe shrugged. He wasn't into the subtler aspects of interior design.

The third and largest was the master bedroom, Jack's bedroom now. Dusty and neglected, the pitiful remnants of female occupancy were depressing: a pretty three-sided mirror over a wicker dressing table, and a little wicker chair, all thick with dust grimed into the white woven surface. A picture of red poppies on the wall beside the mirror, perfectly positioned between two pale, bare rectangles. In the drawers a comb, hair curlers, a faded valentine excessively sentimental and signed "Jack." Four pairs of delicate, lace-edged silk panties that perhaps Natalie had thought would not be in keeping with her new life. The bed was unmade, the sheets and blanket tossed half on the floor, the white sheets yellowed and smelling sourly of sleep. The stacks of newspapers and dog-eared paperback books near the door leaned drunkenly against a cardboard box filled with electricians' catalogs. Joe stopped, in his search for an escape, to fight open the top dresser drawer, pulling the knob with his front paws while bracing his hind paws against the lower drawer. Dulcie, growing more concerned about a way out, headed for the kitchen.

There, leaping up on the kitchen counter, she pawed at the window. It, too, was nailed closed and boarded over. The man was crazy as a rabid coon. When, trotting into the musty bathroom to try the smaller window, she found it just as immovable, a cold panic filled Dulcie. Padding nervously to the living room, she paused in the archway, looking.

Grim. The tired upholstered couch and matching chair and scarred end tables looked as if they had been recently hauled in and plunked down with no thought to arrangement or comfort. This couldn't be how Lori's mother had left her home. The fireplace smelled of old, wet ashes. On the bookshelves that flanked the fireplace, a few cheap paperback books lay bent and bedraggled, their yellowed pages dog-eared, their cheap covers filmed with dust. The two small windows above the bookcases were as heavily boarded over as the others.

But in this room she could smell the scents of more recent human occupancy—male sweat, unwashed hair, stale beer and cheese. The old, faded easy chair directly across from the TV was creased with use, its ottoman standing at an angle as if someone had just risen and left the room. She prowled tensely, all her instincts keeping her ready to run or fade under the nearest chair.

On the end table by the easy chair lay the remote, its buttons dust free from use, but the spaces between the buttons sticky with grime. Last night's newspaper lay crumpled on the floor beside the chair, on top of it an empty cup smelling of stale coffee. She imagined Jack sitting here hour after hour mindlessly watching TV, shutting his child out of his life, effectively abandoning her.

The coffee table and two small end tables held no accessory. She imagined small figurines arranged on the coffee table, little porcelain boxes or ashtrays, delicate treasures in keeping with the little group of oval-framed flower prints that remained on the wall at one end of the couch. The other three walls were decorated with a variety of oval and rectangular blanks where the small floral print of the wallpaper was brighter. The woman's touch had been removed; the house was a shell. On the lower shelf of one end table, a little white-and-pink vase stood forgotten. When Dulcie stuck her nose in, it smelled of sour, evaporated water and wet, decayed leaves. At the bottom, in a thick brown residue, lay three dried-up flower stems.

She prowled the windowsills peering out at the solidly nailed plywood. She checked the bathroom and kitchen windows again, then approached a door at the end of the kitchen that must lead to the garage. Sniffing underneath, she breathed in the damp smell of sour, musty boxes and old clothes. Leaping at the knob, she swung and kicked.

Beneath her swinging weight, the knob turned. She kicked against the molding and, to her amazement, the door swung into the room, creaking with rusty complaint, carrying her with it. Not locked at all! Jack had grown careless since Lori ran away. Dropping down, she leaped down the two steps into the garage, into the musty stink.

The concrete floor was icy beneath her paws. She considered the smelly boxes piled against the walls, with their contents spilling out. Atop one box lay an abandoned toaster and an old hot plate caked with grease. Leaping onto the workbench among a clutter of string and rope, three six-packs of beer, and scattered tools, she reared up to paw at the window with its new glass.

It was locked, as well as nailed shut. She dropped down to the floor again and studied the side door, but it was secured by a dead bolt, she could see the metal through the crack. Staring above her, she considered the electric garage-door opener that was mounted on the center of the ceiling. The usual small metal box with its long metal track. Lori said Jack had disconnected it.

Now that Lori was gone, was it working again? Had he reconnected it, after Lori left? But why would he? It wasn't like he could park in there. Caught apparently in deep depression or something worse, why would he even remember the garage door?

Just below the light switch beside the inner door was the little button that should operate the mechanism. No trick at all, with the cardboard boxes piled against the wall, to reach the button and press it. Leaping atop the stacked boxes, she crouched until they stopped teetering, then pressed.

Nothing. Not even a click to indicate a flow of electricity. She pressed the button three more times, bruising her paw. She was about to drop down again when she thought to scan the ceiling directly above her.

And there it was, in the smooth ceiling. A second attic door, leading to the space above the garage, a rectangle of plywood set into a wooden molding.

The other attic door had been loose, Jack Reed knew Lori couldn't get out through the attic, so why would he nail this one shut? And she could see no new nails at the edges. Maybe Reed had even taken cruel pleasure in imagining Lori climbing unsteadily up onto the flimsy cardboard boxes, reaching up, straining to move the plywood and climb through—only to discover that the crawl space led nowhere. That, after searching among the dark and the spiders, there was, after all, no way out. And Dulcie hated Jack Reed. If he had appeared before her just now, she would have leaped in his face clawing and biting.

Instead, she leaped up as powerfully as she could, striking the door with her front paws. She felt it give before she dropped back, and she saw a little line of unpainted wood where it had shifted position. She leaped again, and again it moved, leaving a wider crack. Apparently this one had no hinges. Crouched atop the musty boxes, waiting for her skipping heart to slow, she leaped and pushed it one more time, opening a crack as big as her paw.

Certain that they could get through, she dropped down again, feeling relieved and smug, and returned to find Joe.

He was still in Jack Reed's bedroom, pawing into the stacks of newspapers and paperback books and catalogs. She knew better than to ask what he was looking for; neither cat knew. Glancing at Joe, she padded past him to search through a pile of Reed's folded jeans, patting at the pockets and slipping her paw in.

All the pockets were empty. Together they searched Jack's dresser drawers, working as efficiently as any pair of thieves, then investigated the high closet shelf. They snooped along in the dark beneath Jack's hanging clothes and prowled among his shoes and heavy work boots. They searched under the bed among the dust mice and peered up at the cheap flat bedsprings, poking their paws in among them. They found nothing. Coming out again to study the electric plugs above the baseboards, they reared up to sniff at those possible hiding places. The lack of opposing thumbs, their inability to use a screwdriver to remove a switch plate or pry off a fascia board, was maddening. In their attempt to detect some hollowed-out secret cache, and not knowing what kind of evidence they were looking for, they could only sniff those suspicious areas and thump them with a paw, listening to the faint, empty echo.

But a cache of what? Drugs? Weapons? What *were* they looking for? If Jack had killed his brother, he hadn't taken much care with Hal's billfold and belt and ring. Why would he be careful about hiding anything else? Moving on to Lori's dark little room, with its one small, boarded-up window, again Dulcie imagined Lori as a prisoner there, locked inside her own house. She imagined the child curled up on her bed reading the fairy tales that stood on her bookshelf. Perhaps in her imagination trying to invent an exciting adventure story to cloak her father's mistreatment.

Except that Lori, despite her love of fantasy, or perhaps because of it, was at heart a true realist.

Feeling enraged for and weepy about Lori, she watched Joe fight open the top drawer of the little chest. Leaping onto the chest to look, she waited while he opened each of the three drawers in turn. The first yielded only the child's tattered T-shirts, some little socks, one with a hole in the heel, and two pairs of jeans so small that Lori must long ago have outgrown them. The other two drawers offered little more. A nightie, a heavy sweater, some spelling and arithmetic papers that were graded A or B.

But then in the bookcase, on the bottom shelf beneath a stack of oversize picture books, three shoe boxes were lined up. Nosing the books aside, they pawed the lids off.

The first held an old rag doll, a tiny battered teddy bear no bigger than a newborn kitten, and the picture of a woman who was surely Lori's mother. Natalie Reed, it said on the back. She had dark brown hair like her daughter, and the same huge dark eyes. Beneath the picture, wrapped with tissue paper, were a faded cotton apron printed with blue flowers and a dime-store strand of pearls with a flimsy bit of bent wire for a clasp. Was this Natalie's legacy to her daughter? Was this all that Lori had left from Natalie Reed's life?

But Lori herself was Natalie's legacy. In Lori, Natalie Reed had created, with her love and caring and teaching, a treasure of great value, a treasure to be cherished.

In the second box was a small album, the kind with old-fashioned black pages. Joe, lifting the pages one at a time with his claws, adeptly flipped them. Pausing before four photographs arranged on a single page, he let out a chittering hunting cry, raucous and loud. His yellow eyes had grown huge, his muscled crouch over the pictures as predatory as a stalking lion. "*Voilà, Dulcie!* Look at this! Wait until Harper and Garza see this!" He stared at her, all sparks and fire, his paw pressing on the page. "Talk about the heart of the matter! Talk about cracking the case!" Shifting from paw to paw, the tomcat rumbled with crazy purrs. "I think," Joe said, hardly able to be still, "I think we just cracked both cases!"

# 29

The minute the weather cleared, Ryan's building crew began to work again on the Harpers' new living room, leaving Charlie and young Dillon finishing up Charlie's studio. Having installed and mudded the drywall, Charlie couldn't wait to paint the walls and move into her new space.

Now it was nearly noon; Ryan's crew had the living room walls framed and were waiting for a lumber delivery, and for the crane to lift the heavy beams into place. She and the four carpenters and her uncle Scotty were kneeling beside the corner of the new foundation where she'd spread out the blueprints when she heard the lumber truck turn into the long drive. Rising, walking out to show them where to drop the load, she was only vaguely aware of the phone ringing inside the house.

Waiting for the truck to back around, she scanned the pasture to make sure the three dogs were safely confined before the lumber was dropped. Rock stood at the fence huffing softly, watching every move in the yard. The big silver Weimaraner was protective of Ryan even in a work situation, and that was all right with her. But the big dog was consumed with interest, too. As curious as any cat, she thought, grinning.

Rock had been a stray, abandoned and uncared for. A beautiful, purebred dog who should have been treasured. She was still amazed by her good luck in finding him—or, in Rock finding her. Motioning the truck into position, she was watching its bed lift and tilt to drop its load when Charlie came out the back door looking distressed, her freckles dark across her pale cheeks. Ryan nodded to Scotty to take over, and turned to see what was wrong.

"It's Genelle Yardley, they took her to the hospital. She fell. Wilma found her unconscious, on the floor by the bookcases. Sprawled out of her walker as if she'd been reaching for a book. Wilma called nine-one-one, and started CPR." Charlie had a large, flat package under her arm.

"No one was with her? I thought the senior ladies—"

"They're in and out all day, they never leave her for long. Susan and Gabrielle are still in the city. Cora Lee fixed her breakfast this morning and ate with her, then left. She said Genelle had unexpected company, a little girl, a neighbor child, I guess. When Mavity went down half an hour later to clear up the breakfast things and make her bed, the child had gone. Mavity left Genelle resting on her chaise on the porch with a comforter over her. She always wants to be outside. See as much of the world as she can, I guess," Charlie said sadly. "Little things, her flowers, the birds . . .

"Wilma stopped by about forty-five minutes after Mavity left; she found Genelle, lying by the bookcases. She hadn't wheeled her oxygen over with her, so when she fell, she couldn't reach it. Half a dozen books were scattered on the floor around her, volumes of Celtic myth."

Charlie looked at the newly delivered lumber and beams, at the framed walls. "It's going to be a wonderful room, Ryan. I'm going into the village to mail these drawings, then by the hospital, see if I can lend any moral support. Dillon's in my studio, sanding."

"I'll look in, make sure she doesn't sand the paper off the board. Give Genelle my love. I guess she won't get her tea party on Monday."

"I wouldn't bank on that. Genelle's tougher than she looks. That woman wants a tea party, she'll have a tea party. Though she might prefer a smaller group, not *all* the Friends of the Library."

"What if she doesn't leave the hospital?"

Charlie shook her head. "Then we'll have the party there. If these are Genelle's last few days, then we'll have a catered tea in the hospital. All the fixings, all the flowers and goodies the inn can put together." Clutching the flat package between her knees while she pulled on her coat, she turned away to her van.

**PULLING AWAY UP THEIR LONG,** private lane, Charlie thought about Genelle trapped in a hospital bed when she'd rather be tucked up under a comforter on her own terrace, the sea breeze on her face, the color and smell of her garden around her. She wondered which of the neighbor children had come visiting. Most kids didn't want to be around sick people, didn't know what to say to them. Turning onto the hillside highway that led down to the village, she looked out at the sea, thinking about death. Thinking about Genelle's tenuous tie to life. And fear touched Charlie, fear of what came after.

*What are we?* she thought, chilled. *Do you just go out like a light when you die? Or* is *there something more?*

If there was an eternal life, was it like that great rolling sea that stretched away below her? Flowing forever to endless shores, carrying uncountable dead souls like swarms of plankton to new lands? Carrying each one to a new challenge beyond their old, discarded life? And she had to laugh at herself. She'd never thought that any one religion was the only right one, that all others were misinformed. That seemed so silly. But she guessed that no doctrine was going to call departing souls "plankton."

Well, her own soul wouldn't be lost just because of her irreverent imaginings, she'd never believe that, either. Any intelligence vast enough to create this world and all in it had to be more easily amused than angered.

Below her the hills were like emerald from the heavy rains. She never tired of their brilliant green curves, which dropped and rolled below her. At home, the horses couldn't wait to get out into the pasture to gobble up the new grass—Max would let them have just so much, then shut them in their stalls again. Horses, like some people, would indulge themselves until they were sick. *Like I am with chocolate*, she thought. And she thought about the kit, also with a sometimes obsessive appetite, and she smiled and said another little prayer that the kit kept safe.

CROUCHING OVER THE BLACK PAGE OF THE ALBUM, Joe and Dulcie studied the photographs of Lori's family. Joe was still grinning, like the Cheshire cat. But this wasn't Alice's fantasy, this was real. What they had found was real. Shocking. Amazing. Very real.

The four names were neatly captioned in white ink on the black paper. The photograph showed Lori at about five or six, an elfin child with big, dark eyes. Natalie and Jack were young, a handsome couple with their arms around each other. "That must have been a while before Lori and her mother moved away," Dulcie said. "But who's the other man? Who's Hal?"

"Jack's brother," Joe said. Hal Reed stood with Jack beside a company truck emblazoned with "Reed, Reed, and Vincent." Below the company name was painted "Jack and Hal Reed. Bruce Vincent." Vincent, the third partner, was not in the picture.

Joe looked at Dulcie, his whiskers and ears close to his head, his yellow eyes slitted with triumph. "You didn't see the other pictures, the ones the kit found, that Harper and Garza dug out from under that cottage."

She looked at him, trying to be patient.

"Harold Timmons, Dulcie! I swear, Hal Reed is Harold Timmons. He was in the pictures that Kit found, standing next to Irving Fenner."

"I don't—"

"It's the same guy. Harold Timmons served time in those L.A. killings. Harold Timmons is Hal Reed. Jack's brother."

She stared at him. "Lori's uncle Hal."

"Lori's uncle Hal. Convicted in the L.A. killings."

"Is that . . . Is that why Jack locked her up? Not to keep her captive?" She looked at Joe, her green eyes huge. "But to keep her safe from Hal? But Hal's gone. Jack—"

"And maybe," Joe said, "to keep her safe from Irving Fenner, too?"

The two cats were quiet, thinking about that. "Where is she?" Dulcie whispered. "Where's Lori? Alone, in the library? And Fenner's out there."

Closing the album and gripping it in his teeth, Joe lifted it back into the box and nosed the lid into place. "Let's get out of here. We can—"

"Call from my place," she said. "Now, Joe. I want out of here now."

Galloping beside her to the garage, Joe was acutely aware of Dulcie's sudden uneasy feelings. Slipping into the garage beside her, he watched her leap to the top of the piled boxes, leap again, and he followed her up and through. Clawing at the plywood, pulling it back into place behind them, he was tense to get to a phone, get Harper over there to toss the Reed house—before Jack Reed, too, developed a sense of impending crisis.

Within minutes they were out the attic vent hole and into the oak tree. Even as they sailed from the tree to the ground, the hairs along Joe's back hadn't stopped bristling. But they were out of there, thank the great cat god for that, and were racing for a phone. They were scorching through the bushes when Dulcie stopped, stood looking at him.

"I'll make the call," she said softly. "If you'll hightail it over to the station, be there when Harper picks up."

"What's the difference?"

"I don't know. See what this call stirs up," she said softly. "Maybe we'll find out what Hyden was so excited about." She didn't know why, but she wanted him to be there. This case was Joe's baby, Joe had followed the cops when they retrieved the newspaper clippings, he was the one who had seen Harold Timmons's picture. "This is your party. Well, and Kit's party, big time. Go on, Joe. Go on over to the station."

Joe grinned, nosed her ear, and took off up a pine tree to the rooftops, heading fast for Molena Point PD. And Dulcie, watching him disappear across the roofs, turned and raced away through the tangled gardens, heading home. She had no idea the kit could have used their help just then. No idea that as they had fought their way out of Jack Reed's house, the kit was holding another lone vigil—that Kit wasn't finished with her surprises.

**KIT WAS TROTTING ACROSS** the roofs when she heard loud, angry voices on the sidewalk below. The sounds of two men arguing, plenty of shouting. Racing to the edge, leaning over with her paws in the gutter in a morass of rotting leaves, she peered down over the china shop's sign.

Two men stood below her, toe to toe. The tall man was really angry, shaking the little man: It was *Irving Fenner*. The kit froze, watching. She still didn't understand why, after he'd killed Patty, Fenner hadn't run away. Except, he'd wanted Lori. Now that he'd lost Lori, was he again looking for the child? But surely Fenner didn't think he could stay in this small town for very long without the cops finding him. That he'd been able to hide until she found him quite amazed the kit. Peering closer at the logo on the tall man's uniform, she realized that was Jack Reed. Her ears sharply forward, her whiskers bristling, Kit listened. Reed was saying, "You came up here to kill Patty, you bastard! I hope the cops—"

"You going to turn me in, Reed? Like you did in L.A.?"

"What're you doing here, what're you after?" Jack looked across the street at the library. "You watching someone, Fenner? *Lori!*" He grabbed Fenner and shook him. "What have you done with Lori?"

"You think I'd fool with your kid, Reed, after you blew the whistle on me?"

Reed shook him harder. "You were after Lori, even back then. Sick, Fenner. You're sick." He pulled his fist back. "Where is she? Where's Lori? What've you done with her!" He twisted Fenner's arm behind his back and marched him to a white truck. A pickup truck, a "Vincent and Reed" truck. People on the street just stood, looking.

Kit swallowed, trembling. Crouching, with her paws in the leaves getting soaked, she watched Reed shove Fenner in the truck, then swing around into the driver's seat. The next instant, they were gone. And Kit took off over the rooftops, heading for the nearest phone.

ATOP WILMA'S CHERRY DESK beside the sunny window, shielded from the neighbors' view by the white shutters, Dulcie spoke into the speaker of Wilma's phone. The deep-toned living room, with its crowded bookcases, stone fireplace, rich paintings, and oriental rugs, always eased her, always calmed her anxieties. As she described for Max Harper the photographs of Jack Reed and his family, she imagined Joe Grey crouched above Harper's desk, listening. Imagined Harper and the gray tomcat joined in spirit by their mutual and intense objective. Giving Harper the location of the album in Jack's bedroom, she wondered how long it would take him to get a warrant. If the judge was in his chambers, maybe not long.

"Will you tell me your name?" Harper said, as he always did. "Tell me how to get in touch?" This was a ritual question to which Harper no longer expected an answer. Likely he'd never stop asking. Giddily, Dulcie wanted to tell him her name, wanted to say, *Oh, you can reach me at Wilma's. If I'm not home, leave a message. Or call Clyde, Joe will pass it on.*

Right. Having said all that was necessary for the case at hand, she terminated the call, pressing the speaker button, then sat staring at the electronic instrument, already feeling lonesome. She loved hearing Max Harper's voice right in her ear, close and personal. Loved the feeling that Molena Point's police chief was her secret friend, loved the giddy amusement of mystifying him. Loved knowing that he would never learn the identity of his two snitches. Seeing Captain Harper nearly every day, when she was in her dumb-animal guise, she always felt such a delicious high. She loved knowing that she and Joe and Kit had passed on to him the latest secret intelligence; for Dulcie, these were among life's most amazing moments.

Gloating over her morning's work, she had turned to leap down when, from the kitchen, she heard her cat door flapping, and then the thudding gallop of Kit racing through. Kit burst into the dining room and under the table as if bees were after her, nearly decapitating herself on the chair rungs. Through the living room like a runaway freight train and up on the desk—a streak of dark fur and streaming tail that nearly knocked Dulcie off the edge of the desk.

Crouched on the blotter, the kit pawed at the phone in a frenzy, pawed at the speaker button nearly exploding with impatience, and punched in the number that Dulcie had just dialed.

• • •

**LORI, HURRYING UP INTO THE HILLS,** heard the courthouse clock strike noon. She was hungry again, in spite of her big breakfast with Cora Lee and Genelle and her cake and milk at Jolly's. Mama would say she was making up for lost time. When she thought about Pa snatching that man up and into his truck, she still didn't know what to make of it. What did Pa know? Did he know the beetle man had kidnapped her? Or was it something else? But she had to smile, because Pa was sure mad. She didn't like to think about what was going on, maybe she didn't want to know.

It was nicer going up the hills in the daytime, among the pretty cottages and with the sun so warm on her back. Seemed like forever since she'd felt really warm. The way seemed shorter, too, than when she'd climbed up in the cold dark with the wind pushing at her, and afraid of every shadow. When she saw the tall Victorian house ahead, with its gingerbread and its *Secret Garden* wall, she ran the last block, could hardly wait to be inside.

Letting herself in the gate, she didn't see Genelle down on the terrace. Maybe she was inside, maybe Cora Lee had come back to make lunch. Something nice and hot. Mama used to make bean soup and corn bread with cracklings. Crossing through Genelle's tangled garden, her stomach gurgled. Pushing through between tall clumps of brown grasses that were all frondy on top, stepping carefully around clumps of bright-red flowers, she listened. The garden was very quiet now, even the birds were still. Along the stone walk that wandered down to the terrace, tiny butter-yellow flowers bloomed. They had been closed this morning. And all across the garden, among the other plants, there were bushes of bright-yellow daisies that didn't seem to mind the cold. There was no one on the terrace.

The long stone veranda was empty, the little round table

was bare. Not a cup or dish, and the chairs were pushed carefully in. On the chaise, Genelle's quilted comforter was wadded up and abandoned. Where was Genelle? Was it Genelle for whom Cora Lee had gone off in such a hurry, had something happened to Genelle? Quickly Lori moved to the glass doors, peering in.

The glass doors were closed, and there was no light within. When she tried the door, it was locked. She knocked, then put her ear to the glass.

No sound, nothing. Had Genelle gone back to sleep, maybe on a couch? Shivering, she knocked again, then moved down the terrace to the end and tried the heavy wooden door that must be the front entrance. She rang the bell first, then knocked. When no one came, she tried that door, but it, too, was locked. Lori shivered, turned, and made her way up the garden ducking under small trees and tall bushes, working her way around the house until she found a back door, and then another sliding one on the far side. Both were locked. She would not ordinarily try to get into someone's house, but something was wrong, something had happened to Genelle. Was this why Cora Lee had left so upset and not come back?

When she was certain that she couldn't get in, she returned to the terrace and curled up on Genelle's chaise under the comforter, covering herself totally, wondering what to do. She worried about Genelle and thought about her wanting a secret garden. She didn't know where else to go. Even outdoors, in the garden, she felt safer than on the street. Genelle had to come back sometime—if she was all right. Or else Cora Lee would come, she thought with a chill. But beneath the quilt she grew warm at last, deliciously warm. Waiting for Genelle, Lori slept.

# 30

**Slipping into Molena Point PD on the** heels of a hurrying rookie, Joe was poised to gallop down the hall to Harper's office when he was treated to sounds of revelry. Loud male laughter from the direction of the coffee room, then Detective Davis's sharp retort. His nose twitched to a medley of deli-rich scents. Hot pastrami and melted cheese, and the herbs and spices that so distinguished George Jolly's pizzas. As Harper made some remark about Detective Davis's birthday that drew laughter, Joe trotted down the hall to the coffee room.

He peered in among a forest of uniformed legs, mirror-polished black shoes, and a few dark skirts above black shoes and stockings. He was crouched to race on down the hall to Harper's office when he was snatched up, lifted into the air by strong hands. He caught the scent of dogs and gunpowder as he was swung up to Detective Garza's shoulder.

"Hold still, tomcat. I'll fix you a snack; otherwise, you'll get stepped on."

Joe was so amazed, he couldn't have moved if he'd wanted

to. He even kept his claws in. Dallas Garza was not a cat person, Garza was a dog man deeply enamored of fine English pointers. Though Joe had to admit that since Garza had joined the department, the detective's attitude toward cats had undergone something of a sea change. Joe's week spent freeloading in the Garza cottage while he eavesdropped, and of course made nice with purrs and good manners, had softened the detective considerably. Now, giving Garza a friendly sidelong glance, Joe lay across his shoulder, limp and obliging, as the detective headed for the buffet table where Max Harper was talking with Davis. Several officers grinned and reached to pet Joe. He had, he thought modestly, made some real inroads in departmental attitude. For tough cops, these guys did have a soft side. Dallas had started to fill a small paper plate for Joe when Harper's cell phone buzzed.

Harper picked up, listened for a moment, and nodded. "I'll take it in my office, Mabel." He left the coffee room quickly, double-timing it down the hall. Joe glanced at the offering that Garza was so thoughtfully preparing. If he dropped down from the detective's shoulder now and followed Harper, Garza was going to wonder.

He waited impatiently as Garza prepared the plate, deliberating between roast beef with garlic or roast chicken. *Come on,* Joe thought, fidgeting. The detective glanced at him. "Keep your shirt on, tomcat." Finally settling on a little of each, Garza was headed across the crowded room, drawing amused glances, one hand on Joe to steady him, when his pager went off. He glanced down at it, then headed down the hall and into Harper's office, where he swung Joe unceremoniously to the floor and set down the plate. Talk about service. Right where he wanted to be, a ringside seat, complete with lunch. Harper, glancing up at Garza, switched on the speaker.

Over the speaker, Dulcie's voice was soft and clear. Whenever he heard Dulcie on the phone talking to an officer, he got the belly-dropping feeling that they'd recognize her voice, but then logic would kick in and he'd relax.

Wolfing his buffet selections, he belched delicately and stretched out on Harper's leather couch. This was just too good, this was the way an undercover type should do his work, waited on by the law, even down to a fine lunch. Lying in comfort and in plain sight listening to his partner's sweet voice as she relayed vital information, he thought that even the selection of the couch itself, and its placement, had been accomplished with his personal influence. Charlie had picked a model that stood high enough off the floor so a cat didn't have to rupture himself scrunching underneath, and she had placed it near enough to the door so he and Dulcie or Kit could scoot under with a minimum of fuss. Charlie and Joe together had worked out the furniture plan. This was the only police chief's office in the country, to Joe's knowledge, that had been designed to accommodate feline surveillance.

At the desk, the captain was very still, his lean, leathery face keen as, listening to Dulcie, he scribbled notes. When Dulcie had told him where to find the photo album, she ended with, "I'll be waiting, Captain Harper, to see how this shakes out." There was a little click that left Joe scowling. Dulcie was getting nervy, too arrogant in her attitude. Who did she think she was, Kinsey Millhone?

But it was Harper's response to the call that caused Joe to become rigid, that made him stare at Harper, wide eyed, before he caught himself and turned away to diligently wash his hind foot.

"Harold Timmons!" Harper repeated, grinning. "Harold Timmons, aka Hal Reed! What do you bet our caller has just IDed the latest body for Hyden?"

*What body?* Joe thought. Those were children up there. Was that what Hyden had found just before he and Dulcie raced away? An adult corpse?

Garza's square Latino face was solemn. "I'll call California

State Prison, get Timmons's dental records, let Hyden know. See how soon the lab can take a look. You want to bring Jack Reed in for questioning?"

"Let's see what the lab gets. We can keep an eye on him. What I want now, with this connection to Fenner, is—"

The phone rang again. Mabel said, "You'll want this one, Captain. A woman again. Won't give her name." Mabel sounded only faintly irritated. Joe gave a little prayer of thanks that Wilma's caller-ID blocking was working. Wilma had had some trouble with it, until she raised sufficient hell with the phone company. He expected Dulcie's voice again, but it wasn't Dulcie.

"I just saw that little man again, the one who killed Patty Rose. The man who left the pictures that you got from under that house." Kit's voice was not as low or modulated as Dulcie's, she was nearly shouting into the phone. So wired that, over her feverish message, did he detect the hint of a purr? Harper and Garza stared hard at the phone.

"He was talking with Jack Reed, right there on the street. In plain sight. Arguing, and Reed was really angry. Reed said, 'You came up here to kill Patty! What a fool.' And he thought Fenner had hurt someone named Lori. Fenner said, 'You think I'd fool with your kid, Reed, after you blew the whistle on me?' Then Reed grabbed Fenner, shouting that he was sick, and twisted Fenner's arm behind him and shoved him in his truck, a white truck, a 'Vincent and Reed' truck."

"How—"

"Captain, Lori means a lot to Jack Reed. Find that man, Captain. Find Fenner. I hope he burns for what he did to Patty Rose." There was a click, and the line went dead.

Joe lay on the couch, heart pounding, trying to look half asleep. What was it about females? Did they have to make editorial comments?

So Jack Reed had Fenner. But where? He tensed when Harper called for four units to watch Reed's warehouse and shop. As the captain and detective hurried out, double-timing it down the hall and out the back door to police parking, Joe raced out the front on the heels of another officer and around the side of the building.

He was crouched to leap up an oak tree and across the rooftops to Jack Reed's when he was rudely snatched up—for the second time that day. Jerked right off the ground. Yowling and snarling, Joe twisted around to face his housemate and lifted an armored paw. Clyde wasn't going to stop him, there was no way he was going to miss seeing this one come down.

***"OH, CHILD! IT'S FREEZING OUT HERE!"*** The words came through Lori's dream as soft as velvet. Pulling the quilt tighter around her, she was propelled suddenly through her dark, alarming dream into the safe place she'd been trying so hard to reach. She felt herself lifted up, wrapped in the soft comforter. Warm arms held her safe, and she smelled Cora Lee's jasmine scent.

Safe in Cora Lee's arms, she woke fully. Cora Lee carried her into Genelle's house, out of the cold, bright wind, and set her down on a sofa and tucked the comforter around her. Kneeling beside the couch, Cora Lee looked at Lori, her dark eyes worried. "Oh, child. I looked everywhere for you. No one found you in the library! *No one looked for you!*" she said, biting every word. "I went straight there from the hospital to get you. That woman—that Nora Wahl! She did nothing! She told no one. Didn't even look for you. I can't believe she . . ." Cora Lee's dark brown eyes flashed with such anger that Lori had to swallow a laugh. The tall, honey-skinned woman was even more beautiful when she was mad.

"Oh, Lori! You came to Genelle running from that man, you didn't tell us, and now . . . Who is he? He's out there somewhere looking for you? And you were waiting here all alone." Cora Lee grabbed her up again, hugging and rocking her as if she was a tiny little girl.

"What happened?" Lori said softly, dreading to hear what Cora Lee would say. "Why did you—"

"It was Genelle, they took her to the hospital. She fell, and was unconscious. I've just come from there."

Lori pulled away, staring at Cora Lee.

"She's feeling stronger already," Cora Lee said. "They think she'll be all right. She . . . She insists she wants to come home."

"How did she fall?"

"She had stepped away from her walker, couldn't reach it or her oxygen. There, by the bookcase, maybe ten minutes after Mavity left. Mavity Flowers is my housemate, one of them. When our friend Wilma got here, she found Genelle on the floor, and she called nine-one-one."

"My mother . . . She had oxygen," Lori said. Then, "Genelle is going to die?" The emptiness was all inside her. Like the hollow dark dropping away in her dream.

Cora Lee hugged her again, speaking into her hair. "It will soon be Genelle's time, Lori, but maybe not quite yet. We all have our own time. I don't think that's the end of us at all, how could it be?" She looked intently at Lori.

Lori swallowed, trying to push back the hollow darkness. She managed a watery smile. "Genelle said she can talk about death if she wants, she can say anything she wants. She . . . told me . . . she keeps wondering what's next."

Cora Lee nodded.

"She told me . . . this world is a nursery," Lori said.

"A nursery for souls," Cora Lee said. "That when we're born we dive down into this world and swim the best we can. Does that seem logical to you?"

Lori didn't answer.

"She says that it's here we learn how and why," Cora Lee said. "That makes sense to me. I find it comforting."

"Can I see her? Can I go to the hospital?"

"Genelle would like that very much."

Lori didn't realize until she said it that she couldn't do that, that Pa might find her. Except, if he'd taken that beetle man somewhere and was so angry, maybe he wasn't looking for her at all right now. Maybe he was too busy.

Maybe that man would tell Pa about the basement, she thought, her heart sinking. And Pa would go back to the library looking for her and find Uncle Hal's billfold. Then he would be mad.

"What?" Cora Lee said. "You don't want to see her?"

"Would we go in a car, and right into the hospital?"

Cora Lee nodded. "We will. Just let me get her things together. You don't have a cold or the sniffles? They won't let you in if you're sick."

"I'm okay. Cora Lee? I don't want her to die."

Cora Lee turned away, not speaking. And Lori thought, *I didn't want Mama to die. But that didn't make any difference.*

JOE DUG HIS CLAWS HARD through Clyde's jacket into his tender flesh. "What the hell are you doing!" he hissed in Clyde's ear. "Drop me. Put me down." He couldn't remember when he'd clawed Clyde like this, and he wasn't sorry, not even with Clyde's blood on his claws. Clyde pulled him off fast and held him away as if holding a bomb about to explode. His expression was shocked, embarrassed. He looked around to see if anyone could hear them, but they were alone. "I wanted . . . I guess I interrupted something important?"

"Damn right you did. They're about to bust Patty's killer, he could be the same guy who did those kids." Behind Clyde, Max

Harper's police unit sped out from behind the station headed in the direction of Jack Reed's house. "Hurry up, Clyde. Where's your car?"

Clyde didn't move.

*"You have wheels?* Where's your *car*!" Joe looked across the parking lot until he spotted a flash of red nearly hidden between two trucks. "Come on! You can drop me off, you can at least do that. Come *on, Clyde*. This is the guy who shot Patty—"

"I'm not taking you where there's shooting."

"I didn't say there'd be shooting. Put me down, then!" He started to fight again, ready to leap onto the oak tree. Clyde grabbed the nape of his neck like a kitten, so enraging Joe that he screamed and yowled and was about to bloody Clyde's face.

"Stop it! Stop it, Joe! This is me, Clyde!"

"Put me down or I swear you're hamburger!"

Clyde stared at him, shocked, then took off running, clutching him, swinging into his car. He dumped Joe on the seat. "Where . . . ?"

"Jack Reed's place."

"Why would—"

"Will you hurry! My god, Clyde . . ."

Clyde started the car, spun out of the lot. "Hang on. And keep your claws out of the upholstery."

Joe considered the expensive white leather beneath his paws, brand new, as soft as velvet and far more costly. The cherry red 1926 Rio was worth enough to keep Joe in smoked salmon for twenty decades; even one claw mark, according to Clyde, would decrease its value. Swinging a U-turn, Clyde followed the police units at a decorous pace that drove Joe crazy. "Could you step it up a bit?"

"You want me to get stopped for speeding?"

"If I can't slip in behind those guys' heels, I'll have to go through the attic, drop out of the crawl space right in their faces."

"How do you know?"

"Already been in there. Already done that. There's no other way in. Damned house is boarded up like a prison."

"I'll take you in through the front door."

"This is a bust, Clyde, not a Saturday-afternoon ball game. You're not going in through the front door."

Clyde just looked at him.

"Keep your eyes on the road. You're a civilian. Even if you are Harper's best friend you can't go charging into a police bust. Even if you were carrying, you—"

Slowing for a stop sign, Clyde looked at him hard. Joe wished sometimes he *could* carry, that a cat was equipped with more effective weaponry than claws and teeth. Clyde slowed at Jack Reed's street, looked up toward Reed's house. The block was dominated by police units. They could see Reed's truck parked farther on; Reed was just getting out. Harper and Garza stood on the walk waiting for him, Max's hands at his sides.

Pulling around the corner, Clyde slid to the curb. Joe was pawing at the door handle when Clyde snatched him up again. "You can go under the house, I'll pull a vent cover off. You can—"

"Won't work," Joe said. "Grids are nailed tight; Dulcie and I already checked." This was amazing, this was for the record, that after their San Francisco caper, Clyde would even think to help him again.

Hauling Joe out of the car, clutching him close, Clyde cut through the neighbor's backyards, approaching the blinded Reed house with its plywood-sealed windows. Moving along the side of the house, they could see, out front, the tail end of one police unit.

"Just drop me, Clyde, and get out of here. I can hear all I want from the bushes," he lied. Feeling Clyde's distracted grip loosen, he made a powerful leap and was free, diving for cover.

From deep in the bushes he hissed, "Get out of here before one of those cops sees you. You could never explain this to Max."

Clyde gave him a look, but he turned and left. Joe didn't relax until he heard the Rio pull away, the sound of its engine fading in the direction of the village.

# 31

"GENELLE'S ASLEEP," WILMA GETZ SAID, taking Lori's hand. Lori watched the former parole officer uncertainly, then glanced up at Cora Lee. She'd seen Ms. Getz in the library. Did Ms. Getz remember her from when she was little and she had gone there with Mama? Did Ms. Getz know who she was? A parole officer had to be nosy, had to be the kind to ask questions.

There were two other women with her, a small wrinkled woman who always wore a white maid's uniform—Lori had seen her around the village—and a tall, redheaded woman who was younger and had freckles. They were sitting in a small waiting room at one end of the hospital corridor, a flowery room with magazines, nothing like the empty, medicine-smelling corridors. Cora Lee drew Lori to a couch and introduced them, using only Lori's first name. Lori tried to mind her manners. Mavity Flowers lived with Cora Lee. The redheaded woman's last name was Harper; Lori was sure she was the wife of the chief of police. Oh boy, she'd really stepped in it. Even if Pa hadn't told anyone else that she was gone, by now he might have asked the cops if a runaway child had been found. And the chief's wife would likely know all about that.

Mrs. Harper wasn't dressed like Lori thought of a cop's wife; she wore faded jeans and a pale-blue sweatshirt over a green turtleneck, and muddy, scuffed boots that smelled of horse. Her hair was really red, long and kinky, and was held back with a piece of brown yarn crookedly tied. When she rose and left the room, Lori was afraid she'd call the station. She'd *said* she was going for coffee, and to see if Genelle was still sleeping.

"Sometimes," Mrs. Harper said, "the nurses get busy and forget to come tell you when someone's awake." She looked at Lori. "They have cocoa. Or a Coke if you'd like."

"Cocoa, please," Lori said, swallowing.

Cora Lee said, "Mavity and Wilma and Charlie and I have already seen her. She got sleepy, but we thought we'd stay in case she wanted company again, or maybe a malt from the cafeteria, something besides hospital food." The waiting room was like a pretty parlor you'd see in North Carolina, with peach-colored walls and a flowered couch and matching flowery chairs. The only thing missing to make it into a little southern parlor, like their Greenville neighbors who had nicer houses than they did, was doilies on the arms or little figurines on a shelf. Sitting on the couch between Cora Lee and Ms. Getz, Lori didn't like to think that Genelle might not go home again. Mama died in a hospital. Alone.

"She asked for you," Ms. Getz said softly. "She's already stronger than when we brought her in."

"She was by the bookcase when she fell?" Lori asked.

Ms. Getz nodded.

"Why was she by the books, all alone, and without her oxygen?" Lori had such a sinking feeling Genelle might have been searching for a book for her, because they'd been talking about books. Because Genelle had asked if she'd read *Roller Skates*, and Lori had said no. "What book was she looking for?"

"She . . . I don't know," Ms. Getz said quickly. "Quite a few books had fallen."

Cora Lee was studying Lori, her brown eyes deep and caring. "You know she has a lung disease, one that cannot be cured. It makes her weak, Lori. Easy to take a fall."

Lori nodded. "Cancer," she said softly. And she thought, *Like Mama*.

Cora Lee said, "As pressure in the lungs increases, one *is* apt to faint. It's not surprising that she fell. But what the doctors are looking at now is an increased pressure in the heart, too—pulmonary hypertension.

"Genelle doesn't want to do anything radical. She's willing to take her medication, but . . ." Cora Lee put her slim hand gently on Lori's arm. Her nails were perfect ovals, not too long, prettily rounded, and polished a pale coral. "Does it make sense to you, Lori, that Genelle doesn't want surgery? Doesn't want any huge and cumbersome effort to prolong her life? That she doesn't want to linger when it's so hard for her to breathe, and will become harder?"

"It makes sense," Lori said, hurting inside. "What *could* the doctors do? What do they want to do?"

"They could put a shunt in her heart, to open the vein wider so there's less pressure. Genelle doesn't want to do that."

Lori tried to understand how Genelle felt. "I guess . . . I guess she's not afraid."

"No," Cora Lee said. "She's not afraid. Genelle holds a clear vision of what she believes comes next, when we leave this world. I can only believe her, I have no reason not to."

"Nor do I," Ms. Getz said. She smoothed Lori's hair with a surprisingly gentle hand. She was a tall woman, and slim. She had what Mama would call good bones. She was wearing faded jeans, freshly washed and creased, a white turtleneck sweater that looked soft enough to be cashmere, and a tweed blazer with little flecks of pale blue among the tan and cream. Her brown boots were well polished. Though she had more than enough wrinkles to be a grandmother, she didn't look like a grandmother. She looked tougher and stronger than grandmothers in books and movies. Lori had never known either of her own grandmothers.

"Over the years," Ms. Getz said, "Genelle has collected works written by many scholars and medical people about an afterlife. Well, you can find proof of anything if you try; there's no way to know until we get there—but I'll throw in with Genelle."

Lori liked Ms. Getz. She talked to her, as did Genelle and Cora Lee, not as a child. They didn't talk down to her the way that welfare woman did. The little wrinkled lady in her white uniform, Mavity something, watched them and said nothing. Lori couldn't guess what she was thinking. She had no idea that there was another presence in the room until she heard a deep and steady purr. Looking around her and then down into Ms. Getz's shopping bag, she laughed out loud.

A pair of green eyes looked up at her from the depths of the bag, and Dulcie purred louder. Ms. Getz said, "Genelle was asking for my little cat, so I smuggled her in. You won't tell?"

Lori laughed again. "I won't tell." And as Lori leaned over to pet Dulcie, Mrs. Harper returned to say that Genelle was awake and they could see her, one or two at a time. "You go," Mrs. Harper said, touching Lori's shoulder.

Following Cora Lee, Lori felt cold and afraid. Afraid to see Genelle here in this hospital that, beyond the pretty parlor, was chill and unfriendly and smelled of medicine and sick people. Passing the partly open doors of the rooms, she could see people propped up in metal beds, or lying flat and pale with tubes sticking out, as if they were already half dead. Some were watching TV, though, and that was nicer.

GENELLE YARDLEY WAS SITTING UP in bed beneath a white blanket and white sheets, reading a little paperback book that looked like all the weight she could hold in her pale hands. But when she saw Lori, she smiled, laid her book open across her lap, and put out her hand. Her smile shone bright, and her faded brown eyes looked so pleased that Lori didn't dare be afraid or uneasy.

"Will you read to me?" Genelle said when Lori sat down beside the bed in a straight wooden chair. "My eyes grow tired, even my hand gets tired. Do you know this book?"

Lori shook her head.

Genelle handed the thin volume to Lori, her finger marking the place. "I'm not very far, you could start again, I'd like that. It's a story written for grown-ups, but maybe you'll like a bit of it."

Lori opened to the first page, and was at once drawn into the story, "'The baloney weighted the raven down,'" she read, "'and the shopkeeper almost caught him as he whisked out the delicatessen door. Frantically he beat his wings to gain altitude, looking like a small black electric fan. An updraft caught him and threw him into the sky. He circled . . .'"

**Cora Lee watched the child** and the old woman for a moment, then slipped away, quickly returning to the waiting room, to Wilma and Charlie and Mavity.

"I don't think she needs us anymore, for the moment. Moral support is wonderful, but a child with a book is better. Except . . ." She looked at Wilma. "Genelle was asking earlier for your little cat again. Maybe she and Lori would both like to have her there."

Amused, sharing a secret look with Charlie, Wilma rose with her shopping bag. "I'll just hang the 'Do Not Disturb' sign on the door so no nurse walks in and finds a cat in the hospital. Who knows what that would stir up."

**In Genelle's room,** Wilma settled into a small upholstered chair and set Dulcie's shopping bag by the bed. Dulcie, looking out, met Lori's pleased glance, but Lori didn't stop reading. When the door was securely closed, Dulcie reared up out of the bag and jumped onto the bed.

Genelle wasn't as pale as Dulcie had expected. Lori sat close beside her on a straight chair, her feet dangling, her voice soft but clear. "'One mausoleum was set away from the others by a short path. It was an old building . . .'" As Lori read, Dulcie nosed the blanket and slipped underneath, out of sight. Gently Genelle reached under and stroked her ears.

"'The front door itself was open,'" Lori read, "'and on the steps there sat a small man in slippers. He waved at the raven as the bird swept down . . .'"

Dulcie purred and dozed, listening. This story always made her smile. Genelle was smiling, too.

"'The raven was puffing for breath a little and he looked at the small man rather bitterly. "Corn flakes weren't good enough," he said hoarsely. "Bernard Baruch eats corn flakes, but you have to have baloney."

"'"Did you have trouble bringing it?" asked the small man, whose name was Jonathan Rebeck.

"'"Damn near ruptured myself." The raven grunted.

"'"Birds don't get ruptured," said Mr. Rebeck a little uncertainly.

"'"Hell of an ornithologist *you'd* make."'"

Dulcie thought Lori seemed to like the story, and surely she liked being allowed to read swear words. Dulcie put her head on Genelle's hand, purring. The sound of the child's voice and of a good story cheered them all, made the sterile room seem less like a hospital.

And it wasn't until much later, until Genelle slept again and Lori and Cora Lee had left, until Dulcie and Wilma were alone in the car that Wilma said, "She's been hiding in the library, right? That's what you didn't want to tell me."

Dulcie looked innocently at Wilma.

Turning out of the parking lot, Wilma reached to stroke the little tabby. "That's where you've been going, when you disappeared downstairs into the library basement. When I couldn't find you anywhere. That's where you've been when I thought you'd gone on out your cat door, then you would appear so suddenly, among the stacks."

Dulcie practiced making her green eyes wide, and knew she was fooling no one.

"I found tabby hairs on the basement air vent," Wilma told her. "Tabby hairs on the bricks behind the little bookcase. I wondered what you were up to. And then, I've seen Lori in the library carrying armloads of books, but she hasn't checked out any books. I didn't think too much about that until just a little while ago, when one of the staff called me.

"She didn't want to tell the head librarian. She'd found the bricks in the wall poked in every which way, and some of them out on the floor, leaving a gaping hole. When she got a flashlight and looked in, someone had hidden a blanket in there, and a thin mattress and a backpack."

Wilma looked sternly at Dulcie. "Had to be either a very clever homeless person or a child."

Dulcie licked her shoulder and said nothing.

Wilma turned onto their street. "No one has reported a child missing. I would have heard that. Nancy Barker also said she saw a man in the basement as she went down. He said he was looking for the large-print books, but something about him made her uneasy."

She looked hard at Dulcie. "Does Cora Lee know anything about that man, know who Lori's hiding from? Does Genelle? Whatever's going on with that child, Dulcie, whatever you've been keeping from me, it's time to spill it."

Wilma's tone let Dulcie know that her patience was at an end. That Dulcie had no further choice but to tell her.

# 32

**Jack Reed watched cop cars approach** the house from both ends of the street. Sitting in his truck, he had a wild thought to bail out and take off running, get away through the backyards and up into the hills.

But they'd have him, he couldn't keep running forever. Soon as they got in the house, saw what was there, it would be over. He didn't know how much they knew about the buried bodies, or, in fact, what they knew about Fenner. He was tired, so damn tired. Tired for a long, long time. Settling back in the seat, he watched two squad cars pull to the curb and two more come up behind them. Harper was in the lead car. Jack knew he had to get out of the truck and go let them in. No point doing anything else. A sour relief filled him, heavy as lead. But a feeling that eased him, too. Maybe he could sleep now. Maybe.

But what would happen to Lori?

If he hadn't swung by the house after lunch to pick up some light-fixture catalogs for a client, would Harper have broken in? Did he have a warrant? Likely he did, Harper pretty much went by the book. He sure as hell hadn't brought half the department out there without a warrant just to knock on the door and question him. What did they know? What were they after, exactly? He watched Harper step out of his unit. The tall, thin chief was in uniform, not in his usual jeans and boots. He stood on the sidewalk looking toward Jack, waiting for him. Harper's hands were at his sides, calm and relaxed, but ready, his thin face drawn. Slowly Jack got out.

As he headed cross the yard, his work shoes crunched on the gravel as loud as gunshots. There was a detective with Harper, guy in jeans and tweed sport coat. Dallas Garza. Jack knew who he was, moved down from San Francisco PD. Square, smooth Latino face as solemn as death. Jack felt nothing but exhausted, he'd forgotten how to feel anything much, really didn't care anymore.

Even if he'd seen them before he turned onto the street, they'd have found him. You want to run, you had to make plans. Money, food. Cover your tracks. Even Lori had made better plans. Harper and Garza stood on the porch waiting, both men grim. He got out, wondering, if he ran, would they draw on him? A crazy, light-headed excitement filled him. *That was the answer. Do it. Run, end it here! End it now!*

Suicide by the cop, they called it. He stood at the bottom of the three steps looking up at Harper and Garza; then he moved on up, his keys in plain sight in his hand, stepped past them to unlock the door. He'd known Max Harper ever since he moved to the village. He'd thought sometimes of going to Max, telling him the whole thing. But he didn't have the guts. It was when Natalie left and took Lori that he shut down.

Before that he'd done the only thing he knew to do. Shut the kid in. Natalie hated him for that. When he heard that Fenner was out on good time, he'd locked her in, locked Lori in the house. But then he had to look at the two of them, Lori and Natalie, their dark eyes hating him. He'd run the business, done his work, come home at night to that. But he'd had no choice, the law couldn't protect Lori even if they knew, even if they tried. Natalie thought he could do something different. But what? There was nowhere to send Lori where Fenner wouldn't find her if he wanted. What could either of them do? And then Natalie took Lori and left him, the two of them, and he thought maybe they'd get away all right. It was best that Natalie did that. Wasn't his burden no more.

But after they ran away he shut down for good. And then Natalie died and Lori was back and it started all over again. What could he do but keep the kid in? Live with her hate. Because Fenner knew about her, Hal'd told Fenner she was smart, the letters Hal got while Fenner was in prison, Fenner knew. Didn't they censor that stuff? Then Fenner got out the second time; he saw Fenner in the village and then Patty Rose was shot . . .

Unlocking the door, he pushed it back and stepped inside, moved back against the open door so the law could enter. He'd thought, when Patty was killed, of going to Harper. But he'd kept looking for Lori, real worried, didn't want to put Lori in more danger, with Fenner out there somewhere. Then that morning early he saw her go in through the library window, and he knew she was all right, knew where she was hiding. And then he saw Fenner watching the library, and that put the fear in him.

Harper and Garza had moved on into the room, stood facing the couch where Fenner sprawled facedown in splattered blood. Spinning around, Harper drew on Jack and backed him away from the open door, backed him against the wall.

Garza checked Fenner for dead, but they all knew he was. Jack stood cold and silent while Harper cuffed him and then called the coroner. He wondered if he'd get life. Didn't want that, he'd rather die. He prayed for Lori, though, couldn't remember praying since he was a kid.

Little Lori, she'd been hiding in the library all that time. Bright. Maybe she'd do all right, in spite of the mess he'd made.

Likely hid there in that walled-up place that went under the alley. When he and Hal first started the business they'd worked in the other building rewiring the two apartments and the store. Pulled old dead wires out, had to go in the library basement to make sure they were already cut loose.

Four more cops came in, men he knew. Stood around him while Harper snapped a leg chain on him. What did they think? He wasn't fighting no cops. He watched Garza and a uniform move away to clear the house. *Clear the house of who? They know it was me.* He guessed cops had to follow procedure. Harper stood looking at him like he expected him to say something. He looked at Harper and felt nothing. What was the point of anything? You were born, stuff happened to you, and you died. What was it all for? Natalie had said, *You don't care about anything! You don't care about your own child.*

He cared about Lori, but she wouldn't believe that. And what difference had it made? Except, Lori was still alive. He never knew why Fenner wanted Lori or those other kids. He knew what Fenner said, what Hal'd said. But he never could figure the rage that filled Fenner.

Coroner's car was pulling up. Harper had left the front door open. Jack stood with his back to it, his cuffed hands behind him rubbing against the rough wood. In a minute they'd put him in a squad car, take him over to the jail. Maybe he'd get a private cell, not have to talk to anyone.

He didn't feel Fenner's kind of rage when he beat Fenner, he just wanted Fenner to end. And he didn't want no farting around with some sharp public defender, either, trial strung out forever trying to get him off with a couple of years. He'd never been cuffed before, never been in jail, let alone prison. He didn't look forward to that, to the gangs, the harassment. He moved aside as two medics came in, and the coroner behind them. As they knelt over Fenner, Harper nodded toward the door.

Jack moved outside ahead of the chief and down the walk

and slid into the squad car ducking his head under Harper's firm push. Cops didn't want you to hit your head, didn't want a charge of brutality. He waited unmoving as Harper snapped his leg chain to the floor. Wanted to make some remark about all this security, but he remembered about the guy in Sacramento, slipped over the seat back of a CHP unit while he was handcuffed, cop left the key in the ignition. Guy took off with the black-and-white, and that left the CHP boys red faced, and that made him start to smile. Not much made him smile anymore.

Driving him to the station, Harper didn't say a word. Marched him inside, took him right on into an interrogation room—room the size of a walk-in closet, no windows, and a barred door. Small table where you could lean your elbows, and two folding chairs. Surveillance camera mounted high in one corner. Whoop-de-do, he was on TV. He didn't think they could use a recorded interview in court. But what difference? Didn't make no difference. Harper sat down across from him.

He studied Harper's quiet brown eyes. Wished he could face the man not as he now was, but as the old Jack Reed. He and Harper'd played poker together once in a while, killed a few beers when he, Jack, did some wiring up at Harper's place. Wired his little barn, four stalls facing each other across a covered alleyway. Put in lights in the alleyway and the one stall Harper used for a tack room, and floods outside.

That was the old Jack Reed, drinking beer with the police chief. Jack Reed with a beautiful wife and a beautiful little girl. Harper sat waiting. Jack looked back at him feeling nothing until Harper began with the questions. Started off talking soft and easy, then when Jack didn't say much, Harper shot the questions at him. Jack was answering as best he could, trying not to get mad, when a big gray cat came down the hall, stood looking in through the barred door. Big gray cat with white markings. When Harper turned to see what he was looking at, the cat slipped away, was gone like it had never been there.

Harper turned back, looking steadily at Jack. Jack couldn't tell if Harper knew Lori'd run off, but he started asking about Lori.

"It's the weekend, Jack. There's no school. She playing with friends? You want to tell me where?"

"They're out somewhere, a bunch of kids. I don't know where. They came by for her."

"Kids from school? You just let her run around in the village without telling you where she's going? Does she go to school every day?" Harper must know she didn't.

"What is this, Max? If you brought me down here to book me for Fenner, then get on with it." Though of course Harper would ask questions, seeing the windows all boarded up. As little as Jack cared anymore, he could see the tangle he was making. Maybe better just to lay it out for Harper, why the plywood over the windows, why he'd killed Fenner. He was going to burn anyway, if not for Hal, then, sure, for Fenner.

And then Lori would be alone and she'd have to go to child welfare, she'd have no choice. Well, they'd take care of her, state paid them to do that.

"Why the plywood, Jack? What's that all about?"

He was thinking where to start, how to start, when the cat appeared again pressing against the bars peering in. Gave him a shiver down his spine, that cat, so he found it hard to talk.

***REED DOESN'T WANT TO TALK** in front of me,* Joe thought. *Was I staring? Made him nervous? Dulcie says I stare at people so hard they get shaky. Oh, right, one little cat can make a grown man shaky.*

*Well, he's not going to talk with me watching him. Whatever the reason, the guy's tongue-tied.* Backing away out of sight again, Joe lay down on the cold tile floor. He could hear, behind him up the hall, Mabel Farthy dispatching a patrol car to a drunk fight. No one needed a drunk fight in the middle of the day, in this village. It wasn't like they had any real bars, just restaurants that served drinks. He thought Mabel probably had Fenner and Harper on her monitor, maybe with the sound turned down.

In the other direction, on down the hall past the interrogation room in Dallas Garza's office, he could hear the faint echo of Harper's voice where Garza and Detective Davis were watching on the closed-circuit TV. Clyde would give a nickel to be here, Joe thought, would be as anxious to hear Reed's story as Joe himself.

It was only after Clyde was convinced there wouldn't be any shooting at Reed's place that he'd loosed his grip on Joe and let him out of the car—with the usual sigh of resignation. Clyde had had no way, though, to gracefully hang around, with cops all over the place; Joe guessed he'd gone on back to the shop to work on one of his vintage cars.

Well, Clyde could hear the story tonight when Max and Charlie came over for dinner. That was why Clyde had shown up at the station in the first place, when he'd snatched Joe up from outside the front door—to invite Max and Charlie to dinner because Charlie's new car had arrived.

Everyone but Charlie knew that Max was shopping for a new vehicle for her, one she could use for her cleaning business, for ranch work, or for hauling paintings to exhibits. Max was as anxious as a kid, wanting to surprise her. The small red SUV had been delivered yesterday to Clyde's shop, and would be sitting in Clyde's driveway when they got there for dinner.

Slipping to the bars of the interrogation room again, Joe peered in. Immediately Reed stopped talking and stared at him. Joe, even before Harper swung around to look, bolted away down the hall toward Garza's office and inside beneath the detective's printer stand, where he made himself comfortable on a small rug that Garza had brought from home and that smelled like dog. Both Garza and Davis had their backs to him, watching the monitor that was mounted high in the far corner.

Davis, curled up in the tweed easy chair, had her shoes off and her feet tucked under her. The chair had also come from Garza's house—the city of Molena Point didn't pay for luxuries; the chair, too, smelled like dog, the smell so immediate that it was as if the framed photographs of Garza's English pointers that hung on the walls had acquired an additional dimension. On the screen, Jack Reed was saying, ". . . almost from the time Fenner began that group in L.A. Don't know what it was about those people that drew Hal to their ideas. He was never strange, as a kid. Shy, maybe. A sort of misfit in school, a follower—"

"And that's why you killed Fenner, because he'd influenced Hal, involved Hal in the killings. And Hal . . . ?"

"I killed Fenner to keep him away from Lori, keep him from killing Lori like he did the others. And Hal . . . that was rage. I saw that dead child, Hal standing over her . . . a black rage. I purely lost it.

"But I wasn't sorry afterward. I knew . . . felt like . . . there was more than one body down under that garden. I thought back about Hal's fishing trips, and was sure of it." Jack looked at Harper. "Fenner . . . I don't know if he was ever sane. I don't know why that L.A. judge didn't give him life. Lock him up or fry him, keep him off the street. Just because those others wouldn't testify against him, would never say he was involved . . . The cops knew he was."

Davis mumbled something to Garza, and shook her head. As if she agreed, as if LAPD or the DA should have tried harder. Maybe Fenner was free to kill Patty Rose because some squirming L.A. judge didn't have the *balls* to make the DA dig farther, and to lock Fenner up for life. Joe wondered how many more kidnapped children and young women were murdered because of an unrealistic attitude on the part of a few state and federal judges or inept juries.

Certainly neither detective looked like they were sorry that

Jack Reed had done Fenner. Garza rose and poured two mugs of coffee, handed one to Juana, and sat down again. On the screen, Reed was describing, as best he knew, Irving Fenner's history, and Reed's view of Fenner's twisted motives. For over an hour, Joe lay beneath the printer table fitting Reed's story together with the facts he already knew.

To believe that extra-bright children would grow up to force the world into some kind of slavery dictated by geniuses was so twisted that it made Joe want to claw everything in sight. To believe those children should be eliminated or forcefully diverted from their intense interests made him wish he'd done Fenner himself. No one ever said Joe Grey was an altruistic do-gooder. In his view, the very children Fenner had killed might have accomplished great and wonderful things in the world.

He knew from his own metamorphosis, from ordinary cat to a speaking, sentient being, the value and wonder of clear and perceptive thought. To kill a child who had a sharper, clearer view of the world was to kill what life was all about. When the interrogation was finished, when Jack Reed was led away to be locked in a cell, Joe left the station still out of sorts. So grouchy that even that night as Clyde prepared dinner, he felt snappish and bad tempered.

"What's with you? What happened after I left Reed's?" Clyde said, tearing up greens for a salad.

"They arrested Reed. What else?"

Clyde turned to look at him. "I provide you with taxi service direct to an in-progress police raid. Chauffeur you right to the scene. Don't tell me, 'They arrested Reed'! What happened?"

"I hardly saw any action. Place was swarming with cops. Medics. The coroner."

"Medics, Joe? The coroner?" Clyde waited, his hand raised as if he'd swat Joe.

Joe grinned. "Reed killed the little bastard, killed Fenner dead.

I only got a glimpse of Fenner as they carried him out, limp as a dead rat, blood all over, before they pulled the sheet over him."

Clyde smiled, lowered his threatening hand, and opened the oven to test the corn bread. "And they took Reed in?" Joe nodded. Clyde pulled out the oven rack, slipped a knife down into the middle of one golden mound, and held the knife up to the light. "And I suppose you hightailed it right on back to the department, heard the whole interrogation." Joe glanced at Dulcie, crouched beside him on the deep windowsill. She smiled, and kept her silence.

Clyde turned around to look at Joe. "Well? What did Reed say?" He checked the other loaf, then removed them, setting them on a rack to cool.

Joe shrugged. "Jack talked about Fenner, his sick mind, why he killed those kids. It's too bad Fenner won't stand trial—for Patty, for those dead children." He turned to wash a hind paw. "His death will save the state a lot of money. But a lot more information would come forth if he stood trial. Make people think a little. Where's the kit? She's the one who found Fenner, she ought to be in on this."

"She's with Lucinda and Pedric," Dulcie said. "They'll be along. They brought us down from Harper's earlier. No one wants to miss the fun; Charlie doesn't get a new car every day." Charlie had needed reliable wheels for a long time. When her crew used her cleaning van, which was fitted out with every possible cleaning apparatus and with tools for household repairs, Charlie had to drive an ancient car of Max's that was less than dependable.

"I wonder," Dulcie said, "without the kit, *would* the cops have found Fenner? It's amazing that Fenner was able to move around the village for two days after he killed Patty."

"Slick," Joe said, watching Clyde toss the salad. "Or lucky. He must have ducked every time he smelled a uniform."

Clyde smiled knowingly.

"What?" Joe said.

"Street patrol picked up Fenner's car. I talked with Max. They found a kid's baseball uniform in the trunk, with the insignia of the junior high on it. A kid's jacket emblazoned with fluorescent pictures of Michael Jackson, and a kid's school backpack."

"Kit sure didn't see him in those duds," Joe said. "She'd have told Harper that."

But Dulcie was shifting impatiently from paw to paw. "You said you heard it all, the whole interrogation. What else did he Reed say?"

Joe watched Clyde stir the bean soup. It smelled good on this cold winter night. "Harper's going to tell you, he'll walk you through the whole interrogation. Doesn't he always? I'd just be repeating it."

"Come on, Joe."

Joe sighed. "He killed Fenner because he was afraid for Lori. He killed Hal in a fit of rage because Hal had killed a child. Can't say I blame him. They were crazy, criminally insane. That cult . . . Sick minds who thought they were saving the world." He considered Clyde's scowl. "No one said I have to take a moderate view of the world. I'm a cat, no one expects me to temper my judgment with civility. I sometimes wish the courts could see the world through feline eyes. Sure would simplify life. In a cat's view, Jack Reed would get a medal for killing Fenner, not be subjected to endless police interrogation and prison." And he turned to wash his hind paw.

Clyde was still scowling. "You have to balance civilized human law against the fire in your belly, Joe. If we all went by the fire in *your* belly, we'd be living like cavemen. Look at some countries—torture and rape because there's more corruption than civil—" A loud knocking at the door caused Clyde to immediately turn on the kitchen TV in case anyone had noticed voices; they heard the front door open. "Dinner ready?" Max shouted.

"In the kitchen," Clyde yelled over a newscast. And their friends came crowding in, bringing the wet, icy wind in with them, pulling off boots and coats in the kitchen. Max and Charlie, and Dallas, then Lucinda and Pedric and Wilma directly behind them, Lucinda carrying the kit inside her coat, warm and snug. Joe heard Ryan Flannery's truck pull up, then Davis's VW. Ryan and Davis were last through the door, Davis bringing wine, Ryan bearing a large bakery box. Shutting the door, shutting out the wind, they hurried into the kitchen. Ryan set the box on the counter, giving Clyde a hug and a kiss on the cheek that made Dulcie smile.

"New project?" Charlie said to Clyde, nodding toward the front drive where a canvas-covered vehicle sat, presumably a newly purchased antique car in need of tender attention. Clyde was always buying a "new" relic—rusty, neglected, begging to be restored.

Clyde nodded. "New baby. Didn't have room at the shop." He turned away, setting a covered tureen on the table. The newly remodeled kitchen was twice the size of the old one, and a great place for company. Ryan had not only torn out the wall to the unused dining room, she had added a handsome Mexican tile floor, redone the kitchen cabinets, and installed a bay window over the sink where the cats could supervise the cooking while remaining out of the way.

Joe watched his friends fixing drinks—wine for Lucinda and Pedric—and wondered when Max would unveil Charlie's new car. Watched them gather around the big table to dish up bean soup and salad and corn bread. Joe and Dulcie and Kit, settled in the bay window with their three bowls of soup and crumbled corn bread, glanced at each other with satisfaction.

Lori Reed was safe again, and Fenner was dead. And maybe

Jack Reed would get an easy sentence if the court was sympathetic. Dulcie and Kit looked at each other, both lady cats wishing Lori Reed was there with them, among their friends, with her own place at Clyde's table—though Lori was enjoying her own hot supper tonight with Cora Lee and Mavity and the two dogs. Lori would sleep in a warm bed tonight, before the fire in Cora Lee's upstairs bedroom in a home where, if she chose, she might enjoy a far longer welcome.

# 33

"WHAT *WILL* HAPPEN TO LORI REED?" Lucinda asked after supper, as the little party crowded around the warming blaze in Clyde's living room. "If Jack Reed gets life, or the death sentence, does she have anyone else?"

"No other family," Wilma said. "And I don't think the child will tolerate being sucked back into the welfare system." This statement from Wilma drew startled looks. "But," Wilma said, "I don't think she'll have to; I think Cora Lee would be delighted to give Lori a home."

"What kind of sentence is Reed likely to get?" Lucinda said.

Wilma shook her head, as did Max and Dallas. There was no telling, given the circumstances. "Anything from ten years," Harper said, "for manslaughter, to life for two counts of second-degree murder."

"How's Lori taking it?" Charlie said.

"Stoic," Wilma said. "Quiet. She's with Cora Lee now, but when Genelle is out of the hospital, Lori wants to stay with her." Wilma had chosen to sit just beside the hearth, in Joe's personal, clawed chair that Clyde had covered with a blanket for the occasion. "Lori knows the whole story," Wilma said. "Hal's fishing trips, the L.A. murders. But she seems all right about it; she's a strong child."

Max settled back into the leather couch, close to Charlie. "Patty would be pleased to know Fenner's dead, that her daughter and grandchild are, to some degree, vindicated.

"Maybe she knows," Lucinda said. Full of supper, Lucinda and Pedric had cozied down together on the leather love seat, while Ryan and Clyde and Dallas sat on floor pillows before the hearth. Detective Davis had curled up at the end of the couch, next to Charlie, pulling off her shoes, tucking her feet under.

Harper shook his head. "Twisted, bitter people, all with some kind of vendetta against society—against children. The idea that children with superior intelligence are against God's law. Crazy as a pet coon. And that guy was teaching elementary school. First school let him go in the middle of the first semester; that was in Orange County. He moved up north to Redding, started again as if he was just out of graduate school. All forged degrees. Lasted a full semester before they dumped him. DA's been on the phone all afternoon talking with school districts. Fenner's background fell through the cracks until a school in San Bernardino began to ask questions, did some checking. That's when he moved to Denver, changed his name, went to work for children's services, another string of forged degrees and references. No one checked. They needed help, and he sounded too good to question.

"There, four children disappeared from outlying towns. Never found. Investigating officer looked at Fenner but dismissed him. These kids weren't on Fenner's caseload, and they seemed to have no connection to children's services. Officer had no real reason to investigate Fenner. And with no bodies, no blood work, no lab . . . Fenner remained in Denver for another two years, then we lose track of him.

"Now Denver is looking at those cases again, pulling those

old files. Next we know of him so far, he's in L.A. Marlie's husband, Craig, gets involved with him." Max had told them over dinner about the L.A. case. "Stories filled the front page for weeks." When Harper glanced idly up at the bookcase, Joe slit his eyes nearly closed and laid his chin on his paws, as if dozing. Dulcie had curled up next to Joe, her eyes closed. Kit faked a yawn, but at the back of the bookcase her tail was twitching with interest.

"The L.A. bodies were found early on a Sunday morning, someone had seen a light in the church the night before, inside the boarded-up windows. Called the police. L.A. checked it out and left, but were back the next morning. Twelve children buried together in the wall of the church, Conner among them. His shirt was gone, and his shoes. He'd died of strangulation."

Atop the bookcase, Kit nuzzled closer to Dulcie and Joe.

"When Hal got out of prison, Jack thought that if he got him away from L.A. and into their own business, he'd straighten out, forget his crazy notions. When he realized Hal hadn't forgotten, he was wild with fear of what Hal would do. And he didn't know where Fenner was. Prosecution couldn't make Fenner, not one of his followers would testify—not for the murders, not for influencing them, or for any involvement with the cult. Refused to say he was the cult leader. Every one of them protected Fenner right down to the end. Best the DA could do was accessory, based on circumstantial evidence.

"Dorothy Street was about ten at the time of the murders, a family friend. After Marlie was killed, I think that in many ways Dorothy took her place for Patty. Patty badly needed someone.

"When Fenner was released, Patty knew but didn't think he'd come here. Parole department in L.A. is grossly overworked. Even if he'd failed to report, they might have had no reason to believe he would head up here, after Patty." Max finished his coffee, set his cup on the coffee table, and put his arm around Charlie, drawing her close.

Lucinda said, "If they proved that Harold Timmons—Hal Reed—killed one of the L.A. children, why did he get only a few years?"

"They didn't prove that Timmons killed any of the children; no one in that group would testify against another. Only Craig Vernon and Kendall Border got murder one, through fingerprint identification."

Pedric said, "So when Harold Timmons had done his time, he and his brother, Jules, moved up the coast to Molena Point and changed their names to Hal and Jack Reed."

Harper nodded. "Jack thought Hal would be all right if he could keep him away from groups like that, that he'd be okay without Fenner. I guess he was, for a while.

"Jack met Natalie, married her. Two years later, they had Lori. Jack says he really believed Hal had thrown himself into the business and was through with anything related to offbeat religions—but said he kept a close eye on him.

"Several years after they started the business, Hal started going salmon fishing up around Seattle and Tacoma, at first booking trips with a local travel group. Jack thought that was good for Hal, a different kind of interest, and he encouraged it.

"Hal wasn't living with Jack and Natalie then, but in a small apartment a few blocks over—the house the senior ladies now own. When Lori was not quite six, Jack went over there one night during a bad storm. All the electricity in the village was out. One of their customers had a flood, wet wires, a mess, wanted someone to get that part of the building cut off before the power came back on. Jack needed some help, and when he couldn't reach Hal on the phone, he went over to see if he was home yet from Seattle.

"He found Hal out in back digging in the garden. He shone his flashlight on Hal, and on a child's mutilated body. Jack said he grabbed the shovel from Hal, hit him and hit him, just beat him and wouldn't stop.

"When he finally did stop, he stood in the pouring rain staring at Hal and at the dead child. He knelt by Hal, by his dead brother." Max looked around at his friends, leathery face drawn into lines of sadness. "Jack stood there awhile, then buried Hal, and buried the child."

The three cats, atop the bookcase, were as still as stone, imagining the grisly scene.

"He didn't know if there were other graves. Thought there must be, but said he didn't want to know. He went home and threw up. For about a week, he couldn't keep any food down, didn't sleep, wouldn't talk to Natalie. That was the beginning of his strangeness, his fear and depression. He began to worry about Lori. If she went down the street to play, she had to tell him exactly where she was going, who she'd be with, which yard. He'd always ask if she'd talked to any strangers—had begun to worry that Fenner was somewhere near. He checked with L.A. probation and parole, learned that Fenner wasn't out yet and when they expected he would be. And all the time, he was eaten up by guilt, guilt that he hadn't suspected Hal, that a child, maybe more, had died. Guilt that he'd killed his brother. He began to buy the Tacoma and Seattle papers, and soon knew there was more than one missing child.

"He knew he could ease the parents, that he could put an end to their uncertainty. But he did nothing. And as Fenner's release time drew near, Jack was consumed by fear for Lori. He knew if he told police where to find the missing children, they'd find Hal as well. Not only would Jack go to prison, he imagined that Fenner would hear about the case, figure out why Jack had killed Hal, and that as vindictive as Fenner was, he'd be sure to come after Lori. Also, four of the L.A. cult members had not been charged; they were on the street and Jack worried that Hal might have been involved with them in Seattle, that they might come after Lori, too, as retribution for Hal's death.

"When Fenner was released, Jack says he was a basket case,

eaten up with fear. Didn't want to go out in the evening and leave Lori with a sitter, didn't want Lori to go to school. Natalie insisted on school, but Jack insisted that Lori had to be driven and picked up, nothing after school, no playing with friends.

"When Natalie lost patience with this, she left him, taking the child with her. It was about then that Fenner went back to jail on another charge.

"When Natalie died six years later of cancer, Lori was sent to a dozen foster homes before she told her caseworker she had a father. Shortly after she gets back to Molena Point, Fenner is out again. Jack thought he saw him once, in the village, and that's when he boarded up the house.

"This was about three weeks before Fenner killed Patty. As unstable as Jack had become, he may have saved Lori. But then, about a week after Jack boarded up the windows, Lori ran away. Hid in the library basement."

Joe glanced at Dulcie. *You found her,* his look said. *You helped her, Dulcie.* Below them, Lucinda wiped away a tear. "Fenner might have been a mental case," she said, "but he was also pure evil."

"Jack has Fenner's letters to Hal, from prison," Max said. "Hal had told him Lori was extra bright. Hal grinding his own ax, I guess. Getting back at Jack for whatever imagined reason, or maybe to impress Fenner."

No one asked how the department had known that Jack had found Fenner. Everyone present was either law enforcement, so knew Harper had received a tip, or if not with the department, then was conversant with other information regarding certain anonymous sources.

But Harper looked around at his friends and frowned. "We have a witness," he said, and he waited.

No one said anything.

"Witness who heard Jack and Fenner arguing on the street, saw Jack rough up Fenner and shove him in his truck. A young woman," Harper said, studying each of his civilian friends. He looked at Clyde, at Wilma, at Lucinda, at Dallas's niece Ryan. He glanced down at Charlie. "A witness who, I'm sure, will refuse to come forward."

Davis said, "These two snitches are starting to make me nervous."

Harper looked at her. "A lot of cases won, Juana. A lot of convictions." He leaned back, stretching out his long legs. "And however this plays out for Jack Reed, he seems easier in his mind."

"So many deaths," Lucinda said.

"Patty fought Fenner's kind in her own way," Harper said. "Most of Patty's holdings go to enlarge her children's shelter and add an accelerated school. Her trust will set up a scholarship system where any child who is bored in school and unchallenged can come there to learn, tuition free." He looked at Lucinda and Pedric, at Wilma. "I've told Jack there are several people who want to take Lori, give her a home in case he gets a long sentence. He'll be arraigned in a day or two. After that, until the trial, he'll be out on bail, under electronic home confinement. The judge was very understanding about setting that up. Lori can be with him during that time.

"Who knows, he may get a short sentence and parole. Meantime, Cora Lee French is there for her. Cora Lee spoke to me this afternoon. Cora Lee loves that child."

"We haven't had dessert," Ryan said, swiping at a tear as she rose and moved toward the kitchen. But Max pulled Charlie up from the couch and headed out the front door.

"Hey," Charlie said. "I want dessert."

"Don't worry, you won't miss dessert."

She let herself be guided outside and down the steps, to the drive. Behind them, everyone crowded out onto the porch, but Clyde moved quickly past them, to flip the canvas cover off the hidden vehicle.

Charlie looked at Clyde, puzzled. She stared at the shiny

new red Blazer. "This doesn't need restoring. *This* is your new project?"

Clyde smiled. Max stood watching her. A card was stuck under the windshield wiper. She removed it and opened it, then looked up at Max. " 'Happy early birthday'? What—"

"It arrived early." He handed her the key.

Clyde, watching them, was almost as pleased as Max. He and Max had considered a four-year-old Jaguar convertible trade-in, a vehicle that both men had greatly admired. Maybe during a light moment, Max had imagined himself tooling around the village in Charlie's flashy Jaguar. But both admitted that Charlie couldn't haul her paintings or half a dozen bales of hay or two big dogs or extra housecleaning equipment in a Jag convertible. Then Clyde had found the two-year-old Chevy Blazer that, while not quite politically correct, got good gas mileage and gave Charlie ample hauling space.

Charlie spent the next half hour hugging Max, examining the car inside and out, and ended up bawling on his shoulder. The three cats, crouched on the porch, had to shut their mouths tight to keep from laughing. Their loud purrs did attract several glances. It was only later, alone in the kitchen, that Charlie tweaked Joe's ear and stroked Kit and Dulcie. "You knew!" she whispered. "All three of you. You little stool pigeons knew, but you never once let on! How can you be such snitches, but you never say a word to me!"

Joe looked up at Charlie, his yellow eyes innocent and round. Kit lashed her tail and smiled. Dulcie said softly, "But it wasn't really a secret at all, everyone knew. Ryan and Dallas. Wilma. Lucinda and Pedric. Davis, the entire department. Everyone knew but you, Charlie."

# 34

LORI HAD NEVER BEEN IN A JAIL OR EVEN A police station, only in the reception lobby of Greenville juvenile, and that was as ugly as a hospital and stank of disinfectant. This police station, though, smelled like fresh coffee. Cora Lee took her inside and left her there and said she'd come back to get her.

She'd washed her hair before she came to see Pa, and Cora Lee had loaned her a brand-new red sweatshirt and even bought her a pair of new sneakers. The little lobby had counters on two sides with a green plant on each of them. There was a barred door at one side, the door of a little cell; she could see the cot inside. She looked in thinking Pa would be there, but the cop who let her in said that was just a holding cell.

She didn't want to go back into the real jail. But it turned out she didn't have to. He told her to wait, and two officers brought Pa up to the front. Pa looked thinner, and whiter. Like maybe he hadn't eaten or slept very much. He didn't have on special prison clothes like in the movies. *Not yet,* she thought, getting scared. Just his own jeans and plaid shirt and work shoes. She stood looking at him and didn't know what to say. But Pa knelt right down and put out his arms, so she had to hug him, and she felt all funny inside.

The officer took them into the holding cell and shut them in. She didn't know if the door locked when he closed it. He stood outside the bars, and another cop came to stand with him. There was a woman officer behind the counter. What did they think, that Pa would make a break for it? Lori wondered how Pa liked being locked up the way he'd locked her up. Then she was ashamed of herself, ashamed of thinking that. Pa sat down on the bunk on the stained mattress, and put out his hand to her. "Lori?"

She sat down where he could take her hand but couldn't put his arm around her. She looked at him and didn't know what to say. He said, "I'm sorry, Lori. Sorry I locked you in." He tilted up her chin so he could look at her. "I was scared for you. Scared that man would find you, the man who killed other children. I didn't know what else to do. Didn't know how else to keep you safe. Then when you ran away, I was more scared. I looked for you, and looked for Fenner. I had no one to go to. Or thought I didn't," he said sadly.

"I know. I'm sorry, Pa. That I ran away. Maybe if you'd told me . . ." She looked at him then, and felt all teary. "I thought . . ."

"You thought I didn't love you."

She couldn't talk.

He pulled her over almost roughly and held her, and she started to cry and couldn't stop. He handed her the big red handkerchief he carried in his pocket to wipe his hands on the job. She blew her nose, then sat hiccupping. Pa pulled her close again, held her safe, like when she was little.

"I think the judge will give me home confinement, Lori. After arraignment, until the trial. If I can come home until the trial, will you help me take the plywood off? And wash the windows?"

"Yes, Pa! And clean the house. We can do that together."

"We can. I've been gone a long time, haven't I?"

"Yes, Pa."

"And now, I don't know how long I'll be home. You know I'll have to go to prison."

She nodded. She knew it but she didn't want to know it. "For how long, Pa?"

"No one will know until after the trial. Until I'm sentenced. I have to stop thinking of you as a little girl. We're going to have to make some decisions."

"What decisions, Pa?" She looked hard at him. "I'm not going back to juvenile. I'm not."

"What, then?"

"Cora Lee French wants me to live with her. Until . . . until you come home again."

"Cora Lee French. The Little Theater singer."

She nodded. "Cora Lee, and Mavity Flowers and two other ladies. In—"

"In *that* house," Pa said, his light brown eyes wide with surprised. "Would you be all right with that?"

"I . . . I think so. I don't have to think about . . . those children." She shivered, but she wanted to make him understand. "They're not there, Pa. They're somewhere else, those children. Somewhere new and bright. They don't care about that place. Even if they did care," she said, "even if they came back sometimes, it would be all right."

"I see," he said, as if he didn't see at all.

"And Cora Lee and Mavity, I would be happy in that big house with them. They even have two dogs, Pa. Two nice big dogs."

Pa smiled for the first time, and hugged her and rumpled her hair like when she was little. And she thought maybe it *would* be all right. She meant for it to be all right. Maybe Pa wouldn't be in prison very long. Cora Lee said that when you were twelve, life was a tangle of choices. That sometimes you had to make really hard choices, that that's what growing up was all about. Lori guessed that Pa was right, she couldn't be a little child anymore. At least not all the time.

**POTS OF CYCLAMENS** lined the tearoom windows, red and pink brighter than Christmas candy, their colors shutting out the stormy sky. A blustery wind rattled the glass but within the cozy, paneled room firelight blazed. Before the licking flames on the brick hearth, a table had been set with high tea. The aroma of hot, savory party fare, of broiled crab sandwiches and little broiled sausages on toast, and of rum cake and other rich sweets mingled with the scent of brewing tea. The guest of honor sat at the head of the table. She had come directly from the hospital. She wore a red cashmere dress, warm and soft and becoming. Her white hair was freshly washed. She was tucked into a wheelchair, a red blanket over her knees, her oxygen tank hooked rakishly to the side of the chair in the manner of a ranger's rifle carelessly slung from the saddle.

The party was smaller than originally planned, cozier, less formal. Wilma Getz represented Friends of the Library but she did not plan to make a speech. On Genelle's left, Lori was seated where she could see the fire; on her right, with her back warmed by the blaze, was Lucinda Greenlaw. On down the table from Lucinda were Mavity Flowers, Wilma, and Cora Lee French. Down from Lori sat Ryan Flannery and Charlie Harper, both the younger women polished and scrubbed and wearing the first skirts either had had on since New Year's—and Dillon Thurwell, who was all cleaned up, too. Dillon wore a pale blue cashmere sweater, a matching skirt, pumps, and sheer stockings. The ladies were all decked out in party finery and Genelle was enjoying every minute, though she often had to hold up her oxygen mask to breathe at all comfortably.

Genelle watched the waiter, in his white crisp jacket, refill her teacup. This young, strapping fellow looked like he spent his off hours surfing, maybe lived for surfing, supporting his habit with this steady job. It made her both frightened and glad that this young man would be surfing and partying in Molena Point long after she was gone. She watched the three cats, tucked up complacently on the window seat among a tangle of bright brocade cushions. Frowning, she studied the far corner, where the cats were looking, all three very still, their ears sharp, their eyes wide with some secret excitement. Dulcie's green eyes blazed suddenly, then slit closed with a little smile; and Genelle thought that a warmth touched the room more compelling than the heat of the fire, a presence as powerful as had, once, so graced the silver screen. This did not frighten Genelle, but made her glad.

She thought about Patty planning the menu long before she died, and she wished she could eat more to please Patty, wished her digestion along with all her bodily functions had not turned so delicate. *Part of the process,* she told herself. And she told Patty, *You were lucky in that respect.* No sense being sentimental. Surely this life, as seen now from Patty's side of the veil, occupied only a tiny moment, a fraction of a second compared to the unknowable eternity that lay beyond.

The waiter went on around the table filling teacups, then turned away. Genelle sugared her tea, breathing in the delicate, steamy scent. Beside her, Lori laid a hand on hers. "It's not as formal as I thought. I didn't want to come, in my jeans and all, and not know how to act."

"Your red sweatshirt is elegant!" Genelle said, laughing. "And your manners are elegant, too. I *am so* glad you came!" Even laughing made her weak. She took a breath of oxygen, like some old wino, she thought, nipping at his bottle.

"It's Cora Lee's sweatshirt. It smells of jasmine. Cora Lee wants me to live with her after . . . while my father's away. But now, before the arraignment hearing, until they let him leave the jail, I could stay with you. If you'd want me. If I could maybe help out."

"I'd like that," Genelle said. "Our friends are taking turns staying at night, but you could help a lot. You could read to me, too. And as for your living with Cora Lee, I think that's a fine plan." She looked hard at Lori. "Would you like to live there?"

"I'd love it." Lori grinned. "And I sure am tired of camping in that basement."

Genelle helped herself to oxygen again. "Your pa loves you, Lori. He was terrified for you, he felt he had no other choice than what he did."

"I know. But if he'd told me—"

"What would you have done? If he'd told you?"

"I don't know," she said, surprised. She'd have to think about that. "I guess Pa didn't have much faith in the law to protect me, though."

"Sometimes the law can't do as much as they'd like. Your pa did the best he knew how. And he does love you. No matter where your pa is or what happens, he will keep on loving you." Genelle reached from her wheelchair to put her arm around Lori.

"At Cora Lee's," Lori said, "there's a window seat looking down. On the canyon where . . . I told Pa it didn't make any difference. But I guess maybe it does."

"Only you can decide that," Genelle said. "Whether you want to live where you can see that gravesite. Only you can know how that will make you feel."

"That's what Cora Lee said." She looked up at the waiter as he offered a tray, and she took four tiny crab sandwiches. "I guess it would be all right," she said stoicly. "I guess you learn to live with stuff." When a second waiter appeared, she took six little sausage sandwiches.

Grinning, Genelle thought, *She'll be all right, Lori will be all right.* And when she looked down the table at Cora Lee, Cora

Lee smiled, watching Lori with true affection. Across the table, Charlie and Ryan shared a satisfied grin.

But Wilma was watching the cats. As was Lucinda. And Genelle understood clearly the look that flashed between the two women and the cats: Joe and Dulcie and Kit were just as pleased for Lori as were their human friends. And Genelle thought, certainly not for the first time, that there was more in the universe, far more, than most folks imagined—or cared to know. She sipped her tea, and nibbled a sandwich, and when again she looked into the shadows, she imagined that she heard Patty laughing.

**GENELLE YARDLEY DIED** three days after her tea party, died quietly in her bed in the middle of the night. At the moment of her passing, a warm and gentle breath moved through her house and garden, pushing away the windy gusts that rocked the night. For a moment, it seemed, the wind was still. In the next room, where Wilma and Lori slept, the windows stopped rattling. Lori woke and sat up in bed, reaching for Dulcie. The little cat stood on the bed looking out to the garden, then turned to look at Lori and pushed her head against Lori, purring.

Taking Dulcie in her arms, Lori held the tabby cat tight. Across the room, Wilma woke. She saw the child sitting up clutching Dulcie, and she knew. Even across the village, the kit, sleeping between Lucinda and Pedric, woke and sat up. With one soft paw, Kit woke the old couple and looked at them and could say nothing.

And, blocks away in Clyde Damen's upstairs bedroom, Joe Grey woke hissing and backing into the pillow and into Clyde.

"What?" Clyde said, rolling over staring at the tomcat. "You have a pain? I told you, you ate too much shrimp."

Joe only looked at him. He didn't know what was wrong,

didn't know what to think. Didn't know how to look at what he had sensed in his dreams.

In Genelle's house, Lori and Wilma listened, then rose and went to Genelle's room. She lay unmoving. There was no hiss of oxygen. Reaching out a gentle hand, Wilma felt Genelle's pulse; she waited a long time, trying Genelle's wrist and then the artery in her neck. Bending, laying her face against Genelle's ribs, she listened for a heartbeat. At last she shook her head, covered Genelle more warmly, and gently covered her face.

**GENELLE YARDLEY WAS LAID TO REST** on a little hill at the edge of Molena Point cemetery. It was midday, and sunny, with a brisk wind off the sea. Genelle's view would be down over the rooftops of the village to the sea, if anyone thought she would linger to enjoy that earthly vista. After everyone who had gathered had at last turned away and gone, after the grave had been covered and the sod laid over, and it was evening and growing dark, the three cats came down from the oak tree.

They had waited a long time for the tractor to fill in the grave, a utilitarian process they didn't much care for, and for three workmen to lay the squares of sod. But they had still felt the sense of Genelle there with them. Almost, Dulcie said later, as if she laid a gentle hand on Dulcie's head. Now the cats, backing down out of the oak tree, stepped right onto Genelle's grave, onto the freshly laid new grass. They stood very still, listening. Facing into the wind. And they said their own cattish prayers for Genelle Yardley.

Though they knew she didn't need prayers. They looked up at the darkening sky and at each other and wondered not only where Genelle would go now and where life had come from in the first place, but wondered about themselves. Where *they* had come from, and who they were, and where they would go at some future time.

"Wonders," Dulcie said softly, "that we are not yet meant to know."

Kit stared at Dulcie, round eyed. Joe Grey licked his paw and fidgeted and didn't like to think about this stuff.

But suddenly the wind died again. All was totally still, the wind still. The cats waited.

They felt warm; they felt loved; they felt like laughing. And then at last they turned away, moving as one, and padded solemnly down the grassy hill, toward the village. Toward this life again, toward their own warm hearth fires; and they walked close together, so close that their shoulders touched, and their whiskers and ears touched, and their very cat souls joined with something huge that moved with them as they slipped away through the falling dark.